I0657770

A Nautical Conspiracy

A Will and Betsy Black Adventure

ABSOLUTELY AMA⚡ING eBOOKS

Habent Sua Fata Libelli

ABSOLUTELY AMAZING eBOOKS

Manhanset House
Shelter Island Hts., New York 11965-0342

bricktower@aol.com • tech@absolutelyamazingebooks.com
• absolutelyamazingebooks.com

All rights reserved under the International and Pan-American Copyright Conventions. No part of this publication may be reproduced, stored in a retrieval system, or transmitted in any form or by any means, electronic, or otherwise, without the prior written permission of the copyright holder.
The Absolutely Amazing eBooks colophon is a trademark of
J. T. Colby & Company, Inc.

Library of Congress Cataloging-in-Publication Data
Beckwith, David
A Nautical Conspiracy
p. cm.

1. FICTION / Mystery & Detective / Cozy / General. 2. FICTION / Mystery & Detective / Amateur Sleuth.
3. FICTION / Mystery & Detective / Women Sleuths.
Fiction, I. Title.
ISBN: 978-1-955036-49-8, Trade Paper

Copyright © 2023 by David Beckwith
Electronic compilation/ paperback edition
Copyright © 2023 by Absolutely Amazing eBooks

June 2023

A Nautical Conspiracy

A Will and Betsy Black Adventure

DAVID BECKWITH

ABSOLUTELY AMAZING eBOOKS

Other Will and Betsy Black Books
by David and Nancy Beckwith

A Hurricane Conpiracy (Book 1)
A Calculated Conspiracy (Book 2)
A Narcotic Conspiracy (Book 3)
A Cosmetic Conspiracy (Book 4)
A Jamaican Conspiracy (Book 5)
A Ransom Conspiracy (Book 6)
A Cover-Up Conspiracy (Book 7)
A Demonic Conspiracy (Book 8)
A Treasure Conspiracy (Book 9)
A Cruising Conspiracy (Book 10)

Available at fine booksellers

AbsolutelyAmazingEbooks.com

Jamaican Sine Paiting

PROLOGUE

Part of the majesty of living on an island is seeing the pinks, reds, and sometimes oranges and turquoises that the sinking sun projects as it drags itself beneath the horizon at sunset. On an occasion, when the banks of clouds have congealed, you think that there is no sunset. Sometimes on these evenings, something else happens. At the last minute, the flailing sun might pass a crease in a cloud causing light to pour through and bounce over the crystal blue ocean before disappearing again as quickly as it came. This was mostly wasted on Oney, Which Flava, and Twinie, who took nature's upcoming magic show for granted and were oblivious to the fact that they had a front row seat to observe mother nature's daily extravaganza. All that mattered to them was that they were hot and uncomfortable.

The sun was getting low in the sky, but despite the heavens being dotted with wispy white clouds, the day's heat still seemed to radiate from every surface on the boat, even the shaded ones. When Oney looked straight ahead, the sun was always in his eyes even though it seemed to be emanating from a northerly direction. No matter which way he turned, he still had to squint, but he could still feel its rays' warmth on the back of his neck. He glanced over at Twinie. Twinie's long shadow pointed away from the sun's red-tinged rays. A gap was opening between Twinie and his shadow. The lower the sun got, the more the gap lengthened, making Twinie's silhouette become increasingly exaggerated. Another gap seemed to be gradually opening between the horizon and the rim of the late day sun. The progression

1

towards sunset seemed slow now, but he knew that when the sun finally surrendered for another day, night would arrive rapidly.

Which Flava mused that after sunset, this summertime Friday night should be a dim one since there was only a quarter moon out. But dim was never dim enough if one was trying to engage in a surreptitious activity.

The *Spirit of the Seas* drifted lazily and aimlessly with the current a mile and half off the Jamaican coast. The water lapped against its hull as it gently rolled with the waves. Low volume Reggae emanated from boat's radio but would still be heard clearly to others since the music was magnified as it danced off the water's surface. The *Spirit of the Seas'* port of call was the Black River in remote St. Elizabeth Parrish. The crew's instructions from Shower Posse big cheese, Harry Dog, had been for them to deliver the boat to the obscure, backwater, posse-owned river marina and boat ramp after sunset and tie it off there. Another posse member would then pick them up and ferry them back to Kingston. The next morning, Harry would bring a trailer and then drive it to a properly outfitted posse owned garage. At this secure facility, the fiberglass boat would be partially dismantled, and its secret cargo would be unloaded and transferred back to Tivoli Gardens. If it were not necessary to damage the boat too badly, the fiberglass might be patched, the boat reregistered, and then the boat would be resold. Otherwise, it would be scrapped.

The three low-ranking, not-so-bright young gang plebes, Oney, Which Flava, and Twinie, had not been told that the boat contained contraband. It was none of their business. If they were smart, they'd just do what they were told to do. Harry Dog had purposely concealed the fact that the boat was transporting a hidden cargo. The fewer people who knew the better.

After all, Harry Dog reasoned, *Loosy goosey chatty-chatty* **(talk)** *sink ships. And if these fass-think* **(impulsive)**, *trickster* **(con artist)**, *teifs* **(thieves)** *know the value of what di boat smuggle, di fool* **(the fools)** *might unna* **(wanna)** *make what would prove for they to be an unwise and deadly move. At they age, a long term taut* **(thought)** *is what to do after breakfast tomorrow. Mi must delegate, but I canna tie up dog wid a chain of sausages.*

A Nautical Conspiracy

The Shower Posse don, Dudus Coke, was ruthless and pitiless in his sadistic, lethal revenge against dishonest underlings. When Harry Dog dispatched them on this mission, he only told them that their job was simply to deliver a boat that Don Dudus wished to give to a friend as a gift. It was to be nothing more than a routine boat delivery.

Since this mission had forced him to cancel a sure seduction that he had had arranged for what was destined to be a weekend of hard-partying, all-nighters of booze and loud, uninhibited sex with the angel Delicia, Twinie brought the tools of seduction he had planned to use — Wray and Nephew overproof rum, Red Stripe beer, a supply of cocaine, and, of course, ganja. And primo powder it was — gleaming white fish-scale coke. He sighed has he lamented that she wouldn't wait for his return. Instead, she would go to the street party with someone else and afterwards be writhing and howling in the arms of her date. What a waste! He got a boner thinking about what he was missing.

No use letting the weekend go a waste. After all, it's only a boat delivery. And too, after all, mi not getting any younger. Mi be twenty-two in August. Life be short and should be lived to the fullest.

Harry had instructed the three menials to wait until the marina closed at dusk to bring the boat in. He told them that the marina had been left unlocked, and that once their mission was completed, they were welcome to drink a few beers from the marina cooler while they waited for their ride to arrive.

As they killed time waiting to complete the boat delivery, the impatient youth soon became bored, and time seemed to drag. Would dusk never come?

Will I get back to Kingston in time, go to the Shower Posse sponsored Tivoli Gardens street party?

What a fuckery (injustice)! Why wait? Time a waste, Twinie reasoned as Oney reached into the boat ice chest for a cold brew.

Oney's street name had been derived from the fact that he had lost one ear in a confrontation with a mongrel pet dog as he tried to break into a widow's home. Twinie's stemmed from his close appearance to the son of a woman who his father was rumored to have once had a fling with.

He handed a brew to Which Flava, who instantly perked up. His appetites for food, drink, sex, narcotics, or good times were voracious, thus his street name.

"Looka, mon, what mi bring. Wan some?"

He held up the bottle of Wray and Nephew overproof rum and a gallon-sized Ziplock bag of fish-scale cocaine.

"Ya, mon," Which Flava almost shouted. "Does a magga (**mongrel**) dog hab fleas?"

"No, mon, but yu do," Twinie said and began laughing as poked Which Flava in the ribs playfully.

With no further delay, they retired to the boat's cabin.

Friday night's been saved.

As the boat floated aimlessly, another scenario was unfolding. The drifting, anchorless boat had gotten the unwanted attention of the Marine Division of the Jamaica Constabulary Force. But not just the regular patrol, but instead a special crew that was its secret task force.

As a response measure in its battle to fight terrorism, the United States Coast Guard had formed their Marine Security Response Teams. These teams were the Coast Guard's equivalent to the U.S. Army's Green Berets or the U.S. Navy's SEALS. Their boats were of varying lengths and makes and purposely feigned to look like a wide variety of commonly found civilian vessels. The crew members also did not wear uniforms. Their dress was totally irregular — t-shirts, shorts, high-top sneakers, and baseball or fishing caps. Some had dreadlocks. The goal was to blend in and therefore be visibly invisible.

Since twenty percent of the illegal drugs entering the United States came through Jamaica, the American military secretly trained an elite squadron in the Jamaican Constabulary Force to use the same methodology. This invisible "enemy" is what the drifting Spirit of the Sea had inadvertently attracted. The partying gangsters didn't know it, but they were being observed from afar through binoculars as the curious squadron tried to determine if everything there was on the level or if it was a boat in distress that needed assistance.

At last, the patrol decided to be on the safe side, and that they should check things out. They quietly and silently approached the stern of the Spirt of the Seas. Reggae music in the cabin continued to play a familiar tune that seemed out of place. The officers' presence was not acknowledged even when they silently pulled alongside. They stealthily boarded the *Spirit of the Seas*. Despite their sea legs, they had a hard time keeping their balance since something seemed to keep rocking the boat. What the task force saw when they rounded the cabin surprised, shocked and at the same time, tickled even them. The threesome on the boat seemed hyperactive and oblivious to their presence. No wonder the boat was rocking. The occupants were arm in arm facing in the ocean off the bow drunkenly swaying and doing stumbling dance steps in the dusk as they caterwauled "Hava Nagila" to an imaginary audience. Which Flava's bouncing dreads suddenly reminded the patrolman of an ultra-Orthodox Jewish man's side curls or payas and made him wonder, "A Jewish Rasta? Surely not."

Little did he know that the happy inebriated threesome had no idea what the song's significance was. They had heard it played more than once at a resort hotel in Kingston. All they knew about it was that it was a lilting, catchy tune that seemed make people want to dance and party. And they had never been known to shy away from a party of any kind, even if they didn't understand why.

One patrolman was dreadlocked as well. He tapped Oney gently on the shoulder with his baton.

The sweating Oney turned and squinted at him through dilated eyes. When he saw the patrolman's dreadlocked hair, he became delusional, and a drug-induced hallucination took hold. He screamed, "Eels!"

It seemed that the patrolman's dreadlocked eels began to hiss and spit green goo at him. When he looked at Which Flava, Which Flava's dreads now turned to eels as well, which began to snap back at the patrolman's hair in retaliation. Gradually a toothless mouth began to form around the eels. The mouth became a haggard face. The face was the old woman Oney had been trying to rob when her dog mauled him. But now she had become a duppy crone with flashing eyes. To him, she suddenly began to look like the wicked witch from Oz as her nose grew and purple snot shot from it and hit Twinie. In reality, he had simply poured his rum and ice on Twinie. The hag's mouth yawed open again and regurgitated more eels.

The eels began to snarl, and bark in harmony in a canine voice, "Oney! Oney! Mi only hab one ear. Mi spell calls for I to have a matched pair for mi potion to work. Mi tek your other."

Memories flooded his addled brain about the mongrel dog that had bitten off his right ear. Now eels were about to take off the one ear he had left. The ear shifted to the back of his head as it tried to hide from the eel's vicious teeth. Oney cupped his hand over it in his effort to shield it as he reached for the knife in the scabbard on his belt.

The officer karate chopped Oney's arm so hard it spun him around into Which Flava, delivering a gut punch that made Which Flava throw up a torrent of rum smelling vomit that soaked both Twinie and Oney. Twinie swung back, missed, and spun out of control — taking all three drunks pitching headfirst into the ocean.

Once the unlucky threesome was rescued, officers easily found on the console what was left of the coke. It was still in the original gallon sized Ziplock bag. There was plenty there to justify prosecuting all three as dealers not just as users and abusers and making the boat legally subject for confiscation. They zip-tied Which Flava, Twinie, and Oney and towed the *Spirit of the Seas* back to a preapproved location for processing.

An "official" Constabulary Force boat met the officers there and impounded the Shower Posse's boat. The three gangsters were driven to the Marine Police Station in Kingston to be booked and charged. The ride that Harry Dog had sent to pick up the unfortunate trio discretely observed the events from the shadows of the marina, and as soon as everyone had left, he called Harry Dog to report that the boat delivery had been botched.

Harry Dog already suspected that something was amiss when the tracking device he had installed on the boat showed it leaving the marina's locale. The call merely filled him in on the reason why.

HO MADE CHUTNEY

Chapter 1

The air was still fresh and balmy but was beginning to heat up as a late morning in Kingston prepared to surrender to a soon-to-be-hot afternoon. The sky was almost completely white with billowing clouds with a celeste blue peeking through only when it was allowed to. A slight breeze blew. An occasional bird darted back and forth. Harry McLeod paid little attention, however, as he silently drove along. The momentary shade from the buildings that he was passing alternated with the flashing sunshine from the open spaces between them. Harry had a knot in his stomach that seemed to swell as he passed each familiar landmark. He obliviously passed the Tower Street Adult Correctional Center, a place that normally brought back unpleasant memories; then past the Jamaica Stock Exchange, a building he had never been in; followed by the National Gallery. He then noticed a sign for the Marine Police Station. *This* got his attention.

"Dutty bumboclaats! Yu ca licky-licky mi batty (**Dirty butt-wipes! You can kiss my ass!**)!" the on-edge McLeod aka Harry Dog mumbled as he shot the sign a middle-finger salute.

He was headed for the Island Squeez Diner on Harbour Street for a lunchtime meeting with Dudus Coke that he was not looking forward to attending. Christopher "Dudus" Coke was the legendary second-generation cutthroat who was the leader of Kingston's Shower Posse, the most powerful street gang in Jamaica. Dudus was viewed as a combination "Robin Hood" and "Godfather" by the people in Tivoli Gardens, the slum neighborhood where the Shower Posse was domiciled, and reverently called "The President" or sometimes simply "Presi."

On one hand, Dudus was a generous community benefactor who paid school fees for children, helped provide aid for single mothers to help raise their children, sponsored street dances, promoted young entertainers' careers, and supported any other causes he considered worthwhile. On the other hand, he was also an iron-handed dictator or "don" who demanded respect as he enforced his self-made laws and was the sole judge and jury when local disputes occurred. When he deemed it necessary, he lethally enforced his will as he kept peace in Tivoli Gardens and the surrounding ghetto neighborhoods. In reality, Dudus was a vicious, merciless, sociopathic extortionist, smuggler, drug mogul, and gun dealer whose future had been launched when his own legendary father, Lester Coke, known by the street name of "Jim Brown," mysteriously burned to death in his Kingston prison cell the night before his scheduled extradition to the United States. The commonly accepted story was that this event was orchestrated by powerful corrupt people with lots to lose if Coke's insider knowledge about the dark side of Jamaican graft and dirty politics ever became documented public knowledge, and that this was their last opportunity to ensure his silence before he left Jamaica and possibly cut a deal with the American authorities. Until his arrest and conviction, Jim Brown had been regarded as the undisputed "don" of Tivoli Gardens.

"Jim Brown" had previously risen to power after he contracted the posse's talents to the Jamaica Labour Party to kill or maim its enemies to insure election results. After his father's untimely death, the twenty-three-year-old Dudus had assumed command of the posse.

Wise leaders of other gangs often gave wide berth to Dudus if they wanted to ensure their own safety. He was now more powerful than Jim Brown had ever been, both domestically and abroad. His poisonous tentacles extended into many levels of Jamaica's government, and he had received many millions of dollars of rigged contract awards and kickbacks over the years.

Jamaican gangs are called posses because of Jamaicans' enamorment with American western movies. While the Shower Posse's home had always been the Edward Seaga sponsored 1960's slum redevelopment project Tivoli Gardens in West Kingston, its tentacles eventually extended to such far-flung areas as New York, New Orleans, and New Jersey. The Shower Posse's name was derived from its reputation of showering its enemies with bullets. Whereas in the early 1970's, Jamaican posses' primary revenues came from helping political parties get the "right" vote in elections, modern posses such as the Shower Posse were diversified. Their revenues now came from such crimes as drug and arms trafficking, bribery, loan sharking, gambling, racketeering, blackmail, and murder.

As rough as the current Tivoli Gardens was, it was still not as bad as its predecessor, Back-O-Wall. In the 1950's, the Rastafarian settlement Back-O-Wall had become unchallenged as the worst, most dangerous slum in the Caribbean. Three communal standpipes and two public bathrooms served a population of over five thousand people. Edward Seaga and the Jamaica Labour Party entered the community in 1961 and redeveloped the area into Tivoli Gardens. With Jim Brown's assistance, Seaga and the JLP never lost an election in Tivoli Gardens before his 2005 retirement.

By the millennium, despite Seaga's efforts, problems persisted that were largely attributable to persistent poverty and Jamaica's growing role in the development of widescale international drug trafficking. Tivoli Gardens had become a garrison community that was the scene of repeated confrontations between gunmen and law enforcement. It was regarded as a territorially rooted homogeneous voting community where political support was regularly exchanged between local politicos and the don for lucrative contract awards and other social welfare benefits.

It was only fitting that Tivoli Gardens was in West Kingston, the home of (or should I say the dumping ground for) the Caribbean's largest garbage dump; the largest public cemetery, the largest market, and the primary maternity/public hospitals of the English-speaking Caribbean; Kingston's blood bank and railroad yard; over ninety-nine percent of its funeral parlors; and was the site of Jamaica's largest power plant and oil refinery.

Harry McLeod's street name was Harry Dog. Though he had no official title, he was ranked in the upper echelon of the Shower Posse hierarchy. Harry was a naturally violent, unmerciful bull of a man who had schemed his way into Dudus's inner circle. His savage reputation, sour disposition, unforgiving nature, and long memory were such that rarely would many other Shower Posse members risk opposing him and take the chance of being viewed as his adversary. An oft repeated fictious story that Harry did nothing to dispel was that he had once even executed some family members who crossed him. Even though Harry Dog was not especially imaginative or innovative, because of his lethal and unsavory reputation, he was often Dudus's go-to man when Dudus had special projects.

As he drove to the restaurant, Harry Dog had had his radio on low as a distraction, but when UB40 began singing "Rat In Me Kitchen," it brought to mind Dudus' possible reaction to Harry Dog's pending report concerning the unexpected events of the night before.

He gulped and mumbled to himself as he prayed, "Pleas (**please**), Jah. Mek da President be ina understan mood and na jump ta blame mi."

When he heard no celestial answer, he sighed and beat his fist against the steering wheel.

Things had never been quite the same between him and Dudus since his failure to find the Genovesa's treasure. The treasure *had* been a long shot. Dudus seemed to accept that fact. What he couldn't accept was the number of men Harry lost or had had maimed in this losing effort. It might not have stung so bad if this had been an isolated loss. But making it worse, the Shower Posse had once again lost face to Colonel Ferron Winter, the Maroon leader in Accompong.

Why did it have to be Colonel Winter?

The Colonel had already cost Dudus millions in the Highway 2000 fiasco and forced Dudus to spend even more money rebuilding his political network after many of the politicians he had been keeping in his pocket "on retainer" had either gone to prison or had fled the country. When the world saw him become vulnerable in this highly public travesty, it had made him seem weak and exposed. The members and leaders of rival posses who had harbored jealous, unrealized ambitions might become abruptly emboldened. Then, rubbing salt in the wound, The Colonel had beaten Dudus a second time in the Genovesa affair. And made things worse by grinding in his victory by fabricating clues that sent Harry Dog and his crew on a wild goose chase to look for a treasure that didn't even exist.

How much face can someone afford to lose?

And to top it all off, Harry's secret side deal with Weasley Lineitem, the shyster accountant, had blown sky high in the confusion of it all.

Thank the Lord that Dudus never found out about my Weasley deal. Or mi wouldn't be here today, worrying about da upcoming luncheon. ... Or of mi secret promise to da batty hole **(asshole)** *Colonel Winter that mi'd never interfere in da Colonel's business again ... a fuckery* **(bullshit)** *pledge if I ever made one. ... But da Colonel canna* **(can't)** *expect mi to honor it.*

Colonel, yu can suck mi hose.

Harry flew another middle finger salute to the absent Colonel.

After all, mi made da agreement under duress. But, if either da Colonel or da Presi found mi not keeping mi word ... mi'd be buried somewhere up in the boonies of the Cockpit Country. Mi just gotta mek damn sure da neber **(that never)** *happen.*

Harry Dog's musings concluded when he saw the street sign for Harbour Drive, where the Island Squeez Diner was located. His thoughts reverted to the spin he was going to need to put on his report to Dudus.

The Island Squeez Diner was located on the second floor of the KDP Building. The outside of the building had three white stucco archways leading into the building. Harry Dog walked up to the waist-high, six-foot long latticed welcome kiosk on the sidewalk. It was partially covered by a black and white striped awning. Signs advertising some of the restaurant's featured dishes lined the front. A neatly shorn, short-haired host in a black golf shirt and a white Red Stripe baseball cap greeted him. Harry asked if Dudus had arrived yet and was told that Dudus was already upstairs at a table. Harry then climbed the stairs to the second floor and was shown through the CruiserZ Lounge down a hall called the Treasure Wall. The hall contained framed newspaper and magazine articles that had been published over the years about this well-established restaurant. He was shown to Dudus' table out on the balcony. Dudus pushed back his chair and rose to shake Harry's hand. He had already ordered an amber Appleton rum on the rocks. Harry told the clean-cut, young waiter to order one of the same for him. The waiter left menus for them to begin deciding on what they would order.

Dudus did not rush into business. He and Harry Dog both examined their menus. Both had decided what to order by the time the waiter returned with Harry's drink.

"Are you gentlemen ready to order?"

"I think I know what I want," Dudus said. "Harry, have you decided yet?"

Harry Dog nodded and deferred to his superior. "After you."

"I'll take the stewed pork with mixed vegetables."

"I'll have the boiled turkey neck over oriental vegetables," Harry Dog said.

"Both are excellent choices," the waiter replied and reached for their menus.

"Oh, Leroy. I'll take the bill," Dudus said to the waiter.

"Of course, Mr. President."

"By the way, Leroy, how is your mother? … And your little brother … Claude? … ?"

"Thank you for asking … and remembering his name. She's fine, and he's still in school. We really appreciate all you have done for our family."

"Excellent. Glad to hear that. Not surprised. After all, de chip neber (**never**) fly far from de block."

The waiter smiled and said, "And, Jah willing, blood follow vein."

Now it was Dudus' turn to smile.

After the waiter left, Harry Dog almost began to talk business, but Dudus's gave him a look that clearly said lunch first/business afterwards and commented on the weather.

The waiter soon returned. Dudus's meal consisted of a medley of bitesize chunks of pork mixed with peas, corn kernels, carrots, onion, string beans, and peppers swimming in a rich, thick brown sauce. Harry's lunch was a turkey neck that had been sliced into pieces about the size of an oxtail serving and had been dipped into what appeared to be the same brown sauce as Dudus' pork with a variety of stir-fried Chinese vegetables on the side. They ate silently, and when they were finished, the waiter promptly retrieved their dirty plates.

Dudus turned to the waiter and said, "That was excellent, Leroy. Bring us each a cup of coffee. Leave the tab. And then, would you see that we're not disturbed? We have some matters to discuss privately."

"Oh course, Mr. President. My manager wishes to make this a complimentary luncheon."

"Thank him for his generosity, but I don't want to take advantage of him. I'm sure he'll be in a position to grant me a favor, if necessary, down the road."

"As you wish."

A second waiter appeared almost instantly with two cups and poured their steaming Blue Mountain coffee.

Harry Dog thought to himself, *One day, I'll command that kind of respect.*

"Now, I'll listen to your report. I hope … for your sake … it is a good one."

Harry Dog shuddered. Dudus Coke's radical and sudden mood swings were legendary to his subordinates. People who displeased The President were then sometimes found in boxes in some remote part of Kingston hacked to pieces. Harry was glad that they were in a crowded downtown public restaurant.

"Mr. President, last night we had an unexpected encounter with the water patrol."

Dudus said nothing. He simply glared at Harry Dog and waited for him to elaborate.

"They approached our boat because it idled at sea waiting for the time for it to dock. They boarded and found contraband. The boat was impounded, and the crew was arrested."

Dudus's countenance seemed to darken as he began to seethe.

"What do you mean they found contraband? That boat was supposed to only contain cash. Cash that would later be laundered by Mr. Lineitem. I never authorized it to transport product."

Harry Dog began to sweat and to dab his forehead with his napkin.

"The captain took it on himself to hold an ill-conceived social event."

"Did you know about this before their departure?" Dudus said quietly, with a hard edge on his voice.

"Uh. No, sir. I did not. I found out after the fact."

"Your soldiers are that undisciplined? Or let me rephrase that thought. This is all the control that you have over the numbskulls who answer to you?"

Harry Dog bowed his head and stared at the table. His foot spastically tapped and twitched under the table. He knew better than to make a lame excuse. Dudus did not do well with excuses. They only dug the hole deeper. He knew what he had to do. He had to get that boat back, no matter what. This would never blow over otherwise.

"Let me make sure I understand this correctly. One of our boats carrying millions of dollars that would not have attracted the authorities' attention if it had arrived when it was scheduled to, was confiscated because it was being used as a party boat by a rahtid (**damned**) fool. And now, I'm out a boat as well as millions of dollars."

"Uh. … Yes, sir. Sorta."

This is not going well.

"What do you mean sorta, bloodclot ediat (**fuckin' idiot**)?"

"Law enforcement only knows that it confiscated the illegal product. They think it was a simple smuggling operation. The money was well hidden in a secret place in the boat. No one but us knows about it or suspects that it exists. All we have to do now is to get the boat back."

"And where is the boat now?"

"Sir, it's being kept at a government impound yard in Kingston. It will be auctioned."

"And when will that be?"

"I don't know. ... But the good news is that the boat can't be traced back to you."

"Whoopee, shit! Good news! You pumm pumm cheese dumb-rass pussywool (**stinking dumb-ass pussy**)! So, it's good news that I've lost a valuable boat with little hope to recover it and millions more in cash that I may or may not ever see again. And if I do see it again, it may months or years down the road. ... And then only if by some miracle I get the boat back by exposing myself and competing for it at a government auction. And you don't think my motives for wanting to recover the boat won't be suspected?"

"Oh, you wouldn't have to bid on the boat yourself. I'll hire a shill to do it for you."

"*You* just don't *know* how comforting I find that, yah bumbaclaat batty boy (**you fucking faggot**)."

Harry Dog said nothing. Until Dudus calmed down, anything he might say would only exacerbate the situation.

"Those ediats (**idiots**) ... "

Dudus did not need to finish the sentence but instead slashing his index finger in the air for emphasis in a dramatic manner across his own throat as he stoically pronounced the threesome's fate.

"I won't have to. Jah beat us to it. It turns out that the coke was laced with Fentanyl and all three died from cardiac arrest on the way in to book them. Since the authorities have no reason to suspect that there is anything on the boat other than the product they confiscated during an ill-fated party, the boat shouldn't be tainted in their eyes, and I'll see if I can accelerate the date for the boat auction using some of my contacts," Harry said.

"You've got about as much chance, batty-hole (**asshole**), of doing that as a jackass has of winning a horse race. I'll use my connections to take care of it myself."

"As you wish."

"By the way, what's the name of the boat?"

"The *Spirit of the Seas.*"

I'm glad I wasn't the Spirit of the Seas' *captain.*

REDIATUR
EXPERT IN
CLEANING AND
REPEATING

Chapter 2

Harry drove away from his luncheon with Dudus relieved that it was over and that he had survived it but second guessing himself with I-should-have-said thoughts. Should he have told Dudus that he had delegated the mission to Bigga Ford, and that it was Bigga who had chosen the young bloodclot ediats **(damned fools)** who had foolishly blown it? His mind churned as thought after thought rushed to displace the previous one.

No. That probably would have served no purpose. Considering the value of the boat's hidden cargo, that would have just said to Dudus that I didn't take the mission as seriously as I should have. And besides that, Dudus hates excuses. It'll only serve to make me look weak. As Dudus has often said, bucket wid a 'ole a bottom, 'ave no bidness pond riverside **(a bucket with a hole in the bottom has no business being used to dip water out of the river.)**

And I would have made a permanent enemy of Bigga, who Dudus clearly favors. He's enough of a rival as it is. That's all I need is to have one more person pissed off at me right now. Then knowing Bigga all too well, he would do everything in his power to get even, and I'd have to be looking over my shoulder for the rest of my life.

I did right by just keeping my bloodclot mouth shut. What counts now is that I make things right. That's what will finally get me back in The President's good graces. I need to spin this setback so that in the end I prevail. After all, weh

16

no kill, fatten **(If I've eaten something that it hasn't killed me, it will then nourish my body).**

He did wonder if Bigga had orchestrated the whole washout just to make him look bad with The President. He quickly dismissed that thought, not because Bigga was ethical. He knew better than that. Bigga just wouldn't take that kind of risk.

No. Acting facety **(nasty or ill-mannered)** *would have just bite mi batty* **(my butt)** *since ebry day debble help teef, wan dyah God wi 'elp watchman* **(for every day that the devil helps the thief, one day God will help the watchman).**

Cornwell "Bigga" Ford was a rising star with the Shower Posse. His street name was derived from his girth. Bigga was not only six feet four inches but also weighed over 400 pounds. Everything about him was oversized — his hands, his feet, his features, and as he liked to brag to people, his self-proclaimed male genitalia, the latter being something his colleagues were willing to take his word for and that he had never been called upon to prove. What he had proven time after time was that his appetite was as big as his belly.

Bigga's rise to posse stardom was primarily attributable to his success after he had planted the concept with Dudus of establishing a Shower Posse chapter in Newark, New Jersey. He then volunteered to move there to make the idea become a reality. This had turned into a very lucrative venture for The President and moved Bigga into his inner circle. But Bigga was street smart enough to know that this boat fiasco could easily undermine his past successes.

Harry Dog's cell phone rang. It was Bigga calling.

"How'd yu meeting with da Presi go?"

"Not good, not bad."

"Did my name come up?"

No, mon. I keep you out of it. … But he make it clear, dis gotta be fix."

"Count on me. I 'elp yu fix."

"Yu betta if yu wanna stay out of it."

"Where are yu now?"

"On Spanish Town Road."

"Meet me at Café Dolche in fifteen minutes."

"Why?"

"Mi'll explain when we get there."

Café Dolche was a one-room, no-frills coffee and pastry shop. It had a vertical glass display counter to entice customers to order more than coffee. The menu and prices were posted on a black wall sign behind it. The no-nonsense, durable tables and chairs were steel with flattened, mesh-type, expanded metal surfaces. Both the tabletops and the chair seats and backs were fabricated from the heavy-duty open design often used on both lawn furniture and gratings.

Harry Dog arrived first. He took a table and waited for Bigga. Bigga arrived almost immediately thereafter.

"Do you want anything other than coffee?" Bigga asked.

"Naw, mon. Just had lunch."

This didn't stop Bigga from ordering food for himself. He ordered a whole freshly baked stout bun and cheese plus a large coffee for himself. A stout bun and cheese is an oblong dark dense loaf somewhat reminiscent of a fruit cake. The main ingredients are stout, raisins, cherries, ground up miscellaneous fruit peels, and prunes. It's sweetened with both cane sugar and honey. He had the waitress bring him a knife so he could slice it into slabs. He offered Harry Dog a piece. Harry shook his head.

"I'm full. I just had turkey necks and Chinese vegetables at the Island Squeez."

Bigga lumbered up to the counter and told the attendant that he needed some pats of butter. He brought them back to the table and began to slather some on each piece. With every bite, he ate half a slice. Before it was even swallowed, he was spreading butter on the next piece.

Harry Dog just watched as the stout bun and cheese disappeared. As on edge as he was, he wouldn't have been hungry even if he hadn't just finished lunch. The way that Bigga inhaled the bun, he felt like that even if he hadn't been stuffed, there wouldn't have been enough there for them both, and he might have lost a finger if his timing was off if he reached for a piece.

"So, what'd yu want to talk about?"

Harry gave him a sanitized overview of the luncheon discussion. Bigga chugged down the rest of his coffee, burped, and said, "Mi might have a diversion until yu get da boat back."

"What's dis yu shit, nigga? Yu di one rounded up these druggie bumba ras clot bowcyat **(druggie dumb ass faggot)** ragamuffins not mi."

"OK, den, wi. Name call not solve problem. Wi gotta stick together. OK? Remember mi son, Dagwood?"

"Paul? Yu neber talk 'bout he."

Very few people knew about Paul Daewood (street name Dagwood) Ford's existence. When Bigga had conceived of the idea of setting up the New Jersey Shower Posse chapter and had briefly gone there to live, he had met Desimone, a local prostitute who had brothers who were gang members. With her assistance, he was able to recruit the membership nucleus the posse needed to get going. Bigga had also had a brief affair with Desimone. The result was his son, Paul. As it turned out, this had been the only child Bigga was to ever father. After returning to Jamaica, he regularly sent funds to help support his New Jersey "family." He occasionally visited them when business took him back up that way. While Paul's existence was not a total secret, he was known only to a few people, some of whom Bigga confided in and who agreed to hold his confidence and a few people who simply found out by accident. Bigga made sure that they knew that loose lips would not be in their best interest either. Harry Dog fell into the latter category.

"We bot' know why. Paul street chil' **(child)** not yard chil'."

"How old Paul be now?"

"Paul be 20. Soon be 21."

"Wow! Time sure fly. He still lib **(live)** wid he mutha? Is he still in school?"

"Naw, mon, to both. He graduate from Essex County Vocational. Learn computers."

"So, what's dis have to do with wi' wi problem?"

"Paul work as night janitor for da office building where da American DEA hab office. He use he computer howdy-do to get into dere computer's classified files. He mek list of they underground agents and der locations. Da President would give a lot to hab dat list. And if wi' the ones to bring he da list, he maybe be willing overlook da boat axxident or at least buy wi more time to recover da boat. An' mehbe, wi eben look lak heroes to he."

"So how wi get it from Paul?"

"Paul get scared dey get on to him. Plus, he hate New Jersey. So, he leave dere ahead dat happen and move to Florida. He now do janitor work at sumthin' called Sugarloaf Lodge. But he allas wanna be in Jamaica. He say he will only gib **(give)** da list to wi if wi help he get 'ere **(here)**. He even hab a plan. He wanna tek tourist boat to da Dry Tortugas and have wi make arrangements to pick he up dere."

"OK, dat's possible."

Paul has the same moralistic values that his father has, Harry Dog thought after they left the café.

A born conniver like his father.

Then he smiled and mumbled under his breath, "Oh well, wha' yu expect. Da turd donna **(don't)** fall far from da bird."

This Artist Di This
Type Of Work To
Highlight The Good
News Of God's Work
In The Lives Of Men
And Woamen Today
K.L. Rankine

Chapter 3

Let the sun shine; let the sun shine in; the sun shine in.

Will Black merrily sang to an invisible audience as he carried his coffee and his I-Pad out onto the back deck to his Little Torch Key home to join his wife, Betsy.

She clapped, and he replied with, "Thank you, thank you very much. And for my next number, the timeless standard, Tiptoe Through the Tulips ...."

"Shhh, ... there's a boat going by."

She was standing at their wooden railing, looking out over the canal at a neighbor's fishing boat as it putted past their house. The neighbor waved. Betsy waved back. Will put down his coffee cup and I-Pad, walked up behind her, wrapped his arms around her from behind, and nuzzled her neck. The neighbor smiled. Betsy looked slightly embarrassed. Will waved at the neighbor with a thumbs up, his arms still around Betsy.

"You're sure perky this morning," Betsy commented.

"What's there not to be perky about? I'm in a place I love with the woman I love. The weather is beautiful. My coffee is hot, and it's Saturday. Life don't get no better than this. If it does, it might just overpower all my senses."

"Will, my darling, double negatives may be OK in math, but they're not in English."

Will didn't reply but began to sing again when the boat had passed by.

Here I am. Rock you like a hurricane. Here I am. Rock you like a hurricane.

He swayed and shuffled his feet with his arms still around her before spinning her around to face him.

"That's what I want to do to you, madam, after we have this dance," Will said as he straightened his right arm out horizontally with his fingers intertwined in hers and slid his left hand from around her waist upwards, massaging the area between her shoulder blades."

Will began to sing again off key.

> *Can't you feel me closin' in, honey?*
> *Can't you feel me schoolin' around?*
> *You got fins to the left and fins to the right.*
> *And you're the only girl in sight.*

"Down, big boy. Go drink your coffee and behave yourself. Do I need to switch you to decaf? By the way, what do you mean, the only girl in sight?"

"Well, I *am* nearsighted."

Wilson and Betsy Black had met in Mobile when they both worked in the downtown financial district. Betsy worked for then nationally chartered WB Bank as a commercial banker; Will was an investment broker for RST Securities, a New York Stock Exchange member firm. She was a native Mobilian; he was from the Mississippi Delta. They had a dreamlike courtship and then married. The stars fell into place with both of their careers and when Will was offered the resident manager's position in Vero Beach, Florida, Betsy was able to arrange a transfer to join him there. A year later their daughter Lexie was born. After Lexie graduated from the University of Miami, the Blacks found themselves to be empty nesters and at a crossroad in their lives.

Once again providence stepped in. This time it was Betsy who was offered a career opportunity when the job as area president of WB's Monroe County banks became available and her superiors approached her with a very lucrative package should she want to take their reins. Will investigated RST and found that they had long wished to have a Key West presence. He proposed that they let him give it a try and after the plan was approved by corporate, coat-tailed Betsy to the Keys. While life had been good in Vero Beach, it became even better in Key West.

Will and Betsy were now approaching middle age and were empty nesters. But their lives were far from empty. They still revered each other, and this esteem had given them to an ever-increasing understanding of themselves. This respect carried over into their community. Their daughter, Lexie, had launched a successful career and was self-sufficient. They each managed profitable branches for their employers in an industry that they were delighted to be a part of. They were comfortable financially. Their health was good.

The Blacks were blessed to live during the prime of their lives in a blissful tropical region that most people had to wait until they retired to enjoy or save all year to temporarily visit. Many people would never do either. There had been some obstacles and challenges along the way. They had had many unanticipated business and non-business-related adventures, often requiring them to draw on reserves that they didn't know they possessed as they defeated or derailed the plans some truly underhanded or dangerous people.

Their forays into Jamaica had led to making friends and lasting contacts that they would cherish for the rest of their lives. When all was said and done, theirs had been a very satisfying life. But best of all, Will and Betsy had accomplished all of this as they fell deeper in love with each passing year.

"So, if hanky-panky has been ruled out, I guess I'll just have to call my standby date and invite her to the "Meeting of the Minds" concert today?"

"Where'd this 'I' baloney come from? Sometimes I think when that when the judge married us, I should have asked for a jury."

"OK, so much for my companionship dilemma. I'll just cancel my date. I'd rather take my wife anyway. By the way, do you know what the teacher's minister told the high school teacher when she confided to him that she had a problem? He said, naturally, after all, you are a math teacher."

Not being easily defeated in a verbal joust, Betsy wasn't ready to surrender the banter exchange yet without getting the last word. It started with a loud, exaggerated sigh designed for emphasis.

"And speaking of math, do you know what the triangle said to the circle?"

"Tell me."

"You're so pointless."

"Cute. It's a shame parallel lines have so much in common since they'll never meet."

"And to think we were happy for twenty plus years, and then we met each other. So what time and where, your majesty?"

"Casa Marina. Two o'clock, my queen. That's when Sunny Jim comes on."

"Remember when we almost hired him to play for Lexie's Quail Valley graduation party in Vero?"

"How can I ever forget? He was available and affordable, but Lexie said she'd rather have a DJ play the canned music that the kids were listening to at the time instead of his "old folks" music. Now, he's a headliner at Key West's Jimmy Buffett Parrothead festival. I hate to see his prices nowadays."

"If you could get him at all."

"Speaking of Buffett ..."

"I should have let you seduce me. Then I wouldn't have had to listen to your witticisms. And I'd save time since it would be over quicker. Let me sniff that coffee. You sure it's not Irish coffee?"

"Nah! But drinking wouldn't have saved you, just delayed the inevitable. You can't hold a good man down when he's on a roll."

Will only got an eyeroll in return, so he coughed and cleared his throat loudly into his fist before continuing.

"Now to get back to my latest story that I was getting ready to tell before I last heard from the Peanut Gallery, the FBI was holding a strategy session when one of the agents asked, 'After we find Jimmy Hoffa, can we please try to find Jimmy Buffett's damned shaker of salt?'"

Will and Betsy drove downtown in the early afternoon. After struggling to find a place to park, they checked in at the welcome table, picked up their festival "goody-bag," walked through the hotel and out to the hotel's private beach.

Everywhere they looked, they saw jubilant Jimmy Buffett fans and had to jostle their way back towards the beach stage where Sunny Jim would soon play.

"Maybe we should have gotten here sooner," Betsy whispered to Will.

The party was well underway. They looked to see if there were any locals that they recognized but saw no one. It was mostly a baby boomer crowd which seemed to mostly be out-of-towners. At first, loud tropical shirts seemed to be everywhere, but when Will looked closer, he could tell that the crowd seemed to be somewhat evenly split between people wearing Jimmy Buffett t-shirts and those wearing Hawaiian shirts. Flip-flops seemed to outnumber sneakers almost three to one.

Novelty hats abounded. They saw both skull caps and baseball caps with parrots mounted on them. There were woven palm frond hats with so many decorations that it was hard to see the fronds beneath it all. Also, Margaritaville baseball and long-billed fishing caps, striped Mexican sombreros with pom poms, Margaritaville straw fedoras with Jimmy Buffett quotes on the hatbands, Luau Margaritaville headbands some of which were headbands with parrots mounted atop them. Wide-brimmed flower-decorated women's straw hats, and graphic bucket hats. Beneath these colorful hats were all descriptions of ostentatious sunglasses. Bling and fake pirate earrings abounded.

And of course, beverage-filled plastic glasses and cups of all descriptions and beer galore.

"Are we the only people here who aren't half soused?' Betsy asked.

"No, I think I saw one other person. Every Corona beer in the state of Florida must have been bought and shipped down here for this weekend. And I should have gone long lime futures."

"Parrothead holy water."

"Since you brought up holy water, I assume you know how to make it. … You boil the hell out of it."

"I never thought that our usual somewhat casual clothing would ever seem out of place, but I do now," Betsy said as she stared all around her, causing her to ignore Will's latest joke.

"What you want to bet tomorrow's big seller will be aspirin and Tylenol? Ain't gonna be able to buy a bottle countywide for love or money."

They heard the announcer tapping on a stage microphone, testing to see if it was live.

"Let's try to get closer to the stage," Will said as he began to thread his way through the boisterous crowd of fans. Betsy followed the path he was trying to clear. They didn't get far.

Sunny Jim's band came up onto the stage, and the announcer made his opening remarks. Will thought one of the guitar players looked familiar. Then he saw something else that he had seen many times. He nudged his wife and pointed.

"Is that Howard Livingston's antique Johnson boat motor on stage?

"Looks like it to me."

"And am I hallucinating, or does that guitar player look familiar?"

"You're right. That's DV Craig, the musician friend of your schoolmate, Tom what's-his-name, …

"Hamilton."

… who we met on your class reunion cruise. But I guess we shouldn't be totally surprised. After all, he did play with the Beach Boys on the road and he was part of the Landsharks, the Jimmy

Buffett tribute band at Disney World and Universal. Maybe he works for Sunny Jim now."

"He doesn't have to work."

Davis Victor aka DV and Cecelia aka Cee Cee Craig were a wealthy, young, middle-aged Orlando couple. Her father's company had the Budweiser distributorship that was the exclusive provider of Anheuser-Busch products for Disney World. Her father was now deceased, and the largest block of stock was now owned by his trophy wife widow, who was not much older than Cee Cee. Cee Cee owned the next biggest block of shares. Neither woman cared for the other, but they were forced by circumstance to at least be civil to each other on the surface. Both were de facto officers of the corporation, though neither of them actually worked, but the company still gave both ladies a very generous income plus other perks. Basically, both were handsomely rewarded by the company's working management not to show up for work or meddle in the company's day-to-day affairs, their sole duty being to attend an occasional board meeting. Cee Cee was a semi fitness junkie who had earned a ASFA certification as a self defense instructor but only used it for personal development.

DV had been a guitar player and keyboardist who had no net worth until he met Cee Cee at Disney and married her. Now he only played music as an avocation. The Craigs had hit it off with the Blacks when DV assisted Will's celebrity classmate in entertaining their classmates during their cruise ship reunion.

The announcer's next statement answered the question for them.

"And we have a special guest playing with Sunny Jim today, down from Disney World, the very talented veteran of the Beach Boys' band and great all-around guy, DV Craig."

DV stepped forward and raised his hand, waving to the audience. The crowd cheered. Sunny Jim stepped up to the microphone and told his fans how great it was to be back in Key West again.

"Arrrrrrrrgh and welcome! You parrothead and pirate lads and lassies!"

Before Jim began to play, to warm up the crowd, he told a couple of pirate jokes.

"Do you know what the ocean said to the pirate?"

27

The crowd yelled in unison, "No, what?"

"Nothing, it just waved."

The crowd booed playfully.

"And do you know how much a pirate pays for his earrings?"

"What?"

"A buck—an—ear!"

"Booo!"

"And last … and best, what's the rating on a pirate's favorite movie? …. Arrrrrrrrgh!"

Before they could boo a third time, the steel pans in Sunny Jim's band launched into one of his familiar tunes, "Life in the Laid Back Lane."

A cheer so loud ensued that it almost drowned out the music. The party was underway. Almost before the final note quit resonating, Jim started his next number.

Loud, loud, loud, wild and loud. He's the tropical shirt wearing king.

"That ought to be an anthem for this crowd," Will said looking around. Some people began to dance. Others just hoisted and often spilled whatever beverage they were drinking.

DV joined Sunny Jim at the microphone for the next number.

Oh, Jamaica, Jamaica me, Jamaica me crazy. Oh, ho, Jamaica.

The catchy refrain made crowd begin to chant along, a few at first, but more and more joined in each time it was repeated until everyone seemed to be singing.

"If you'll remember, Discovery Bay is where DV told us that he and Cee Cee had bought a villa."

"I remember," Betsy said. "Cee Cee must be in this crowd somewhere. Let's see if we can find her."

The band rolled into the next number, another crowd pleaser.

Gimme water and white, white sand. Blue water, blue, blue water.

Once again, these lyrics were repeated over and over again, causing the crowd to once more to get boisterously into the act. Even after the last note had died, some inebriated fans continued to warble the words.

"And now we have a special treat for you," Sunny Jim announced.

Cindy Livingston began pushing Mile Marker 24s signature Johnson outboard to the middle of the stage. Her husband, singer/songwriter Howard, followed her with his guitar in one hand, grinning and waving to the crowd with the other. He and his band had become Key West local icons and Keys good will promoters over the preceding decade. He took his place next to DV with Jim's band. The highlight of Howard's concerts was when he cranked the ancient boat motor, which had been specially rigged with a blender, and made margaritas with it. The pitcher of margaritas was then auctioned off to the highest bidder as a charity fundraiser, and the auction winner was presented with a limited edition pale blue Howard Livingston baseball cap that only auction winners owned.

"Hang loose," Will told Betsy. "We want to see this."

Sonny Jim continued, pointing at the motor, saying, "But today, Howard's not going to be making margaritas as he usually does, but *'mangoritas'* instead. And when he finishes, he will present the pitcherful to the lucky person who has bought it for the price of a charitable donation."

The band began to play Sunny Jim's song "Mangorita" as Cindy packed the ingredients in the blender and cranked the Johnson outboard.

Mix it in the blender and its mangorita time.

This lyric was repeated over and over during the course of the song once again bringing the enthusiastic audience in into the act in mass.

When the song had ended, Will said, "Now, while Jim's doing the auction, let's go find Cee Cee. Bet she's near the stage."

Will was right. After about five minutes of looking, Betsy spied Cee Cee and began waving to get her attention. Soon they were all together, hugging. Cee Cee waved to DV up on the stage until she could get his attention, and when she had done so, pointed dramatically at the Blacks. She pointed at her watch and mouthed "afterwards." DV game them all a thumbs up to let her know that he understood her message.

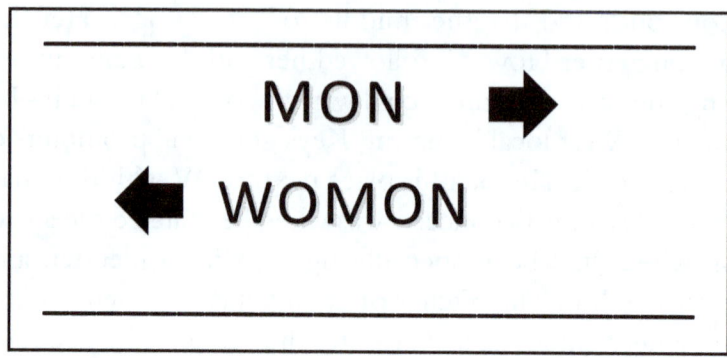

Chapter 4

The Blacks along with Cee Cee enjoyed the remainder of Sunny Jim's concert. After the final number, "Thongs in the Key of Life," they waited while DV helped the band clear the stage, pack up his own guitar, and say farewell to Jim and the crew. Then after they had exchanged pleasantries, DV suggested that they go somewhere quiet so they could visit.

"Ever been to Two Friends on Front Street?" Will asked. "Good locals' hangout."

"Can't say that I have," DV replied.

"They have a guitar player in their front room by the bar, but we can get a table in the dining room adjacent to it. It should be quiet enough to talk there. By the way, you into raw oysters?"

"Absolutely. Is Two Friends walking distance?"

"Sure, but we'll take our car instead since Two Friends has their own parking lot behind the building. I'd just as soon not have to fight this crowd later to retrieve the car here. We're talking about just a few minutes' walk from Mallory Square."

"Give me a few minutes to take this guitar back up to our room first," DV suggested. "Is there anything you need for me to get out of the room while I'm up there, my darling?"

"I'm good. I'll wait with Will and Betsy here in the lobby."

Two Friends' parking lot was small, but they found a parking place since most people were still at the "Meeting of the Minds.' A long sign along the roofline to the open-air bar/café advertised, "BREAKFAST LUNCH DINNER." The roof was mounted atop stained rough-hewn logs that were load-bearing vertical supports that had been wrapped periodically with decorative nautical rope. Below the open-air windows was bamboo wainscoting. One solid unpainted, rough plank wall was draped with hanging commercial fishing nets. Below the nets, a water feature dripped through limestone rocks into a long narrow trough.

Will and Betsy led the Craigs through the small front room that served as a bar. They greeted Danny Hughes, the owner, introduced the Craigs, and then found a table in the dining room. The guitar player had just arrived and was setting up to play. Since it was before dinner hours, most of the epoxied, wooden-slabbed, round tables in the open-air dining room were unoccupied. They selected a table with a view the street.

"How's this?" Will asked.

"Looks good to me," DV said and Cee Cee agreed.

A Hispanic looking waitress approached their table and welcomed them. They could hear the musician in the other room introducing himself and starting to play "Coconut Telegraph," the first song in this afternoon's gig.

"My name is Maria, and I'll be your server. Drinks are half price right now during happy hour, beers – buy one, get one free, and we have half price wings and oysters. Happy hour ends at six."

"I don't know about you guys, but since this is Jimmy Buffett's big Key West weekend, I'm going to order a margarita," Will said.

When he saw the group nod, he told the waitress, "A round of margaritas for everyone. And bring me a dozen oysters on the half shell and the fixings to make my own cocktail sauce. Anyone want to join me?"

Everyone nodded once again.

"Then a dozen for each of us and put it all on one bill, mine."

When the waitress left, Will said, "I bet you could teach that boy a thing or two about how to play "Coconut Telegraph."

31

DV smiled, "Maybe, but it's after hours, and I'm off of work. Do you know how many times I've played that song at Disney and Universal?"

"No, how many?"

"Lost track, but more times than I can count. Would you believe that when the Landsharks started, there wasn't a Jimmy Buffett fan in the group? And then ironically that's how we ended up making a living."

Will laughed and said, "Who'd a thunk it?"

"Sometimes, if you're savvy, you simply play what the crowd wants to hear, and they always seem to want to hear Jimmy Buffett."

Cee Cee entered the discussion at this point and said, "Pardon me if I brag on my husband a little bit. When the Landsharks were playing at Disney, Buffett came over to hear them one night. He liked what he heard so much he hired them on the spot to play at his Margaritaville at Universal. After that, things really began to take off for them."

Before anyone could comment, their drinks arrived. Will held his high.

"Here, here to the Landsharks. And a toast as well to friendship, ocean breezes, not making Jamaica mistakas, and Jimmy Buffett."

"Here's to you. Here's to me. The greatest friends upon the sea. And if, perchance, you disagree, then screw you. Here's to me!" DV countered.

"Hear, hear. Up yours too. Now bring us up to date on Jamaica," Will said.

"Well, we found our dream villa, Mount Corbett, in Discovery Bay," Cee Cee said in an excited voice. "We'll soon be closing on it."

"I hate you. I'm so jealous — Princess Alice's old Jamaican home! We know the property well and at one time looked at it. It just wasn't in the cards. Between our jobs and Lexie's schooling and all our other responsibilities, the timing was just wrong. Sundance, the villa that the bank rented for us when Betsy was on assignment there, was just a short walk down the same hill. And our dear friends, the Davises, lived on Primrose Lane just above it.," Betsy said.

"That's one of the reasons we're in Key West right now," Cee Cee continued. "DV agreed to help Sunny Jim out at the Buffett festival, and we planned to go on down from here to close on the property and assess what else we need to do."

"Hot diggity damn! Boy, oh boy, is that exciting! Betsy and I really miss that place. I don't know how to describe the feeling. It makes us feel like we belong. I guess that's why they have the motto, 'Welcome home'. You just don't know what it feels like every time we land in Mo Bay, deplane, and see our friends Henry and Rose waving back. Though I kinda hate to have to admit it, I was almost ashamed that for security reasons on one recent dangerous affair, we had to more or less sneak into the country and not tell them about it until later. We were fulfilling an obligation to help out a friend."

"… who had risked his life against some very powerful men to help us out when I was working there," Betsy interjected.

"Not just powerful but ruthless as well," Will added. "It was a power struggle with a lot at stake."

"I want to hear that story."

"You will, but not today. I promise, I'll make a happy hour story out of it one day soon."

The waitress arrived with their oysters and the makings for their cocktail sauce. The table got quiet while they passed around the horseradish, ketchup, tabasco, and lime wedges so each person could customize their sauce with the heat that matched their own taste.

Will put a sauce-covered oyster on a saltine and raised it in a mock toast to the group.

"Do you know what they call a male oyster? … a boyster, which makes an alpha male oyster … boisterous," he said.

"Please dear, they're eating."

"And that makes an oyster party animal a joyster," Will added.

DV wasn't to be outdone. He speared an oyster and held it up for all to see.

"Over the lips and through the gums, look out tummy, here it comes."

"You too," his wife groaned. "Betsy, maybe you and I need to go powder our nose, and let our husbands just embarrass themselves instead of all of us."

She looked around and looked back at Betsy before saying, "Or I see an empty table across the room. Shall we take it and leave the Smothers Brothers to duel it out by themselves?"

Everyone laughed.

"But back to Jamaica," she said. "Seriously, we've got to get you down to Mount Corbett, sooner rather than later. You have an open invitation."

"I'm going to just as seriously hold you to that. By the way, our old staff at Sundance knows the staff at Mount Corbett. I'm assuming you'll be keeping them," Betsy offered.

"For the time being, and hopefully, forever," DV said.

"We're still in touch with Leva and E.J.," Will contributed. "Hell, they evolved from staff into family. I'll let them know who the new owners of Mount Corbett are and let them know that we're friends."

"Thanks. And there may be something else you can do for us right now," DV continued. "We'd like to get a boat to keep down there and also a car. Who should we talk to who won't screw us over?"

"As for the car, my buddy, Henry. Henry's a professional driver and pretty damned smart. But let me make another suggestion. Depending on your transportation needs, you may just want to keep him on retainer to drive you around. At least until you get to know the place. That's what we did. Jamaica's a very dangerous place for a novice to drive. Those people drive like they have a death wish. You drive there on the wrong side of the road with one hand on the steering wheel and the other hand on your horn. And blind curves ... huh ... Jamaicans think that's where you're supposed to pass. Jamaicans have a saying about the overtaker meeting the undertaker. And animals ... they just walk out on the road in front of you. Ever hit a goat? Take my word for it, you don't want to. And I haven't even gotten to the subjects of potholes and steep shoulders yet. You could disappear in some of their potholes and wind up coming out of the bottom of them in China."

"Surely you exaggerate."

"You think? Not much. Anyway, I'll get hold of Henry about the car. As far as the boat is concerned, we have a very dear friend, Colonel Ferron Winter, who will have ideas concerning the best way to acquire a boat. He's the elected leader of a faction who call themselves the Maroons. The Maroons' tentacles and influence run very deeply through the fabric of the island. I'm not sure if we owe him more or vice versa, but who's counting. He made Betsy and me honorary Maroons, and we look at him as our honorary stepfather. Since his responsibilities are time-consuming, you may hear from one of his lieutenants, Mikey Mo Mullins. I would trust my life to Mikey Mo."

Betsy laughed and said, "In fact, we have."

"Yes, we have, my dear. More than once. So, when are you leaving?"

"In the morning on the Jet Blue flight at 9:50 to Sangster in Mo Bay. Get there at two something."

"Damn, I'm jealous."

```
NOTICE
ANY STRAYAWAY ANIMALS
WILL BE SHOOT
DONKEY COW GOAT
```

Chapter 5

Will called Colonel Winter and filled him in on DV's request. Then he called Henry Davis and arranged for him to meet the Craigs at the airport. A couple of weeks elapsed before he heard from anyone again. Then one day Will's phone rang. It was DV.

"Will? DV Craig. We heard from both Henry and Mikey Mo Mullins. You don't know how much we appreciate your introducing us to Mikey Mo and Henry Davis. They have made things so much easier than they would have been otherwise. By the way, Mikey Mo sends The Colonel's regards. Henry did as well."

"Glad to hear that. Henry's not only a great guy, but he knows the ropes down there. Not only did he become a great friend, but he saved our bacon more than once. You'll find if you haven't already that he doesn't just know stuff; he knows people — and I mean the right people — in addition to his understanding of human nature."

"We took your advice and contracted him to drive us for the time being. I'm beginning to understand your comments about Jamaican drivers and road conditions. And you didn't say anything about how easy it is to get lost down here, but, damned … it's nice to have someone driving who knows his way around. If I'd been doing all the driving, I'd probably have been in an accident by now. I'm beginning to understand Jamaica me crazy. The drivers are the crazies, and if it weren't for Henry, I'd probably be as crazy as they are by now."

36

"People up here don't believe me. They think it's just some of Will's bullshit. You have to have been there to know that I'm really a little old truthteller who's telling it like it is. What about the boat?"

"Mikey Mo lined us up with a boat broker in Kingston. English dude named Price Wright. Ever heard of him?"

"Nah! But that doesn't mean anything. What counts is that The Colonel knows Mr. Wright, or he wouldn't have recommended him. Colonel Winter's never steered me wrong."

"Wright's going to be an answer to a prayer. He seems to be a birddog who can smell value and then get a rock bottom deal on it. That's exactly the kind of person we need to be dealing through. Man, I owe you for arranging an introduction to someone reputable."

"I know what you're saying. Betsy and I dealt with a few people when we were newbies first moving to the Keys who I wouldn't deal with again. We had our first home sound system installed by a Bar-Don Electric. He totally screwed up the wiring and then wouldn't stand behind his work. Mis-wired our house and fried an expensive amplifier."

"I hear you, my friend. By the way, you didn't tell me that Henry used to live in England."

"Yep — he and Rose lived in London actually — for a goodly number of years before getting homesick to return to their Jamaican roots. They still have dual citizenship. His background is quite colorful, actually. He flew in the RAF and at one point was a driver for some of the royal family. He was also a general contractor. She sewed for some fashion designer. They still have a daughter who's a schoolteacher in London and another one who's married to a career Nigerian government employee."

"And now he just drives a tour bus? Seems overqualified for that."

"Hey! What can I say? I've never seen his balance sheet, but he has a nice house and seems to never want for anything. I'm guessing that between the money he made and his retirement benefits, they easily maintain a standard of living that more than adequately meets their needs. He drives now just because he likes to and loves dealing with people. Henry wouldn't make a good recluse."

"He certainly has people skills. You were right when you told me about all the people he knows — and I've yet to run into anyone who doesn't seem to respect Mr. Davis."

"I never did ask you what kind of boat you were interested in buying."

"Oh, something that will sleep six people. Something big enough that we could take a longer trip in with friends if we wanted to. Something with a galley, and of course, beds … naturally a decent head. I like catamarans."

"Motorboat, I presume."

"Sure. I'm not into sailing. That's too much like work."

"I see y'all have thought this out. You're not just pulling something out of your ass. Any luck so far?"

"Actually, yes. The boat broker seems to have a line on something that will fill the bill nicely. He found what sounds like a winner coming up for government auction. A cat with a galley. It's a thirty-five-foot Gemini Legacy. Fourteen feet wide. Square-top mainsail. It's got twin Yanmar diesel engines. Three private bedrooms. Can sleep up to six people. Shallow draft — less than three feet. Sounds perfect for us. It's called the *Spirit of the Seas*. I told him to go for it. He'll represent us at the auction next week."

"That's exciting. Good luck. Keep me posted on whether you get it or not."

"Absolutely. None of this would be happening without you."

"Oh, we got so sidetracked on the boat, I forgot to ask. What about Mount Corbett?"

"It's done. We are now proud owners of a Jamaican villa."

"You're just full of good news. You got a sho' nuff wiener with that one. It's one hell of a house, and the grounds are magnifique."

"I couldn't agree with you more. Cee Cee thinks we've died and gone to heaven. So much has gone right that I can't imagine anything going wrong."

"As we say in the South, don't get overconfident and put your mouth on it. Or as they say in Jamaica, 'Chicken deh merry, hawk deh near' **(The happy chicken is what attracts the hawk)**."

PLEEZE NO GANJA SMOKING IN THE BAR

Chapter 6

Many rivers to cross
But I can't seem to find my way over
Wandering I am lost

Wesley "Weasley" Lineitem turned up the radio when he heard the opening strains of the Jimmy Cliff classic begin to play on his car radio. He hoped that the song would distract him and improve his mood. His finger trembled slightly as he initially hit the radio button, accidentally switching the station, and held the volume knob down a bit too long after turning it back. The radio momentarily blared.

"Song tells the bloodclaayt truth," he mumbled and then added, "Wa **(Why)** do mi let Harry Dog talk mi into dis ting **(thing)**?"

Instead of making him feel better, all the blaring song did was to make the headache he'd been nursing that morning worse. The sun shined directly into his eyes, making him see stars. He veered briefly onto the shoulder of the road, spraying gravel on the car's underside as he reached to turn it off.

"Wa? Cause mi a rahtid ediat **(damned idiot)**, thas wa."

Weasley was Harry Dog's personal accountant as well as being a certified tax attorney. He had also been Harry's coconspirator on occasion when Harry was trying to pull a fast one on someone else or even a score. Despite his professional status, Weasley was a natural born, professional liar who did not muse for long or often over moral dilemmas.

He and Harry Dog had hit a sizable score together when he had set up a refining company for melting scrap gold. The source of the gold was cash purchases of unsalable pawnshop jewelry that he bought to launder some of the Shower Posse's illegal monies. His inspiration had been cloning a similar successful operation that El Chapo Guzman of the Mexican Sinaloa Cartel had devised to launder his cartel's illegal profits. The scam was to set up a series of dummy corporations which then bought the gold with Shower Posse money in a sham transaction for cash from the refinery after it was processed. Dudus was in effect buying back his own gold at market prices. He would then store the untraceable gold until a later time when he could sell it on the open market and declare a capital gain on his tax return. Voila! Dudus's dirty linen was now clean as a hound's tooth.

And all this for a two percent commission. What Dudus didn't know was that this was a padded price since half of it went back to Harry Dog as an under-the-table kickback. Harry called it his Jamaican IRA, affectionately known as his irie IRA.

Weasley's street name wasn't derived from his character, though that certainly would have been appropriate. Instead, it came about because he reminded many people of rodent or a mongoose. His close-cropped hair sat on top of a long neck that protruded from an elongated, tubular, yet still muscular-looking body. His torso was mounted atop short, squatty legs. Despite his attempts to smile behind wire-rimmed glasses, his alert, piercing eyes had a wily, sneaky look. Weasley's sharklike grin was hyenalike and carnivorous.

After the *Spirit of the Seas* fiasco, Dudus had used his government contacts to make sure the boat was included in the upcoming government auction and had informed Harry Dog of the auction's date and time. He left no doubt that he expected Harry to do whatever it took to make sure the boat was returned to the posse. But Harry Dog had an undisclosed dilemma. He didn't bring this up with Dudus because any excuses on his part would just denote weakness and laxity and infuriate Dudus more than he already was. Harry Dog knew that he would never be allowed to attend the auction personally. He was too well known as a thug by the law enforcement community. Everyone allowed into the auction had to be vetted before admittance, and Harry knew there was no chance that he could pass an inspection under his real name.

Harry had another problem as well. It wouldn't be smart to go to Bigga for help even though Bigga owed him big for keeping his role in the whole calamity a secret from The Presi. Bigga had the same problem with the law that Harry did. It was no secret what a thug he was. And Harry's stomach knotted every time he thought about the dutty batty creases **(dirty ass-cracks)** that Bigga had sent to do the last job. They were why he was in this mess to begin with.

He secretly wondered if Bigga had submarined him on purpose to make him look bad with Dudus. After all, the truth of the matter was that while they might feign on the surface to be friends who were playing on the same team, they were rivals who were both trying to move up in the dog-eat-dog world of the posse where only the strong survived. And he couldn't afford to pitch Bigga under the bus in a kneejerk reaction just because he suspected possible treachery. He might be wrong. And then Dudus would then think that his retaliation against Bigga was just a desperate effort to find a scapegoat for a fuckery in an assignment that The President had clearly assigned to him.

And you could bet your bottom dollar that Bigga would be sure to get even — somewhere, sometime — when Harry least suspected it. That's all Harry needed, to be looking over his shoulder constantly dodging one more enemy. He had enough enemies already. But this fuckery wasn't going away. The President had made that clear.

So, what do I do? I'll call on my pal, Weasley to get me out of this jam. Weasley's a professional man. And he's educated. Hell, he's both a lawyer and an accountant. And he doesn't have an arrest record. And I'm sure that Weasley knows better than to try to screw over me. I've got too much on that infant-killa (cradle-robber). I know all about his kinky obsession with minors and odda sketels **(other sluts)**. *Yep, no one knows as much about Weasley's dirty laundry as I do.*

And Dudus views Weasley different. He's not a member of the posse. … And never will be. He's just hired help. And hired help's disposable. A wah di ras **(what the fuck)**, *if push comes to shove, I can always dump Weasley under the bus.*

Weasley continued to smolder with resentment against Harry Dog as he drove along. The resentment festered in him as he thought about the trip to the beach with the sweet young Cheyenne that he had had to cancel today and the pumm pumm **(pussy)** he had planned to get afterwards.

Mon o mon! Di gal have one nice piece ah chest yu see **(You should see the tits on that gal.)**

Instead, I'm going to a boat auction. I told that bobo **(fool)**, *Harry Dog, that I don't know anything about boats. Never even owned one … or wanted to own one. Don't know one kind or model from another. And I don't have the slightest idea what one's worth.*

But oh, no. He rass cleat head eaz **(He's too damned stubborn to listen.)**.

I can see it now. I pay too much for the rass clot thing, and then it's my ass on the line with Dudus. Dudus has got more money than Jah. So, why does he want this secondhand piece of shit? He could afford to buy ten boats — and new ones.

Weasley's head began to throb even worse than it had when he left. He started feeling breathless with anger.

What's the name of this tub again? Spirit of some rass thing. Or was that Spirit of the Season? … Spirit of Spain? … What if it doesn't have the name printed on it? How'm I supposed to recognize it?

Weasley stopped for a light. The light changed, but he sat there absorbed in his negative thoughts until the car behind him blew his horn to urge him to go on. He absentmindedly hit his turn signal but then kept on going straight with it continuing to blink. The other driver tooted at him again. He answered by holding up his middle finger and then gunned the car.

A half hour later, Weasley arrived at the impound yard where the auction was to take place, checked in, and was given a bidder number and an auction program. His participant number was forty-two.

Weasley accidentally dropped the sign-in pen on the ground after the lady handed it to him and had to pick it up. He felt dizzy, his equilibrium seeming slightly off when he bent down. He attributed this to his irritated frame of mind. The briefcase full of cash Harry had given him suddenly seemed heavier than it had when he had put it in the car. He looked for a place to sit down or something to put the briefcase on, but the auction had provided no chairs or tables. People meandered around. Some did a last-minute examination of boats; some looked over the program to try to determine when a particular item might come up for bidding; some people circled items of interest; still others chatted in small groups with people they knew. He assumed those people were regular participants.

Weasley just stood off to one side alone and waited impatiently. He wiped his sweaty brow on his sleeve. He finally saw a familiar face, Price Wright, the boat broker.

He managed to get Mr. Wright's attention and walked over to shake hands with him.

"You're the last person I expected to see here today," Wright said just to make small talk.

"Same goes for you. Whazz-up?"

"Oh, It's just another day at the salt mine for me. I'm here to see if they're selling any boats that might match what a client of mine is looking for. Who knows? I might get lucky and find just what he has in mind within the price range he wants to pay."

"Well, good luck."

"You too."

I wish this rass headache would go away.

A man and his assistant arrived. The assistant was the same woman who had checked him in.

"May I have your attention please? We will begin the auction in three minutes. This will be a standing auction. You will follow me as a group to the item being auctioned. You will then have two minutes to view each item. Notice that I said view. You will not be allowed feel or handle the item being auctioned. The time for you to have done that expired yesterday. I will open the bidding, which will be our suggested minimum or floor price. If no one bids, then the item will be carried over to a future auction. My assistant will assemble the details about the winner when the bidding has ceased, and I have awarded the boat. She will give you an invoice that you will take to our cashier who will give you a temporary title. The settlement date for payments is today before you leave. We do not take checks. American or Jamaican Cash is the only acceptable medium of exchange. The exchange rate is today's rate set by the Bank of Jamaica — .0086. We will not be auctioning the boats in the sequence in your program but instead in the order that they are being stored in the yard. Are there any questions before we begin?"

He looked around.

"No? Then let us proceed. The first item to be auctioned is number sixty-seven. That is six — seven."

The briefcase was making Weasley's fingers feel numb and weak, so he set it down by his feet. 67 was not the item he had been sent to buy so his attention riveted to the auctioneer's attractive assistant's ample bustline. His thoughts turned again to Cheyenne, but he found himself not seeming to have the attention span to focus long on either woman. His mind felt foggy, and his thoughts wandered aimlessly. As the bidding commenced, is left knee twitched and then his ankle itched.

*Rass **(Damn)** mosquito*, he slurred.

He tried to flex the itching knee and scratch at the same time. When he did, he lost his equilibrium and kicked over his briefcase. He lost his balance and came down hard on the shaky knee, spitting out his saliva-covered top denture. It toppled into the red clay dirt.

"Fuc ... ah ... mmm ... wha di ...," he inadvertently slurred nonsensically. The left-side of his mouth felt suddenly heavy, and he couldn't 't form words. With frustration, he put his hand under his chin and tried to push his jaw back up into place. The only thing he accomplished was for his bottom teeth to dig into his top gums. He grimaced and let out with more unintelligible syllables.

The auctioneer heard Weasley's unintentional, impaired utterance and thought he was attempting to bid. He pointed at Weasley and announced, "Four million six Jamaican from bidder number forty-two. Do I hear five?"

Four million eight hundred thousand Jamaican came from another bidder, followed by five million.

Saved, Weasley thought as he squatted on his haunches swaying drunkenly as he leaned over to try to recover the errant denture.

As he leaned, his glasses fell off. His legs suddenly felt even weaker, and he plopped down on the ground to continue feeling around him to try to retrieve his missing teeth. He somehow found them.

'Ere the rass tings **(Here are the damned things.).**

He jammed the dirt-coated dentures back into his mouth before he could drop them again and tried to stand. His equilibrium was off once again, and he swayed forwards.

He reached out to stabilize himself and accidentally grabbed the leg of the beefy man in front of him. He tried to use the man's leg to regain his balance. One hand became entangled with the chain that secured the man's oversize back-pocket wallet to his belt. As Weasley continued to topple forwards, he pulled the man's already low-riding loose pants down his legs exposing the fact that the man was going commando. The man jerked forwards thinking that a thief was trying to steal his wallet, pulling Weasley's head into his ass crack. When Weasley butted him, the blow jarred loose a wet fart into Weasley's face. The brown residue dripped down Weasley's nose and leaked into his open mouth. The now livid man pivoted and spun around to confront his would-be thief. Weasley's feces-covered nose slammed into his hairy, sweaty crotch the moment he turned. The man's thatch of pubic hairs tickled Weasley's nose, causing him to sneeze. Just as he did, the man's fist slammed down on Weasley's head, causing him to bite his tongue, gag, and then throw up on his unfortunate victim. Weasley saw stars and ducked back to avoid another blow, slinging his dirt, puke, and spit covered teeth like a projectile down the man's pants leg.

"Yu tin kyu wan licky-licky mi buddies, renk batty bwoy? Licky-licky me? Licky-licky dis instead (**You think you wanna give me a blowjob, dirty faggot? Blow this instead.**).

He tried to raise his work-booted foot to kick Weasley but instead tripped on his own pants that were by now hugging his ankles. Weasley zigged in the other direction to avoid the expected kick, toppling spreadeagle, sending them both to the ground on top of his glasses.

Before the man could recover, Weasley suddenly found the energy to rise. He threw a handful of dirt into the man's eyes, grabbed his briefcase, and fled towards the rear of crowd. The bystanders looked one with both astonishment and amusement, not believing the scene they had just witnessed.

Weasley ducked behind a boat to catch his breath. When he thought he was safe, he let the crowd of bidders sweep him along as they followed the auctioneer the short distance to the next boat to be auctioned.

As he stood there panting and squinting, Weasley heard the auctioneer announce, "And now number eleven, one — one, "The Sprite …."

Did he say spirit? Shit! That's Dudus's boat.

Weasley tried to listen, but his ears were still ringing from the blow to the head. Without his glasses, the name on the boat was also a blur. The rest of the announcement seemed garbled, but he wasn't really listening since his head throbbed worse than before.

"The auction will begin in two minutes."

Oh, thank you, good Lord. The boat Harry Dog told me to buy. Let's get this over with so I can get the hell out of here before something else happens.

"We will begin the bidding at five million Jamaican."

"Five million one," Weasley impulsively yelled almost before the words were out of the auctioneer's mouth.

The man who had been involved in Weasley's debacle saw who was bidding. He smiled. *He wants this boat? This is my chance to even the score with dat renk, dutty pussywool* (**stinking dirty wimp**) *by artificially jacking up the price of the one he wants.*

"Five million five."

"Siss millon," Weasley countered unintelligibly.

Harry Dog had given him twelve million Jamaican to work with, even though he didn't expect Weasley to have to spend it all. The Sprite should have come in less than that since it was ten feet shorter than the *Spirit of the Seas*. Harry Dog had neglected to tell Weasley the length of or the type of boat he was bidding on since he thought the program should make the boat's identity clear. With the muddled state of Weasley's mind and his limited boat knowledge, it probably wouldn't have made a difference anyway. All Weasley knew was that he was not supposed to fail to buy the boat Dudus wanted.

"Six million five."

Weasley momentarily forgot the next number. Concentration was becoming increasingly difficult.

"Siss millon," he blurted out.

"The last bid was six million five," the auctioneer reminded him.

"Oh yeah! Rass. Sebben den," Weasley slurred back, his face feeling even more numb.

"Eight."

Weasley's face began to tingle even though his body felt limp.

Why won't the bastard just let me buy it?

"Ettt – fibe."

"Nine."

Gwey and fyah fi yu, batty crease **(Fuck off and burn in hell, asshole!)***! Mi tol to get das boat or it mi ass.*

Weasley hesitated. The opposing bidder noted that fact and smiled.

"Ten."

Might as well shoot my whole wad and get this over with.

"Twelve."

The auctioneer pointed that the other bidder, who grinned and shook his head from side to side. The auctioneer rapped the gavel down.

"Sold to bidder number forty-two for twelve million dollars Jamaican."

Weasley's competitor and adversary gave himself a round of applause and flew his middle finger at Weasley. Revenge was his. He had just conned Weasley into paying a twelve million for a boat probably worth no more than seven.

Weasley, on the other hand, breathed a sigh of relief. Success was his, or so he thought. He could report back to Harry Dog that he had bought the boat Harry Dog sent him to buy. He silently congratulated himself on the fact that he had gotten it before he had run out of money.

Batty hole didn't know that with one more bid he could have had it since mi was tapped out. Dis oughta buy mi some browning points with The Presi.

Chapter 7

After Weasley finalized the boat purchase and received the appropriate documentation, he drove away, relieved that his role in the boat affair was over. His hands shook, and his head continued to throb. With a trembling finger, he managed to put his phone on silent. He suddenly felt short of breath again, and his vision blurred. He saw Jack's Jerk, pulled over on the side street next to Jack's, and killed the engine to give himself a chance to catch his breath. That's the last thing Weasley remembered until he heard someone tapping on the car window.

"Yah OK, mon? Yu need 'elp?"

He acknowledged the good Samaritan, cranked the car, and drove on.

Harry Dog tried unsuccessfully to dial Weasley for an update. He finally gave up and decided that he would just go by Weasley's office the next morning.

He purposely waited until midmorning to go. Weasley was not known to be an early morning person. When he walked in, Weasley's latest assistant, Yolanda, was just hanging up the phone. She had only worked there for a few weeks and did not recognize Harry.

"Da boss in?"

"Dah was just Mr. Lineitem on the phone. He won't be in today. He's sick."

"Wa yu mean, sick? Wi hab bidness (**business**) together. Wen he be here?"

"Mr. Lineitem's in da hospital."

"Wah? Wah wrong wi he?"

She shrugged her shoulders.

"Wich hospital?"

"Andrews Memorial on Hope Road."

Harry was suddenly concerned for Weasley's health.

"Tank yu," he said, almost over his shoulder as he turned and rushed back towards the door.

"Wait, Mister," Yolanda called out.

"Wha?"

"Yu gwine to the hospital?"

"Uh-huh."

"When Mr. Lineitem called, he axxed me to bring de tin box on his desk over on mi lunch hour. Will yu take it, since yu're going anyway?'

"Wha's in it?"

"I dunno, but he wanted it."

"Sure."

She retrieved the box and handed it to Harry Dog. He snatched it out of her hands and then didn't even say goodbye as he slammed the door behind him.

Pat's Flowers was on Old Hope Road. Her number was in Harry's phone since he had dealt with her in the past. Unfortunately, mostly to order flowers for funerals for former associates. He dialed ahead on speed dial and told her that he was on his way to the hospital and needed to pick up some flowers for a friend.

"Use yu judgement. I be at yu store shortly. Yu got candy? Get he a box of choclates."

Then he remembered Bookophilia was also on Old Hope Road just before Pat's.

Mi get mi good pal some reading material too. Go der fust.

After he had picked up Weasley's presents, Harry Dog found a parking place at Andrews Memorial Hospital and carried his good will offerings into the reception area. A large sign in the Seventh Day Adventist facility announced DEDICATED TO HEALING THE WHOLE PERSON.

Riight! Yu bet! Dey dedicated all right. Dey dedicated to suck de whole person's whole money from he like a buddy buoy **(gay person)** *wanna suck mi hose dry.*

Harry watched the fish in the large fish tank from a green Naugahyde covered chair while the receptionist checked with the nurses' station to make sure that Weasley could have visitors. When she had verified this, she then told Harry that Weasley was in room 151.

Harry Dog opened Weasley's door and walked in with a big sharklike grin on his face.

"Some people will do anything not to have to go to work," he said and laughed. "So, wha happened to you?"

"Tell me I had a stroke."

"You gonna be OK?"

"I tink so."

"Since yu are mi fren **(friend)**, mi brought you some stuff."

He approached Weasley's bed and handed him the magazines and candy. He put the vase of flowers on a table across the room.

"Yolanda sent over da tin box you wanted. Wha yu wanna mi do wid it?"

"Just put it on the table next to the window."

"And mehbe dis'll make you feel betta," Harry said and handed Weasley a get-well card he had picked up at the bookstore. Weasley opened the card.

It contained a heavily made up, grimacing, obese, middle-aged black woman in a low-cut, scoop-necked nurse's uniform that exposed most of her huge cleavage. Her floozie-looking, highly teased blonde wig puffed out beneath a white nursing cap. She held an oversized hyperthermic needle in her meaty right hand. The fat first finger on her left hand pointed directly at the card holder. The caption read, "You're sick? Looking for sympathy?" The inside of the card read "You'll find it in the dictionary between shit and syphilis."

Weasley, who still felt weak, barely smiled.

"So, did you make it to the auction?"

"Of course. And got the job done."

"Great. I knew wi could count on you."

"Get mi briefcase out of the closet. Da paperwork's in dere."

"What'd yu have to pay for it?"

"It was tough. It took all the money yu gave mi. Some battyhole started a bidding war. He doesn't know it, but he backed down just in time because mi was running out of money. One more bid, and he would have had mi."

"I'll never tell. That's what bluffing is all about — the guy whose buddies are the biggest."

Harry Dog retrieved the documents from Weasley's briefcase. He gave them the once over, and then his lip curled in a snarl.

"Looks like these papers have a misprint. It says that the name of the boat is the 'Sprite'."

"Yeah. Das the one you told mi to buy."

"I didn't tell you to buy the 'Sprite.' I told you to buy the '*Spirit of the Seas.*' yu dumb fuck."

Harry kept reading the papers.

"It says this is a thirty-two-foot boat. The '*Spirit of the Seas*' is forty-two foot."

"My glasses got broken," Weasley stammered. "Plus, my head was killing me."

Harry's voice rose, and he began to shake the papers in Weasley's face.

"I'm the one who's going to kill yu — yu stupid SOB. And if I don't, The President will. You paid twelve million Jamaican for a thirty-two-foot boat? … And you let the one you were supposed to buy get away from you?"

"I tried to tell yu I didn't know nothing about boats!"

Weasley suddenly felt like he was about to have a stroke all over again. Until this moment, he was so sure he'd done the right thing, even as impaired as he had been.

"So, who bought the *Spirit of the Seas?*"

"I dun know. Mi left after that. My head was killing me."

"You better be glad you're in a hospital. If you weren't, I put you in one. … Or in the goldamned cemetery. How could you fuck up this bad?"

"I didn't know. I thought they were the same — just a misprint."

"Wait'll I tell Dudus this. I'm not taking this fall for you. You just going to be one dead four-eyed, high-tone bush-nigga. I've got a half a mind to take these flowers and use them to ram dis choclate so far up you ass that you'll be shitting choclate bunnies till Easter."

Harry abruptly turned without saying goodbye or get well and slammed the door as he exited the room.

Chapter 8

Weasley felt like he wanted to throw up. This was not the meeting he expected. He had expected to be treated like a hero by both Dudus Coke and Harry Dog. He had thought his reputation and stature would be enhanced. Instead, he now had to find a way to redeem himself.

How was I expected to know that there'd be two boats with almost the same name? But now, how can I earn The President's forgiveness when I'm in the rass **(damned)** *hospital? I gotta tink this out.*

He felt like the breakfast he had eaten might come back up.

But what could I do even if I weren't in da hospital?

His regular hospital nurse came in and administered a medication. Weasley dozed back off.

A nightmare ensued. In it, he saw himself tied shirtless to a chair with Dudus leering down at him. Dudus was holding a smoking soldering iron. Harry Dog was leaning against the wall, picking his teeth with a toothpick, grinning like he was about to enjoy the scene that was about to ensue.

Dudus suddenly spoke and said, "Mr. Lineitem. What should I do with you? Where should I begin?"

He tested the iron to see if it was hot by touching one of Weasley's nipples. He seemed satisfied when Weasley tried to jerk away and cried out as a pain shot through him.

Dudus's hat suddenly grew into a dirty, black, Rue style, open-crown hat with a flat stiff brim. His face got angular and pockmarked and was suddenly covered with a scraggly beard. Before Weasley's eyes, Dudus became a black spitting image of Fagin from the movie "Oliver." Like Fagin, his eyes lit up in a wicked grin that seemed to be boring a hole in Weasley.

He suddenly began to sing. Harry Dog began to change his appearance. Weasley blinked. Harry Dog had become Bill Sikes. Sikes joined Fagin, and the two of them held hands as they did a jig around Weasley's chair.

We're reviewing the situation
We're bad 'uns and bad 'uns we shall stay
You'll be seeing no transformation ... or forgiveness
It's not wrong to be a rogue in every way

Then Fagin put his face right up to Weasley's and spoke, saliva dripping onto Weasley's face.

"Should I forgive and forget? After all, anyone can make a mistake. Or should I burn the name of the *Spirit of the Seas* into your chest, so you won't forget it again? Maybe on your forehead instead. Maybe even on your ass."

Harry Dog aka Bill Sikes' eyes lit up.

"Boss, let me help!"

Fagin then sang by himself.

I think I'd better think it out again.

About that time, the boat broker, Price Wright, walked into the room. He became the Artful Dodger and began to sing to Fagin and Bill Sikes.

I don't want nobody hurt for me.
Or made to do the dirt for me.
It's getting far too hot for me.
There is no in-between for me.
But who will change the scene for me?

He pointed at Weasley with his middle finger, from which a long fingernail began to burst forth. It glowed and smoked like a second soldering iron.

Everything went black. When Weasley woke, he found out he had soiled his hospital bed.

I've got to get out of here and find Price Wright. He's in the boat brokerage business. He should know who bought the Spirit of the Seas. *And if he doesn't, he'll know how to find out. I'll bribe him if I have to. Or if that doesn't work, I'll dig up some dirt on him and blackmail him. Everybody's got something to hide. Maybe I'll get even and burn him with a soldering iron since he tried to do it to me.*

Weasley felt suddenly elated and compelled to sing out loud. He warbled one line off-key to conclude Fagin's song.

Now, I won't need to think this out again.

He felt so inexplicably euphoric that he defecated on himself again.

The nurse overheard him singing and poked her head in the door.

"Are yu OK, Mr. Lineitem? Do yu need to go to the baffroom?"

"As a matter of fact, mi did hab a axxident."

```
┌─────────────────────────────────────────────┐
│          Notice — PUBLIC BAR                 │
│    OUR PUBLIC BAR IS PRESENTLY               │
│         NOT OPEN BECAUSE                      │
│          IT IS CLOSED                        │
│                          manager             │
└─────────────────────────────────────────────┘
```

Chapter 9

Weasley spent the remainder of the day plotting his escape from the hospital. He decided he wouldn't check out. He didn't have the money to pay the hospital bill anyway, not if he had to spend his own money to dig out of deep kaka by replacing Dudus' boat.

Dunno wha de big deal is. A rass **(damned)** *boat's a rass boat.*

But he'd worry about the rass bill later. He just had to get out of there and find Price Wright before the vindictive Harry Dog or Dudus sent some thugs back over to the hospital to punish him for screwing up.

Weasley retrieved the tin box from his office and opened it, smelling the contents. Now, thanks to Harry Dog, he had just the tool he needed to facilitate his jailbreak from Andrews Memorial. He would make his escape that evening.

Tonite, mi outa here. Rass. Sure am glad mi on de fust floor.

The tin box was filled with fresh chocolate chunk cookies. But not just any tollhouse cookies. These had been generously laced with ganja. He was tempted to taste one but resisted.

Maybe just one … No. Mi'll need a clear head if mi going to make dis work. Bidness before pleasure.

And this was not just any ganja. It was primo-primo weed — Lamb's Bread — Bob Marley's favorite variety. Marley prized it because

57

he said it was unusually uplifting and made him energetic. ... And best of all ... it was a product of Jamaica.

Buy made-in-Jamaica first. Support yu local Rasta.

And in a gourmet batch of cookies. Not just choclate chip but choclate chunk made wif Reese's pieces.

Weasley had baked them himself only the day before the auction. And even better, he had accidentally spilled double the usual amount of weed in the batch.

Mi almost hate to give dese away, but yu do wha yu hab to do. Dis do be an emergency.

Temptation was just too much for him to resist. He stuffed a whole cookie in his mouth and gobbled it down. Shortly thereafter, he felt lightheadedly happy. The sun came in the window and an aura *surrounded* the get-well card that Harry Dog had brought him. Suddenly, inspiration struck, and the obese black nurse on the front of the card smiled at him. She spoke to him and told him that by hook or crook he somehow needed to disguise himself.

"Get a nurses' uniform," she advised.

Tank yu Jah (God) for sending mi my own guardian angel.

He sniffed the cookies again. Euphoric!

Heaben on earth.

He smelled them one last time. The scent caused him to sneeze and then drool into the box. He turned those cookies over.

He blew a kiss to the nurse on the card for helping him form a plan. She winked and blew him a kiss back. She sucked seductively on one of her pudgy fingers.

This was more than Weasley could stand. He got an erection and began to sing the old Platters' song "Heaven on Earth" back to her in return.

Heaven on Earth
Alone with an angel, is living with dreams come true
Heaven on Earth
I know that it happens only when I'm with you.

The fat nurse smiled and bent over, shaking her ample bosoms at him as she licked her pouty red lips. He could see her name tag for the first time — Nevaeh Claire. Nevaeh's halo highlighted nursing cap which she tilted downward seductively over one eye. She winked. He felt hot and feverish all over. She took note and began to cool him by fanning him with angel wings that seemed to appear from nowhere.

Yes! He was now completely convinced that he had been right. God had indeed sent this seraph down from heaven and assigned her specifically to be his guardian angel. With Nevaeh on his side, he couldn't go wrong.

Yes, mi gon need to steal a nurses' uniform to wear out of here. But lucky mi. Di custodian's closet is right across the hall. And hit's not locked. Mi remembers seeing clean uniforms and towels on da orderly's cart.

The orderly's cart wasn't there, but the housekeeper's was. She had left her cart in the hall as she changed the beds down the hall. Weasley didn't see what he needed on it. When he was sure he was not being observed, he used the cart as cover and sneaked a peak into the closet across the hall. As he had hoped, clean nurses' uniforms were being stored there. He grabbed the first one that looked like it might fit and crept back to his room. He jammed it under his mattress.

Step one completed.

Weasley sniffed the box again. He took one out and stared at it lovingly. His erection returned, and his mouth watered. He rubbed the cookie along his cheek. It felt velvety.

He looked at the nurse again, and grinning, she nodded her approval.

OK, just one more for mi. Dey too good not to eben get a few to sample.

Nevaeh winked and made a circle of approval with her index finger and thumb.

He started to take a third cookie, but Nevaeh rubbed her first fingers rapidly in an "x" across each other, shook her head, and spoke to him in a husky voice for the first time. She sounded to him like Mavis Staples with a Jamaican accent.

"What sweet nanny goat a go run him belly (**the things that seem good to you now can hurt you later.**)."

He nodded his comprehension and said, "Mi undastan. Crayben choke puppy **(the results of greed are grief, loss, and destruction.)**."

Neveah smiled and replied, "Gud. Mi glad yu undastan **(understand)**."

He obediently put the third cookie back in the tin box.

Weasley waited until his live nurse came into the room for a routine check later that afternoon to put his plan into action. He didn't want to seem too anxious and give her a reason to suspect that anything was amiss. He also knew that his timing needed to be right. It would probably take an hour or more for the cookies to deliver their desired high, but then he knew from experience that after that, the high could last after that for up to twelve hours.

If mi lucky, da ganja's effect should last through a major portion of da night.

He waited until the floor nurse had come in to take his temperature.

"Mrs. Donald, yu and everyone here has been rilly, rilly nice to mi. Mi got sometin special for yu and da rest of da staff. Hope yu enjoy dese fresh cookies as much as mi enjoyed baking dem. Hit a fambly recipe."

He handed her the tin box full of cookies.

"I baked 'em de day before mi came to da hospital, and I wan yu to hab dem while dey still fresh. Dere's plenty to go around. Be sure and share 'em wif the orderlies as well. All of yu hab treated mi so gud, so mi wan to show my appreciation. Yu hab a tough job, and mi sure people don't say tank yu often enough."

Mrs. Donald thanked him profusely and took the cookies back to the nurses' station. Each time a different staff member came to his room after that, they thanked him all over again.

Step two into getting mi batty **(bottom)** *de hell out of Dodge ... or should mi say Andrews Memorial. Le' dey party begin ... mi rass* **(damn)** *well hope so anyway.*

Now Weasley's dilemma was timing his exit so that he didn't get caught. The answer hit him — the pager to summon the nurses. He'd find some bullshit reasons to call the nurses from time to time. If he hit the pager repeatedly and no one answered, it probably meant that the ganja had taken hold, and it was time for him to go.

But doubt refused to go away. His fears of getting caught seemed to grow as the afternoon progressed. He visualized himself being roughed up by an overexuberant, muscular orderly. This caused his stomach to knot and churn. More doubt set in. He began to wonder if his plan had a chance of working.

One ting for certain, I can't be here when Harry Dog and his men come back.

Finally in an effort to calm down, he ate the second cookie he'd saved for himself. Neveah nodded her approval. By dinner time he began to feel calmer and better.

In the early evening, Weasley buzzed the pager as a test for someone to pick up his dinner dishes. No one came. After a few minutes, he hit it again. Still no one. He tried a third time. Still nothing.

Eureka! It's time for me to move out. Adios, Andrews Memorial.

Weasley donned the nurses' uniform and put on a surgical paper face mask to hide his identity. The uniform turned out to be much larger than it had looked when he had snatched it from the supply closet. It hung loosely like a sack on his frame and was too long.

Weasley eased his door open and peeked out. He could hear a radio playing at the nurses' station. He thought he heard Neveah's voice.

Good sign.

He crawled barefoot on all fours down the hall, pushing a wheelchair in front of him for cover. The nurses' uniform was so big that his knees kept getting tangled in it until he toppled over frontways, falling spreadeagle into a dirty dinner tray that still had leftover apple sauce and mashed potatoes and gravy on it. It had been left for pickup on the seat of a second wheelchair parked in the hall. His front and face came up covered with leftover squashy goo.

In a gut reaction, he swiped at his wet front as he grabbed the wheelchair to try to get his arms back under him so he could rise. The wheels weren't locked, and it shot away of him, raring up on two wheels, careening into the wheelchair that he had been using as cover. The tray rattled to the floor. Crockery and glasses shattered, sounding to him like an explosion.

Weasley thought his heart would stop. He waited nervously to see if anyone in the nurses' station had heard the crash. When no one came, he now spider-crawled drunkenly on all fours down the hall, zigzagging to try to avoid getting cut by stray broken pieces. He suddenly felt out of breath and gasped for air.

The radio in the nurses' station got louder as he crawled closer to it. He squatted, raised his head, and risked a peek. The nurses and the orderlies were merrily eating cookies and dancing with Neveah. They were swaying back and forth with their arms waving over their heads and singing "I Want to Take You Higher." The cookie tin looked almost empty.

When Neveah saw Weasley, she shooed him on. Then she bent over with her hands on her ponderous knees, wiggling her hefty butt at her dancing partner. Her knees and heels were twisting sharply in and out in a Charleston-like manner as she crisscrossed her knees with her pudgy hands. Her massive rear end bounced up and down, distracting the other dancers and blocking any view of him.

He hurriedly crawled on past the station unobserved to the end of the hall that led to the outside. He stood up and fell against the door's push bar before he could regain his equilibrium. The door opened so fast that he fell out into the humid night air. As he continued to stagger with his arms waving to regain his balance, he stubbed his toe, sending him plunging blindly headlong into a bougainvillea bush with the dress now wrapped around his head.

Mi free! Mi made it!

He pulled the card with Neveah's picture on it out of his pocket and kissed it. She blew him a kiss back.

Weasley clawed his way back out of the hedge. The thorns gouged and ripped his billowy dress. He finally disentangled it enough to slip it back over his naked, now scratched up body. He again felt lightheaded but was so elated that he didn't even feel the scratches the bush had left on him.

He glanced around. There was no one in the parking lot.

Tank God! But now, how in da hell do mi get outta here?

There was a bike rack about ten feet in front of him. He checked the bikes. They were all locked to the rack with one exception — a standup push scooter that stood to one side. He hadn't been on one of those since childhood, but it beat walking. He grabbed it and winced as he tentatively made his way across the level parking lot. Each time that his bare left foot and stubbed toe hit the uneven, pebble-strewn pavement, a pain shot through both.

At first, he pushed gingerly towards the edge of the parking lot to get to the street. The street, however, wasn't level with the parking lot since the lot was on the crest of a hill.

Suddenly he found himself not on level ground anymore. The scooter picked up momentum as it rushed down the slope into the dark. Weasley panicked as he realized that if he tried to slow or stop the scooter, the rough street surface would shred the sole of his bare left foot.

As the scooter picked up speed, the nurses' uniform got twisted in the scooter's wheel. It wrapped itself around the spokes, jerking Weasley's torso forward until he was hugging the handlebars as the uniform entangled itself in them as well. He bent over and tugged back. The dress refused to free itself so all he accomplished was to lift the now billowing dress and pull the remaining portion of it over his head. He found himself not only blind but with his naked backside totally exposed.

As he continued to battle the cursed uniform, Weasley had no choice but to just try to steer and hope for the best. He managed to barely keep his balance until he hit a curb. The scooter went one way, and Weasley went the other. When he dinged spreadeagle into a parked car, his bladder let loose. His knees hit the car first. He ricocheted off the ground. The jarring landing on an adjacent duplex's grassy front lawn knocked the wind out of him.

Could things possibly get worse? He soon found out.

Suddenly, every bone and joint in his body seemed on fire. He was in a fire ant bed. The ants crawled in mass into Weasley's sweaty crotch and crack, under his arms, and onto his head. They began to bite. He began slapping wildly until a new searing pain radiated from his groin as he accidentally whacked his own scrotum.

He bit his tongue.

Weasley's guardian angel greeting card nurse fell out of a torn pocket. He glared at Neveah like she had let him down when she was supposed to be protecting him.

Neveah responded with a headshake and a shrug and said, "Jah and his angels can only do so much to protect dumb-asses and fools."

He tore the card in half.

When the pain had subsided enough for him to move, Weasley rolled the scooter onto an expanse of grass as far away as he could get from the ant bed. He gave the scooter a once over to see if it was damaged. It seemed fine.

Now naked, Weasley sat in the soothing cool grass, faced the street, and tried to untangle his ripped and tattered-apple sauce-mashed potatoes and gravy-urine soaked, grass-stained dress from the spokes and kickstand of the scooter.

Weasley didn't realize it, but he was being watched from the house behind him by a hooligan teenager and his floozie girlfriend. They were home alone since the hooligan's mother was out for the evening with his latest "uncle." His gang-member, big brother was also out looking for trouble with his pals. The car that Weasley had crashed into belonged his brother, a fact that the teen found somewhat amusing.

The two young people had gotten into the boy's mother's ganja stash and were already flying high when Weasley arrived.

The two drug-high teens were highly amused at what they had just seen. It was better than any movie, and this show was free. Up until now, their evening had been totally boring, but that was about to change.

Jah done send mi a sucka to play wif. It's party time!

The wannabe rude boy decided to have some fun at Weasley's expense that would impress his girl with his manliness at the same time.

And maybe, he thought, *we'll pick up a dolla or two from this punani* **(pussy)**, *and we can buy a boktle of overproof rum.*

Weasley finally got the now tattered nurses' dress untangled from the scooter, covered himself up with it loincloth-like as best he could. He now looked like he was wearing a giant diaper. He tore some strips off a ripped part of uniform's hem and wrapped them around his bleeding, push-off, left foot. He tested the raw foot to see if he had enough padding on it before getting back on the scooter.

He began to shove himself slowly and painfully down the street. By the time Weasley had gotten part way down the block, the boy had gotten out his two-person Segway from behind the house. It was the transportation he used for his parttime job as a drug mule for his brother. He and the girl took off in pursuit of Weasley.

Time to hab a little fun.

His trollop girlfriend held onto him from behind. When he caught up with Weasley, he started circling and taunting him.

"'Hey, ole mon, where yu get yu driver's license? And de way yu dress, yu must be goin' to a strip club. Or do yu tink yu Tarzan? If you really Tarzan, gimme a yell."

Weasley stuck out his third finger.

"I've always wanted to go to a strip club, but I ain't got no money. Tink yu could loan me some?"

He began to circle Weasley again, popping him with the lanyard that held his keys.

"Is dis de way dey dress to do what dose clubs call S and M? Or yu tryin' to turn a trick? Ain't yu too old to be inta dat shit? Bet yu canna even get yu buddy up no more."

He popped Weasley again.

"Cat got yu tongue? Yu don tink mi serious? Gimme yu money. Louisie, show granddaddy here yu blade."

The girl whipped out a switchblade.

Weasley had not been having a good night up to now. He hurt all over, and, worst of all, his guardian angel, Neveah, had let him down. The taunting sent him completely over the edge.

Time to teach dese punks some manners.

The kid wouldn't let up. He was having too much fun.

"I gotta betta tought **(thought)**. Since I don know you name, instead of yu lending me yu money, why don yu jus gibe it to mi instead. Den I won't hab to hunt yu down to pay it back."

That was the straw that broke the camel's back. Weasley pointed behind the kid and yelled as loud as he could, "Watch out! There's a car coming up behind you."

The diversion worked. The kid turned to see what Weasley was referring to, but nothing was there. When he turned back around it was too late to defend himself or veer out of Weasley's way. Weasley rammed the kid's Segway with his scooter and then decked the young hoodlum with a crunching roundhouse punch. He snatched the lanyard out of the kid's hand and slashed the girl's cheek with the keys on the end of it. Blood erupted. The rowdy and his girlfriend both hit the street with a thud. The now not-so-tough kid held his jaw and whined.

"I tink yu broke mi jaw."

"Yu nose about to be nex."

The girl just whimpered and grabbed her bleeding cheek.

"Git."

The kid and the girl took off running.

Weasley uprighted the Segway and rolled down the street on it in the opposite direction, disappearing into the night to go look for Price Wright, the boat broker.

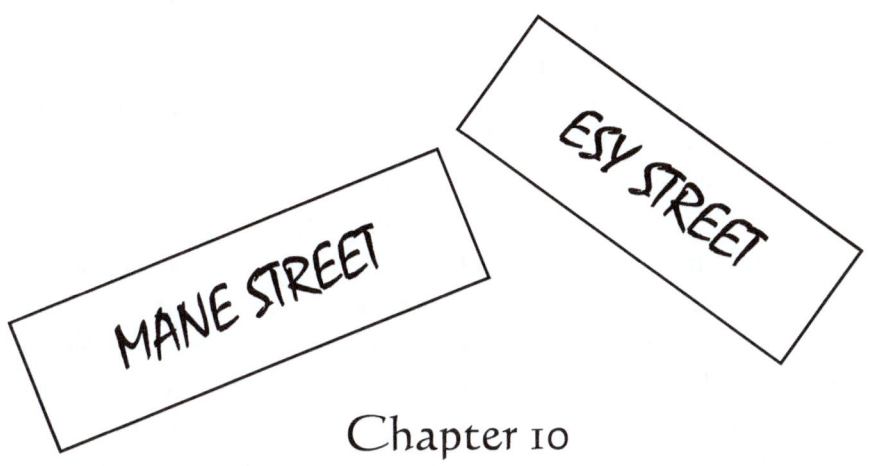

Chapter 10

Will Black was out in the yard trimming and watering some plants when Betsy brought the phone out to him. It had been over a week since they had had rain, and things were beginning to wilt.

"Got a call for you."

"Tell 'em I'll call them back."

"It's DV Craig."

"Oh, OK, I'll take it. Why don't you finish watering this croton, and I'll talk to him? You mind?"

"Of course not. Nothing's too good the man who's the peanut butter for my jelly."

"Crunchy or smooth?"

"Sometimes I like smooth, but then again, some crunch certainly can add a little zest."

He handed Betsy the hose, and she handed him the phone. He took the clippers and walked around the house and sat down in a chair on the dock.

"DV. Great to hear from you. Calling from the land of sea, sun, and rum?"

"I wish," DV said. "Try Orlando instead, but not for long. Thought I'd give y'all an update before we head down. And don't forget my open invite. Me casa, you casa."

"Duly noted. Sounds like things are moving along on schedule."

"Yes, they are, in large measure thanks to your help. We closed on the house, and we've found a boat."

"How's Henry working out?"

"Man, oh, man. I can't thank you enough for that introduction. … And Mikey Mo Mullins too."

"Good reliable men, both of them."

"Your friend, The Colonel, got Mikey Mo to line us up with an English boat broker, Price Wright and then used his connections so Mr. Wright could get into the most recent government repo boat auction. He found just what I had in mind. A boat called the *Spirit of the Seas*. It's a forty-two-foot catamaran powered by two 320 horse diesels. Sleeps eight. Got a head, galley … everything Cee Cee and I wanted in a boat. And he got us a helluva good deal on it. So good in fact that he's been getting some calls offering to buy it from us at more than what we paid … and from more than one person. Can you imagine that? If I'd been greedy, I might could have set off a bidding war, and we would've flipped the boat and made a nice chunk of quick change. And people say that a boat's a hole to dump money down."

"Did you seriously consider selling it?"

"Naw! Hell no! It's just what I had hoped to find. … We're not in the boat business. … And I don't need the money. We bought this boat to enjoy it. Hopefully with you and Betsy."

"I hear you. I guess it's kind of like flipping a house that you love. You've gotta live somewhere. If you flipped it, you'd just have to go find some place to go, and you might not like your new find as much as what you've already got."

"He said one guy has kept calling back over and over and got kind of rude when he didn't get what he wanted. Acted like a he was some kind of big shot. Some guy named Harry McLeod."

Will's radar went up.

Harry Dog? Oh, shit! How the hell did he get into this picture?

He almost said something but decided better until he could get to the bottom of what was going on.

"But you told him you didn't want to sell? Right!"

"Yep. That's what I told Mr. Wright to tell him. But he kept calling back and raising his offer. And then Price started getting calls from some accountant named Wesley Lineitem. Said he was representing a client who was looking for a boat just like this.

Oh, double shit! Weasley? You gotta be kidding! What the hell is going on here?

"What a name for an accountant? I thought Price was joking with me when he told me the fellow's name. Said he also has kept calling back as well and sweetening *his* offer. Wright said he was most insistent. Is there some shortage on boats that I don't know about? ... The accountant wanted Mr. Wright to give him my phone number so we could talk about it direct. Even said that he'd fly to Orlando if he had to ... if that's what it took to close a deal. Then he got persnickety. He told Wright flat-out that he'd cut him out of any deal unless he helped convince us to sell. Said he'd make me an offer I couldn't refuse. Sounds like the Godfather, doesn't it?"

You just don't know how on target you are.

"Wright didn't give him your number, did he?"

"Told him he'd have to get my permission first."

Hallelujah! Weasley and Harry Dog both! And competing against each other? That don't sound right. Those two work in cahoots with each other as a rule. Something's going on, and it can't be good.

"DV. I hate to cut this short, but I've got a business call that I've been waiting for coming in. May I call you back? It'll be later."

"Sure. No problem, mon. Just wanted to update you. ... And to thank you again."

Will hung up and headed around the house to tell Betsy about his conversation.

I've got to get hold of Mikey Mo or Colonel Winter.

Will ran around the house full blast yelling, "Betsy" at the top of his lungs.

Betsy dropped the hose.

"Will, are you hurt? You cut yourself with those clippers?"

"I'm not hurt, but the Craigs might not be so lucky soon."

Will repeated his conversation with DV.

"Oh, my God," Betsy gasped. "Harry Dog and Weasley? Both! I thought we were through with those creeps."

"So, did I. I get chills thinking about getting back involved with Dudus Coke and the posse."

"We got off lucky in our past altercations, but we easily could've not been so fortunate."

"We were fortunate because we had friends in the know on our side. You know damned good and well that Dudus's has never forgiven you for wrecking his swindle kickback program on the Highway 2000 program. That not only cost him a lot of money, but he had to rebuild his whole network of on-the-take politicians and cops after that," Will said. "And I haven't mentioned the face he lost both in and out of the posse."

"I did what the bank sent me down there to do, protect their interests. And when we helped The Colonel wreck Dudus's hopes of getting even by stealing the Maroons' Genovesa treasure.

"And Harry Dog ... he hates us with a purple passion. On both occasions our interference caused him to become Dudus's scapegoat."

"Well, he deserved to be."

"I'll let you tell Harry Dog that."

"And Weasley ... that crooked snake. We all but wrecked his money laundering kickback scheme."

"I'm not sure who among that bunch hates us the most."

"And ... God forbid ... if they find out that the Craigs are our friends ...."

"... I hate to think."

"Our friends kept us from going from the frying pan into the fire with those hoodlums. Now it's our turn now to do the same thing for DV and Cee Cee. Can you get off to go down to Jamaica?"

"I'll make time," Will said.

"I wonder what those ass-wipes are up to this time. You better call The Colonel."

"No shit, my darling! And the sooner the better. That's exactly why I didn't say anything to alarm DV. I need to talk to The Colonel first."

BEWARE FALLING MANGOES

Chapter 11

"Colonel? Will Black."

"Will. What a pleasant surprise! I told my wife I had an inkling that this was going to be a good day, and now I know why. How's your lovely wife and daughter?"

"Both are doing great, but I got a phone call today that may not have been so great."

"Tell me about it."

"We met a couple from Orlando on a cruise ship that my high school class had chosen for one of my reunions. He's a professional musician with a band under contract to do regular gigs at Disney World. … and he's more than just another itinerant musician. He and his wife are very well-heeled.

"Long story short, we bonded after they told us that they wanted to buy a second home in Jamaica … which they have now done. They bought Mount Corbet in Discovery Bay."

"Yes. Mikey Mo mentioned them to me. What was their name again?"

"DV and Cee Cee Craig. I introduced them to Mikey. I also introduced them to Henry Davis."

"I'm aware of those things as well."

Shoot! I don't think the Colonel ever misses much. I guess that's why he is who he is.

"Best I remember, I also referred him to Price Wright, the boat broker."

"Yes, sir, you did. And that's the reason I'm calling you."

"Mr. Wright didn't work out to their satisfaction?"

"Oh, he worked out very well. You might say almost too well. With your assistance, he participated in the auction of confiscated boats in Kingston. Wright found just what the Craigs were looking for and got them an attractive deal on one."

"So, what's the problem?"

"Since the auction, Mr. Wright has been barraged with phone calls from both Harry McLeod and Wesley Lineitem making increasingly high offers for the boat. Both are very insistent. And they appear to be competing against each other."

"Now, that *is* interesting. Harry Dog and his creepy shyster pal, Weasley? My, my."

"Weasley even insisted on talking to my friend direct. And threatened Wright with retribution if necessary and threatened to fly to Orlando to negotiate with the Craigs in person."

"Sounds like they're desperate. What you want to bet, that both are being squeezed by Dudus Coke? And we both know he can be merciless. I'd better investigate this."

"Thought you'd say that."

"What's the name of the boat?"

"The *Spirit of the Seas*. The Craigs are planning on taking the boat themselves from Kingston up around Port Antonio to Discovery Bay."

"By themselves?"

"Actually, they asked Betsy and me to join them, but we haven't accepted their invitation yet. As much as we'd like to, I told them it would depend on our schedules."

"I don't have to remind you that if your friends have stumbled into Shower Posse business, they could be in extreme danger."

"I'm haven't forgotten. That's why I'm calling you."

"If you care about your friend's welfare, you might want to accept their invitation. You have experience in dealing with Dudus and his thugs. I can't assign my men to protect them for who knows how long just on the suspicion that that bunch is up to something, but I'm not going to ignore the situation either. The Craigs will never be safe until they either sell the boat or until we can get to the bottom of what is really going on with it. I'll talk to Mikey Mo. He'll get back to you. Thanks for the head's up. And don't worry, my friend. I'm not hanging you out to dry. I'll assign some men to watch those creeps and intervene if they try something. You're too dear to me to put you at unnecessary risks by leaving you in an untenable situation."

"I appreciate that. I hope I'll hear from Mikey Mo asap. These are nice people who don't deserve to be dragged into a posse mess."

"I feel somewhat responsible since I'm the one who introduced the Craigs to Price and partially arranged for the boat buy."

"Sir, you had no way of knowing."

"By the way, don't say anything about any of this to your friends. I don't want to alarm them yet or have them go off and do something halfcocked that they'll regret. We know our adversary pretty well, but the Craigs'd be in way over their heads."

"They've hired Henry. He'll help us protect them. He's come through for us on more occasions than I can count."

"You're right. Henry's a good man … and a savvy one. I'll get Mikey Mo to brief him."

"Great."

"I hope we'll be seeing you soon in Accompong. Having a victory drink with the Craigs. In the meantime, for God's sake please stay safe and don't underestimate our opponent by getting overconfident.

"Remember, 'Noh care how boar hog try fi hide under sheep wool, 'im grunt always betray 'im.'

"Will, thanks for calling."

"As usual, your insight hits the nail right on the head, sir. And thank you for being such an excellent mentor. And don't worry that your advice is going on deaf ears. I hear you loud and clear and once again I'll heed your words. And I'll also keep in mind something else you taught us. 'Sorry for maga (**mongrel**) dog, maga dog turn round and bite yu'."

"Which is also, so, so true, my friend. Harry Dog is indeed a maga dog. Unfortunately, there's no other way to describe him. And I doubt if he'll ever change."

"No, I don't guess he will. He is what he is. Once a scumbag; always a scumbag. No matter how often a leopard bathes, he'll never wash out his spots. God bless you, sir, and thank you again for everything you've done."

```
┌─────────────────────────────────────────┐
│                                         │
│        This Is The Back Door            │
│     The Front Door Is In The Back       │
│                                         │
└─────────────────────────────────────────┘
```

Chapter 12

Will filled Betsy in on his conversation with Colonel Winter.

"So, The Colonel wasn't aware of the Harry Dog and Weasley situation. I feel better now that you've talked to him," Betsy said. "I guess now we just wait for Mikey Mo."

"I told DV I'd call him back. Why don't I just call and tell him that things have worked out so that we can join them in Jamaica."

"And don't even bring Harry Dog and Weasley up?"

"Bingo. At least not until we have a better handle on what's really happening."

Will dialed DV's cell phone.

"DV. Will Black. Is the invitation to join you in Jamaica still open?"

"Is a frog's ass watertight?"

"And don't forget, he also always comes down when he jumps up. We would love to join you for an irie holiday."

"Fantastical! I can't wait to tell Cee Cee. But we're probably a month out from going down. We've got some things to take care of here in Orlando first. Plus, I told Mount Corbet's former owner that I would give him ample time to take care of his affairs there before I booted them out once and for all. They're trying to find a rental to move into until they can decide on what they want to buy."

"That time frame works better for us as well. After all, we are working stiffs. Both Betsy and I need to make sure we've got all our bases covered at work before we traipse off on a vacation. We both had some time off coming that we would've probably used as a staycation otherwise, but I'll take a vacation in Jamaica instead, ... any day of the week. Just be sure you give me a call as soon as your plans begin to firm up."

"Will do."

"One other thing, if you don't mind another suggestion."

"Every suggestion you've made to date has been a wiener ... and I don't mean Oscar Mayer. What you got in mind?"

"This isn't for me but for you. As long as you've got the boat out of the water, why don't you get it inspected at a shipyard and hopefully detailed at the same place? If they don't do detail work, I'm sure they'll guide you to someone who does. You need to make sure the boat is seaworthy and let them fix anything that needs fixing before you take it out to sea and possibly get caught in a dangerous situation or in the hands of a shade tree mechanic.

"And by getting it detailed now, you won't have to do a damned thing to it when you take delivery. You're going to have enough on your hands familiarizing yourself with your new toy without having to deal with maintenance that the previous owner might have ignored on top of everything else. If I had to guess, if the owner let his boat get confiscated by the government, he may not have been the most responsible individual in the world.

"Some things are a helluva lot easier to deal with on dry land, and the peace of mind is going to be worth a lot. Plus, both the shipyard and detailer have the equipment they need to do the jobs right and will warranty their work."

"You're right. After all, I'm just a guitar picker married to a debutante. I'm beginning to understand why you were the brightest puppy in the litter," DV said.

"And one more thing. You didn't get a trailer with the boat, did you?"

"Nope. Just the boat."

"Either the shipyard or the detailer will probably haul it for you. When we got ours detailed in the Keys, the detailer came and picked it up and then brought it back when he was done."

"You're full of good ideas. Thanks."

"One other suggestion. Get Price Wright involved in finding the shipyard and detailer. Since he's both local and in the boat business, I'm sure he's been down these roads before. ... And get him to look at the job when it gets done. ... Even if you have to pay him something extra. ... You want some local eyes and ears that you trust to make sure the job gets done right. It can be rough enough dealing with trades people in this country, but as you're going to find out soon enough, dealing with them down there is whole different story. Especially if you're possibly ... or should I say probably ... viewed as a gravalicious bakra mus mus.

"IE?"

"A greedy white slave master boss."

"Comforting."

"Since Wright's local, he knows how to deal with local help."

"Another good idea. And I've got one of my own. While the previous owner and the staff are still there, we might use the month to do some interior painting that Cee Cee wants to do. Then it'll be finished by the time we get there."

"Possibly but maybe not. You need to go into Jamaica with your eyes open to avoid disappointment. I don't want you to think I'm a buttinsky know-it-all, but if you've got the time, I'll tell you a couple of tales about my Jamaican learning experiences. Betsy and I were once much like you are now. While we had visited Jamaica for short periods as vacationers, we had never actually lived there for the extended timeframe that it takes to truly understand the dynamics of the people and the country. Our perspective changed when Betsy's bank sent us down here to live while she was on a special assignment."

"Your disclaimer is duly noted."

"Sundance, the villa that the bank rented for us, needed some overdue maintenance and updating. Leva, our cook, finally convinced our absentee landlord to let her hire someone to do these things, and I naively volunteered to be the eyes and ears of the owner. Shortly before we were to begin interviewing potential contractors, Betsy and I were invited to a neighborhood cocktail and dinner party where we met an expatriate American. He told me that before the work began, I needed to take time to understand the Jamaican tradesman mentality. He was so right. So now, if you will allow me to, I'll share this same information with you."

"I'm always open to learn. To put the thought in the proverb form Jamaicans are so fond of, 'If you beat your head against a wall, it will be your head that'll break, not the wall."

"Very well said. My philosophical friend, Mr. Davis would approve of that observation. "First, you need to understand that 'soon come' is not merely an expression; it is a national mindset."

DV smiled and nodded.

"Next, you need to understand the components of a typical Jamaican workweek on a day-by-day basis.

"Monday is spent recovering from the previous weekend and contemplating life's challenges.

"Tuesday is dominated by preparations for Wednesday, which is the nationally accepted workday.

"On Wednesday, you will see your tradesman hard at work noodling, inspecting, and then ciphering on his hands. Palms are Jamaica's legal pads. He will write entire columns of numbers on the palms of his hands which will be of little use since these numbers will soon be obliterated. This will cause him to write additional numbers on his hands. While this might save paper, crucial information like phone numbers, names, and other facts will inevitably be lost.

"Much conversation and urging will then ensue about the proper positioning of things, leading to endless discussions about the ever-rising cost of building materials or, in your case, paint. A paid helper will then be sent to search for the essential missing components needed to complete the job. Hours will pass, and the helper will finally return empty-handed telling the contractor and homeowner that the vital pieces 'soon come.' By then the workday will be finished.

"Wednesday evening is spent with rum and friends celebrating another hard week's labors.

"Thursday is then spent preparing for the upcoming weekend.

"On Friday the party begins.

"Saturday is reserved for music and dancing. Protocol forbids them to think of tools and toil since Saturday is a time to party and celebrate life.

"Sunday's pace becomes more mellow. It's the time to think about going to the beach or engaging in romance. The day culminates in a Sunday night party.

"Monday requires resting and recovering from the weekend and once again sorting out life's issues.

"No problem, mon. There is plenty of time to prepare on Tuesday because Wednesday 'soon come.'"

"That seems somewhat cynical."

"I was skeptical too when I first heard that analysis. Sarcastic maybe. Pessimistic perhaps. But somewhat truthful and on target, more probable. Mr. Davis clarified the matter further for me from a slightly different perspective. Do you want to hear his take, or are you tiring of my babble?"

"Actually, it's just getting interesting … and thought provoking. You seem to be on a roll, so have at it."

"Mr. Davis' observations stem from the Jamaican proverb that says, 'Dog say 'im won't work, 'im wi Sidone and look, for 'im must get a livin'.'"

"Which means?"

"If a person can't make an adequate wage, he should simply sit and watch."

"OK?"

"This coupled with several other Jamaican proverbs should give you a clue as to the origin of an entrenched, counterproductive work ethic that resulted from slavery and its aftermath. If a worker doesn't feel that the reward measures up to their effort, they should expend as little energy as possible."

"Explain."

"At the core of these proverbs is the underdogs perception that work doesn't always yield benefits to the laborers.

"Now couple those proverbs with one that says 'Bakra's **(white man's)** work neber **(never)** done. To be more specific, since a white man's work is never done, there's no point in trying to do it.

"This proverb also implies that work is viewed as bakra's business, making work the act of working for someone else, thus making wholehearted work a betrayal of the worker's own interests. Therefore, the worker can rationalize that since work is a futile activity, it simply doesn't make sense to engage in futility."

"Talk about conveniently convoluted rationalizations."

"Oh, I'm not done yet. Since honest labor is not rewarded fairly, trickery should be used to survive. Once again, there's two Jamaican proverbs dealing with this issue.

One says, 'yu neber **(never)** see empty bag 'tan **(stand)** up.' The other says, 'Yu neber see full bag bend.' In other words, the hungry worker is too empty to stand while the well-fed worker is too full to bend.'"

"Hmmm."

"As you will soon learn, this same nonwork philosophy has sometimes been adopted by Jamaican government employees, making them an ongoing challenge to deal with. The government is seen as a faceless bakra to which one is not personally accountable. Government work is never done, so why try. There is even a proverb that says, 'government work neber done.'"

"If you're trying to discourage me, you're doing a damned good job of it."

"That's not what I'm trying to do. I'm just trying to get the Jamaican perspective across to you, so you'll understand why and how things are done down there."

"And also, why it's important to have a local looking out for me."

"Exactly right."

The Good Book
Says! The First
Day Of The Week
Cometh Mary
Magdalene Early
When It Was Yet
Dark, Unto The
Seplucure

Chapter 13

DV dialed the phone number that he had been given as Price Wright's private land line.

"Price S. Wright Yacht Sales."

"Mr. Wright. DV Craig from Orlando."

"Good morning, Mr. Craig. Everything good with you? What can I do for you today?"

"I'm doing great, Mr. Wright. I'm calling about the *Spirit of the Seas*. Would it be possible for you to find someone to inspect and also detail the boat for me before I take delivery of it?"

"Absolutely. I know some excellent shipyards and boat detailers in the Kingston area. A good idea, I might add, to do it before you take it out. Plus, that way it'll be both reliable and pristine when you get it."

"Would one or the other trailer the boat to where it needs to go? I don't have a trailer, and even if I did, I'm not down there."

"Loyalist Cove Marina has some trailers. I'll see if they have one that'll handle this boat, and if they do, I'll see if I can get them. They do have a fulltime mechanic, but they don't do detailing themselves. They sub it out to a related company owned by another member of the family."

"Great, and since you're local and I'm in Florida, will you contract the shipyard or detailer and supervise the work? I'll be glad to compensate you for your time."

"Not a problem. Since you're a client there will be no additional charges for my services. Once again, I compliment you for planning ahead. As a foreigner, you're vulnerable to workmen who promise more than they plan to deliver. I'll make sure that the detailer isn't a fly-by-night and does a thorough job for you. Plus, I'll inspect his work before he gets paid. I know what to look for since I've performed this service for other clients. That's the advantage of dealing with a full-service broker with the years of experience that I've had."

Wright smiled. He wasn't being completely candid with DV. He was not a good Samaritan working for nothing. There would be a good payday in it for him. While there wouldn't be a disclosed add-on charge, the price DV would be paying would be padded with a markup so that Wright could receive a prearranged under-the-table cash kickback from the contractor. Also, the supplies that the detailer would use would be purchased at wholesale but billed to the client at retail with the spread being shared with Price. Last of all, if another workman were brought into the picture to do repairs on the boat, a similar kick-back arrangement with Price would be in place. In actuality, detailing was a nice source of side income for the broker. The good news was that Price did attempt to conscientiously represent the boat owner and make sure he got what he was paying for.

Both DV and Price would have been shocked if they had known that Price's private line was not as private as either man thought. Their conversation was being monitored by not just one person but three. Harry Dog, Weasley, and Mikey Mo were all listening in.

Two of them, unbeknownst to the other had broken into Price's office and bugged his phone. Weasley had used a different tactic. He had bugged Price during an appointment with him. He had investigated whether Price could sell the Sprite, the boat Weasley had bought by accident so he could recover at least some of the money he had paid for it. Then he planned turn this money over to Harry Dog as a peace offering in an effort to get back in his good graces again before Harry totally ruptured Weasley's relationship with The President.

It was probably a miracle that the threesome had not either run into each other or seen each other's bugs in the process in the process of tapping Price's phone.

Everyone was motivated by his own overlapping but self-serving agenda.

Mikey Mo did not want to disappoint Colonel Winter or the Blacks since Will's phone call to The Colonel had given him a heads-up about Weasley and Harry Dog's unexplained interest in the *Spirit of the Seas*. His allegiance and loyalty to both ran deep. And then therefore, since the Craigs were friends of the Blacks, they were Mikey Mo's friends as well. On top of that, he was curious to find out just what Dudus Coke might be up to this time. He wondered if Harry Dog had reneged on his pledge to The Colonel not to involve himself in The Colonel's business again after their problems with Harry during the Genovesa affair.

But then he mused, *Technically speaking, this could be interpreted as not being The Colonel's business. If anything, The Colonel might just be inserting himself this time for a change into Dudus' business.*

Harry Dog had a different motivation. Dudus was giving him absolute hell over the way that the boat had been lost to begin with. But he had made the mistake of delegating what should have been a routine mission to Biggie, unfortunately for him one of Dudus' favorites. And then Biggie had redelegated the affair to Oney, Twinie, and Which Flava — the three biggest numb-nuts on Earth. But they had paid the price for their stupidity.

He couldn't help but smirk sadistically at their fate.

*Oh, how they paid! My main regret is that I didn't get a chance to torture the bumba ras claats (**dumb-ass ass wipes**) myself.*

But then I compounded my mistake by drawing Weasley into the whole affair. But how was I to know that Weasley would have a stroke at the auction and end up buying the wrong bloody boat.

Weasley's motivation somewhat mirrored Harry Dog's — survival.

Otherwise, I might be looking over my shoulder forever, waiting to be possibly gunned down or tortured to death by either one of Dudus' or Harry Dog's sadistic Shower Posse killers.

The threesome each took note of DV's intention to get the boat detailed. This presented a needed opportunity.

Mikey Mo thought that if he could arrange to be present as the new owner's agent when the boat was detailed, ... and he'd pay the detailer for permission if necessary ... he might get a chance to inspect it and find out why the Shower Posse was so hell-bent to get it back. He could then report this information back to The Colonel, and they could decide what needed doing next. One thing was certain. Both the Craigs and the Blacks would be in extreme danger until the mystery was solved.

The Blacks — they're family, and you do whatever it takes to protect family. And the Craigs — since they're friends of the Blacks, that makes them almost like extended family.

And truth of the matter was, on top of everything else, he would enjoy sticking it to Dudus and Harry Dog once again.

In the case of Harry Dog and Weasley, the knowledge derived from DV and Price's conversation presented an opportunity of a different sort. They each came up with the same idea. This gave them a chance to hijack the boat and trailer while it was in route to the detailer's shop and get Dudus off their case by redeeming themselves.

Being selfish and self-centered, neither man gave a passing thought to the idea that by working together they would increase each of their odds of success. That would have been too logical.

Chapter 14

"Mr. Craig? This is Price Wright in Jamaica. How are you doing this morning?"

"Can't complain. Did you find someone to inspect and detail the boat?"

"As a matter of fact, I did. That's why I'm calling. Salty Cove Marina on Port Kingston Causeway can do both the inspection and move the boat. They've got a triple axle trailer that will do just fine. And their captive detailer, Salty Scrub Boat Cleaning, will take care making the boat spic and span."

"Great. And a truck to pull the trailer?"

"They've got a one-ton GMC pickup with dual rear wheels. It could haul a boat double or triple this boat's weight.

"Both companies are related and operate on the same property. The father owns the marina and the son the detail company. The Sleaze family. The father, Sylvester senior, has been in business for over thirty years. You probably won't need to talk to him, but in case you do, he goes by Sizably Salty. Most people just call him Si. They call his son Slightly Salty or Sly. Good people both."

"Their names certainly sound like someone you could trust," DV said, hoping the doubt wasn't creeping into his voice. "You say you know these people?"

85

"Absolutely. I'd let my mother use them ... assuming she had a boat. Si's hourly rate for the mechanic is a hundred and twenty-five dollars an hour for labor. ... Of course, plus parts. He charges a minimum of $150 for hauling plus a mileage fee. For a boat this size, Sly charges forty-five dollars a foot for the exterior work and eighty dollars extra to do each cabin."

Sizably Salty's rate was actually a hundred dollars and hour. Slightly Salty's pricing was actually forty dollars a foot for the outside and seventy-five dollars for each cabin, but what's a few dollars to a rich American.

"For this price, Sly'll wash and polish the boat, apply a sealant to all gelcoat surfaces above the waterline, remove any rust or mildew, and recondition the seats. It doesn't include barnacle removal, but we don't have that problem anyway."

"Sounds good. What about the cabin?"

"Vacuum, give the cabin a complete wipe down, clean the mirrors, clean the refrig and sinks, the galley counters, and clean all vinyl surfaces."

"Sounds thorough."

"Oh, it is. Both'll do a good job. They warranty their work for six months. Now, if it's a go-ahead, give me a credit card number. They require 25% up front."

"When can they do it?"

"If these terms are acceptable to you, Si told me he'd send Sly up here to pick up the boat Thursday afternoon."

"Book 'em."

DV finalized the arrangements and hung up. Price called Si and Sly back and scheduled the job.

"I told him a buck and a quarter an hour for the mechanic and forty-five American for the exterior and eighty bucks for each cabin. Put that on your billing. And don't forget your old bredren (**brethren**) Price when it comes to the difference."

"Price, one of these days you're gonna get caught. You know that, don't you?" Sly said.

"But until that day comes, 'weh no kill, fatten' (**As long as I keep eating something that doesn't kill me, it will keep nourishing my body.**)."

Thanks to multiple bugs, Harry Dog, Weasley, and Mikey Mo were all able to listened in. All three smiled at Price's rationalization of his under-the-table deal. Weasley also smiled to hear that the Sleaze's owned a GMC pickup since using On Star would simplify his hijacking plans.

The boat inspection and detailing presented the opportunity each of them had been waiting on.

Game on.

Mikey Mo immediately called Colonel Winter and updated him.

"Do you know Si Sleaze?" he asked.

"Not very well, but I do know Sly's mother-in-law, Gertie Teaser. And I do remember Gertie's daughter, Ima, when she was a kid."

"You mean to tell me that Ima Teaser grew up to become Ima Sleaze or Mrs. Slightly Salty Sly Sleaze? That's kind of like trying to say Peter Piper picked a peck of pickled peppers."

"Truthfully, officially it's Mrs. Sylvester Sleaze Jr. That's his birth name."

"Which is not much better. But back to my original conundrum. Do you think you could arrange for me to be there to inspect the *Spirit of the Seas* while it's being detailed? I'm sure DV'll back up my reason to be there if we're forced to get him involved … which I'd rather not do."

"I agree. I'll do my best."

"Respect. Sir, your worst is better than most people's best."

"I'm just an old man just trying to live by the golden rule. After all, scratch an old woman's back, and she'll let you taste her pepper pot."

Within a few hours, The Colonel reported back to Mikey Mo.

"Talked to the senior Sleaze and told him we know the new owner, and he wanted you to clean out the boat's lockers and cabins and collect any items possibly left by the seller. He said he doesn't have a problem with that. He's sending two drivers. One to drive the trailer and one to drive a vehicle with a wide load sign to escort the *Spirit of the Seas* to his shop since some of the roads they'll be travelling are narrow and not very good. Said if you'll be there when they pick the boat up, you can ride with one of the drivers. He hopes to pick it up early at sevenish before traffic gets bad."

"I'll be there."

"Call me when you're done, and I'll send someone to take you back to your car."

"Thank you, sir."

JAH LOVES YOU AND JAH DOES NOT MAKE MISTEAKS

Chapter 15

Mikey Mo was not the only outside participant who planned to be present for hauling the *Spirit of the Seas*. Both Harry Dog and Weasley had listened in on Price's conversation, and each individually made his own plans as well.

Harry Dog's plan was a simple one. They'd use an On-Board Diagnostic Scanner to hack into the computer system of the truck and take it over. They'd plant an OBD-2 device in it and then set up an ambush afterwards. They'd then set up a con to get the driver to stop. When the driver got out to see what was wrong, they'd use the OBD to kill the engine and then hijack the truck and trailer. It would only take seconds to plug the device into the truck's OBD port. They just had to make sure they didn't get caught while they were doing it. This would require a diversion.

He decided to send three of his men to do the job. He chose Mighty Mouse, Hi-top, and Monkeyman for the mission.

Mighty Mouse got his street name because he was only 4'7" and had big ears that stuck straight out from the side of his shaved head. What made him look even more abnormal was that he was a gym rat who took steroids and had bulging muscles — making him into kind of a black, sawed-off hybrid between a bald Alfred E. Newman and Vin Diesel.

Hi-top was the direct opposite of Mighty Mouse. He was 6'5", rail-thin, had dreads, and wore custom high-top sneakers with marijuana graphics on the sides. His street name was embroidered in script over the top of the graphics on each shoe.

Monkeyman got his nickname from his lifelong ability to shimmy up coconut trees with seemingly little effort. He would have a machete gritted between his teeth as he did so. When he got to the top, he would grasp the trunk of the tree tightly between his knees. He would then use the machete with one hand to whack off bunches of coconuts while he held onto the tree fronds with the other hand.

Harry's diversion was for the tall Hi-top and the short Mighty Mouse to find some excuse to start a loud argument with each other. The mismatch was sure to attract attention. While everyone was watching the show, Monkeyman would sneak over and plug the device into the truck's OBD port.

They would then lie in wait up the road to ambush the truck. Monkeyman would roll a plastic five-gallon bucket under it as it travelled by. When the driver stopped to see what was wrong, they'd use the app on their smart phone to kill the engine, knock the driver unconscious, then recrank the pickup, and take off with the truck and the boat. They'd then deliver the truck and boat to Harry Dog at a prearranged location.

Weasley's plan was of a similar nature. The only difference was that he planned to accomplish the same thing using GM's On Star satellite system since he was working alone and it required no installation.

Harry's men arrived at the impound yard at the appointed time. Mighty Mouse, Monkeyman, and Hi-top walked in separately. Hi-top pretended to be looking up at the sky while the already low Mighty Mouse was purposely bending down. He then "tripped" over Mighty Mouse, sending them both sprawling on the ground.

"Watch where yu walk, yu hi-pocket, gumpy jewraffe," Mighty Mouse said as he stood back up.

"Who yu call a gumpy jewraffe, yu mofo, short-pocket munchkin. Yu a freak of nature."

"Yu got room to talk, yu lanklet, knee-grow skypra."

"Mi knock yu ona ground, but Jah already beat me to it, shortbus."

"Batty bwoy (**queer**)! … rent-a-dread (**fake Rasta male whore**)!"

"Nuh ramp wid mi (**Don't fuck with me**), bloodclaayt. Mi knock yu on yu lickle raas (**little ass**)."

"Jus try."

Hi-top pretended to take a swing at Mighty Mouse, but Mighty Mouse easily ducked under it. He pretended to hit Hi-top in his "buddies" but made sure the blow glanced over harmlessly to one side. Hi-top doubled up like Mighty Mouse had connected.

While all this was occurring, Monkeyman sneaked over to the driver's side of the GMC pickup, opened the door, and quickly plugged in the OBD-2 scanner. When he went to close the door again, the door slipped out of his hands and slammed, attracting Si's attention. Si pulled the pistol he habitually carried with him.

"Get away from my truck."

He shot his pistol into the air. He was immediately surrounded with security personnel with weapons drawn.

Monkeyman took off across the yard and tried to climb and vault the chain link fence. As he attempted clear the barbed wire at the top, his pants caught on it and ripped. Monkeyman made it over the fence but left part of his pants behind. He kept running, not knowing that Si was not pursuing him.

He ran in the back door of the first unlocked business he came to. It led into the back of the Taboo Go Go Club, straight into a hallway outside of the strippers' dressing room. The employees always kept the door unlocked so they could sneak out and grab a smoke when the urge hit or when they wanted to have a confidential conversation with each other.

The Taboo Go Go Club was unusual in that it employed female strippers but alternated by presenting female impersonators in between the strippers' acts. Occasionally both performed together. And both served as bartenders and waitresses as needed.

Thursday was open mike for amateurs. Since the club's turnover was great, they used these afternoons to preview for new talent.

Monkeyman plowed straight into the auditioning Fiona Flamefly as she walked towards the stage to audition her act. Fiona had two schticks that made her act unusual. First, she danced with a ten-foot Chinese bull snake that she kept on a transparent plastic leash. At certain points she'd wear the snake like a live boa wrap around her neck as she danced. At other times she would allow it to slither down her body and crawl seemingly uncontrolled across the stage towards the audience only to have her jerk it back with the almost invisible leash just as it got near enough to the customers to make them nervous. The second schtick was the grand finale of her act. The club was instructed to gradually lower the houselights as she neared that point in her act. When the lights were low, she would shoot a flaming fireball from her crotch.

As Monkeyman fled down the hall, he collided with Fiona. The snake was around her neck. As Fiona spun around and attempted to regain her balance, the scared snake wrapped itself around Monkeyman's neck. He panicked and began to scramble to try to get the snake off of him any way that he could. As he thrashed, his knee hit the firing mechanism on Fiona's backup fireball causing it to shoot from Fiona's crotch into his. What was left of Monkeyman's ripped pants caught on fire, and he butted the stripper as he danced wildly down the hall. He inadvertently fled out onto the stage and treated the surprised patrons to a dance much wilder than anything that the Taboo had ever offered before. In desperation, he reached down and grabbed an iced-down bucket of beer on the table nearest the stage and doused the fire. The drunken customers, thinking this was part of a new act, gave him a standing ovation.

A bouncer grabbed for Monkeyman but instead came up with the snake. Monkeyman fled out of the front door of the club, screaming as he continued fleeing on down the street. He decided he had had enough fun for one day and took refuge in a rum bar to get drunk. He rationalized that by now Hi-top and Mighty Mouse had already left him behind anyway.

When the *Spirit of the Seas* was properly secured to Si's trailer, the impound yard gates were opened, and Si departed. Sly and Mikey Mo followed in Mikey Mo's Jeep.

"Which way are you going?" Mikey Mo asked.

"We're in Portmore so I'll go by way of Port Kingston Causeway."

"Wait while I get the paperwork to check you out," said the yard manager.

"No problem, mon."

This delay and the knowledge of Si's route gave Hi-top the opportunity to alter his original plan. Since concealment would be impossible on Port Kingston Causeway and Monkeyman was nowhere to be found, he decided against trying to roll an obstacle in from the side of the road. On top of that, it was possible, he reasoned, that Si would simply run over it and keep on going. He would implement a new, better plan instead. He rushed away and ran by a nearby hardware store to quickly buy what he would need.

Mighty Mouse and Hi-top purposely waited for Si to go through the Portmore Toll Plaza and set up to waylay him where the road forked at Fort Augusta Drive.

He waited for Si to come along and then got in front of him, driving his pickup with the tailgate down while Mighty Mouse laid prone in the truck bed. As they approached Fort Augusta Drive, Mighty Mouse rolled the just purchased five-gallon bucket of red paint off the end of the truck. It hit the road with a splat, and Si ran over it, sending red paint in all directions.

"Ah wha di …?" Si yelled as he attempted to swerve.

Si's reactions were not quick enough, making it too late to avoid a calamity. Red paint covered the underside of his white truck and trailer as well as the road. It also splattered up the side of both the truck and the boat.

Hi-top immediately pulled over on the shoulder, killed his engine, and jumped out to pretend that he intended to be accountable for the "accident" and do the right thing. Si pulled over as well. Hi-top smiled contentedly since with his revised plan he hadn't had to rely on the OBD-2 to shut down Si's engine.

Si was screaming, "A wah di bloodclaat dew yu (**what the fuck is wrong with you**), bongopushdigrasskvaat?"

"Mi sarry (**sorry**), mon. Axxident."

"Sarry! Nanny raas (**my grandma's ass**)! Yu jus chupid (**stupid**)! Look a mi truck!"

Mikey Mo and Sly got out of Mikey's Jeep to assist Si. In the confusion, Mighty Mouse vaulted over the side of the truck and sneaked up behind them with a drawn pistol. Hi-top then pulled his own pistol, leaving the Sleazes and Mikey Mo caught between both guns. As Hi-top held them at bay, Mighty Mouse zip-tied all three.

"Wi take yu truck and get it cleaned," Hi-top said sarcastically. "Wi le yu know wha yu can pick it up."

He laughed at his lame joke.

"Mi find yu and get yu, yu pickled bong belly (**greedy**) mofo," Sly said.

Hi-top laughed again, held up his middle finger, and said, "Gud luck."

Mighty Mouse couldn't resist socking Sly in the stomach.

Since he was short and had trouble with visibility on the long trailer, Mighty Mouse drove Hi-top's truck and let Hi-top drive Si's rig with Hi-top leading the way.

In the meantime, not knowing what had just occurred, Weasley had set up at the end of a curve farther down the road. He planned to hijack Si using GM's On Star satellite system to force the truck to stop. His plan was to kill the GMC's engine, pepper-spray Si, and then take off with the boat.

In his haste to zip-tie Mikey Mo and the Sleazes, Mighty Mouse had made the mistake of tying off their hands in front of them instead of behind. Once the thugs had gone, it didn't take long for Mikey Mo to get Sly to fish his boxcutter out of his Jeep, and free all three of them. They climbed back in Mikey Mo's Jeep, got Mikey's pistol out of the glove compartment, and set off in pursuit.

Weasley sat next to his stolen Segway and waited for the truck to come along. If his plan worked, he'd lose it, but he planned to abandon it anyway since it wasn't registered to him. He had a fisherman's hat pulled down to try to disguise his face. When Weasley saw Si's truck round the curve, he climbed back aboard the Segway, activated the app on his cell phone, and killed Hi-top's engine.

"Ah wha di ...?" Hi-top exclaimed.

He turned the key, and the truck started back up.

"Mi didn't activate the OBD, but it must be interfering anyway. Wi betta take it off da truck completely."

He turned on his turn signal so Mighty Mouse would know something was amiss and pulled over on the shoulder of the road. He got out of the vehicle and got on his hands and knees bending over to try to disconnect the device.

Weasley rode up innocently on the Segway and yelled to Hi-top as he passed. When Hi-top turned, he pepper-sprayed him in the face. He then rounded the truck as Mighty Mouse was coming forward and tried to spray him as well. He mostly missed. Curse words filled the air. Weasley pushed Hi-top out of the way and jumped into the driver's seat of Si's truck. Fortunately, the keys were still in the ignition. He cranked it and floored it, almost hitting both Hi-top and Mighty Mouse. The boat rocked on the trailer, and for a moment it appeared that Weasley might lose it. The truck dug into the soft shoulder as it tried to get traction. Weasley continued to gun it relentlessly.

As the truck spun in the sandy shoulder, Mighty Mouse had the presence of mind to leap up on the trailer's fender and managed to pull his short but muscular frame onto the wobbling boat. The boat continued to sway back and forth, bouncing him back and forth and up and down like a rodeo rider.

Mighty Mouse knew he needed to find a way to regain control of this out-of-control scenario. The boat continued to teetertotter in every direction as Weasley alternated erratically between the road and the shoulder. Every protrusion became a potentially dangerous obstacle as the boat bounced and seesawed. A car coming from the other direction almost veered off the road to avoid a collision. The angry driver shook his fist out of the window.

Once Weasley got the whole rig back into the lane once and for all, the boat stabilized. Mighty Mouse saw a gaffing hook and grabbed it

I'll throw it through the bastard's back windshield.

He reared back to throw it like a javelin just as Weasley hit a pothole. His javelin sailed over the top of the truck's cab and caught in the branch of an overhanging tree. It ricocheted and came sailing back towards Mighty Mouse. He leaped aside as it clanged back down next to him.

"To rass (**Fuck you!**), Jack!" he screamed at it in frustration, as if an inanimate object could hear him.

He'd just have to stop Weasley the way he knew best — with his gun. He clamored on all fours out onto the bow deck of the boat, pulled his pistol out of his pocket, and took aim at the truck's back windshield. About that time, Weasley hit another pothole, and Mighty Mouse's bullet went wide and plugged a street sign instead. Hearing the sound of the gun and then the ping, Weasley inadvertently jerked on the steering wheel again, making Mighty Mouse lose his balance. He tumbled backwards into the cabin, losing his grip on the pistol in the process. It bounced into the galley and wound up in front of the oven. Mighty Mouse spidered back in to get it. Just as he reached for it, Weasley hit another pothole, and the oven door jarred open, whacking the kneeling Mighty Mouse on the back of his head. He momentarily saw stars.

"To rass all of yu!" Mighty Mouse screamed in frustration to anyone, anything, and everything.

Mighty Mouse did manage take control of the pistol once again and then began crawling back to the front deck. He took aim, this time holding the pistol with both hands. The bullet went through the back windshield barely missing Weasley.

Weasley finally realized that he had a stowaway passenger in the boat who he needed to deal with. He slammed on the brakes and pulled over. The boat rocked again, and Mighty Mouse's pistol was thrown over the side of the boat into the dirt.

Weasley jumped out of the truck, pulled his own pistol, and ordered whoever it was in the boat to come out. Mighty Mouse refused to do so but instead leaped over the side of the boat to look for his own weapon. Weasley shot a warning shot. When Mighty Mouse couldn't spot his own pistol, he decided it was time to call it a day. He took off running. Weasley took two shots at him but missed his mark.

Once Mighty Mouse was out of sight, the trembling Weasley jammed his pistol back into his pants. The weight of the pistol made Weasley's pants begin to sag, and he reached down to pull them back up. In his nervous excitement, his finger squeezed the trigger, and he shot himself through his own left testicle. The pain caused him to flinch, and when he did, he pulled the trigger again, this time sending a second bullet slamming into his left calf. The shock and pain caused him to black out.

Mikey Mo, Si, and Sly rounded the curve in Mikey Mo's Jeep, finally catching up to the stolen pickup and boat. They screeched to a stop and jumped out, their own weapons in hand. It didn't take them long to see that no weapon would be needed. Sly reached down and retrieved Weasley's weapon from his bloody pants. Si jumped into the truck to see if it would crank. It cranked right up. Everything seemed to be intact except the broken back and front windshields. He briefly inspected the boat to make sure it was still safely attacked to the trailer.

Mikey Mo recognized Weasley.

"I know this guy. This is Mr. Lineitem, a Shower Posse accountant. Should we take him to a doctor?"

"Rass him!" Si replied. "Da less we hab to do wif he da betta. Mi don **(don't)** wan The President to know wi were eben here."

"I think you're right," Mikey Mo replied. "No use going looking for trouble with Dudus or Harry Dog if we don't have to."

Sly spit on the still unconscious Weasley anyway as a parting gesture and partial retaliation for the indignity he suffered earlier at the impound yard. Mikey Mo did feel sorry enough for him though to anonymously call 110. Sly rode with Si in the truck in case another problem arose. Mikey Mo followed in his Jeep.

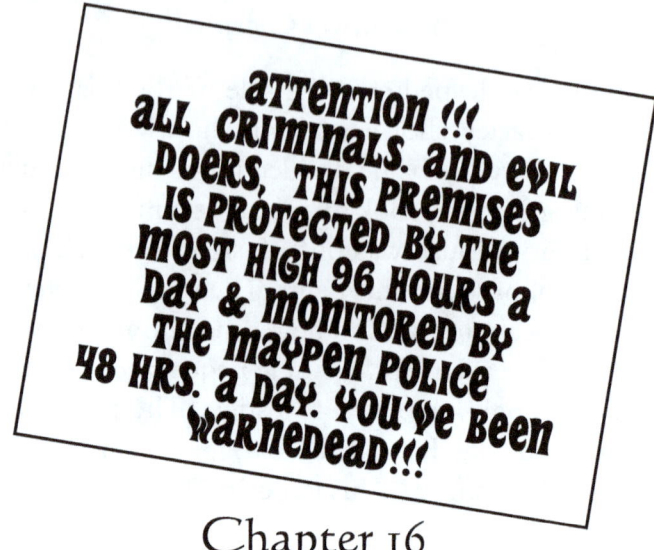

ATTENTION !!! ALL CRIMINALS. AND EVIL DOERS, THIS PREMISES IS PROTECTED BY THE MOST HIGH 96 HOURS a DAY & MONITORED BY THE MAYPEN POLICE 48 HRS. a DAY. YOU'VE BEEN WARNEDEAD!!!

Chapter 16

Mikey Mo debated the meaning of Weasley LIneitem's role in the attempted hijackings all the way back to Accompong the following day.

When he arrived at Colonel Ferron Winter's home, The Colonel was sipping hot tea with his wife beneath the royal poinciana tree in his front yard.

"Gud morning, sir. I had quite an adventure yesterday."

"Tell me about it," The Colonel said as his wife went into the house to retrieve a cup for Mikey Mo. She served him some tea, and then left them alone to talk business.

Mikey Mo gave Colonel Winter a blow-by-blow account of both of the attempted boat hijackings. The Colonel, as usual, patiently and silently listened, not interrupting Mikey Mo with questions.

When Mikey Mo concluded his recitation of the events, The Colonel calmly asked, "Did you have an opportunity to examine the boat once it got to Sleaze's shipyard?"

"Yes sir, I did. I couldn't find anything that seemed unusual about it. Actually, it was quite a nice, well-designed boat that appears to have sleeping accommodations for six or more people on it. I ran my hands across the fiberglass inside and out to feel for rough spots that might indicate a patch job and could find nothing suspicious. I checked all the cabinets for false bottoms and again found nothing.

"Since the Sleazes were already aware of your interest and had already been inadvertently drawn into this affair... oh, by the way, both of them send their regards ...."

The Colonel smiled and nodded.

"... I asked them both to be on the lookout for anything unusual. I went back by there before I drove up here this morning, and neither of them were able supply clues as to this mystery. The senior Sleaze even checked the bilge."

"So, we still don't know why Dudus Coke has an ongoing interest in this particular boat."

"Nope. But now there's an even bigger puzzler. I recognized the hijacker who was working alone. It was Mr. Lineitem."

"Wesley Lineitem, the Shower Posse accountant? Now that *is* a surprise. Not exactly the work that a desk-jockey accountant usually does. Did I understand you to say that you did not know the competing hijackers? Describe them again."

"One was a skinny, dreadlocked tree topper, and the other was just the opposite, a skin head, muscle-bound midget."

"And they pretended not to know each other and caused a disturbance at the impound yard? Hmmm! ... But were later working together? Interesting."

"That's correct, sir."

"And you say there was another unrelated incident at the impound yard as well? Coincidence? Huh! ... Even more interesting."

"Yes sir. A man tried to break into Si Sleaze's truck. Si scared him off with his pistol. The dude went over the fence and disappeared."

"A ... to use your vernacular ... tree topper and a midget ... They both would certainly be rememberable. I should be able to easily confirm my suspicion that they are two of Dudus's thugs. But the question remains — why would Dudus' hoodlums and Dudus' accountant be competing for the same prize? When they both work for the posse? I would normally say that the affair is none of my business except for the fact that I got a phone call from Will Black telling me that he and his wife plan to return to Jamaica once the *Spirit of the Seas* is deemed seaworthy to join their friends on the boat's inaugural voyage from Kingston to Ocho Rios."

"I know exactly where you're going, sir, and I'm on board all the way. The Blacks are not only dear friends but since you made them honorary Maroons, they are also family. And that makes the Craigs extended family. … And we will go to any lengths to protect our own."

"I couldn't have stated it better, my young associate."

"So do we tell them what we suspect?"

"At this point, we have nothing to tell. This may just be a matter of Dudus Coke's ego being bruised because he was denied something he wanted. He *is* a powerful man not accustomed to losing even a minor skirmish."

"Agreed, sir. He is not a good loser. And the fact that you bested him more than once, is why he has such a grudge against you. But what if this is something that Harry Dog is doing without The President's knowledge?"

"That too is also possible. I think we will understand the matter better if I can identify the two initial hijackers and find out if they are part of Harry Dog's team.

"Did I understand you to say that this boat sleeps six?"

"Yes sir."

"Then maybe I'll apprise our friend Mr. Davis that something is possibly amiss and see if I can arrange for him to join the Craigs and Blacks on the upcoming initial voyage. Henry's presence alone may deter any further aggressions. Both Dudus and Harry Dog respect his abilities. Henry will be able to watch our friends' backs and keep us apprised without setting off unnecessary alarms. And of course, you and Henry can have as many of my men as you need to back you up. If something is truly amiss, our adversary will soon tip his hand, and when he does, we'll have the advantage of surprise on our side."

"So here we go again with another confrontation with the Shower Posse. And this time we don't even know why."

"Looks that way," The Colonel said and shook his head. "But what is meant to be is meant to be. We have prevailed against them in the past, and if we are forced to, we'll do it again. I'll get back to you as soon as I'm able to identify the mystery hijackers. And you know what you need to do. But please be careful. Remember, pretty rose got maca jook **(prickly thorn)**.

"And if anyone asks, you have my complete backing and authority."

"Thank you, sir. Let us pray that this is a false alarm, but I'm afraid that it's not."

"Remember my friend. That a prayer from the mouth is no prayer. It is up to us to have the heart to make our prayers come true."

"You're so right. Jah bless."

```
We are not responsible
for shoes left over 30 days
remember  to clean your shoes before
you take it to the shoe man
ATTENTION!!
WE ACCEPT CLEAN
JOBS WE CANNOT
WORK ON DIRTY JOB
SO PLEAS CLEAN YOUR
SHOES AND BRING IT
```

Chapter 17

After Mikey Mo left, Colonel Winter drank some more tea while he digested the information that Mikey had just given him. He did not relish another confrontation with the powerful Dudus Coke, and he knew that the potential fallout could be unpleasant.

Why was Dudus hellbent to get this boat when he could afford a fleet of boats this size?

Hell, with all his illegal smuggling activities, he probably owns a fleet of boats this large or larger.

And this Weasley thing? It was his understanding that Weasley was in Harry Dog's pocket. And he was nothing but a crooked paper-pusher anyway; he wasn't a street soldier. Was there some dissention in the ranks of the Shower Posse? Was there an uprising in the making? Surely not! He couldn't see either Harry Dog or Weasley risking a power grab from The President when they'd be chancing ending up in unnamed graves in the Cockpit Country.

But neither Mikey Mo nor the Sleazes found anything unusual about the boat. It appeared to be just a nice recreational boat.

So here I am risking a war while not having even a clue as to why. But if I must kick over a hornet's nest to protect the people I love, so be it.

He reminded himself of a proverb as he kicked these random thoughts back and forth and evaluated the pros and cons of this latest predicament.

Spit in the sky, and it falls in your eye.

This latest intervention could only lead to more bad blood between him and Dudus, and they already had a history of conflict. When he had first been introduced to Will and Betsy Black by Henry Davis, she was on assignment to protect her American bank from graft when it became one of the leading lenders for Prime Minister Patterson's long overdue upgrade of Jamaica's highway system. It was known as the Highway 2000 Program. Dudus had been part of a consortium of contractors out to milk money from the government's road contracts through kickbacks, overbilling, falsified payrolls, and shoddy workmanship. Not being local, Betsy had not known how far over her head that she was in. Dudus had been willing to murder the Blacks should it become necessary. Other people did die. Before the affair was concluded, the fallout far exceeded just protecting the bank's highway loan. It cost The President a meaningful percentage of his empire.

And then there was the Genovesa treasure hunt where Dudus tried to even the score by this time meddling in The Colonel's business. This intervention became not only costly monetarily and personnel-wise but damaged Dudus' already tenuous relations with Kingston's powerful Spangler Posse. And in a final insult at the matter's conclusion, Colonel Winter had gotten the last laugh and rubbed his victory in as he embarrassed and humiliated Dudus a final time. To a thug like Dudus, this was unforgivable.

Colonel Winter dialed his old friend Henry Davis. They had known each other since childhood when they both lived back up in the hills. On one occasion, Henry had saved his life when as they were playing, and they had accidentally come up on an illegal ganja field. The owner had mistaken them for government agents and had taken a shot at them. The bullet hit a tree near Ferron, and a splinter had ricocheted off and stuck in his shoulder. Henry had carried Ferron back to the village on his back. The doctor there said that this probably saved Ferron's life since otherwise he would have most likely have bled to death. After this, the two friends declared themselves to be honorary cousins for life and even sometimes called each other "Cuz."

He couldn't help but think back on the incident as he prepared to hit Henry's number. The memory made him think of another old Jamaican proverb.

Ebery day debil help tief, but one day God help watchman (**Every day the devil helps the thief but one day God helps the watchman**).

Henry had definitely been his God-sent watchman, and they had been watching out for each other ever since.

"Hang-To (Henry's childhood street name), your old cuz."

"Ferret (Ferron's childhood street name. He had been nicknamed for a rat since he had been known to be quite elusive.), you old rascal. How's things?"

"'No complaints from this old man. You know what they say. No use complaining because it wouldn't change anything anyway. Did you know that the Blacks may be coming to Jamaica for a visit?"

"To visit with their Florida friends, the Craigs?"

"Oh, so you know about them."

"Mikey Mo introduced us. I expect to be doing some driving for them."

"There may be a situation developing that could involve both couples."

"Good or bad?"

"Unfortunately, not good since The President is involved."

"Nothing with him is ever good."

Colonel Winter brought Henry up to date on the rash of attempted hijackings that Mikey Mo had reported to him.

"So, The President possibly has an interest in a boat that the Craigs bought at auction?" Henry mused when Colonel Winter had finished. "Let me talk to some people and see if I can confirm that the two thugs who tried to steal the boat belong to the Shower Posse. If so, what then? Do the Craigs know about the incident?"

"No. I don't think so. I assume you feel the obligation to protect the Blacks as much as I do."

"Do a dog's nuts glisten in the pale moonlight? Of course, I do. Does either couple know about any of this?"

"No. I decided not to alarm them and see if you and I can put an end to it first. After all, I do have some influence with Harry Dog."

"Ferron, old cuz, I hate to remind you, but Harry Dog gave you his word that he wouldn't meddle in *your* affairs going forward. In this case, you'll be meddling in *his*."

"Not if Will and Betsy are potentially caught in the crossfire of a situation that they have merely bumbled into. Then it becomes *my* business."

"I don't mean to question your judgement, old friend, but you shouldn't put them at unnecessary risk by letting them get blindsided. Dudus and his men are too dangerous to take chances with."

"I understand that the Craigs and the Blacks will be taking the boat from Kingston to Ochi. Mikey Mo tells me it sleeps six. Do you think you can get yourself invited to go with them?"

"Only if we tell Will the truth about the reason that I'll be there. After all, he's a guest on the boat too. The Craigs own it. Let me tell Will why I'll be there, and then let him decide if we should alarm the Craigs. I think that's only fair."

"OK, I'll go along with that."

"I'll be back to you. And I assume that Mikey Mo has been apprised of all of this."

"Absolutely. I expect the two of you to work together to do whatever you have to do to protect our friends."

"Ten-four."

And you will try to identify the thugs?"

"No trying to it. We'll find out for sure who the hell they are."

Chapter 18

Additional questions had occurred to Henry since his conversation with The Colonel. Mikey Mo answered them the best he could. The two of them then carefully thought through the scenario facing them. At Henry's request, Mikey Mo also again redescribed the Shower Posse boat hijackers.

"If Harry Dog sends the same twosome in the future, you shouldn't have any trouble spotting them — a skinny shaggy giant and a muscle-bound slick-headed midget."

"Yeah, I'll just have to keep my eyes open for a hairy, lanky, daddy-long-legged giraffe and a skin-headed, pip-squeak gym junkie. That should be easy enough."

"I was thinking more like a long-legged string bean and an optimistic shrimp."

"Why optimistic?"

"Short people are optimistic because they're always looking up."

"Yuk, yuk. And they're also down to earth."

"But they're still dangerous. Why don't you be the one call the Blacks?" Mikey Mo suggested. "Not only have you known them longer than I have, but since we know from experience that the Shower Posse has the capability to tap phone calls, your phone is more likely to be secure."

Henry made the call. He told Will and Betsy at the beginning of the three-way conversation that he was going to avoid the use specific names because of the sensitive nature about what he was about to discuss. He would refer to both the Blacks and the Craigs generically as the "owner" and "friend."

"It has come to our attention that a past treasure hunting competitor is showing an intense interest in your friends' new acquisition."

"Their real estate?" Betsy asked.

"No, the other."

"Hmmm. I see."

"Are you referring to our Tivoli Gardens competitor?" Will asked.

"That's the one."

"Do we know why?"

"No."

Henry then offered to join the Blacks for the upcoming boat trip but told them that he would leave it up to them to suggest that the Davises be invited to join the travel party. They all agreed that it was premature to alarm the "owner" since they did not know them well enough to know how they would react or about the level of their self-defense capabilities.

As Henry reminded them, "We know from experience the other party's mindset and capabilities. The owner does not."

Henry outlined the salient points Will would need to make when he talked to DV to secure the Davises' invitation. He also tried to nail down a specific date. The reasons were many, and they all made sense. First of all, the travelers would all have a free place to stay in Kingston since Henry had already called his son Big Boy and gotten his permission for the party to stay at Big Boy's Kingston villa while they were in the city. Next, they would have transportation.

"The villa's availability on that date coupled with use of a van my son keeps at this address would probably be enough bait to seal the deal. But if not, here's one last advantage of me being included."

He then reminded Will and Betsy that since he knew the Kingston metropolitan area, he could take them to the places they would need to shop to outfit and provision the boat and make sure that they were not pestered or overcharged.

"I know of a date that our mutual DJ friend will be working in Kingston. Let's push this date as our preferred date for you both to arrive in Kinston. This way my wife and I can hitch a ride to Kingston with him and not have my van stuck there once we leave."

"Good idea. Let me get back to you."

"Excellent. We look forward to welcoming you home."

Unfortunately, unknown to either Mikey Mo or Henry, Colonel Winter had already made the mistake of calling Harry Dog and had warned him to lay off any future attempt to steal the *Spirit of the Seas* since this would once again put him in the position of meddling in Maroon business. He did not explain why, making Harry Dog wonder just how this could be so. Harry immediately dispatched a man to bug Mikey Mo's car and thus subsequently overheard Mikey Mo and Henry's follow up conversations. But since Henry was the one to have called Will and Will was the one to have called DV, Harry Dog still didn't know the names of all the parties involved. He decided that he would have to send Hi-top to the airport on the appointed date to clarify that fact. Then he could decide his next course of action.

Harry Dog dispatched Hi-top to the airport the day that the Craigs and the Blacks were scheduled to arrive. Harry Dog told him Will and Betsy's ETA and text-messaged Hi-top Henry's picture. Hi-top picked up Monkeyman to back him up, and the two went to the airport together. The two hoods loafed around the airport and soon became bored. For fun, Monkeyman then shoplifted some candy bars from an airport kiosk to kill the time. Hi-top began to play the Fishdom video game on his smartphone. He soon became frustrated since he couldn't get beyond level 2 and began looking at YouPorn instead.

Henry and Rose arrived, and Hi-top saw them. He accessed Harry Dog's text message and showed the photo to Monkeyman. He agreed that this was who they had been sent to watch. Hi-top texted Harry Dog, telling him that the quarry had been spotted. He and Monkeyman then split up and follow Henry and Rose around the airport, trying hard not to be seen. Henry found two unoccupied seats and then went to buy some tea for Rose and him to drink while they waited.

Since Hi-top was 6'5" it was hard for him to stay concealed. Henry looked for a short muscular person but didn't see one. This puzzled him a bit since he expected Hi-top to have a short accomplice. He bought two teas and brought them back to where Rose was holding their seats. Neither of them noticed Monkeyman lurking within earshot.

"I can't wait to see Will and Betsy," Rose commented. "It seems so long since we've spent time with them."

"You're right, my dear. Remember when we stayed with them in Vero Beach, and they took us to Disney World. That was such a wonderful trip. That was the first time I'd ever been in a Home Depot. I had never seen a hardware store that big, even when we lived in London."

"We have certainly made some memories together. We even survived the posse invading our home and kidnapping them. It was a wonder that any of us lived through that night."

"We probably wouldn't have if Dudus hadn't been holding them for ransom to try to get the clues on how to steal the Maroons' treasure. But Mikey Mo and E.J. came through and saved the day and made 'em pay. Yep! The Blacks are about as close to being family as anyone I know."

"My dear, they are family."

Monkeyman's ears went up. "Will and Betsy Black" — now he knew who the Davises were here to pick up."

He worked his way back over to Hi-top and whispered to him what he had just learned. Hi-top sent the name to Harry Dog in a text message.

Harry Dog went ballistic.

"Ah wah di ...? Da rahtid renk **(damn stinking)** Will Black and his dutty gyal **(dirty bitch)** wife! Wah dey hab to do wif dis affair? If dey nuh ramp wi mi again, mi see dey fyah fi yu dis ya time (**I'll see that they burn in hell this time.**)."

Harry Dog quickly texted Hi-top back and told him not to lose the Blacks no matter what unless he wanted to suffer Jah's wrath and his as well. He warned him about the ramifications of screwing up again and reminded Hi-top that it was him and his men who had blown the hijacking mission. As usual, Harry Dog's memory was short. He conveniently forgot to disclose that the hijacking would not have been necessary if the men that he delegated the boat delivery to hadn't first dropped the ball through undisciplined stupidity. And that Weasley, his second appointee, hadn't failed as well.

Will and Betsy's plane landed five minutes early. They walked across the tarmac and into the terminal and after going through customs, were hugging the Davises. About a half hour later, the Craigs plane landed, and Will and Betsy introduced them. Once everyone cleared customs and retrieved their luggage, Henry led them out to Big Boy's van, and they took off for his villa.

Hi-top and Monkeyman followed a discreet distance behind.

DON'T TEACH YOUR GARBAGE TO SWIM

Chapter 19

Henry Davis called Mikey Mo to report that their guests from America had arrived and that he had picked them up at the airport, not knowing that Harry Dog was monitoring the phone call.

"I'm in Kingston presently," Mikey Mo said. "Do you have specific plans for them yet?"

"Not really. They just need to make preparations for their journey. You know, buy provisions for the boat and such."

"As I told you before, I'm emceeing a show at the Jubilee Market at Sir William Grant Park tomorrow. Why don't you bring them by there so that I can visit with Will and Betsy and meet the Craigs? I'm sure you can buy some of what you'll be needing at Jubilee. My show starts at eleven."

Harry Dog listened in on the conversation and called Hi-top.

"I know that if the Blacks and Henry Davis are meeting with Mikey Mo Mullins they are up to no good. You can count on the fact that those batty holes (**assholes**) almost always are. They'll be at the Jubilee Market in the morning. Since you now know where they are staying, get a man over there and plant a bug. I've got a score to even with them. And get your sorry worthless batty over to Jubilee while they're there and find out what they're really up to."

As Henry approached Sir William Grant Park in downtown Kingston, the hustle and bustle became almost frantic. The activities varied from people walking to people with pushcarts trying to sell their wares. The street was jammed with buses and taxis.

After finding a place to park Big Boy's bus, they walked straight into the main market. This longstanding marketplace was named in honor of the jubilee of Queen Victoria. It was a vast area of streets, lanes, and alleyways, with hundreds of stalls offering anything from exotic fruits to rat traps, and CDs with all forms of Jamaican music to freshly caught fish, and of course, the inevitable ganja. A large part of the market consisted of some stalls selling vegetables and fruits and others selling meat and fish.

It was the perfect place for a foodie to be introduced to Jamaican cuisine. The more interesting parts of the market, however, were those where all kinds of other articles were sold. For instance, there were stalls where a person could buy CDs with Jamaican reggae. These stalls had enormous speakers from which tunes of this iconic Caribbean music blared to entertain passers-by. They competed with music coming from other stalls.

There were others where a person could buy sweets. But they were often deceiving. When a potential customer approached them, the vendor would secretly lift the cloth on his stall, revealing a hidden ganja stash, which, in fact, he would be smoking himself.

The market was energetic, vibrant, and colorful — and at times, smelly. Some areas might be spacious, but in others, you would have to squeeze yourself through the crowd.

People were yelling to get the attention of potential customers. In one case, they saw a fierce fight break out between an aggressive vendor and her equally aggressive female customer. Both women screamed curse words as each attempted to try to insult the other as much as possible. Strangely enough, people seemed to be enjoying the fight. One woman finally fled in a fit of laughter, repeating the worst used words to everyone around, screaming at the top of her lungs for the benefit of those who were too far away to understand what was being said.

Cee Cee aimed her camera at one woman who almost snatched it out of her hand. But then another woman stepped up and not only volunteered to pose but wanted to chat afterwards. DV and Cee Cee were in culture shock. Will and Betsy were merely amused.

"I bet you can't guess who one of the primary principals of this market is," Henry said.

Will and Betsy shrugged.

"The Kingston and St. Andrew Corporation. Remember them?"

"Do I ever!" Betsy gasped. "A Dudus Coke subsidiary. That sure brings back memories."

"Holy shit! Does it ever!" Will said. "If it hadn't been for Colonel Winter … and I might add, you and Mikey Mo … The KSAC would have caused Betsy's bank to lose a shit-pot-load of money on the Highway 2000 program, and we'd probably both be dead."

"Small world, isn't it?" Henry replied. "And now it appears we're in over our heads with a boat that Dudus has taken a fancy to. Oh, well, shit happens. Let's go find Mikey Mo."

As they strolled down each aisle taking it all in, Hi-top trailed behind them at a discreet distance. While they were relaxed, he was not. He wondered as he ducked from one booth to the next why Harry Dog as so intent on keeping tabs on these foreigners. They seemed like harmless tourists enough to him.

Since Harry Dog imparted information to his subordinates on a need-to-know basis, Hi-top still hadn't made the connection that two of these people were the owners of the boat that he was supposed to have stolen or that the rest of the party had frustrated Harry Dog's efforts in the past, causing Harry Dog much embarrassment and loss of face with The Pres.

"Do you realize how long it's been since we were in an outdoor market this big?" Will commented as they ambled along. "And I think this one is as big or even bigger than the one we visited in Nassau. Guys, have we ever told you about that?"

"Don't believe you have," Rose Davis said.

"We want to hear about it too," said Cee Cee.

"Well, it was our second year in Vero," Betsy started out. "When we won that drawing for a trip from Peterson Groves to celebrate their fifty-year anniversary."

"I still can't believe that happened. Your mother registered us, and we didn't even know about it until the owner, our neighbor Fred Peterson, called us and told us we'd won."

"That was such a hoot the day he called us. He was trying *so* hard to pretend he didn't know us so people would think that the drawing was on the level."

"I can still hear him now. 'Mr. and Mrs. Black. This is Mr. Peterson, the proprietor of Peterson's Groves, calling to tell you that you are our grand prize winner and have won a trip to Nassau.' He was trying so hard to seem unbiased until you accidentally shot his story all to hell."

"Boy, did I ever. If you'll remember, it was later in the day on a Saturday afternoon, and we had had a beer or two in the pool, and I responded, 'Fred, ... is that you? What the hell's with this Mr. Peterson/ Mr. Black crap? Is this some kind of prank?"

"To which he responded, 'Mr. Black, we *are* on live radio.' ...'"

"You really had a bad case of foot in mouth disease that day."

"Yeah. I stuck my foot so far down my throat that my toes were wiggling out my other end. But Fred *was* partially at fault. If we were going on live radio, he could've warned us in advance."

"*You?* Foot in mouth. I can't believe *that*," Rose said sarcastically with a laugh.

"Oh, yeah. My dear hubby had a bad case of it that day. But he didn't know that we didn't know that my mother had registered us for the drawing and had forgotten to tell us about it. But that faux pas was only the beginning of a chain of events," Betsy continued.

"Who would have ever guessed that Fred's travel agent would screw up our reservation to Atlantis and when we got here, we found out that not only would we not be getting a suite, but that the hotel was full. They said the number on our reservation didn't even conform to their numbering system."

"And you were stomping around that lobby and making a scene like a rabid bull."

Will began to sing a doctored version of the 1950's Leslie Scott/Irene Williams calypso standard, "Crazy Like Mad."

For I am crazy like mad
For I am crazy like mad
Come with me and you will see that I'm crazy like mad.

"Here my hubby goes again. Honey, stick to being a financial advisor. The Mighty Lord Wilson you ain't and ain't ever gonna be."

"So, I was mad. What do you expect? Here we are standing in a hotel lobby in a foreign country on Labor Day weekend like two idiots surrounded by luggage with no place to stay. And if you'll remember, the travel agent in Vero wouldn't take our phone call because she had a customer at her desk. But after the hotel manager saw how mad I was, he did jump to find us a room, even though it wasn't a suite."

"Just to keep you from disrupting their lobby. And remember that drunk dice shooter at Cable Beach who was puking all over the dice table?"

"And going through Burger King's drive-through when we got back in the stretch limo Fred had rented. I thought that the cashier was going to drop his teeth when our driver ordered our Whopper meals and then pulled the limo up enough so we could pay them from the far back seat. I really think that since we were in a limo that he thought he was about to meet a movie star or something. Or maybe the Estefans."

Will began to sing off key.

Memories light the corner of my mind.
Misty water-colored memories of the way we were.

Betsy put her hands over her ears and said, "Will, please. I used to like that song. Let's hope this trip goes better than that visit to Nassau did."

"Every trip with you, my dear, is an irie occasion."

The stalls had a wide variety of merchandise. They saw straw goods, rum, conch shell jewelry, Batiks, t-shirts, woodcarvings, and a wide array of food items. Aggressive salespeople urged them to come visit their stalls.

"Hey, mister. Come in my shop and look."

"Tell me what you're looking for, ma'am. I'll give you a special deal."

"You looked her shop, but you haven't looked in mine. My feelings are hurt."

All around them was the din of people negotiating prices on items that had interested them.

Will began to hear music. It seemed to be coming from an open area across the way.

"Sounds like we're getting closer to Mikey Mo. I wonder who's playing."

An assortment of musicians was rocking away on a floor-level makeshift stage area to a familiar tune, "Funky Nassau."

"I know some of those guys," DV enthusiastically announced. "Those two are Sly and Robbie. They opened for us when I was playing with the Beach Boys. They're playing one of our old numbers we did together. And that's Ray Munnings. He was The Beginning of the End's guitar player. They were the ones who originally wrote and recorded 'Funky Nassau'."

Sly and Robbie's pickup band consisted of an organ, two guitars, a bass, a drummer, and two trumpet players. Will couldn't resist tapping his feet and doing a little shuffle as he listened.

"Remember when the Blues Brothers sang that song?"

"Of course. We've only watched that movie probably two dozen times."

"Boy, island music has sure changed since we moved to Florida. Goombay and reggae to Funk. Come on. Let's get up close to the band. I want to hear more of these guys."

Mikey Mo saw them and waved. After finishing "Funky Nassau," he announced that the band would take a short break.

He left the makeshift stage, hugged Betsy with one arm and hugged Will with the other. Hi-top edged closer to see if he could overhear their conversation. Since he was by far the tallest man in the crowd, his presence did not go unnoticed to Mikey Mo.

One of the hijackers? Why's he here?

When Hi-top tried to take their picture with his smartphone, he further attracted Mikey Mo's attention. And when he raised his Shower Posse tattooed his arms, Mikey Mo could see that he was armed. This confirmed two things Mikey Mo already knew to be true. There was now absolutely no doubt that this thug was one of Dudus' men, and there was also no doubt that he was at the Market for a reason. And the reason had to be no good.

He whispered something in Henry's ear and nodded in Hi-top's direction. Henry studied Hi-top's face, memorizing his features, so that he too would be sure to remember him if he saw him again.

Will turned around to introduce the Craigs, but they were involved hugging up to Sly and Robbie. His mouth fell open.

"Do you know this guy?" Mikey Mo said to either or both.

"Do we ever?" both Sly and Robbie exclaimed. "We go way back. We used to work on the road together."

"Remember when we played SXSW in Austin?" Robbie asked.

"We were hot that day," DV said. "And I don't mean just the weather."

"DV, that's when I became convinced that you white boys weren't to be taken for granted," Sly agreed. "You got time to play a few numbers with us today for old time's sake?"

DV looked at Henry for guidance and said, "I guess that's up to our host. I'm not the one setting the schedules."

About that time Ray Munnings came over. They hugged.

"DV, my brother, time has been good to you. You ain't getting' out of here without jammin'. Don't even think about it."

"I guess the decision's been made," DV said. "Let's make Kingston funky."

"I can't wait to hear you play," Rose said.

"Why don't we do a couple of my old Beach Boys numbers. Do you think your band knows 'Sloop John B' or 'Kokomo'?"

"I think they can manage that," Sly said.

"Then let's get to it," Mikey Mo said. "Time's a wasting. Oh, Henry, before I forget. The Colonel sent with me a list of people and their phone numbers in case you need any local assistance on your upcoming trip around the island to Ochi. Here it is."

Henry took the paper and absent mindedly put it in his back pocket.

Mikey Mo got behind his mike, and said, "Folks, we have a special treat for you today — a reunion of sorts. It just so happens that we have a former Beach Boy in our midst, and he and Sly and Robbie are old friends and colleagues. Give it up for DV Craig. He's graciously agreed to do a couple of numbers with the band."

Robbie lent DV a spare guitar. DV checked the tuning. It was just fine. The band began to play the old Beach Boy classic, "Kokomo."

Aruba, Jamaica, ooh I wanna take you.
Bermuda, Bahama, come on pretty mama
Key Largo, Montego
Baby, why don't we go, Jamaica

People began clapping in rhythm to the band and singing along. Will and Betsy joined in.

Hi-top stood to one side taking the whole scene in.

I might not know the Davises, the Craigs, or the Blacks, but I certainly know who Mikey Mo is. He's Colonel Winter's go-to man. That batty hole was also a major reason I failed to hijack the Spirit of the Seas last week. No wonder Harry Dog sent me over here. If these people know Mikey Mo, something has got to be afoot. And I sure would love to know what was on that piece of paper that Mikey Mo just gave Henry Davis. If I got it and gave it to Harry Dog, and it turned out to be something, it would go a long way into getting back into his favor. But I need to get someone else to get it for me since Mikey Mo knows who I am.

Then he spotted Blind Blake, a local pickpocket.

So Blind Blake is working this crowd. Bingo! He's my answer.

The band finished playing "Kokomo" and after the applause died down, launched into "Sloop John B."

Blind Blake's schtick was pretending to be a blind man with a cane and a seeing-eye dog. But, in reality, he was one of the best pickpockets in Kingston. Hi-top pulled Blind Blake aside and told him what he wanted. Within seconds, they had negotiated a deal, and Hi-top gave him a down payment. Henry had continued to suspiciously monitor the thug. When he noticed the money changing hands, he thought that maybe the gangster was just making an illegal narcotics transaction. If that was the reason, he was here —*No problem.*

He let his guard down a notch and went back to watching the musicians.

Bind Blake waited for an opportunity to purposely bump into Henry at a time that he thought Henry would be distracted with watching the singers. Momentarily Henry thought it was an accident, but then he thought he felt someone reaching into his back pocket. Suddenly it hit him. The harmless blind man was more than a drug dealer.

He's a pickpocket looking to score my wallet.

He stomped down as hard as he could as he spun to confront the thief. He caught the would-be miscreant on his sandaled instep. The robber screamed and his sunglasses flew off, exposing the fact that he was not blind after all.

I'm right! Das pretty rose does hab macca jook **(This pretty rose does have a prickly thorn)**.

With his sight having been miraculously restored, the abruptly unimpaired thief bent over to grab his now suddenly impaired foot. He butted an overweight tourist in her ample belly as he reached around her to grab her buttocks. She almost toppled. The petrified woman ripped a loud, resounding wet, foul-smelling bottom burp and peed on herself as he tried to grab her breasts to right himself again. She shoved him as hard as she could. This sent him careening into an old man in a wheelchair. The man's young, muscular caregiver then slung the Not-So-Blind Blake as hard as he could in his effort to protect his charge.

This sent the hapless con man twisting and reeling headlong into the band's drummer. The walking cane that the pickpocket had somehow held onto throughout all this came thundering down into the bass drum with an earsplitting boom that sent the entire drumkit scattering across the floor. The drummer initially toppled backwards but then bounced back up and kicked as hard as he could, catching the miscreant with a crashing blow into his genitalia.

Now Blind Blake was truly blinded but with pain. All he could see was stars and felt nauseous. He frantically grabbed one trumpet player's instrument and let go with a torrent of putrid smelling vomit down the bell of the horn. He then let go with a second round, spraying any member of the band who happened to be close. He reached for his knife, slashing out at the bass player. The bass player swung his guitar as hard as he could, knocking the thief momentarily senseless and sending the knife skidding across the floor.

The old wheelchair-bound man rolled over Blake's service dog's tail. The injured dog snapped at the person closest to it, sinking his teeth into a tourist's oversized crocodile Hermes purse. The two began a tug of war over the purse, sending its contents in all directions. The dog finally let go, knocking the woman into the person behind her. The furious dog attacked again, shredding the woman's Diane von Furstenberg sundress and pulling it off. As the agitated woman tried unsuccessfully to cover herself, her own bladder let loose. The man next to her slipped in her urine, and his foot caught the dog, resulting in a dropkick that sent the dog head over heels into another couple. The drooling dog screamed and ran off down the corridor and through an open doorway. This caused another panic as people knocked each other over trying to get out of its way.

By the time security go there, the hapless thief was still out cold. They began to pick up the other bodies off the floor and check to see if anyone was seriously hurt.

Rose ran over to check if Henry was OK. Henry assured her he was fine.

After it was all over, Betsy looked at Will and said, "Now, what were we saying about hoping this trip would go smoother than our old trip to Nassau? I almost felt sorry for that unfortunate thief. He won't have much of a sex life for a while."

"Don't. As our good friend here, Henry, is fond of saying 'Ebry day debble elp teef; wan dyah *God* we elp de watchman' or in other words, 'Every day the devil helps the thief; one day God will help the rest of us'."

Henry smiled and gave Will a thumbs up.

"I know. I know, my dear. I said, almost. And I remember something else Mr. Davis is fond of saying, 'Sorry for maga **(mongrel)** dog, maga dog turn round bite yu'."

"Couldn't have said it better myself, dear lady," Henry said. "I see I have taught you both well, my Jam-erican friends."

Only Henry noticed Hi-top slinking off fuming, mumbling about the money he had wasted with Blind Blake.

"Mi sure hope Harry Dog doesn't hear about dis," he mumbled, confirming what Henry already knew.

I knew it. … Shower Posse for sure!

Henry mulled over what Mikey Mo had told him about his encounter with the Shower Posse a few days earlier and wondered about Hi-top's motive. He nodded knowingly as he thought how Blind Blake had turned into Not-So-Blind Blake.

Noh care how boar hog try fi hide under sheep wool, 'im grunt will always betray him (No matter how hard a hog tries to hide under sheep's wool, his grunt will always betray him).

And was it a coincidence that Hi-top seemed to be around when trouble occurred? Coincidence is the word you use when you can't see the levers and the pulleys. And Henry was positive that he knew what controlled Hi-top's pulleys and levers. They were manipulated by Dudus Coke and the Shower Posse.

Chapter 20

The morning sun was shining, and the slight breeze gave the air a fresh feeling as Mighty Mouse and Monkeyman worked their way back over to Big Boy's villa. This portended to be a good day to accomplish their mission, and both felt relaxed as they listened to their car CD. Bob Marley's familiar tune "Duppy Conqueror" played as both puffed away in a lazy, leisurely manner at their ganja spliff. Hi-top had already called them and informed them that the villa's occupants were at the Jubilee Market and would therefore not be home to threaten the mission. Unfortunately for them, things are not always as they seem.

While Big Boy's guests might be enjoying a reunion at the Jubilee Market, leaving the villa indeed unoccupied, that only meant that human opposition was unlikely. But there can be unexpected challenges than the human kind.

About that time, Jimmy Cliff began to sing the classic oldie "You Can Get What You Really Want." This seemed to the two hoods to be an omen. They paid no attention to the song that perhaps would prove to be more appropriate that day, "Too Many Rivers to Cross."

Harry Dog was back in Tivoli Gardens looking at the same soothing horizon. He had music playing as well. Bobby McFerrin sang

"Don't Worry, Be Happy." But Harry Dog had tuned McFerrin out because he was indeed worried, and he saw little reason to be especially happy since he still had to get that renk **(stinking)** boat back or face mortal hell with Dudus.

Instead of just mindlessly puffing away at a ganja spliff, his mind was in continuous turmoil as it churned with one random question after another that he couldn't answer. But his gut told him something new was afoot. And he had damned good reasons for thinking so. First was his out of the blue call from Colonel Winter cautioning him about honoring his previous commitment to stay out of the Colonel's business and mentioning the *Spirit of the Seas*. He didn't remember ever before getting a call from Colonel Winter. So why now?

His mind reverted back to his previous promise to The Colonel that he would avoid future situations that would bring the two into conflict. In his opinion, he should not perpetuously be held rigidly to that commitment unconditionally. After all, his vow had been made under duress. And presently he was only following Dudus's orders.

A man can't be expected to serve two masters.

*What a rhaatid **(hell of a)** mess! How'd The Colonel even know about that bloody boat? ... Or for that matter, the Shower Posse's interest in it? ... Is Price Wright secretly in The Colonel's pocket? ... And why should The Colonel even care? ... Is de old mengkeh **(fool)** now bugging us?... And what's the new owner to him? ... He's not even Jamaican or a bredren. He's a white bakra from America. ... There's got to be a hidden motive there. ... Maybe he knows what's in the boat, and the greedy bastid is trying to steal it from us. ... But how would he know that? If he thinks he can steal from The President, he's gotta be senile or stakki **(a nutcase)**. ... Could the Shower Posse have a mole in it working for him? ... Only a few of our people know what's in that bloodclot boat. ... As I said, what a rhaatid mess!*

Then there was Mikey Mo foiling the hijacking. This brought up even more unanswered questions.

Hell, Mikey Mo doesn't do anything on his own. ... After all, he's Colonel Winter's lap dog and errand boy. He had no reason to even be at the impound yard that day. ... I understand Weasley being there. ... He was trying to save his own ass. ... But Mikey Mo? ... Something doesn't add up.

And then there was Will and Betsy's arrival in Jamaica with the boat's new owners.

Why are they here? … And how do they know the Spirit of the Seas' new owners? And now that bumba das clot **(ass wipe)** *Henry Davis is in the picture? This can't all be coincidental. There's some kind of bloody conspiracy going on. … And by God, I'm going to find out what it is.*

If Harry Dog had known at that moment that the incoming entourage had assembled with Mikey Mo that morning at the Jubilee Market, he would have been even more disturbed. About that time, his cell phone rang. It was Hi-top.

"Boss. Hi-top. You'll never guess who the Americans met with this morning, Mikey Mo Mullins."

Harry Dog's teeth gritted. He bit the ganja spliff he was smoking in half.

Hi-top neglected to mention the misadventure with Blind Blake. Some things are best kept confidential. He had no doubts that this disclosure would have sent Harry Dog over the edge.

But now Harry Dog was convinced he had been right all along. Without a doubt, some skullduggery was afoot, and he had better find out just what it was. Or else.

"Do you have someone bugging their residence like I told you to?"

"Yes, sir, I do. My men haven't reported back to me yet. It should be an easy matter. They're good, reliable men. I'll let you know as soon as I hear from them."

"You did tell them that I overheard where the owners keep his spare key, didn't you?"

"Yes, sir. Just like you told me to. In a hanging basket by the front door."

"Good."

Little did either of them suspect that the bugging was about to run into some unexpected pitfalls.

Monkeyman and Mighty Mouse arrived at Big Boy's villa. Everything seemed quiet so they parked their car. There were no other cars around, and all the lights were out. No neighbors were out and about. And their quarry was expected to be gone for several hours. Conditions seemed to be about as good as they'd ever be.

"Let's get this job over and get the hell out of here," Monkeyman told his partner. "There's a cold Red Stripe somewhere with my name on it crying out to be drunk."

They approached the front door and peeked in a window. All seemed well. The hanging basket was out front hanging from an ackee tree branch, just as Hi-top had told them it would be. But the branch was just a little too high for them to reach up comfortably to fish around in it for a key.

"Why don't I get on your shoulders," Mighty Mouse suggested.

"My shoulders? After all, you're the weightlifter, not me," Monkeyman replied. "Why don't I get on yours? Besides that, my back's still aching from our boat hijacking assignment. I think I must have pulled something."

"Whatever."

What they had no way of knowing was that the hanging basket was the home for a Jamaican red ground racer. The snake was almost a pet to Big Boy. He had affectionately named it Julius Squeezer. Big Boy allowed it to live in the pot since it was nonpoisonous, and it ate rats. He rarely had to go into the pot since he had a key on his keychain, and in case he ever did lock himself out, he kept an old broom handle in the flowerbed to shoo Julius out so he could reach in and get the key. His father, Henry, knew this and had shooed Julius away when he had first arrived with the Craigs and Blacks, but there no way that a home invader would know about this arrangement.

Monkeyman stood on Mighty Mouse's broad shoulders and reached into the hanging basket. Julius had recently molted. He felt around for the key and found it under Julius' molted skin. Just as he grabbed it, Julius wrapped himself around Monkeyman's arm. The shocked Monkeyman began to flail and slap as he tried to disentangle himself. The key shot out into the adjacent flowerbed. The snakeskin dropped on Mighty Mouse's bald head.

Mighty Mouse felt the snakeskin and panicked. Then it dangled down in front of his eyes. He shrieked. This wasn't just a snake; it was a duppy (ghost). And it was protecting Big Boy's villa. He had been told all his life that Ol' Higeses shed their skin before they turned into an owl and sucked the life out of their innocent victims.

But he thought as his mind raced, *This only happens at night. But this is daytime!*

He didn't understand, but he knew he didn't want to die. He continued screaming.

"Da house's haunted. Da snake rilly a duppy. Hit's a Ol' Hige. Hit gonna suck da breath from wi."

As Monkeyman tried to beat Julius off, Mighty Mouse continued to dance trying to shake the snakeskin. He lost his balance and stumbled backwards. He tripped over Big Boy's water hose, throwing them both into an adjacent pink bougainvillea. Monkeyman didn't notice that a thorn had ripped his cell phone loose from his pants. He ground it into the dirt as he attempted to climb out of the thorny plant.

The terrified snake continued to hang on for dear life and it slithered down Monkeyman's prone body and then down Mighty Mouse's shirt looking for a safe haven. It became entangled with Mighty Mouse's bling, leaving its thrashing tail sticking out.

Mighty Mouse shot back out of the thorny bougainvillea, just as Monkeyman attempted to right himself. He screamed for help. Mighty Mouse swatted wildly as he tried to hit the snake, but all his flailing arms accomplished was to knock them both into the prickly plant a second time. Monkeyman staggered to stand again. Mighty Mouse finally got one hand around the snake and blindly tried to fling it. It wrapped itself around Mighty Mouse's arm, and when it finally lost its hold ended up around Monkeyman's neck. This sent Monkeyman into yet another panic, and his bowels let loose.

Monkeyman ran blindly as he tried to disentangle himself once more from Julius. He tripped over a limestone rock and headbutted the ackee tree. Julius continued to hold on and tightened his hold. A dazed, strangling Monkeyman staggered back.

He yowled a round of profanity in a high, screechy, nasal voice. The tone terrified Mighty Mouse. He began to shake and tremble and then began to back away from Monkeyman since duppies' voices were most often in squeaky nasally tones.

"De Ol' Hige has possessed yu!"

Julius now looked for another safe harbor. He slithered down Monkeyman's shirt and wrapped himself around his waist. Monkeyman reached up to his neck to grab Julius, and when he found nothing there, he thought he was finally safe.

This feeling of safety only lasted for seconds since when Monkeyman had headbutted the tree, it upset a wasp nest. Suddenly he had a new problem. He found himself surrounded by a cloud of angry, stinging wasps.

Once again, the scratched and bleeding Monkeyman panicked and ran. He tripped over the same rock and began rolling down the steeply sloped yard towards the street. When he finally quit rolling, Julius decided once and for all that he had had enough and slithered down Monkeyman's pants leg and scooted towards the car. When Monkeyman saw him emerge, he began to shout for Mighty Mouse to shoot the bloodclot renk **(damned stinking)** thing.

"How yu shoot Ol' Hige? Hit not mortal. Wi need Sam de Sham, de obeah man, to put curse on de rhaatid ting."

"But Sam de Sham not here right now to help wi. So, either shoot the rhaatid ting or mi shoot you," Monkeyman yelled back.

The blood from the bougainvillea scratches was running in Mighty Mouse's eyes. When Mighty Mouse pulled his pistol out of his pants, it caught on his cell phone, sending it flying. He pulled the trigger. His shot missed the snake, and instead shot out the car window on the drivers' side before exiting through car's windshield.

Julius was unharmed and headed for cover.

"Let's get the rass **(fuck)** out of here before the law arrives," Monkeyman shouted.

"Yu right. Rass dis house and everyone in hit **(it)**. Hit's cursed."

"By de way, yu face fava shit **(your face looks like shit)**, bald head," Monkeyman told Mighty Mouse.

"Yu tink yu look any betta, rent-a-dread. And yu need to change yu pants. Dey smell like shit."

"Because dey fulla shit … like yu. Mi need a Red Stripe."

"Yu can drink all de Red Stripe by yuself. Mi need a few stiff Wray and Nephews instead."

At this point, they both jumped in the car and gunned it down the street as they tried to keep from getting cut even more from the broken window glass. Monkeyman had yet to notice that his phone was missing. At this point, he really didn't care. He just wanted to get away from this cursed house.

Monkeyman's face was already beginning to swell from his normal allergic reaction to the wasp stings. He could already feel his lips begin to balloon, his tongue begin to thicken, and his eyes puffing up as they swelled partially shut. He squinted to see.

He pulled over into a parking lot and sat silently.

"Yu-sse dribe de c-car," he finally managed to lisp to Mighty Mouse. "Mi habbing trouble seeing. An f-fine a rum bar in a huu-rry."

"Yu not talking too good neither."

"M-mi don c-care wha' Hi-top s-say, mi ne-nebbe goin' back dere, nebbe eber."

"Mi neither, bra."

```
TO ANY PUSSY
HOLE YU CUT
MY CANE I CUT YU
ONE BLOODY CLOTH LICK WITH A BIG
STONE
```

Chapter 21

Hi-top alternated pacing and sitting in his car outside of the Jubilee Market as he waited for Henry to leave with his guests. He almost felt dizzy from his racing heart's adrenaline rush as he rereviewed the events that had just transpired inside the Market. He wished he were somewhere where he could release his frustration. He wanted to hit something or someone or shoot his pistol. He'd even feel better if he could yell at Monkeyman or Mighty Mouse or even kick a dog. Anything. Any kind of release would make him feel better. Instead, he just sat and ground his teeth and mumbled curse words to his empty car.

While he waited, he tried to call Monkeyman and Mighty Mouse to find out if *their* mission to plant a bug in Big Boy's villa had been successful. He desperately needed some good news after the Blind Blake fiasco, but none was forthcoming. He dialed Monkeyman and got no answer. A few minutes later he tried again. Still no response. He sent a text message. Nothing. He cursed some more.

About that time, Hi-top's own phone rang. It was Harry Dog wanting to know if the bug had been successfully planted in the villa as he had ordered. He said one didn't seem to be working. He cursed that Monkeyman was not answering his own phone. Hi-top lied and assured Harry Dog that everything was under control, and that while he didn't have an answer that very minute, he would let him know as soon his men reported in. He was careful not to mention the botch-up at the Jubilee Market, since, after all, this had been an unauthorized mission. Admitting failure would serve no purpose. What was done was done.

Harry Dog's final words were, "Don yu forget, yu fail mi, mi hab yu rass."

At least, Hi-top rationalized after hanging up that Blind Blake was the one currently taking that fall, not him. And while Blind Blake was occasionally useful, the pickpocket was disposable since he was only an associate not an actual posse member.

I should be safe, he thought. *No one but him even knows that I was there. He would never tell anyone I hired him because it would serve no purpose, and no one would believe him anyway. The Kingston police know he's a career thief, con man, and pickpocket. Besides that, it would just be my word against his.*

He asked himself again just why Harry Dog was so interested in these people. There had to be more to this story than Harry Dog had told him.

But after all, Harry Dog's de uptown boss, mi just ragamuffin rude boy.

He was unaware that he had been identified by both Mikey Mo and Henry Davis. Otherwise, he would have had one more thing to grind on his nerves and cause him to ponder as he continued to wait on his quarry to leave the Jubilee Market.

In the meantime, as Hi-top sat out in his hot car brooding, Henry's party was having an enjoyable lunch at a jerk joint in the Market. Afterwards, they took a leisurely stroll from one stall to another to see if there was anything there that might be useful in outfitting the boat. While they bought a few items, they still didn't find everything they would need for the boat.

More than an hour later, the group finally came back out to Big Boy's van. Henry then drove them over to Marine Safety on Norman Road to shop for additional marine items. Hi-top followed at what he thought was a safe distance. Monkeyman still didn't answer his phone.

After making a few more purchases, they headed to the Port of Kingston, where DV had taken a short-term rental slip, to drop off their purchases. DV was also using the occasion to give his guests a first look at his proud acquisition, the *Spirit of the Seas*.

When they arrived, Henry drove them down by the wharf and let them off.

"Take the stuff down to the boat, and I'll join you after I park the bus," he instructed.

Hi-top parked his own car and tried to call Monkeyman again. Still no answer. He finally remembered to try Mighty Mouse's phone. Same result. As he fumed over his AWOL crew, his focus returned to the Blacks and the Craigs. He temporarily forgot that Henry was parking the bus.

Henry's absence didn't register as Hi-top snuck down the dock. Then he spied DV's boat, and the big picture finally came together.

Mutha of God. The Spirit of the Seas — the boat we was supposed to steal last week! That's why Harry Dog is having such a shit-fit!

In the excitement of this revelation, he didn't notice Henry watching from behind him. His cell phone rang. It was Mighty Mouse finally returning his call on a phone he had borrowed from the bartender. Hi-top turned down a cross-dock to answer the overdue callback.

"H-h-h-heeeey! Yu lookin' for wi?" a drunken Mighty Mouse slurred in a raspy voice.

"What's wrong with your voice?"

"Nuttin's wrong with mi voice. Mi's perfectly fine in mi voice."

"Are you drunk or high?"

"Mi's ash sober ash mi's gonna git. And nuffink mi – wait, wait, wait – mi – no – no - oh yeah - nuffink … yu can do 'bout it. Gerroff mi case!"

"Let me talk to Monkeyman."

"He canna come to de phone."

"Why not? He drunk too?"

"He tongue bigger than he mouth, and he canna see anyway."

"Wha de hell you speak about. Put he on."

Mighty Mouse belched in the phone before saying, "Canna … cause of de snake."

"Wha de hell yu speak now."

"And de wasps … and de wasps go partner wi de snake."

"Are you on ganja or cocaine?"

"Wi gotta go now. Ice melt on mi medicine."

"Are you at the hospital or doctor? Which one?"

"Sam de Sham and Rummie's."

"Rummie's! Yu at de obeah man's rahtid rum bar?"

"… Gotta go now."

Mighty Mouse hung up and left Hi-top fuming to the point that he was oblivious to his surroundings. While this conversation was going on, Henry saw something that gave him an idea. There were two buckets of chum on the dock in front of a fishing boat. They contained a mixture of noxious fish attracting ingredients including menhaden, chopped bonito and mullet, mackerel guts, all topped off with spoiled chicken livers and chicken skin. Henry held his breath and moved one of the unwholesome pails into the center of the walkway. He held the other in reserve on the main walkway.

Hi-top turned back towards the *Spirit of the Seas* from the cross-dock. His attention was on both the boat and what he was going to do to Monkeyman and Might Mouse when he saw them again. As Henry had hoped, he wasn't watching where he was walking and kicked the chum bucket, splattering the smelly, slippery concoction all over the dock as well as his feet and lower legs. When he saw what he had done, the already fuming gangster attempted to dropkick the bucket. Instead, he stepped on a slimy chicken liver and fell backwards into the dripping, gooey fish food. Hi-top saw stars when his head whacked the dock.

As he laid there, a circling seagull saw an unexpected banquet and dived down to be the first to feast. Others immediately followed. Soon Hi-top found himself being pecked amid a flock greedily feeding hungry birds.

This is when Henry struck with the reserve bucket. He swished the contents on the prone Hi-top and surrounding area. This new banquet now attracted pelicans to join the party. Hi-top tried to sit and kick and swat his adversaries only to find more joining the food bonanza. His cell phone slipped from his hand and landed in a pile of mackerel guts only to be quickly swallowed by a pelican as the phone began to ring again.

It was Harry Dog attempting to call him once again to scream additional threats.

Hi-top attempted to stand. As he blindly swatted and slapped back and forth at a seagull determined to latch onto a delicious fish head caught in his dreads, he stepped out of his unlaced sneakers, lost his balance, and tumbled into the water.

Henry eased by unnoticed and proceeded down the dock to join his friends. The only shred of Hi-top that remained on the dock was his now empty signature custom sneakers with the marijuana leaves and his street name embroidered on the side. A lone seagull pecked the yummy chum off them.

Henry quietly put Hi-top out of his mind and didn't mention the encounter to the rest of the group.

Once Henry had rejoined the party at the boat, DV announced that now that they were all back together again, he had a proposal.

"Today is special for a variety of reasons. Cee Cee and I are thrilled to be standing here with you our dear new friends by our boat and be on the cusp of sharing an exciting journey on it as we take it from here to our new home on the north coast. Also, this is special since it's our last night in Kingston for a while. But today is also something else even more special. It's *my* special lady, Cee Cee's birthday. Don't ask which one. I'll let her decide how candid she wants to be on that topic. ... after all, we all know how ladies are."

He elbowed his wife playfully before wrapping his arm around her and pulling her into a hug.

"So, let's celebrate all of these things tonight with a special dinner. Henry ... Rose ... you're local. Do you have a suggestion?"

Rose piped up and said, "As a matter of fact, I do have an idea. Gloria's Seafood is an institution in Port Royal. But now its fans don't have to travel there anymore because they've now opened a second restaurant here at Kingston's Victoria Pier on Ocean Boulevard. ... And the icing on this birthday cake ... "

She got a few hisses and boos at the birthday pun.

"... is that they will soon be opening a third unit in the Ocho Rios area where we all live. Why don't we get a jump on Gloria's there and familiarize ourselves with it while we're still here in Kingston?"

Cee Cee said, "Now, I think Rose has an excellent idea."

"My Rose always has good ideas," Henry said. "Our wedding was a good idea. I used to think that the best day of my life was the day that Rose married me, but then came the day when I had two candy bars fall out of the machine at the same time."

"Now I know where I stand," Rose replied.

Will jumped in at that point and said, "Changing what could become a touchy subject, Socrates said 'to be is to do.' And then Jean-Paul Sartre said, 'to do is to be.' Do you know what Frank Sinatra said? ... 'do-be-do-be-do.'"

"What does that have to do with anything?" Betsy asked.

"Oh, nothing. I just seemed like a good time to change the subject."

"I guess you're proof that what they say about romance is true," Rose countered. "Love is temporary insanity cured by marriage."

"Humph! I'm the one who's got to live with him," Betsy responded.

"I'll drink to that," DV contributed.

"Or any other issue on the table," Cee Cee said.

Henry had no trouble finding Gloria's later that afternoon and was fortunate enough to find a parking place in its small on-site parking lot. The first floor of the building housed Devon House Ice Cream. The dining room was on the second floor with an overflow dining room and banquet room on the third level. Despite the late afternoon heat, the restaurant was bright, airy, and cool with a constant breeze from the harbor flowing through the building. The nautical-themed décor avoided being kitschy, and there was an expansive view of Kingston Harbor.

Since it was still early, they decided to go into Gloria's well-designed bar for a happy hour drink. The bar provided a plum vantage point for people-watching as well as a good view of both the harbor and parking lot. The group ordered a round of drinks and toasted to both this occasion and their upcoming trip.

Then Henry noticed something a bit upsetting. He saw Hi-top getting out of his car Since his encounter with the hungry birds earlier, he was limping noticeably.

Oh, shit! Henry thought. *I thought I got rid of that a-hole earlier this afternoon at the port. I wonder how he found us.*

Little did he know that Hi-top had been parked on the street near Big Boy's villa watching for several hours as he waited to track them again.

Henry made an excuse that he needed to use the restroom, but instead he walked downstairs to assess the situation. Hi-top was hobbling along the boardwalk preoccupied by a multitude of issues. He was in a rotten mood since he was still smarting from his encounter with the hungry birds earlier in the afternoon and was not paying as much attention to his surroundings as he normally would have.

First and foremost on his mind was how he could get discreetly near enough to the revelers so that he could gain intel from their conversation.

In addition, he kept thinking, *Damn, damn, damn! Of all the boats In Kingston, — theirs is the Spirit of the Seas.*

No wonder Harry Dog's driving me crazy. The only way I'll ever redeem myself with him is to somehow get my hands on that boat. But to do so, I need to find out what the new owners' plans are for it.

Henry monitored his quarry, assessing if he would need to assail him again, but luck was about to be with him once more. Fate was still with him.

As Henry hit the walkway adjacent to the harbor, a scene began to unfold. A homeless woman with a shopping cart was going through the trash bins to try to recover recyclable items that she could sell. She accidentally unearthed a J$100-dollar bill in the trash. Before she realized what she had found, it began tumbling in the breeze down the dock. Hi-top saw it and went after it, and at the same time, she did too. The woman beat him to it and snatched the bill up before it could blow into the water. Hi-top snatched it away from her and gave her a push. She snatched it back, and a heated exchange peppered with obscenities followed.

"Gwine wif yu, old 'oman! Dat money mine, yu dutty **(dirty)** nigga batty gal **(dyke)**."

"Who you call dutty nigga batty gal, yu waste man **(useless)** rent-a-dread."

"Mi talk about yu, yu rum head boom dog **(drunken whore)**! Yu see anyone else here, or yu too drunk?"

"Gunkona **(Go fuck yourself)**, rude boy!"

Hi-top gave her another shove. She stiff-armed him back and snatched the bill from him once more. He grabbed it back. She grasped his dreadlocks and jerked his head downward into a headbutt while at the same time kneeing him the groin.

He expelled so much air that it left him breathless as he bent over to grab and protect his throbbing "buddies." As he leaned, she gave him still another violent push as she stomped on his instep and stood on his shoes. As he tried to straighten up, she kneed him again for good measure. He lost his balance and tumbled in into harbor, taking the money with him but leaving his expensive custom sneakers where he'd been standing.

Henry smiled and thought, Da *puss an' dog noh have di same luck, but today she definitely da dog with all da luck on her side.*

Hi-top had definitely gotten his just deserts.

She deserves to be congratulated.

He walked up, and the livid woman turned to face off with him as well.

"Yu wan some too, mista? Yu mess wi' Holly Hunter, and mi got plenty lef' fo yu."

"No, Miss Hunter, I saw what happened, and you were perfectly within your rights. He got what was coming to him. I just wanted to congratulate you for standing up to this mugger and to reimburse you for the money that the man stole from you. You were right to stand up for yourself. Obviously, he is not a nice man. Would J$200 be fair?"

He handed her two J$100-dollar bills and made one final comment.

"Yu know what they say about a pickled bong belly **(greedy person)** like he, 'A greedy mek fly follow coffin go a hole **(A greedy fly follows the coffin into the grave.).**"

He quickly turned around before she could respond and backtracked, reaching the stairs leading up to the second floor. When he looked back, Holly was loading Hi-top's sneakers into her shopping cart. She sniffed them before she did so and held them up to examine them closer.

Yes, she thought. *These should bring some money.*

Henry gave her a final thumbs up.

That was worth every penny I spent, he told himself as he returned to the birthday party.

Justice had been served for the third time that day, and the good guys had won yet another round. He momentarily felt a little guilty about what had happened to the unlucky Shower Posse thug.

Those shots beneath the waist must have really hurt. I could almost feel them.

But then he repeated to himself his two familiar proverbs that Will and Betsy had already cited earlier at the Market.

*Sorry for maga **(mongrel)** dog, maga dog turn round bite yu. Yes, he will.*

*And ebry day debble elp teef; but wan day God elp de watchman **(Every day the devil helps the thief; but one day God helps the watchman).** And today's been that day.*

Yes! Justice has indeed been temporarily served and yes, we good guys have indeed won another well-deserved round.

But then he reminded himself, *Just because we won two rounds today doesn't mean that we've won the war.*

Henry returned to the bar as if nothing had happened. As he approached the table DV made an announcement.

"Oh, good. Henry's back. Now I want to make a presentation. Honey, I have a small birthday present for you."

He produced a gift-wrapped gift and presented it to Cee Cee. She tore into it and gasped at what she saw when she opened the box. It was a Breitling Colt Silver Dial lady's' dive watch. The rotating bezel had twenty-nine diamonds embedded in it, and there were even more diamonds on the face of the watch.

"Darling, it's beautiful. ... I think it's the most beautiful watch I've ever seen."

"You deserve it. Cee Cee, I knew I was in love with you when I couldn't fall asleep because reality had finally become better than my dreams. Darling, I love you."

"And I'm one happy woman since happiness is when a woman who finds a true friend and happier yet is the woman who finds that that true friend turns out to be her husband. I love you too."

The Craigs weren't the only ones happy. Henry was secretly happy as well. He just didn't want to cloud the occasion by telling everyone why. He smiled as he thought about how he had helped make Hi-top's entire day a fiasco, and most likely Harry Dog's as well. It had to be one of the most miserable days of both of their criminal careers. If Henry had known about Monkeyman and Mighty Mouse, he would have been even more ecstatic than he was.

He couldn't wait to tell Mikey Mo.

Maybe I can't get revenge on Dudus Coke directly but as the old proverb says, "if yu canna get revenge on smadi **(somebody)***, tek* **(take)** *revenge on associate."*

```
┌─────────────────────────┐
│                         │
│         NO              │
│      VENDING            │
│                         │
└─────────────────────────┘
```

Chapter 22

"Can't I trust you to do anything right," Dudus Coke barked into the phone. "I used to think that you were an asset to my organization, but lately I'm beginning to wonder. First, you lose a boat loaded with a valuable cargo, and now you're too stupid or lazy to correct your error."

"I'm trying hard to get the boat, but we've had a series of setbacks. You know, some bad luck," Harry Dog responded.

"No, I don't know. All I know is that you've failed. Trying doesn't mean shit; succeeding is all that counts. And you're on borrowed time. If I have to send someone else to do your job, you're finished, fassyhole **(a universally dislikable person)**."

"Yes, sir. I understand. I'm not going to let you down. Just give me a little more time."

"My tracker shows that the boat has left Kingston and is headed up the coast. Do you know where it's going?"

"No, sir, but I'll find out."

"You better, menkeh **(idiot)**. And put out a reward for whoever recovers the boat if you have to."

Harry Dog hung up fuming.

God, I hate eating crow with The Pres.

He immediately called Hi-top. He needed to find an outlet to release his frustrations on.

"Where do you stand on your assignments? I still don't have a signal from that house your men were sent to bug. You know that if you can't get the job done, I'll find someone who will. Are you bat dunce **(plain stupid)** or are you just a waste man **(useless)**."

"My men have encountered some difficulties …"

"Difficulties mi rass. Mehbe yu just bafan **(disorganized)**. Mehbe yu not management material and neber were."

"Sir, I'll prove that your faith in me is justified."

"Yu betta. I undastan that the *Spirit of the Seas* has left Kingston. Where is it going?"

"I'm not sure, but I'll find out."

"You're on borrowed time my friend."

He abruptly ended the call. Giving Hi-top grief instead of taking it made him feel a little bit better.

Within a half hour, Hi-top called Harry Dog back and told him he had talked to the harbormaster and was being told that the boat was headed for Morant Bay.

"Get your men on a boat to Morant Bay."

"Sir, uh … I have two little problems."

"You got more problems than that, and you're getting ready to have even more, senseh fowl **(weakling chicken)**."

"My men are balking at going, and besides that, their cover is blown. They say that that they are up against an obeah man who let loose an Ol' Hige on them. They say they were lucky to escape alive. They're also balking about finishing their assignment unless they can get another obeah man to reverse the curse. … And on top of that, neither one of them are boaters."

"Tell them they haven't seen a curse like the one I'll bring down on them if they don't follow orders. I can curse with the best. As far as boats are concerned, I know a Indian already in Morant Bay who owns his own fishing boat. He goes by Captain Curry. His mate is a Chinaman named Lo-Chow Mein. Curry owes me. I'll call him and tell him you're coming. Work out a plan with them. Put out a reward for the boat if that's what it takes. And you better not fail this time."

"We should be in Morant Bay well before lunchtime," DV commented as they left Kingston harbor. "It's only about 25 miles. But before we leave, I have a little something for each of you."

He handed out plastic bags. Each had been labelled with the name of the recipient. When his guests opened their bags, they found a teal-colored baseball cap that had been embroidered to say, "*Spirit of the Seas*." They also found a matching color knit Ralph Lauren collared golf shirt as well as a matching pocket t-shirt. Each had been embroidered with the ship's name. On the back of each t-shirt, it said "CREW" except for Cee Cee's which said "CO-CAPTAIN."

"Where's yours?" Will asked.

DV pulled out one that "CAPTAIN" and donned a three-cornered pirate hat and an eye patch after he slipped his t-shirt on.

"As Mel Brooks once said, 'It's good to be the king.' But I'll settle for being the captain. Now we're ready to go.

"Avast! Me hearties! Let us now depart and conquer the Caribbean. … I hope I got your sizes right. … Not only does it feel good to be the captain, but it also feels good to finally be out on our own boat headed for our new home no worse for wear other than a little excitement at the Jubilee Market."

If you only knew, Henry thought, *how close that came close to not being the only excitement.*

He decided it was a good time to change the topic.

"There's not much to Morant Bay, but it's worth stopping there. We can spend the night on the boat. No use pushing ourselves too hard to try to make it all the way to Bull Bay in one day. Let's enjoy the trip. We can always get there tomorrow."

"I agree," Cee said. "Henry's right. Let's relax and enjoy our trip."

"Good. Colonel Winter has some connections in Morant Bay since it's the home of many of the Windward Maroons. The list that Mikey Mo gave me at the Jubilee Market recommends a couple of restaurants where he knows the owners. Maybe we'll go to one of them tonight. But why don't we just get something light for lunch and then save this evening to go more upscale," Henry suggested.

"Sounds like a plan," Betsy said. "So, what'd you have in mind?"

"There's a branch of Juici Patties there. Why don't we make that lunch? And The Colonel recommends a place named Sue Tru for this evening."

"Have you ever eaten a Jamaican patty?" Will asked DV.

"I'm not sure I have."

"You're in for a treat. Jamaicans eat them for fast food like we eat burgers. You know what an empanada is, don't you?"

"Sure. Kind of like a Hot Pocket?"

"Well, sort of. But patties aren't round. They're crimped, flat semi-circular pockets with a filling. Think of them as orange empanadas with a Jamaican twist."

"Orange?"

"Yeah, they use a blend of egg yolks, annatto, and turmeric in the pastry dough. And the fillings can come in all kinds of flavors. It can be almost anything — chicken, beef, lobster, or jerk. And for vegetarians there are cheese and veggie patties. If fact, there's even ackee and saltfish."

"What's ackee and saltfish?"

"Oh, I see you've still got a lot to learn. It's our national dish," Rose said in a giggly voice. "But we'll make Jam-ericans out of you like we did Will and Betsy. I'll fix some for you when we get to our house. Ackee is an African fruit."

"Juici Patties sounds like a good place to begin our education."

"Morant Bay is also important to Jamaican history. Home of Paul Bogle, one of our national heroes. I'll explain more when we get there."

They arrived well before lunch and docked the boat at the Errol Flynn Marina. After checking in, they were approached by a local cabbie. On the door of his Ford Transit van was a magnetic sign saying Hack's Hacks.

"Ya, mon. Welcome to Morant Bay. Where yu need me to tak yu?"

The baseball-capped driver was a clean-cut, mature looking Jamaican with short hair who appeared to be in his fifties. Like Henry, he had a pencil thin mustache. He wore a pale blue golf shirt and chinos instead of the usual loud Rasta looking apparel. He peered at them through aviator sunglasses. When he smiled, it seemed genuine.

Henry silently appraised him and then walked around the van to inspect the license plate. When he saw it was red and that the number was preceded by a "P," he nodded. He looked for a JUTA decal and found one. He nodded his approval again since now he knew that this was a legally licensed taxi.

"How much to rent your contract carriage for the rest of the day?"

"A hundred and eighty American."

"Too much. I'll pay $120."

"Oh, mon. Yu hurt mi, but mi like yu. $160?"

"$130."

"$150."

"$140, and we'll throw in lunch for you at Juici. And you get half up front."

"Deal. Respect, mon."

They bumped fists to seal the deal.

Henry turned to DV and said, "My friend, In Jamaica you never take the first price offered. Jamaicans expect to haggle to get the best bargain and won't respect you unless you do."

They loaded everyone into the van and prepared to leave the marina. Henry rode shotgun.

"I assume that Hack is your street name," Henry asked. "By the way, I'm a JUTA member as well. In the Ochie area."

"Welcome, mi brudda. But as to mi name, hit kind of is and hit kind of isn't. My birth name is Jersee Hackinsack."

"Hack's Hacks is certainly catchy. Let mi introduce you to my dear friends — Will, Betsy, DV, Cee Cee, and my dear wife, Rose. DV and Cee Cee have recently bought a villa in Discovery Bay.

"OK, Hack. Here's the game plan for our visit today. We plan to have lunch at Juici Patties since they also have Juici outlets on the north coast where DV and Cee Cee will soon be living — and we insist that

143

you join us. And while we're here, I was going to take them to the old courthouse to see Paul Bogle's statue and let them go shopping at Lorna's Crafts. They also want to pick up some fresh fruit to take back to the boat. We planned to have dinner at Sue Tru's."

"Do you mind if I make a few suggestions?"

"Of course not. You're local. We're not."

"Since it's early, let's go to see Paul Bogle's statue before lunch. Since I have conducted this tour many times, with your permission, I'll explain to them why he was so important to Jamaican history. Then we'll go to Juici. Instead of going to Lorna's, let me take you to a shopping area that most out-of-towners never get to experience. And this evening, I would like to suggest that you dine at Longboarder Bar and Grill instead of Sue Tru. There's nothing wrong with Sue Tru, but I think your guests might enjoy Longboarder more."

"Hack, you're our tour guide for the day. Lead on, my JUTA brother."

"You keep saying JUTA. What does that mean?" Cee Cee asked.

"Jamaica Union of Travelers Association."

Hack drove them to the remains of the courthouse. What they saw was the ruins of what once was a very attractive building. He parked, and they got out.

The courthouse consisted of a two-story cinder block and stucco building with matching winding staircases that led up to the second floor from both sides to a central porch with two tall round archways. A masonry wing with corner blocks led off to each side. The bigger-than-life statue of a stern Paul Bogle stood atop a six-to-eight-foot pedestal. His outstretched arms grasped a vertical sword that was hugged to his chest. The sword extended all the way down to his wide-stance firmly planted feet.

Hack began his oft given talk.

"This courthouse burned for the second time in 2007. There has been talk of rebuilding it, but as of now the funds have not been available. You can't tell it now, but at one time the building had a high-pitched roof with a belfry atop of it. It was quite stunning. Sit on the steps, and I'll tell you about the 1865 Morant Bay rebellion that Bogle led."

"1865 was also an important year in American history," DV observed.

"Yes, I know," Hack said. "Your Civil War ended slavery there then. We were actually more progressive here than you were. Slavery officially ended in Jamaica in 1834."

"Hack, I don't mean to interrupt you or be rude," Cee Cee said, "but you appear to be using flawless English now instead of the ... what do you call it? ... pigeon ..."

"Patois," Betsy corrected.

"Yeh ... patois ... when you picked us up."

Hack smiled and paused before replying, "Dear lady, you are very perceptive. I was born in London and was a history major at Goldsmiths. My parents emigrated from Jamaica for economic reasons. After my parents died and I retired from the British military, I chose to return to my roots. When I picked you up, I used the language that tourists expect to hear from a local. But now that I've gotten to know you, I see there's no reason for the pretense."

Rose joined the conversation at this point and said, "Hack, Henry and I emigrated the same as your parents."

Then she turned to Cee Cee and said, "My dear girl, in Jamaica, fluidly alternating back and forth from classic English to street English is quite common, even when we are talking to each other."

"And can happen sometimes even within the confines of one sentence," Henry added.

"So now that we've cleared the air, let's get back to the history of Morant Bay."

"Hear, hear," Will said.

"As I was saying, even though slavery had been officially abolished, life was still not pleasant for freedmen. They lived in poverty and were still treated like second class citizens ... and had little say in how the country was run."

"Sounds like Reconstruction," DV said. "All you needed was some Carpetbaggers."

"Even though about half a million black Jamaicans could supposedly vote and black Jamaicans outnumbered their white counterparts by over thirty to one, only about two thousand could afford the high poll tax to register. Unrest stemming from a series of economic setbacks brought tension to a fever pitch in the 1860's when back-to-back catastrophes occurred."

"Like …?"

"Like massive crop damage from flooding, cholera and smallpox epidemics, and a long drought."

"I guess that would do it."

"All they needed to light the fire was a catalyst. They got it in 1865 when a black man in Morant Bay was put on trial for trespassing on a long-abandoned sugar plantation.

"When this happened, Paul Bogle, a Baptist deacon, marched forty-five miles and led hundreds of people to do a nonviolent protest march on this courthouse. The British answered by shooting and killed about twenty-five protesters. The protesters retaliated and burned the courthouse and some of the surrounding buildings. These events led to a general uprising throughout the parish. So, the British governor declared martial law and ordered his troops to hunt down the rebels. They began to indiscriminately kill anyone who was black — women, children, innocent people who just happened to be at the wrong place at the wrong time. The initial death toll passed four hundred. Then they arrested and executed about three hundred more people, including Paul Bogle."

"Holy mackerel!" DV said. "And then what happened?"

"This led to protests in England. Some Englishmen praised the governor; others damned him. The governor was ultimately relieved of his office and sent back to England. He was then replaced by a moderate mixed-race governor."

"Sounds like the SOB should have been executed himself," DV said.

"I agree, but the rebellion did have consequences that went beyond St. Thomas Parish. It began a period of change that eventually spread throughout the entire British empire. It was the start of Jamaicans who were formerly locked into an apprentice system having the right to choose their employer and profession. It also became easier to qualify to vote. Other reforms followed."

"I thought I knew Jamaican history pretty well," Will said. "But Hack, my friend, this has been very educational."

"I too learned as well," Henry agreed.

"And I now understand why Bogle's picture is on both Jamaican bills and coins," Betsy said.

"He has been officially declared to be one of our national heroes. Well, now that I've got you all in agreement," Hack concluded. "I'm getting hungry. Let's go eat some patties."

```
GOATS
ENTERING
THESE
PREMISES
WILL BE
CURRIED
```

Chapter 23

Hack drove them to Juici Patties. It was a square, modern, clean looking, two-story building with a drive-through for takeout customers. The bright yellow and red, professionally designed sign prominently announced the business they were in.

Hack parked his van, and they walked in. The interior layout reminded everyone of an American fast-food restaurant. A sign on the wall announced the restaurant's mission.

"We attribute our success to work, work, and more work; treating all customers well; providing what they need in a comfortable environment in the most efficient way."

"If that's the truth, no wonder they're successful," Will said. "I know some American businesses that should read and then follow that mission statement."

The patty choices seemed overwhelming to DV and Cee Cee at first. Since this was their first time to eat patties, they chose to go a safe route with ingredients they were familiar with like ground beef and onion.

Everyone ordered their meals, found a table, and began to eat.

"This is good," Cee Cee announced. "And boy, this place is as clean and well-maintained as any McDonald's in the States."

"This company is a true Jamaican success story, and the owner, Jukie Chin, is a Jamaican business legend. He has built a fast-food empire," Hack said.

"Chinese owned? Reminds me of Pickapeppa in Shooter's Hill," Will observed. "Getting to tour it several years ago with Rose and Henry was one hell of an experience."

Rose agreed.

"Jukie Chin got his start making patties in his parents' grocery store in Clarendon. After he had graduated from high school, he began to bake patties for a small Chinese restaurant in Kingston. Now he owns forty-two restaurants like this one across the island as well as a bakery in Canada that distributes his patties to outlets worldwide."

"The mission statement on the wall says it all."

"Says my husband the poet," Betsy commented.

Will and Betsy chimed in together and said in unison, "A poet but doesn't know it. … A Longfellow."

The group laughed.

"As I said, other businesses would do well to emulate that mission statement."

After lunch, Hack said he was going to take them to a shopping complex that was unlike one anywhere else where they could buy some fruit to take back to the boat.

"Lead on, mi JUTA brudda. Yu do good so far."

"Then fasten yu seat belts, wi about to go to Sam de Sham's Home of Bargains."

When they got to their next stop, they saw that Hack had not exaggerated. What they saw almost defied description. It was a hodgepodge four-story building constructed entirely out of ocean-going shipping containers that had been stacked on one another. Some were mounted horizontally; some were mounted vertically. Some were painted red. Some were yellow, and others were green. Some had giant six-foot, gaping, plexiglass covered portholes cut out of their sides. Some had sliding doors. Some had railless extensions welded to them that made verandas of sorts. Some had roll-up garage doors. Some had corrugated metal extensions from their rooflines to provide shade.

Some at the top had no ceiling at all. They could smell the odor of frying food as they walked across the street.

"You weren't lying," DV commented. "I've never seen anything even remotely like this."

"Reminds me of Fred's Beds on Big Coppitt Key, except Fred's is all on one level."

Each container had a homemade sign telling the name of the business it housed. On the ground level was a fried chicken joint. It called itself RFC. There was also a laundromat that called itself "Washie Washie" as well as a rum bar appropriately named "Rummie's."

"RFC?" Cee Cee asked.

"Rasta Fried Chicken," Hack explained.

A hairdressing salon called itself "Damsel Dreads." The souvenir shop was named "Toys 'R Wi." They saw a sign that said "Docta Docta."

"A doctor's office?"

"No, a pharmacy."

"And what is Brooks Brudda? And Sparky Shack?"

"The clothing store and the electronics shop."

"I should have known. So, where's the veggie market?"

"Round to the side — Piggly Wiggly."

"Up top it says 'De Balmyard.' What's a balmyard?"

"A balmyard is where an obeah man lives and practices his craft. This obeah man — Sam de Sham. He owns the whole building."

"An obeah man slum lord," Will said as he began to laugh. "What'll they think of next?"

"What so funny about that?" DV asked. "What's an obeah man?"

"Hack, why don't you tell him. You're better about explaining stuff than I am."

"Let me say up front, that you're in the obeah capital of Jamaica. Obeah began here, and there are more obeah men in St. Thomas Parish than anywhere on the island. Let me also say that there are few Jamaican traditions more openly rejected but secretly embraced than obeah."

"OK? So tell us just what it is," DV said.

"The practice tracks back to Africa but has also often been associated with the Catholic church. The word 'obeah' is used to denote witchcraft, evil magic, or sorcery. A supernatural power is invoked to achieve either personal protection or to destroy a person's enemies. It can be used for either good or evil."

"Sounds like voodoo," Cee Cee commented.

"Somewhat, but whereas voodoo involves group meetings and rituals, obeah is conducted freelance secretly on a one-on-one basis with the obeah man ... or woman ... and the person seeking their help. This is because the British made obeah illegal after they thought it was used to incite the black populace during Tacky's Rebellion in 1760."

"Tacky's?" asked DV.

"Tacky's Rebellion was part of the second Maroon war," Henry explained.

Hack continued. "Obeah is not a religion in the sense that it has its own deities, even though a corollary is its belief in duppies."

"Duppies are ghosts," Betsy explained to the Craigs.

"It's instead a set of ritual practices used to influence the many spirits around us or to cause bodily harm. A person wishing another person ill might consult the obeah man to put a spell on that person using herbs and potions. Some potions might also be used for protection. That's why I said it can be both good and evil. The items used for spells are often sold in pharmacies like 'Docta Docta'."

"As well as ganja," Will added.

"Well, we won't talk about that right now. ... Now, my friends ... enough education. Let's go spend some money and help support the Jamaican economy. The stairs to the upper levels are around back."

```
PLeaSe!!!
no nuDITY
In tHe OFFICe
& GARDen
tHOnGS aRe O.K.

tHAnK YOU
manaGemenT
```

Chapter 24

Monkeyman and Mighty Mouse arrived at Sam de Sham's shopping center desperate to get help from the obeah man. Neither had recovered either physically or mentally from their previous day's run-in with the Ol' Hige that they had encountered at Big Boy's villa. They both felt that it was imperative that Sam de Sham provide them with an herbal perimeter that would protect them and prevent the duppy's return.

"Ol' Hige seek wi down and suck all de air out of wi if wi gib him anodder chance."

"Yu right. Wi should no tekka chance. Mi a young mon and don wan to die tha' way. Dah's for sure."

Mighty Mouse pointed at Rummie's sign and said, "But first mi need to settle mi nerves. Wi should hab a rum before wi go see him. Besides, mi head still hung and fuzzy from what wi drank yesterday."

"Mi agree."

"And mi head getting nappy and itchy. Mi need to go in Damsel Dreads while wi here so mi can get him to wash mi head and shave it clean again."

"Wi got time. Les get a rum drink first before wi hab to explain tings to Sam de Sham. Mi nerves still bad from de duppy attack. And mi body feel like everthin on it be bruised."

They went in the mostly empty Rummie's and each ordered neat doubles of overproof Wray and Nephew rum. Unnoticed to them, Marley's "Duppy Conqueror" played in the background on a cheap CD player behind the bar. Monkeyman still had some ganja with a hint of PCP left over from the drive into Morant Bay. The combination seemed to soothe their aches and pains, so they ordered another round. This soon led to still another round which began to make them hungry. Monkeyman reached in his pocket for another toke but came up short. Mighty Mouse did the same.

"Mi getting hungry since wi sleep too late to get breakfast. Les get some chicken at RFC," Monkeyman suggested. "Mi go get da chicken, and yu hold wi seats."

He went next door and bought them some chicken while Mighty Mouse waited in the bar. The chicken along with another round hit the spot. All they needed now for dessert to make things perfect was more ganja.

"Yu stay here and hab anoder rum. Mi go ober to Damsel Dreads and get fresh. Shouldn't take long."

"Go in Docta Docta and get some more ganja while yu out."

"Yah, mon. No problem."

When Mighty Mouse returned, he looked upset.

"Did yu go to Docta Docta?"

"No, mon. because mi see something."

"Wah wrong yu? You see yu ex-wife?"

"No, mon. Worse. Da duppy find us here. Now he dress up and hide unda a skin tha look like a shirt an' cap da say *Spirit of the Seas*."

Henry had been wearing his golf shirt over the t-shirt. The drunken Mighty Mouse had seen him take it off when his layered clothing had become too warm.

"Wha yu mean?"

"Yah, mon. Mi no lie. Mi see him tek off one of he skin. And now he bring he duppy friends to help he get us. Mi know das who dey is 'cause dey skin say de same ting."

The drunken twosome staggered out of the bar and peeked around the corner into the Piggly Wiggly where Henry and Rose were shopping. Monkeyman squinted through a PCP haze. He tried to read the embroidery, but the Davises fuzzy images jumped and wavered in front of his eyes. Mighty Mouse assured him that he had read the embroidery on the baseball cap correctly.

Henry noticed them staring and glared back. He immediately knew who the twosome was — the Shower Posse thugs who had tried to hijack the boat.

It's got to be. They match Mikey Mo's description exactly — a six foot five Rasta and a bald midget. How many of those can there be? But what are they doing here? This can't be an accident. They have to be up to no good.

Henry's glare scared Monkeyman.

"Da duppy see wi," he gasped.

He began to hallucinate. When the cucumber in Rose's hand began to lengthen and look like Julius Squeezer, the two thugs felt an even stronger need to hide and smoke another joint. Before the duppy could get them, they fled around the building and up the stairs to the second floor and Docta Docta.

A bearded Rasta man in a dirty knit cap was behind the counter.

"Mi need a hit now — a extra strong one. A duppy chase wi."

"Got just what you need. Yu evah lick de toad?"

He bent over and pulled a wire cage from under the counter. It contained several hallucinogenic Bofo toads.

"Yu lick da toad's back and yu duppy problems solved. Five dollahs a lick."

Mighty Mouse immediately gave the clerk a ten-dollar bill. The clerk got two fat, healthy looking toads out of the cage.

"Yu start at de back and lick hard as yu can till you get to his head."

He handed a toad to each of the gangsters. They followed his instructions, leaving a trail of saliva on each frog. He took the toads from them and put them back in the cage.

"Now, go with Jah in peace."

They had barely made it back out onto the stairway when their vision filled with bright white vibrations of circular fractal arcs. An all-pervading hum of overpowering intensity crashed into them both. For a few moments, they were totally oblivious to everything around them.

They felt like they were floating, and they descended the stairs to ground level. They felt no need to analyze what was happening because all their fears had totally vanished. By the time they had made it to the bottom of the stairs, vibrations began to crescendo from both around and within them. They were unified with an infinite matrix of complete ecstasy and joy in an experience no longer bound by human edges. No longer did they fear any Ol' Hige or the Davises but instead felt universal and unconditional love for everyone in love's purest, rawest form.

"Mi hab merged with Jah," Mighty Mouse said to an imaginary audience.

"Yaaaah," Monkeyman agreed. "Mi neber feel like dis afore. Mi habbing a soul orgasm. Mi body crying and yelling with pleasure and joy."

Before either of them realized it, they were somehow lying prostate in the alley behind the building even though they were sure that they had both started out upright. A pool of snot and tears spread from their chins to their eye sockets as each thug literally began choking on joy and gratitude. They both began laughing and crying at the same time in a rhythmic undulating loop of pain and joy.

Henry and Rose watched from a safe distance as Henry filled Rose in on their identities.

"I don't think we'll have any trouble with those two today, but just to be on the safe side, why don't we round up our crew and leave before they possibly come to."

```
AIRLINE TICKET US$200
HOTEL MATCH US$1000
LYING TO YU BOSS J$10,000
SRI LANKA WHOOPING
NEW ZEALAND IN A WORLD
CUP SEMI-FINAL: PRICELESS
```

Chapter 25

Harry Dog again hammered Hi-top on the phone. Hi-top was factually in the dark and didn't know what to tell him since his men were still missing in action after he had sent them over to bug Big Boy's villa. He still did not comprehend the fact that Julius Squeezer had accidentally derailed the bugging attempt and caused Monkeyman to lose his cell phone leading to the subsequent two-day bender that that he and Mighty Mouse had gone on in the aftermath. All Hi-top knew was that for some unknown reason neither of his crew seemed to be on the job and were not answering his messages.

But he couldn't tell his maga dog boss that. Harry Dog was in no mood to listen to excuses or bizarre tales of failure. Sympathy had never been Harry's strong point.

After all, Hi-top thought, *when kitchen dressa tumble dung, maga dog laugh* **(When a kitchen drawer spills, a mongrel dog only laughs.)**.

But he knew from experience that Harry Dog wouldn't laugh. He would just foam at the mouth like a rabid dog and scream a new variety of wild threats. And Hi-top shivered to think of how Dudus would react when and if he ever learned of their failure. He wouldn't warn a person by threatening. He would just escalate his displeasure to the next level.

Hi-top dialed Captain Curry to see if maybe he'd heard from the missing men and was told that they hadn't been in contact.

Something's wrong. I better drag my ass over to Morant Bay and find out what's going on.

He called Captain Curry back and put him on notice that he was coming over and would possibly need the use of the captain's boat.

Both Monkeyman and Mighty Mouse woke up the morning following their drug induced hallucinogenic trip both hung over and disoriented.

"Where wi at?" Monkeyman asked.

"Mi dunno, but mi feel like mi stomach hurt like mi wanna trow up."

"Turn on da light. Mi having trouble seeing."

"Da light is already on. Been on all night."

"Den wah everthin look so dim and colorless?"

"Mehbe yu da one dats dim, not da light."

What the Docta Docta Rasta had not told them the day before was that 5-MeO-DMT, the venom secreted by toads, was one of the strongest psychedelic and hallucinatory drugs in the world. It was six times more potent that its better-known cousin dimethyltryptamine, known on the street as DMT, and its flashbacks and other aftereffects had sometimes been known to last up to six months after it was ingested.

Monkeyman's mind began to flash back to the previous day. Suddenly he remembered the *Spirit of the Seas* clothing that Henry and his friends had been wearing. A light somehow went off in his dim, throbbing brain.

"Da boat Hi-top wanted wi to steal must be here in Morant Bay. If wi succeed in stealing it now, wi be back in da posse's good graces."

"Yah, mon. Yu right. Les wi go find it at da marina."

They drove over to the Errol Flynn Marina and walked around. The boat was nowhere to be found. Monkeyman spoke to the harbormaster.

"Wi was told to meet the owners of da Spirit of da Seas this morning, but mi no see it here."

"Das because yu miss it. Dey just left das morning. Say dey go ta Bull Bay."

"Wi missed dem?" Mighty Mouse said to Monkeyman as they walked back to their car. "What wi do now?"

"No worry. Mi tink of sometin."

"Ya, mon. Yu always good at tinkin'."

Hi-top also arrived in Morant Bay that same morning. Harry Dog had told him that his tracker showed most recent whereabouts of the boat to be at the Errol Flynn Marina. When Hi-top approached the harbormaster, he was given the same information that Monkeyman had gotten. He had missed the boat since it had just departed that morning.

The harbormaster mentioned as an afterthought, "Yu da second person to axk about dat boat dis morning."

"Tall mon and short mon?"

"Ya, mon."

At least he thought, *mi hab narrowed down where mi men could possibly be.* Unlike Monkeyman, Hi-top knew exactly what his next move would be.

He made a beeline for Captain Curry's.

DV felt good as he and his "crew" headed out from Morant Bay. What a beautiful day! It was windy and the sea was somewhat choppy, but all in all, it was a picture-perfect morning. He reminisced about the session where he had worked with the Beach Boys when they recorded the song "It's a Beautiful day" for the "Americathon" soundtrack. It was through that movie that he had met both Elvis

Costello and Eddie Money. He suddenly felt like singing the song out loud, changing the location in the lyrics from L.A. to Morant Bay.

Ooooooooooow!
Livin' down in Morant Bay, such a beautiful day
Whoa, whoa, whoa, whoa
The skies are clear. It's a beautiful day in Morant Bay.

His outburst was met with lighthearted applause and whistles from the rest of the crew.

Yes, everyone had thoroughly enjoyed their brief Morant Bay visit. It had been educational as well, with Hack having been a delightful tour guide. Before parting ways with him, they gave him a nice tip as a reward.

No one in their party had any reasons to be alarmed because Henry had shielded them up until now from any Shower Posse shenanigans. The night before had been capped off by an excellent meal at the Longboarder Bar and Grill, and the sleeping accommodations on the boat had proved to be comfortable enough to satisfy everyone.

DV figured that they should get to Bull Bay sometime in the early afternoon.

Monkeyman saw an unattended Sea-Doo docked behind a seemingly unoccupied seaside villa and had an idea. He jimmied the lock on the villa's back door while Mighty Mouse acted as a lookout. He found just what he needed hanging on a key rack in the kitchen pantry — the key to the Sea-Doo.

The name of the Sea-Doo was "Wet Nuts." Neither thug had a clue at that moment what that name would soon portend — in more ways than one.

Even though Mighty Mouse had never driven a PWC before, it didn't seem like it should be that hard. He'd watched people on them plenty of times.

"So, wha's yu plan?" Mighty Mouse asked.

"Wi catch up to da Spirit of da Seas and den pretend to hab engine problems. When dey stop to help, wi hijack da boat."

It seemed so simple in his still addled mind. He didn't worry about details.

"Ya, mon," the still sluggish Mighty Mouse agreed. "Sounds like dat'll work."

Details had never been his strong suit either, even on a good day, and today certainly wouldn't qualify as one.

"Mi drive," Monkeyman said, even though he had never driven a PWC either.

"No, mon. Let mi drive so yu can be lookout. Mi canna see ovah yu long tall self if mi behind. Besides, yu got long arms to hold onta mi with."

"Yu right. Yu drive."

Within minutes, they departed on their stolen Sea-Doo.

Hi-top arrived at Captain Curry's and explained to him that as he had mentioned on the phone, he'd need to borrow one of his boats. The captain was already committed to a charter set for that morning. He would have balked at letting Hi-top use his good boat anyway.

No problem, mon. Mi no need yu. Mi good a driving a boat. Mi a regular Captain A-rab lak in Mobley's Dick.

Captain Curry rolled his eyes. He had his doubts. The truth of the matter was he didn't want to trust Hi-top with any boat. But Hi-top wasn't going to take no for an answer. He flashed a wad of bills that made Captain Curry salivate. After Hi-top agreed to a rental fee equivalent to what the captain figured to be the replacement cost of his eighteen-foot aluminum outboard runabout, he let him have it. Within minutes, Hi-top was off in search of the *Spirit of the Seas* even though he too had no idea what he was going to do when and if he caught up with it.

Mi cross da bridge wen wi come to it.

Mighty Mouse bounced along going faster than would have been prudent if he had been an experienced PWC driver. He sped up and slowed down jerkily as he tried to get used to the controls. A couple of times he turned too sharply, almost throwing both him and Monkeyman overboard. He hit each wave overly hard time after time.

WHAP!

Each time he did so, Monkeyman would cry out as his unprotected, nerve-filled testicles took a beating each time the boat slapped back down. The stunning pain soon extended up to his torso. He began to feel nauseous and almost vomited.

Ouch! Das one time mi wish mi didn't always go commando.

WHAP!

"Ooh! Yu renk saw-down ediat (**stinking sawed-off idiot**). Yu killing me buddies!" he cried out as they bounced along. Each jolt caused the car keys in his pants pocket to jab his groin. Each time the throb felt like a white-hot knife was stabbing his genitals.

Over the top of another swell and then another …

WHAP!

Monkeyman felt like he was on a roller coaster, and his stomach was about to come up.

WHAP!

He tried to cry out but instead mostly moaned. His head felt even heavier than when he had gotten up that morning, and he was getting dizzy again.

"Yu wan mi to catch up ta da boat or not?" Mighty Mouse yelled over the noise of the Sea-Doo and ocean.

Monkeyman could only groan. He felt like each blow was a charley-horse multiplied by five or someone was pressing down on a bruise in a sensitive area.

WHAP! WHAP! WHAP!

"Ooh! Ooh! Ooh! Fassyhole!

They continued to fly across the ocean. He wondered if he'd be peeing blood by the time this was all over.

WHAP!

"Rahtid batty crease **(damned asshole)**!

WHAP!

"Watch it, lickle bumboclaat **(little douchebag)**!

WHAP!

While Monkeyman was suffering, Hi-top was having his own adjustment problems. First, he had lied to Captain Curry. He was a novice boater. He was a land thug, not a sea thug. Second, he wasn't accustomed to guiding a boat sitting in the stern by the motor using the outboard's steering arm instead of a steering wheel. His idea of driving a boat was to guide it using a steering wheel like he did with his car and giving his car gas with his foot instead of twisting an outboard's steering arm. Third, cars have brakes; boats do not. Last, he did not take into consideration that all his weight, was on the stern of the boat, making for a potentially unbalanced situation in turbulent seas.

Hi-top was oblivious to channel markers. He didn't know what the signs meant anyway and really didn't give a shit. In his haste to find the *Spirit of the Seas*, he headed out as-the-crow-flies, oblivious to the channel. He churned up bottom, almost stalling the boat on several occasions, as he sought go in a straight line to get to deeper water.

"But wah di rass **(What the fuck?)**?" he said each time the motor bogged down. "Did he rent mi a bum motor?"

Only by some miracle was he able to keep from shearing the outboard's prop as he gunned it each time that he chewed up coral and seaweed. At one point, he veered to avoid a startled sea turtle and almost threw himself out of the boat before he could correct it and zig the other way.

"Yu renk **(stinking)** tings should be outlawed," he yelled as he waved his fist at the turtle. "Mi hab de right of way."

Once he cleared the harbor, he had other things to be concerned about since he didn't know how to play the rough waves to his advantage. Too often, he hit a wave head on and found the boat climbing a steep wall of water only to fall off a cliff as it came down the wave's backside.

SLAP!

"Rahtid!"

Hi-top began to feel seasick, and his boat began to take on water. Soon, he had water up to his ankles, soaking his brand new custom-made, ganja-embroidered sneakers. He hit another wave.

SLAP!

"To rass **(fuck you)**!" he yelled to the upcoming swell.

It hit anyway. He almost turned loose of the steering arm before he grabbed it with his other hand. The close call caused him to pee on himself.

He shook his fist at the ocean and yelled, "Kiss mi nanny raas **(grandmother's ass)**!"

He quickly got the sea's response.

SLAP!

He soon saw what he thought was possibly the *Spirit of the Seas* in the distance. A forty-two-foot sloop that was under sail was between him and it. He made a beeline in that direction. He still had no idea what he expected to do if he caught up with DV's boat. He gunned it again.

SLAP!

His ass and lower back hurt.

"Batty crease **(asshole)**! Kiss mi bung!"

The sea responded again.

SLAP!

About that same time, Mighty Mouse also thought he had sighted the *Spirit of the Seas,* and he too veered in its direction. Monkeyman gritted his teeth and held on for dear life.

"Hold on, mi brudda. Dere she is."

"One more shot ta mi buddies, I be gyal **(a girl)**. I be yu sista stead yu brudda," Monkeyman said in a tenor voice through his still gritted teeth.

Monkeyman was hurting too bad to truly concentrate on what Mighty Mouse had just been trying to tell him. Mighty Mouse abruptly slowed momentarily to let the PWC stabilize. Monkeyman slammed forward into his back before slamming back down hard on his sore bottom again.

In the momentary calm, Monkeyman heaved over the side. The salt spray whooshed the vomit back on them both.

He panted, "Awah di rass clot yu chat bout **(What the fuck are you talking about?)**?"

"Da boat. Da boat. Yu soon see. Hang loose."

With no further warning, he shot off in that direction.

WHAP!

"Yu saw-off bat dunce waste man **(short, stupid wastrel)**!"

WHAP!

"Yow! Rahtid yu, buggaman **(Fuck you, faggot)**. Mi kill yu dead wah dis oba **(over)**."

Mighty Mouse saw the same sloop that Hi-top had seen. It was travelling in the opposite direction as the *Spirit of the Seas.* He veered to the port to go around the boat's stern. As he approached it, he could read the boat's name, the "Row V. Wave." He briefly wondered about the origin of the strange name but quickly put it out of his mind since the verbiage was meaningless to him.

WHAP! WHAP!

"Oh, shit! Oh, shit!"

Hi-top approached the "Row V. Wave" from the opposite direction. He turned to the starboard with the intention of doing the same. He'd go around its stern. The sloop continued to tack, distracting both Hi-top and Mighty Mouse, causing them to zig as well. Both had their vision obscured by the ocean spray. When each looked up, they were headed straight for each other.

WHAP!

SLAP!

"Ooooooh, shiiiiiiiit!"

When the two boats collided, Monkyman was thrown over Mighty Mouse's short shoulders. He was suddenly airborne, sailing towards Hi-top. He grabbed Hi-top's dreads while he sailed by. This caused Hi-top to topple backwards into the ocean, frantically taking Monkeyman with him. As he did so, he twisted the steering arm. His boat to begin to circle erratically and almost tip over. The force of the collision caused Mighty Mouse to crash headfirst into the bow seat on Hi-top's boat. The blow rendered him unconscious.

The stunned captain of the "Row V. Wave" circled around and began to try to rescue the hapless thugs.

In the meantime, DV and company continued their journey to Bull Bay completely unaware of the mini drama playing out behind them.

Will piloted the boat. DV pulled out his guitar and sat on the deck entertaining his wife and guests as he played Jimmy Buffett's "Jamaica Mistaca."

Come back, come back to Jamaica.
Don't chu know we made a big mistaca.
We'd be so sad if you told us good-bye.
And we promise not to shoot you out of the sky.

Birtnight Bash Friday
Call Im A Big Deal
Sizzla
Maestro Don-Likkie Danjah
Along Side Stone Love
S. Mart Car Wash
Gutters For Sale etc.

Chapter 26

Dudus Coke checked his text messages from the backseat of his Mercedes Benz G65 Wagon as his driver chauffeured him to Judgement Yard. He was oblivious to the pedestrian stares as the car passed through neighborhoods of shacks so poor that many didn't even have basic utilities. His car always attracted attention since it was reportedly Jamaica's most expensive luxury vehicle. But The Pres took his affluence for granted, though he knew he'd earned it through both guile and ruthlessness.

Judgement Yard is in the so called "garrison" community called August Town. It, like so many Kingston neighborhoods, is divided by local political ideology. Essentially, it is a physical fortress and was once equipped with a rifle tower that had been eventually torn down by raiding police. Judgement Yard's walls are high and made of thick, bullet riddled concrete. The August Town Road homes that surround it are equally bullet riddled, not from just police confrontations but also from longstanding feuds with the Vietnam, Jungle 12, and River sections of August Town.

No one even tries to estimate how many lives have been lost in August Town over the years. Heavily armed police and soldiers continue to patrol the community daily. This contrasts with the calm, peaceful Hope River that runs alongside it. It is in this river that time seems to stand still as many locals still bathe, wash their clothes, and obtain their drinking water from it.

On this day, Dudus was being driven to Judgement Yard to have a meeting with the international reggae and dancehall star Sizzla. Sizzla had founded Judgement Yard and maintained his art studio, his record label, Kalonji Records, and one of his residences there. Sizzla was one of reggae's most bankable stars. He had produced over fifty solo albums plus over fifteen compilation albums as well. His "Solid As a Rock" was a reggae anthem.

The Bobo Rastafarian singer owed much of his success to the support of Dudus Coke and the Shower Posse. He had been born and raised in St. Mary Parish near Bull Bay to strict Bobo Rasta parents. Dudus had helped the teenaged Sizzla get his first job as a sound system apprentice. He had later introduced him to "Bobby Digital" Dixon, the producer who helped him record his first hit singles and later to Homer Harris, who continued to propel him to the top of the charts. Bottom line was that Sizzla owed The President — big time, and today Dudus expected both respect and in small measure to be paid back.

As was Dudus' custom, the meeting was a short one. He did not waste time with small talk, false praise, or preliminaries. Without belaboring detail, Dudus explained to Sizzla that the government had unjustly confiscated and auctioned a boat belonging to him and that his property was currently docked for a brief time in Bull Bay. He needed Sizzla to use his local connections to help Dudus' men right the wrong before it departed. He stressed that time was of the essence. He gave Sizzla both Harry Dog and Hi-top's cell phone numbers and told him to communicate back through Harry Dog. At that, the meeting was concluded.

There was no hesitation on Sizzla's part. He knew exactly what he was expected to do even if he didn't know how he planned to do it. No one ever told Dudus Coke no. Not even an international reggae star. Not if you were smart. You just made the things he desired happen.

The moment Dudus left, Sizzla called his cousin, Pacman, who worked at Danny's Marina in Bull Bay. He then reported in to Harry Dog.

The remainder of the trip to Bull Bay was uneventful for the *Spirit of the Seas*. The same couldn't be said about Hi-top and his crew. While no one was seriously injured by the mishap, each of them blamed the other for their latest failure. When the Row V. Wave let them off back at Morant Bay, they didn't report the accident to anyone. All they could think about was how fast they could head down the road before the owners of the totaled boats discovered their crafts' demises and either had them arrested for breaking and entering as well as grand theft or, in the case of Captain Curry, demanded restitution.

It was only logical for them to head for Bull Bay where they could catch up to the *Spirit of the Seas*. They could get there much quicker than DV's boat since it was only a short car trip. And they were pretty sure that they would ultimately find the boat at Danny's Marina since it was about the only game in town.

Hi-top followed his crew in his car. While he still didn't know about the episode with Julius Squeezer, he suspected intuitively that delegating anything to these two at this point would most likely be a mistake. After all, he did know that they had blown the hijacking. He also rationalized that they were to blame for his boat colliding with the Sea-Doo even though he was as much at fault as they were. But he also knew at this point that his options were regretfully limited.

The inept threesome stopped at the Corn Shop near Bob Marley Beach to pick up some lunch. The menu was scribbled with an erasable marker on a whiteboard hanging behind the counter. Hi-top and Monkeyman each got brown stewed fish that was served with peas and rice, and Mighty Mouse got the cow cod soup with a side order of breadfruit. Since the Corn Shop offered curbside pickup only, they ate their lunch at a picnic table at the beach while they reassessed their next move.

As they were eating, Hi-top's cell phone rang. It was Harry Dog. Hi-top was expecting him to rage, scream, and threaten and was surprised when this didn't happen. Harry Dog very matter-of-factly instructed them to drive over to Danny's Marina immediately and meet with a man named Pacman to work out a plan to recover the *Spirit of the Seas* once and for all. Pacman would be expecting them. Hi-top was relieved when he hung up that he hadn't had to improvise more lies and alibies. He was running out of ideas.

When they arrived at Danny's, they discovered that there were some picnic tables under a royal poinciana tree. Pacman, who had gotten his street name from his oversized mouth and big lips, grabbed some cold Red Stripe's out of Danny's cooler and joined them at one of the tables.

As they took their first sip of the cold, refreshing brew, they took the time to properly introduce themselves.

"Call mi Pacman. Mi cousin Sizzla told mi to expect yu."

"Yu mean Sizzla, da dancehall king?"

Ya, mon. He from Bull Bay. He mi cuz."

The three Shower Posse thugs were awed. They clinked beers. After another swallow, Hi-top began to explain their mission.

"A boat named the *Spirit of the Seas* should be arriving here in a few hours. It was stolen from the Shower Posse. Dudus Coke means to get it back. Yu need to keep it here until we can figure out a way to do so."

"Das simple. Mi just water da fuel. Mi do dat and da boat won go nowhere."

"But then wha?"

"It'll buy wi time. Wi come up wi a plan. Donna yu worry."

"But then?"

"Donna yu worry, Mi got plenty of cousins left to help."

The *Spirt of the Seas* arrived at Danny's Marina before lunch. The trip had been an uneventful one.

"Welcome to Bull Bay," Pacman said as he helped them secure the lines. "How long will yu folks be with wi?"

Pacman would have been an average looking Jamaican except for the turban concealing his dreads. His black t-shirt had a picture of

Haile Selassie on the front. On the back was the flag of Ghana with a five point star of David.

"Only today, my friend," DV replied. "We plan to stretch our legs and have some lunch. I'll get you to top off our fuel tanks while we do so, and then we'll be off for Port Antonio."

"No problem, mon."

"Is there a restaurant near here that you would recommend?"

"Mi cousin, Turbulence, is a licensed operator. He take yu where yu need to go."

"JUTA?" Henry asked.

"Yah, mon."

"That's funny," DV commented. "There's a dancehall artist who goes by that same name."

"Ya, mon. Das him. Mi cuz. He do both. Music run in wi family."

"Surely no one else as big as Turbulence."

"Ya, mon, mi other cuz even bigga. He go by Sizzla."

DV turned to Henry and said, "Wow! It *is* a small world. I've worked a show before with Sizzla."

"If yu a music man, why don mi get him to take you to Bob Marley Beach? Yu can get a good take-away lunch at the Corn Shop and eat it at one of they's picnic tables. Mi dial him now."

"Sounds like a plan."

Pacman picked up his phone and called his cousin. He was there within minutes. Turbulence was a dark skinned slightly above average man who looked taller than he really was because of the beige turban that concealed his dreadlocks. He wore a long, white, dress-like, African-style robe that went below his knees. Draped around his neck was a four inch-wide red, yellow, and green striped knit scarf that hung nearly to the bottom of the robe. Over it all was a medallion of the lion, Ras Tafari, the imperial symbol of the Ethiopian throne. All in all, he commanded a commanding presence.

Pacman made the introductions. After a brief conversation with Pacman, Turbulence drove them to the Corn Shop. Cousin Florence served them.

Most of the party played it safe with chicken dishes, but DV got adventuresome and ordered the curried goat.

When they had found a table at Bob Marley Beach, Cee Cee commented, "A lot of men around here seem to be wearing turbans like yours. And the women seem modestly dressed. Is there some significance?"

Rose stepped in at this point and asked Turbulence, "Sir, would you mind if I explain it to them? Feel free to correct me if I get some of the facts wrong or leave out something pertinent."

"Yah, ma'am. Feel free. Mi not good at speeches."

"Then let me give it a try. There are three factions to Rastafarianism — Twelve Tribes, Nyabinghi, and Bobo. Bobo's wear the turban. The reason that you've seen so many turbans today is that Bobo was started here in Bull Bay, and most of the Bull Bay Rastas are still Bobo till this day."

"Was Bob Marley a Bobo?" Cee Cee asked. "Is that why they call this Bob Marley Beach?"

"Bob Marley was born in Nine Mile just outside of Bull Bay and his favorite place to wash his dreads for his whole life was in the Cane River Falls not far from here. But to answer your question, no, Marley was not Bobo. He was Twelve Tribes."

Turbulence broke in at this point and said, "Not all of us Bobos wear a turban. It must be earned by studying and understanding all the orders of Bobo. Only then are you entitled to wear one."

DV asked, "Is Rasta a religion?"

"Not a religion per se though many of our beliefs are similar to Christianity. Christianity in its simplest form is the belief in Christ, but not necessarily the 'Jesus Christ' found in the New Testament. But instead, the Christ prophesy in the Old Testament book of Isaiah who called the Christ by the name of Immanuel."

"Well put," Rose said and then continued, "Bobo is the strictest of the Rasta sects. Its holy trinity is Marcus Garvey; the black Christ, Holy Emanuel; and Ethiopian emperor, Haile Selassie."

"This is getting interesting," DV said. "Who was Marcus Garvey?"

"He was a Jamaican who founded the Universal Negro Improvement Association early in the twentieth century. They advocated that all blacks worldwide should return to Africa and that it should be forever free of any white rule. We can talk about him another time.

"But back to Bobo. Bobos are peace-loving but are willing to walk in their enemies' blood if it becomes necessary. The word bobo is Ethiopian for warrior. They are only allowed to attend a Bobo church and are vegetarians. They have strict orders to always dress neatly, and the color black can never be subjugated to any other color. They do not condone racial mixing."

She looked at Turbulence and asked, "Have I left anything out?"

"You've been thorough. I might add we always adhere to the teachings of Marcus Garvey. We also fast twice each week and on the first Sunday of every month. Also, we do not eat mangoes or sugarcane."

"I didn't know that," Henry commented.

"I've got a question," Rose said. "Is it true that Bobo's are not supposed to perform music in public?"

"Some of our members believe that."

"But you're a reggae recording artist," DV blurted out.

Turbulence just smiled.

"So is mi cousin Sizzla."

"My husband's in the music field as well," Cee Cee said. "He played with the Beach Boys."

"Mi brotha by a different mutha," Turbulence said and high-fived DV.

"Actually, I've worked some road shows with your cousin Sizzla."

"Mon, wi need to get together and jam."

"Cool. I wish we had time. I'd like that. Maybe in the future."

"Mi and Sizzla are working together tonight at the Wickie Wackie Beach Bar."

"Oh, man. You're making me feel bad. I'd give anything to be a part of that."

Will changed the subject and asked Henry, "So, what kind of Rasta is Mikey Mo?"

"Twelve Tribes," Henry replied. "They're more lenient and conservative than Bobo. They even eat meat."

He then added, "Turbulence, we need to get back and get going."

"Ya, mon. If yu all finished, wi go."

"Yeh, we need to get back so we can leave for Port Antonio," DV said.

"Wi go by one more place. Bobo Hill."

"What's that?"

"Da home of da Bobo Shanti. Yu see. Mi cousin Luton Fyah keeps a house der."

After lunch, Turbulence drove them by Bobo Hill before they returned to Danny's Marina.

They all said goodbye to Pacman and Turbulence and climbed on the boat. Both walked back to the ships' store. Pacman smiled.

The motor cranked and sputtered. Then it died.

```
ZIGGY ROAD STOP
FUTURE WALLMART.
```

Chapter 27

"Wha … the …?" DV uttered.

He turned the key again. This time the motor didn't even try to turn over. It was just dead.

"If you keep trying to crank it, you'll only run the battery down," Henry commented. "We need assistance."

They retied the boat and walked up to the ships' store. Pacman pretended to be surprised to see them as he straightened a shelf of t-shirts.

"Yu forget something?" he asked innocently.

"Our boat won't crank," DV said.

"Mi dunno much about motors," Pacman said as he put on his most innocent face. "But mi hab a cousin, Moto Mouth, who's a mechanic. He works at the local salvage yard. He da only mechanic mi know. Mi can call he. He not far from here."

Fifteen minutes later, Moto Mouth drove up in a rusty old pickup. He too had a turban and a scraggly beard. He was smoking a joint.

DV led him over to the boat and once again turned the key. The motor would not respond.

"Do you know what's wrong with it?" he asked the mechanic.

Moto Mouth pulled the cover off the motor and stood there staring at it as he continued to smoke his joint.

"Mi need to study it awhile."

"How long do you think that'll take? We need to get to Port Antonio today."

"Nah going to happen today."

"How long do you think it'll take you to fix it?"

"Mi nah know. ... Mi leh yu know. ... Might have to order a part. ... Don worry. ... Mi got a cousin owns a part shop."

DV turned to his friends and said, "Looks like we may be stuck here this afternoon."

"Mi hab a cousin, Likkle Miss, who work at a hotel," Pacman said. "She get yu rooms at de Scarlett Guest House. Cousin Turbulence tek yu dere. And mehbe cousin Punchie, who's a tour guide, might be available to take you to the falls."

"More cousins? How many cousins do you have?" Will asked. "Are you kin to everyone in town?"

"Uh … Wi big family."

"Are you sure we're not in the Jamaican Ozarks where everyone is inbred and marries their cousin?" DV asked jokingly. "Don't they call those mountain folks hillbillies? I guess here they call them Bobo-billies."

"And I bet you don't know what they call them in London," Will shot back. "Royalty."

"Or maybe we should call them royal-billies," DV said.

"Or maybe the royal house of Billy Stewart," Betsy suggested.

"Nah, he died. But, boy, he sang one hell of a R and B version of 'Summertime,'" DV said. "He did some shows with the Beach Boys as well back in the early days."

Henry excused himself to take a phone call. It was Mikey Mo returning his call. He told Mikey Mo what the situation was with the boat and how suspicious he found things to be. Mikey Mo agreed, told him he was in Kingston, and would drive on over.

"I'll bring two other men. They'll be in a separate car. Expect me in the next hour or so. I'll arrive alone. I don't want the people at the marina to know that I'll have backup watching the boat until it's repaired. This whole thing smells like another Shower Posse trick."

"Will I know your men?"

"Ya, mon. I'm bringing Tom John and Froggie."

"They're good men. I'll see you in about an hour."

Mikey Mo arrived just when he said he would. He purposely kept any observations or suspicions low key as he evaluated the situation so as not to alarm anyone on either side. Turbulence recognized Mikey Mo immediately since they too had worked music shows together on occasion. They had a brief reunion. Then Turbulence got Pacman to take a picture of him, Mikey Mo and DV together to commemorate the occasion with each of their cell phones. Pacman surreptitiously texted his picture to Hi-top.

"It would be an honor to work with both of you tonight at the Wickie Wackie since you won't be able to go to Port Antonio today. Our gig starts at seven."

DV added, speaking to Mikey Mo, "Turbulence tells me his cousin Sizzla will be there as well. I think it could be fun."

"Sure. Why not? Count me in."

"I can't wait to see you four together tonight. This could be a historic occasion," Betsy added.

As soon as they left for the hotel, Pacman called Hi-top and filled him in on DV's plans for that evening and told him that they'd be at the Wickie Wackie.

Hi-top was thrilled. An idea began to come together in his head. Now he had a plan. Plus, he would finally get payback for that embarrassing and painful day of mishaps when DV and Mikey Mo had performed with Sly and Robbie at the Jubilee Market at Sir William Grant Park.

Yes! What goes around comes around.

He called Monkeyman and Mighty Mouse into a conference, explained what he had in mind, and what their role would be. His next move was to call Moto Mouth and tell him what he wanted him to tell DV about the boat.

NOT RESPONSIBLE
IF SEAGULLS EAT
YOUR FUNNEL CAKE

Chapter 28

To use for their open-air musical performances, the Wickie Wackie Beach Bar had constructed an uncovered, elevated, weathered-lumber deck that was enclosed by a pine two-by-four railing. It was built on vertical creosote posts and overlooked the beach. Its unpainted lumber was warped and twisted. It started out on ground level as an appendage to the rustic, open-air building, but by the time it got to the ocean it was about twelve feet above the sloping beach beneath it. Stacks of large box speakers dominated the ocean end. Running another eight to ten feet above the floor, were two longer creosote posts. Strobe lights were mounted vertically from them and shone out towards the surf.

The beach itself was rough. It was covered literally wall to wall with washed up shells and dark lava rocks. Not far away down the beach, was a tall pyre where each night the restaurant lit a blazing bonfire. Cheap resin tables and chairs had been haphazardly placed on a portion of the deck, but the remainder of it was open so it could be used for a dancefloor.

Sizzla was already there when DV and his party arrived. Turbulence drove them over. The deck and building were not overflowing with people yet, but at the rate partiers were coming in, they soon would be. They easily found a table and ordered an initial round of Red Stripes. After DV and Sizzla reminisced about the afternoon they had performed together at Palm Beach's Sunfest, Sizzla and Turbulence introduced DV to the other musicians, and they began to identify some musical numbers that everyone would feel comfortable performing together.

Betsy spotted Mikey Mo arriving and jumped up to hug him. After everyone had been greeted or had been introduced, Mikey Mo joined the other musicians.

"Since DV's our American guest artist, why don't we do some reggae cover versions of hit songs from the U.S.," Mikey Mo suggested.

Sizzla agreed that it would be fun since after all, many of these songs climbed the Jamaican charts as well. Everyone else quickly concurred.

"But don't ignore Jamaican songs. After all, this is a Jamaican audience, not an American one," DV replied.

"No, mon. We won't," Sizzla said. "We'll have no problem on that front. You'll see."

"Then thanks for the honor. Respect. I'll try not to let you down."

"I've emceed many a show with a playlist with that bias. OK, mi friends, let me make some suggestions that have always worked for me in the past," Mikey Mo said. "Why don't we open with 'Light My Fire' and 'Johnny B. Goode.' Everybody likes them."

"UB-40 did that one, and Peter Tosh's version of 'Johnny B. Goode' is still played on Jamaican radio."

"And we've got to play some Jimmy Cliff," DV said. "I worked with him once in New Orleans and once at Sunfest. How about 'You Can Get It If You Really Want'? Did you ever hear him sing 'Ob-La-Di, Ob-La-Da'?"

"Ya, mon. Either of dem always a winner. Do you know '54-46'?"

"Hell, yeah. Toots is a must. Worked with him once too."

"Yu *hab* been around. How about 'Red Red Wine' or 'Can't Help Falling in Love'?"

"Know them both. We haven't mentioned a Marley piece."

"A lot of them are overworked, but I've got an idea. Ever hear Marley sing 'Go Tell It on the Mountain'?"

"I can see right now," DV said, "that this is going to be *one* fun evening. I've got one last idea for our final number. Do you know "You've Got a Friend?"

"Oh, ya, mon. Good idea. Jimmy Cliff did that one too."

"Then let's get this show on the road." Mike Mo said with finality. "We're not getting paid to stand here and talk. These people want to hear music."

Hi-top had dropped Monkeyman and Mighty Mouse at the marina with instructions not to do anything until he gave them the go-ahead. None of them had much fear that the boat's owners would return since Moto Mouth had emphatically lied and told DV that there was no way the boat could be repaired that day.

Instead, he had spent the afternoon surreptitiously draining the watered fuel tank and putting some STP water remover in it. He sprayed the engine with Seafoam and finetuned it. When he cranked it, it ran like a top.

Pacman gave Monkeyman and Mighty Mouse the duplicate boat keys that he had had made earlier as soon as they arrived. The threesome talked a bit but quickly became bored. They soon began to smoke a little ganja and drink a few Red Stripes with Pacman in the ship's store. Pacman broke out some snacks for them, which he conveniently forgot to pay his employer for. They gorged themselves on CheeZees, banana chips, corn curls, and Pringles. Pacman rationalized that the owner could easily afford the petty theft, and besides that, his bakra **(white slave driver)** boss would never miss them anyway.

Pacman then began to play cousin Sizzla's award winning "Royal Son of Ethiopia" CD, and the group mellowed out to the blaring music as they waited for Hi-top's call that would send Monkeyman and Mighty Mouse into action.

Besides the revelers out on Wickie Wackie's deck, another secondary group assembled on the beach below the deck. Earlier that afternoon Hi-top had called the Wickie Wackie to find out what time the music would begin. When he arrived, he spotted DV's party up top. He mentally counted them to make sure everyone was present. He didn't want to risk another run-in with Henry Davis. After assessing his surroundings, he decided to stay downstairs where he could mingle into that crowd while remaining unnoticed but could still easily keep tabs on the group on the deck in case he needed to warn his men.

One reason that Mikey Mo had been the last to arrive was that he had detoured by the marina to drop off Tom John and Froggie at the marina. Their instructions were to use DV's hidey-hole key to unlock the boat cabin and then spend the night on the boat since DV and company would be staying at the Scarlett Guest House. Their mission was to protect the *Spirit of the Seas* from any riffraff should it become necessary.

When they walked down the pier to the boat, Tom John and Froggie heard familiar lyrics to the title song on Sizzla's album coming from the ship's store,

> *What does it worth, without love?*
> *put away your distrust and your grudge*
> *words without work is not enough ...*

They ambled down toward the boat. They kept looking around to see if they were being observed but saw no one. They walked back and forth unnoticed until they located the boat. Froggie found the key while Tom John kept a lookout, and then they climbed aboard. Before long the gently rocking boat and warm cabin had put them both to sleep.

When it was completely dark and the music set was well underway, Hi-top called Monkeyman's cell phone. The plan he had devised was ingenious in its simplicity. Even two numb nuts like Monkeyman and Mighty Mouse should have no trouble pulling it off. He had already done the hard part. He had bribed Pacman and Moto Mouth to make duplicate copies of DV's boat keys. He had made sure that DV had been told repeatedly that the boat was nonoperational. Only he and Moto Mouth knew that the boat's engines were instead in top form and filled with fresh fuel.

All Hi-top's men had to do was use these duplicate keys to crank and then hijack the unoccupied *Spirit of the Seas* in the dead of night and take it to a predetermined boat house controlled by the posse. They didn't even have to be sneaky since Pacman was in on the deal anyway. What could be simpler? Since DV and his party were staying at Scarlett Guest House and spending the evening jamming at the Wickie Wackie, no one would never suspect foul play until the following day when they came back to check on the boat. By this time, it would be too late. The boat would be sequestered far, far away.

Simple. Direct. Straightforward. Fool proof. What the hell can go wrong?

He didn't get a good feeling, however, when he heard Sizzla blaring in the background as he tried to talk to Monkeyman. His first doubts began to creep in.

"Wha yu?" he demanded. "Yu betta not be inna rum bockle (bottle)."

"Na, mon. Wi in da ship's store waiting for yu ta call."

"Then turn that rahtid ting down. It time for yu to go to work. Are yu ready?"

"Ya, mon. No worry. Wi on it. Gotta go now."

Before Hi-top could chastise him further, Monkeyman hung up.

Monkeyman and Mighty Mouse partially walked and partially staggered in the dark down the pier to the *Spirit of the Seas*. Monkeyman climbed over the gunwale to get aboard first. The next thing he knew he was flat on his back with the breath knocked out of him with Mighty Mouse on top of him.

"Get off of mi, yu lickle waste mon," he managed to gasp.

"Sorry, mon. Mi shoelace got caught in da boat cleat."

"Mi shoe about to be so far up yu rass, pipsqueak, da mi shoelace wrap around yu tonsil."

"Be cool. Mi movin'."

"Ouch! Da mi fingers yu steppin' on."

"Sorry, mon."

"Ediot! Yu mek me drop da boat key. Now wi gotta find it."

They crawled around on all fours looking for the key.

"Mi got it," Mighty Mouse announced.

Monkeyman tried to snatch it from him, but Mighty Mouse had his thumb in the loop at the end of the key's coiled lanyard cord on the dead man's safety kill switch. When Monkeyman snatched, it stretched the cord, and when Mighty Mouse shook it loose from his finger, the key zinged Monkeyman in his left eye, blurring his vision.

"Ow! Yu mowly **(stinking)** lickle quashie **(low life)**! Dat hurt! A wah di bloodclaat dew yew **(What the fuck's wrong with you?)**?"

"Yu say yu wanted da key. Mi get it for yu. Yu dunna like it, den gunkona **(go fuck yourself)**."

Monkeyman jammed the key in the ignition, but the motor wouldn't crank since he had forgotten to attach the dead man's switch.

"Ah wha di …? Now wha's wrong?"

By this time Tom John and Froggie had been alerted that they had uninvited visitors and silently approached them as they assessed the scene. Froggie grabbed Monkeyman around his dreads and yanked. When he did, Mighty Mouse charged head down and head-butted him in his testicles. He screamed and released Monkeyman. Tom John grabbed Mighty Mouse by his ankles and swung him around, this time making him head-butt Monkeyman in his groin.

Monkeyman expelled a projectile of partially digested banana chip, Pringle, CheeZee, and corn curl laden vomit as he grabbed himself in pain. By this time Mighty Mouse had righted himself again and charged Tom John. Froggie was behind him and had by now recovered enough to grab the gaffing hook. He swung it at Mighty Mouse, catching him on his rear end and shooting him forward. Mighty Mouse tripped on Tom John's outstretched foot and careened into the water. As they watched Mighty Mouse flounder, Monkeyman leaped over the side of the boat onto the dock and took off running until he disappeared into the dark. Neither of Mikey Mo's men pursued him since all that they cared was that he was gone. Mighty Mouse dogpaddled under the pier and hid there. When he had recovered enough to move on, Mighty Mouse pulled himself piling by piling away from his adversaries until he reached the shore. Then, he too disappeared into the dark. Pacman never came out of the ship's store since in his addled state, he couldn't hear the battle over the top of the CD.

So much for Hi-top's foolproof plan. If he only knew as he listened to DV, Turbulence, and Sizzla play at the Wickie Wackie that he had just had further proof that that he had two fools working for him.

About that time, the musicians launched into a Jimmy Cliff all-time favorite.

So as sure as the sun will shine
I'm gonna get my share now, what's mine
And the harder they come
The harder they fall, one and all
Ooh! The harder they come
The harder they fall, one and all

Hi-top ordered another Red Stripe and thought that his ordeal with the rahtid boat had finally come to an end. He could finally redeem himself with Harry Dog and Dudus.

```
┌─────────────────────────────────────┐
│                                     │
│           NOTICE                    │
│        "NUH PARK                    │
│         OUTSIDE.                     │
│      TIEF RAMPANT"                   │
│              MANAGEMENT              │
│                                     │
└─────────────────────────────────────┘
```

Chapter 29

Mikey Mo's phone rang.

"It's Tom John."

"Lemme call you back in a bit. I can't hear you for the music. I'm emceeing a show."

As soon as he could, he went into Wickie Wackie's men's room and returned the call.

"You were right to have the boat watched. We just had intruders try to steal it. We ran them off. No damage was done."

"Do you know who they were?"

"No, but one was tall with dreads. The other was short and bald with big ears."

Mikey Mo knew immediately who Tom John was talking about. The Shower Posse thugs were back.

"Good work. Stay with the boat the rest of the night in case they come back. I'll be there in the morning. By the way, good work."

Shortly after Mikey Mo's call, another call was being made to Hi-top.

"Boss, dis Monkeyman."

"Have you captured the boat? Speak up. I can't hear you over the music."

"Sure. Dis betta? … Good. No, mon, wi didn't. It's got armed men guarding it. Wi didn't even try."

"How many men?"

"Four that we saw. … But could a been more. And they were armed to the teeth. We'll have come up with anudder plan to steal it some udder time. Pacman says it's leaving for the Errol Flynn Marina in Port Antonio as soon as dey find out for sure dah it's fixed. We'll get it there."

"Did they see you?"

"No, mon. Wi was careful."

"And you didn't do anything suspicious."

"No, mon. Like mi say, wi was careful. They don suspect nuttin."

"Da posse hab an ally in Port Antonio who can probably be of local assistance. Her name is Queisha Hamilton. Her uncle was Neville Hamilton Senior."

"But he long dead."

"Dah's right. As is her cousin, Neville Junior. And yu know who put dem in da ground? Colonel Winter and Mikey Mo Mullins with the help of da same bakra Betsy Black who is now on da Spirit of da Seas. Queisha would do anyting to get eben. Plus, she owes Dudus big time."

"Mi tought da Hamiltons lived in Browns Town."

"Not after her uncle and cousin were murdered. Da Colonel made sure her life there became a living hell afterwards, and Dudus helped her move to Port Antonio and got her a job at the hospital there. He also supported her until she could get back on her feet. As I say, Queisha owes da President big time. Here's her phone number."

"Wi be sure ta get with her when we get there."

Hi-top called Pacman next. He backed up Monkeyman's story. And he said he had an alternate plan involving his cousin Slam Dunk. He briefly outlined his idea. Hi-top told him to get Slam Dunk over to the marina the first thing the next morning.

The following morning after breakfast, DV, Henry, and Mikey Mo went down to check the boat while everyone else remained behind at the hotel. Mikey Mo called The Colonel from the hotel and gave him an update on the latest attempt to steal the boat. The Colonel quizzed him for details, including the names of some of the locals in Bull Bay they had been dealing with. They decided not to alarm the rest of the crew yet of the latest botched attempt on the boat with the exception of Henry.

When they got to the marina, Pacman proudly announced that Moto Mouth had repaired the boat so that it ran, but that he had not been able to get all the parts he needed so he couldn't guarantee how long his work might last. He introduced them to another of his cousins who just happened to be there. He went by Slam Dunk. Then he gave DV a bill for docking, fuel, and Moto Mouth's services.

"Moto Mouth does not feel good about that engine since he couldn't get all the parts he needed. He suggested sumtin mi totally agree wif. Mi cousin here has worked for Moto Mouth and is a pretty decent mechanic in his own right. His widowed mama lives in Port Antonio. She's recovering from some recent surgery, and he wants to go check on her. If you will take him with you as far as Port Antonio, if the engine breaks down, he'll know what to do and will be there to help you. And you'll be helping him at the same time. Ya know, one hand washes da udder."

Before DV could answer, Mikey Mo's phone rang. It was Colonel Winter. Mikey Mo walked away so they could talk in private.

"The manager of the marina — you told me he goes by Pacman. Is his real name perhaps Patrick Manson?"

"Yes, sir. I believe that's right."

"Thought so. And the mechanic who goes by Moto Mouth. What's his birth name?"

"Haven't heard it mentioned."

"But he's a relative of Pacman's?"

"Yes, sir. Where are you going with this?"

"Where I'm heading is this. I'm sure that Moto Mouth is really Maurice Manson, and yes, they are really cousins. They are also cousins to the singer Sizzla …"

"Yes, sir. He was here last night playing with his cousin, Turbulence, our driver … and DV …"

"The whole family is deeply indebted to Dudus Coke. Dudus got Sizzla his first job in Kingston as a sound system apprentice and later introduced him to Bobby Digital. Don't trust anything any of them suggest."

"You must have ESP, sir. Pacman just suggested we give Slam Dunk, who's another of his cousins, a ride to Port Antonio, and in return, if necessary, this cousin will patch our motor back together if it breaks down again since they were not able to obtain all the needed parts yesterday."

There was silence on the other end of the line.

Finally, Mikey Mo said, "I hear you. I'll handle this situation, sir."

He hung up and signaled Tom John and Froggie that he needed to talk to them privately. They walked up to the parking lot with him, and then he returned alone.

"Well," Mikey Mo said to Slam Dunk. "Welcome aboard. I guess if DV's going to have you as his guest until Port Antonio, you'll need to earn your Red Stripes."

He laughed, put his thumb up to his mouth, and tipped his empty curved fingers towards his nose.

"Mind helping bring some Red Stripe from my car down to the boat?"

Pacman and Slam Dunk both smiled. Mikey Mo had taken the bait. Hi-top's plan was going to work. And if everyone was drinking beer, it was going to be even easier than he thought.

Yowzah! Yowzah! An easy-peasy slam-dunk! A lead-pipe cinch, piece of cake that was gonna be like shooting fish in a barrel!

Since Slam Dunk was armed, once aboard, all he had to do was choose a good time to commandeer the boat, dump everybody ashore, and take off to the Shower Posse safe house that Monkeyman and Mighty Mouse had been instructed to use. … And make himself some easy money.

But that's not what Mikey Mo had in mind. When they got back up to the parking lot, he instructed Slam Dunk to get the cases of beer out of Tom John's trunk. After he opened the trunk and leaned in, Tom John and Froggie slipped up behind him and pinned his arms behind his back while they disarmed him and took his phone. They then shoved him in the trunk, slammed it, and drove away. The next time Slam Dunk would see blue sky again would be when Mikey Mo's men would dump him on the shoulder of a remote bauxite road in the John Crow Mountains a couple of hours away and then drive off.

Mikey Mo waited before returning to the boat and regretfully telling everyone that Slam Dunk sent his apologies, but he had remembered that he had a previous unbreakable commitment that he had forgotten about. Sadly enough he realized that he wouldn't be able to depart until the following day. So as bad as he hated to do it, he had suggested that they leave without him. He would have to make other arrangements to get to Port Antonio. Pacman was baffled, but since Slam Dunk had left without a word, he didn't know what to say or do that wouldn't raise suspicions.

When Turbulence had delivered the rest of their party to the marina, everyone said their goodbyes, and the *Spirit of the Seas* departed. DV noted that it seemed to be running just fine. Moto Mouth was being too cautious. He was a better mechanic than he gave himself credit for.

As Mikey Mo drove away in his car, he called Colonel Winter.

"Slam Dunk is no longer a threat. He decided that it was not the best time to visit his mother since he needed to satisfy another commitment in the John Crow Mountains first."

Pacman called Hi-top and told him that he wasn't sure what had just occurred, but that apparently Slam Dunk had had second thoughts and had unexpectedly backed out of his assignment.

"And I thought he was so excited about making some extra money. I guess you just never know about some people," Pacman concluded.

PURSUVERUNCE PAY

Chapter 30

Mikey Mo's phone rang again a few hours later. It was Colonel Winter.

"Yes, sir."

"I've have been following up on some of the information you gave me earlier, and my phone calls have yielded two results. First, effective immediately, as a result of my calls, Patrick Manson, the man you know as Pacman, is being informed of a career interruption. He will no longer employed by Danny's Marina. And second, as soon as the authorities can locate him, Maurice Manson will be served with an official citation for running an unlicensed commercial establishment from a property zoned as residential only. His establishment has been posted with an official notice informing him that he has until the end of the month to move everything he uses to run said business off the property. The notice states that there will be a stiff fine if he does not comply and that the ultimate risk is that he could be incarcerated. A notice has been posted on his door stating these things."

"Man, oh man, sir. That didn't take you long."

"I am not without influence on that end of the island. Mi lilly **(little)** axe can still cut down big tree when need be. I assume our friends are now safely on their way to Port Antonio."

"Yes, sir. They are."

Slam Dunk walked several miles down the deserted road after John Henry and Froggie let him out. His body was bruised from the bouncing he took in their trunk. He was thirsty. He was just about as angry as he had ever been in his whole life. He had no cell phone or weapons to use to break into anyone's house. God forbid, if he ever saw any houses! And finally, the disrespect he had been shown was unforgivable.

Someone is going to pay.

And he rationalized that the bakra, DV Craig, had to be behind it all. He had to be the one who hired Mikey Mo and his thugs and put them up to mercilessly and without provocation attacking him, an honorable working man.

In the meantime, Pacman was feeling some of the same emotions. He had just been informed that his services would no longer be required at Danny's Marina. The owner had sent his bookkeeper to collect Pacman's business keys along with a locksmith to change the locks on everything he had had a key for. The bookkeeper went through the box of Pacman's personal belongings to make sure he wasn't taking anything that didn't belong to him and made him empty his pockets on his desk before he would pay him his partial wages in cash. The bookkeeper also wrote down the serial number on Pacman's pistol. He was then escorted off the property and told never to return for any reason. Noncompliance would be treated as trespassing and dealt with accordingly.

He treated me like trash. I have never been disrespected this bad in my whole life. Someone is going to pay.

Monkeyman and Mighty Mouse stopped by a roadside rum bar on the way to Port Antonio and got roaring drunk. Since both felt bruised and sore, they rationalized that rum would help ease not only their physical aches but assuage the blows to their egos as well. Mighty Mouse probed his tipsy companion to make doubly sure that Hi-top didn't know what really happened the night before. As they got drunker and drunker, they justified their failed assignment every way that came to mind. It was Hi-top's fault, not theirs.

Whack!

Monkeyman twirled the boat keys that he had somehow miraculously manage to hang onto as they talked, occasionally slapping the table with the coiled dead man's switch to emphasize his points, not even noticing when he whacked Mighty Mouse's fingernail. It began to throb turn purple.

Whack!

"He told wi dah da boat was unguarded, and that dah was no danger of the owner returning. Dah bullshit! Dese people are well guarded by both an obeah man spell and duppies as well. Wi neber had a chance. Wi tried to tell dah fool Hi-top dah but da fool no wanna listen."

Whack! Whack!

Monkeyman had accidentally whacked him again.

"Ya, mon, yu right. ... Ouch! Watch it! Dah rahtid key hurt. ... Mi saw da snake in Kingston. He tried to kill yu and mi both. And de spell put on wi at da market in Morant Bay. Dah was no axxident. Dah was a obeah spell. But wi still gotta get to Port Antonio and get da boat and break da spells before anyone in da posse finds out wha really happened last night."

Pacman's phone rang. It was Slam Dunk. He was still trying to contain his rage. He had managed to come upon a shack in mountains and had promised the Rasta owner that he would pay him J$50 if he would let him use his phone. But Tom John had taken all his money. Now he needed Pacman to come rescue him and pay the man his J$50. He put the owner on the phone to explain to Pacman how to find his house. After they hung up, he and the Rasta chilled out together with a joint.

Pacman picked up Moto Mouth and the two of them managed to find Slam Dunk. The Rasta invited them to join them as he and Slam Dunk got higher and higher. Both readily accepted. That was the only thing Pacman remembered until the following morning when he recalled his lengthy rant from the night before as he had told his companions how he had unjustly and through no fault of his own lost his job at the marina and how he had been disrespected and treated like a common criminal as he was escorted off the property.

"Dey eben had da locks changed and took notes on mi pistol. Wah dey tink mi am? A dutty tief! Dey can all kiss mi nanny dutty, brown rass **(my granny's dirty, brown ass)**!"

When Pacman arrived back at Bull Bay, he dropped Slam Dunk off and then took Moto Mouth home and let him off. As he was backing out, he heard Moto Mouth begin to scream profanity. He jumped out of the car, forgetting to put it in park. It began to roll and backed into a fifty-five-gallon drum before he could jump back in and put on the brake. Moto Mouth ripped the citation the authorities had taped to his door off and was running around like a wild man.

"Summady reported mi to John Law, and now deh say mi outta bidness. Das all yu fault."

"Dunna look at mi, mon. Das gotta be da doings of da dutty bakra **(white man)** dah own da boat. He musta done dat to hab to keep from paying yu to fix he boat."

Pacman conveniently neglected to tell Moto Mouth that DV had paid the bill, but that Pacman didn't have a chance to see that Moto Mouth got his money before he had gotten sacked.

"I got nuttin to keep mi here, and now neither do yu," Pacman announced. "Les go ta Port Antonio and get eben with da bumboclaat **(douchebag)**."

"Ya, mon. Mi in. Les go. Mi grab some Red Stripes outa da fridge for da trip first. Mon, it's hot out here. So leh wi chill in mi swimming pool first while we tink tings true."

"Yu gotta pool?"

"Ya, mon."

Moto Mouth had a cistern liner on the salvage yard that was partially filled with rainwater. It was in front of the bow of a rusty, once-white, homemade pontoon boat that was on a trailer with flat tires. Bird droppings covered the boat's warped, raw-wood deck. The pontoons had been fashioned from fifty-five-gallon drums that had been banded onto the frame in a linear manner. A hole had been bored into the deck, and an over-the-hill saltwater fishing rod protruded vertically. On its top end, Moto Mouth had attached a tattered, once-black flag with a faded yellow pirate happy face. It said in all caps, "HAVE A IRIE DAY, MATEY." Protruding from the boat's bow was an eight-foot two-by-twelve.

"Does dah tink really float?"

"Ya, mon. Mi call it mi Ship-faced Titanic Too."

"Wah's dat?" Pacman asked as he pointed at the board.

"Das mi diving board. When Mi use it, mi call it walking da plank. … But mi woudna recommend diving off of it headfirst. But if it mek yu nervous, yu can use da ladda dere."

He pointed at a rickety, unattached extension ladder that he had left permanently dangling into the cistern. Pacman looked at it doubtfully, not sure whether it would teeter or slide out from under him if he attempted to climb down it.

"Oh!"

The water was tinged with green algae.

"Da water's no blue."

"No problem, mon."

Moto Mouth picked up a couple of containers of Clorox and dumped them into the water and then threw the empty containers out into the salvage yard.

He began to add some more water into the cistern liner by turning on the water hose that he had dangling into it over the edge. Then he threw in some patched car inner tubes. Last he dropped a latched Igloo ice chest full of cold Red Stripes and a Ziplock of ganja into the cistern and let it float freely. He turned on a boombox that dangled from a pulley by a rope and lowered it partially into the cistern.

"Yu tink only white folks got a resort. Welcome to da Last Resort."

He quickly stripped and yelled "Last one in is a pumm pumm (**pussy**)!" before jumping. Pacman shrugged, stripped, and followed.

Once in the water, they unwound their turbans and dunked their freed-up dreads. They then spent the next several hours drinking Red Stripes and burning weed while they listened to "The Best of Weed Song" collection on Moto Mouth's boom box. Sizzla's "Smoke the Herb" began to play. By the time DJEasy's reggae mix entitled "Weed Meditation for Ganja Smokers" came on, they were merrily singing along. When Peter Tosh began to sing "Legalise It," they wailed, yowled, and high-fived each other in agreement. The trip to Port Antonio would have to wait until another day.

The *Spirit of the Seas'* trip to Port Antonio turned out to be a pleasant one.

"We have a slip reserved at the Errol Flynn Marina, and the guest car from Trident Hotel will pick us up there," DV said.

"Weren't we at the Errol Flynn Marina in Morant Bay?" Cee Cee asked. "Is everything around here named for him?"

"Shortly after World War II ended, Errol Flynn's sailboat, the Zaca, developed mechanical problems and he had to put in at Port Antonio. This was the start of his love affair with Jamaica, Rose said."

"Funny how fate works," Cee Cee commented. "Did he actually move here?"

"He and his wife, Patrice Wymore, maintained their first residence on Navy Island near Port Antonio. At first, they lived on a boat anchored off the coast. But according to the legend this changed after he won the island in a poker game and decided to build them a home there. The wild jet-set parties he held there are as legendary as the story of how he obtained the island to begin with. Because of him, this part of Jamaica attracted the jetsetters, people like Noel Coward, Ian Fleming, and J.P. Morgan among others. Coward and Fleming ended up building homes in Jamaica as well."

"Wow! Who owns the island now?"

"The Jamaican government. They keep it private. It's a good-sized island — over three hundred acres. Flynn also owned a 2,000-acre estate here in Portland. Also built a mansion on it as well. Patrice still lives on it where she raises cattle and coconuts. Oh, and I almost forgot, Flynn started a very exclusive boutique hotel he named GeeJam. Its guest list has been filled with celebrities over the years."

"Like who?"

"Oh, Grace Jones, Sharon Stone, Katy Perry, Alicia Keys, and Rihanna are a few of the more recent names who come to mind."

"But back to Trident. You'll meet Patrice later today," Betsy said. "She also owns the gift shop there."

"You're kidding! Really! Do you know her?"

"As a matter of fact, we met through Mr. Levy who owns the hotel. We're all going to have happy hour together this evening on the hotel's Verandah Terrace."

"This Trident must be a pretty swanky hotel."

"Swanky to me means hoity toity and pretentious. Trident is relaxed. Let's just call it five-star. But in its own way, it's a legendary as Patrice is. In the old days people like Bette Davis, Ginger Rogers, Audrey Hepburn, and William Randolph Hearst stayed here. More recently it has attracted Tom Cruise, Johnny Depp, Denzel Washington, and Whoopi Goldberg among others."

"I can't wait."

They docked at the Errol Flynn Marina, and the harbormaster, Dave Dingle, known locally as Ding Dong, called one of Trident's guest cars to take them to the hotel. The thirty-five-acre hotel property was surrounded by a tall nondescript white wall with a stylized "T" on it and tall wooden gates. The long driveway was flanked with fifty-year-old casuarina trees.

The main hotel was a sprawling one-story gleaming white building with a Jamaican-Georgian exterior. This building contained a screening room, an art gallery, a boutique, a gym with a Jacuzzi, a yoga deck, a masseuse parlor, a library, a main dining room that specialized in Jamaican and Japanese cuisines, and multiple indoor and outdoor bars.

"Gee willikers!" Cee Cee commented. "Mr. Levy seems to have thought of everything. Even a yoga deck. I wonder if they have a yoga instructor."

"Gee willikers? I haven't heard that since Batman used to use it," Betsy said. "Are you into yoga?"

"Personal fitness is kind of a hobby of mine. I'm an ASFA certified self-defense instructor."

"That's good to know. I hope we don't have to call upon you to use your skills, but I do feel better knowing that you know how to take care of yourself if a situation demands it."

The hotel claimed to have the finest selection of rare cognacs and Cuban rums in the Caribbean. Flanking it were thirteen spacious one-and two-bedroom studio villas. Each had its own private plunge pool and terrace. The area behind the hotel contained terraces but was dominated by an immense Olympic sized pool surrounded by a massive white deck that overlooked the jagged cliffs that hovered over the coastline. Between the cliffs was a sandy path that led to a pristine, private, champagne-colored beach.

"This is breathtaking," Cee Cee gasped. Even though the Davises and the Blacks had stayed here before, they were always awed to see it again, especially through the eyes of a newcomer.

When they walked into the lobby, they were greeted by a formally dressed clerk.

"Welcome to Trident. My name is Shantiqua. She pointed at a plush seating area. Please have a seat. May I offer you a glass of chilled coconut water? Also, please take a towelette to freshen yourself before you check in."

"Gee, these feel great. They're ice cold and smell like lemongrass, and I think this glass is crystal," Cee Cee commented. "I'm going to like this place."

Shantiqua patiently waited for them to sip their coconut water and to towel off before sending a bellman to inform Mr. Levy that his special guests had arrived. Before he left, the bellman introduced himself as Travis.

Mr. Levy was an older man slightly below six feet who wore glasses. He was wearing a white guayabera shirt that did not hide his paunch. While he was not bald, he had the usual receding hairline and thinning hair one would expect of a man his age. After a warm, sincere greeting, the low-key hotel owner told them that he wouldn't detain them but would let them check in and freshen up from their trip. They would have plenty of time to talk during happy hour.

"Travis will handle your bags and escort you to your rooms."

Will spoke up at this time and said, "Guys, since there's six of us, I reserved one two-bedroom villa that sleeps four and one junior villa which sleeps two. If you don't mind, DV and Cee Cee, I thought we'd let you have the one-bedroom villa so you guys can have your privacy. We'll take the larger one with the Davises since we've travelled with them on many other occasions and know we're compatible.

"And that way you'll have your own private, heated pool in case you feel like catching up on a little honeymooning."

Will gave a playful leer. Betsy punched him gently in the ribs. Henry just smiled.

The Craigs both agreed that this arrangement was fine with them.

Both of their villas were spacious and breezy and had imported wooden floors. The villas were primarily white, accented by high-end, dark-wood, mid-century Scandinavian, and modern designer furniture. The bathroom was equally spacious, and each villa had both an indoor and an outdoor tub. The glass living room doors led onto a private deck and pool. Great care seemed to have been taken with every detail, from the eclectic art to the latest in wi-fi, a flat-screen TV, and Egyptian cotton towels, robes, and slippers. There was even a JBL boom box in each villa.

After they all got unpacked, Will and Betsy were too keyed up just hang around their villa.

"We've got time before the cocktail hour," Will suggested to Henry. "Why don't we see if the Craigs want to walk over to Trident Castle while we're here?"

"Good idea," Henry agreed. "You girls want to come with us?"

"Of course," Rose and Betsy said.

Within five minutes the Craigs joined them for the short ten-minute walk. They cleared it with Shantiqua before they left, and she called to let the castle security know that a guest was coming their way. Earl Levy walked in and when he overheard their intention, offered to personally show the castle to them. As they strolled along, he began to tell them the history of the castle.

"I was originally an architect by trade. I consider the castle to be my premier accomplishment. It's on seven acres. I originally designed it and had it built for the German Baroness Fahmi, but by the time it was completed, she had had some financial setbacks and could no longer afford it. So, I ended up with it and used it for a while as my private residence. Nowadays, it gets rented mainly for special events and as a filming location."

"Would I know any of the movies?" Cee Cee asked.

"Ever see 'Our Man Flint'?"

"The James Coburn spy spoof?" DV asked.

"The one and same. It was one movie partially shot here. I don't take most guests into the house, but since you're friends of the Blacks and the Davises, I'm going to give you a special tour."

Soon they were standing in front of the castle. The baroque Austrian style mansion's Rocco stonework was a stunning vision in white. Ivory turrets jutted against the sweeping Caribbean sky. A pair of massive stone alligators guarded the majestic stone steps that rose up to its grand entranceway.

"Before entering the castle, it is traditional for a first-time guest to make friends with the guardians and to guess their sex," Levy said.

The Davises and the Blacks smiled. They had already been through this exercise.

"Golly, Mr. Levy. I don't know. How *are* you supposed to tell?" Cee Cee asked as she admired one of the alligators.

Levy took her hand and put it in front of a long, rectangular space beneath the one of the guardians.

"To make friends just slide your hand under here and scratch the gator's belly, and your question will be answered."

She slid her arm up to the elbow, as DV slid his hand into the void on the other one. A shocked look came on both their faces. He snatched his arm back out, but she continued groping.

"This ain't my week for boys," DV announced.

"This boy's hung like a Jersey mule," Cee Cee finally said. "His erect maleness has room to carry multiple cups of coffee as well as a dozen donuts — all at the same time, and if this big boy ever died after an overdose of Viagra, they wouldn't be able to close the coffin."

"Speaking of Viagra," Will said. "Did you hear about the two thieves who broke into the drugstore and stole their Viagra? They tell me now that the cops are looking for two hardened criminals."

DV refused to be outdone. "Did you know that a penis is the lightest thing in the world? Even a thought can raise it."

"What do you mean, light? Not Leroy here," Cee Cee responded.

The rest of the group began to laugh and tease them both.

Mr. Levy unlocked the door and invited them to enter. The interior of the castle was as overwhelming as the exterior had been. The massive, multistory entry had a dramatic tile floor of large black and white alternating tiles laid in a diamond pattern. There was an opulent ballroom with a grand piano, an exquisite massive dining hall, a professional kitchen, spacious multiple living rooms and drawing rooms, a photography studio, and a myriad of stairways and terraces, many overlooking the property's high jagged cliffs.

"These cliffs remind me of Big Sur," DV commented.

The rooms were decorated with antiques from all over the world. There were Roman statues and exquisite gleaming chandeliers. Out back was a Romanesque deck and pool that Mr. Levy called the "Mood Pool," a helicopter pad, and a petite private chapel.

"How many bedrooms does it have?" Cee Cee asked.

"Eight," Mr. Levy responded. "Let me show them to you."

Each large bedroom had a massive, canopied bed with a full-sized sofa made into the footboard and a hug private bathroom with every possible amenity.

"This would compete with anything at Newport," DV observed. Levy beamed.

Mr. Levy let them wander and explore. Finally, he announced that happy hour was approaching and suggested that they return to the hotel. Soon they were comfortably seated on the Verandah Terrace. A waiter whispered a message in Mr. Levy's ear.

"Our guest is here," he announced and rose to greet her. They kissed on each cheek.

"My friends, may I introduce you to Patrice Wymore Flynn?"

Errol Flynn's widow was probably approaching eighty, but she was still a stunning former Hollywood actress who looked younger than her age. She was slightly taller than an average woman and stood confidently erect. She had let her hair go salt and pepper. She exuded self-confidence in a way that made a person think of Lauren Bacall. The Davises and the Blacks had met Patrice before. She let them know warmly that she remembered their past encounters. Mr. Levy then introduced her to the Craigs. A waiter pulled out a chair for her, took her drink order, and soon they were engaged in a relaxed conversation.

DV commented, "Your husband was certainly a legend."

"Oh, he certainly was, and yes, he could throw a party. But people don't realize that he fought with the studio constantly over his image. He could often be a shy fireside-and-slipper man."

Next the conversation turned to Errol Flynn's involvement with the tradition of river rafting on the Rio Grande, and she asked if they planned to take advantage of it while they were staying at Trident.

"My husband did not invent river rafting. He simply resurrected it and brought it back into fashion. For years, Jamaicans used to bring bananas down from plantations on long bamboo rafts to ocean going ships that were waiting at the mouth of the river. In fact, to be perfectly honest, it was one of our banana growing friends who thought it would amuse Errol's guests to see they process that bananas went through to get from the upper reaches of his banana plantations to where they could bed loaded on a ship for export."

Mr. Levy then volunteered the use of Trident's guest car and driver if they wished go rafting the following day.

They all agreed that it sounded like it would be fun. When things broke up for the dinner hour, Mr. Levy stopped back by the front desk and asked Shantiqua to give each couple a glossy brochure on the Rio

Grande rafting as he told her to also have the hotel car and driver available for them the following day.

```
STOP!!!
BEFORE YU DECIDE TO
BREAK INTA MI HOUSE
STAND OUTSIDE AND GET
RIGHT WITH JESUS
TELL HE YU SOON COME HOME
```

Chapter 31

By the time Pacman and Moto Mouth got to Port Antonio they were in an alcohol and ganja induced haze and had convinced themselves that the owners and guests of the *Spirit of the Seas* were guilty of every heinous thing they could think of including secretly being evil Arab terrorists who were responsible for global warming. They made a pit stop by Pieyaka's Reggae Bar to relieve themselves so they could refill their "tanks" with additional rum before heading to the Errol Flynn Marina. They walked down the dock and confirmed that the boat had arrived.

Pacman knew the manager, Billy Budd, from both dealing with him when he worked at Danny's and from the fact that Billy had at one time been married to his cousin, Abeba.

"'Ello, bredren," Pacman said when he saw him. "Wah gwaan? Yu remember Moto Mouth?"

"Ya, mon. Bwai, ya done know she mi deya gwaan easy **(I'm just here taking it easy.)**"

"Mi see da Spirit of da Seas be here," he said, trying to appear both surprised and casual. "Dey were mi guests until yesterday. Nice folks. Mehbe we can 'ello. Dey on da boat?"

"No, mon. Dey stay at Trident. Da hotel send car to pick dem up."

202

"Too bad. Just wanted to say 'ello. Wi get outa yu hair. Good to see you, mi bredda."

Now Pacman knew where his quarry was staying. When they were out of Billy Budd's earshot, he commented to Moto Mouth, "Now yu know why mi do da talking. Mi know how to talk and taste mi tongue (**I know how to think before I speak.**). Now wi know where dey at and Billy Budd's none the wiser. Now wi call our cousin Shantiqua. She work at Trident."

A quick call to Shantiqua with the same lie quickly revealed DV and company's plans to raft the Rio Grande the following day. He bumped fists with Moto Mouth. That was going to be a perfect place to get even for their causing both Pacman and Moto Mouth to lose their jobs.

The following morning everyone took their time getting going for the day. Their suites were so luxurious that they hated to leave them. They had had a delicious dinner in Mike's Supper Club, the hotel's gourmet restaurant, of fried yam and mackerel pâté, followed by grilled red snapper in a soursop sauce that had been accompanied by callaloo and a medley of lightly steamed veggies. It had been topped off with a triple chocolate mousse that was served beneath almond crumble. Everyone agreed that they would probably never be hungry again, but by mid-morning the following day their appetites had returned. Since the hotel's policy was to serve guests anywhere on the property, they decided to eat breakfast on the same verandah that they had enjoyed for happy hour.

The staff pulled together two tables, and suddenly seemingly out of nowhere the hotel's general manager, Dwight Powell, appeared along with a white-gloved waiter to pull back the ladies' chair and welcome them.

When they were seated, he asked, "Would you prefer an American breakfast or a Jamaican one?"

The group was unanimous in going for the Jamaican breakfast.

"Then I'll instruct the chef to make scrambled eggs, fried bammy, salt fish and baked beans, callaloo, yams, boiled green bananas, and of course, Blue Mountain coffee. Enjoy."

"What's bammy?" Cee Cee asked.

"A nutty-flavored, starchy dish made from yucca root. You'll like it," Powell replied.

Pacman and Moto Mouth were not dawdling over an elegant Trident breakfast like DV and company. They had driven up to the Rio Grande the night before and had spent the night in their car smoking more ganja and chasing it down with overproof rum. Their cousin, Hitman, was currently working as a Rio Grande raft captain. They wanted to make sure they got the chance to talk to him before the *Spirit of the Seas* crowd arrived there. Hitman was an aging former posse soldier who had "retired" after age began to make his job harder and harder to do and the Shower Posse became less and less forgiving when he didn't deliver the same results that he had been able to deliver when he was younger and more agile.

When they arrived, Hitman was sitting a picnic table drinking a Red Stripe. He was a wiry, slightly taller than average man in his fifties. A dirty, tattered baseball cap sat atop his close-cropped hair. He had a ragged goatee. He was barefoot and wore knee-length plaid shorts. His faded green t-shirt said "Jamaica Where It All Started" and had a map of Jamaica with a star showing the location of the Rio Grande.

When they walked up, Hitman waved his hand in front of his nose and said, "Mon, yu smell ripe. When da las time yu bathe yu body."

Moto Mouth sniffed his underarm before saying, "I dunna smell nuttin. Yu must be smelling yuself."

Pacman sat down, lit up a fresh reefer, and made the expected socially correct inquiries about Hitman's family before getting down to the business at hand. He tilted, and a silent but deadly fart inadvertently slipped out when he plopped down. Hitman slid down the table to put some distance between him and his reeking guests. Pacman then told Hitman that DV had stolen a boat belonging to the Shower Posse and that Harry Dog was under immense pressure from the President to get it back. Hitman nodded knowingly. He well remembered the way Dudus could get when he didn't get what he wanted.

Pacman then gave Hitman a highly one-sided account of how their attempts at recovering the boat had cost both him and Moto Mouth to unjustly lose their jobs. Then to spice up the story even more, he added that he and Moto Mouth had gone up and above board do everything DV asked them to do, but that DV had framed them so that he wouldn't have to pay them for their services. He then told Hitman that this bakra thief would be visiting the Rio Grande that morning. He asked Hitman if someone should be allowed to get away with not only gypping hardworking, well-meaning locals but to then making them lose their jobs as well.

"We're not asking you to do anything. We'll take care of da pickled bong belly (**greedy**) fassyhole. Mi describe dem to yu and gib yu they name. I just wanna make sure dey on yu raft."

"How many?"

"Six."

"Dah will tek more dan one raft."

"Mi mainly after getting even with da boat owner."

He peeled off some Jamaican dollars.

"Give dis to da ticket agent and keep some of it fo yuself. Wi be waiting round one of da bends in da river. By da way, lemme swap cell phone numbers in case mi need to call yu. Will yu call mi when yu see dem arrive? And, by da way, mi brudder, tanks. Respect."

"Ya, mon. No problem. Mi tek care of mi end. And while yu wait, why dunna yu jump in da river and wash yuself off."

"Ya, mon. Mi gaan (**I'm gone**) now. Lickle more (**See you later**)."

"Lata. Walk gud (**Take care**)."

Pacman and Moto Mouth rode down the riverbank on a dirt road adjacent to it looking for a place to ambush their quarry. They were oblivious to the brilliant tropical sun that beat down on the river, illuminating its lush green, sloping banks. Women washed out their breakfast dishes in the clear, cool stream as men with Red Stripe coolers set up to sell beer to the current day's tourists. They came upon a wide place in the river that had rope dangling from a mahogany tree. He called Hitman back and described where he was setting up, and he and Moto Mouth sat back and lit up another reefer. He smelled himself again and decided that Hitman just must be getting soft in his old age.

Preteen barefoot, shirtless boys were setting up a beer stand as well as a row of woodcarvings and calabashes to sell to rafters. Later when they would see a raft approaching, they would swim out with both a cold Red Stripe and a locally carved souvenir in hand to try to sell both to an impulsive tourist who would often buy one or both simply for the novelty of it since it would give them something to talk about when they got back home from their vacations. The boys would later give the raft captain a kickback. It was an honor system, and it worked since the penalty for dishonesty was, if a captain spread the word that he had been shorted, to be banned from the river.

Mr. Levy's driver drove the *Spirit of the Seas* crew to the river, and they arrived before eleven. Hitman spotted them immediately and made a beeline out to their car to welcome them. Since he was required to be licensed and his license could be at risk, he gave them the false name of Stoogy so he could cover his tracks in case things went wrong later. He told them that he was a senior captain and volunteered to be their captain for that day's trip. All they had to do was ask for him, and he would take care of the rest of the arrangements. Instead of sharing the money with the ticket agent or the other captains, he instead bought each captain a beer and then kept the rest of the money for himself. He didn't mention that Pacman had nefarious plans for the party that possibly could endanger them as well. After all, he rationalized that he didn't know what Pacman's plans actually were. He then walked out of earshot, called Pacman, told him that contact had been established and that they would soon be on their way.

While they waited, Mr. Levy's driver arranged for their tickets to be charged to Trident's account and told them he would be waiting with the car at their departure point when they arrived at the end of their rafting adventure. They then sat under a spreading royal poinciana with their new captain and listened to a ragtag band that was serenading arriving tourists for tips. The band didn't play the angry reggae of Kingston but the carefree, old-school calypso of Harry Belafonte. Hitman explained to them that their trip would between two and half and three hours and that their cruising speed would be about three miles an hour. Anytime they wanted to stop and take a brief swim, all they had to do was tell him. DV asked him if tourists were allowed to pole the raft. The answer was of course, "Yah, mon, and I'll snap your picture."

Soon each couple was sitting on the love seat of their twenty-five-foot bamboo raft and found themselves gently rolling down Jamaica's largest river. Hitman powered them with a long bamboo pole that he used to propel the vessel and steer it through both the vast choppy waters and mild rapids. He regaled them with local lore and information about the river's flora and fauna. He pointed out one especially wide place in the river and called it Lovers' Lane. The vegetation along the river was thick and verdant with an abundance of gold and green bamboo clusters along side coconut and breadfruit trees, rose apple, flame of the forest and countless other flora.

Pacman and Moto Mouth waited at their chosen spot for their quarry to arrive. Pacman's plan was one that he thought would appeal to Harry Dog since the Shower Posse had derived its name from its reputation of showering its opponents with bullets. Pacman and Moto Mouth waited on opposite sides of the river. One of the higgler boys had shown them an extra length of rope that had been left in case it was ever needed as a backup to the one hanging from a tree. Pacman immediately purchased it and instructed Moto Mouth to attach it to a tree limb on the opposite side of the river. He tied a loop for their feet at the end of both ropes. Now each of them would have one arm free to shoot as they swung out. The plan was that he would swing from one bank while Moto Mouth would simultaneously swing from the other one as the raft passed by. As they crossed each other over the raft, each of them would open fire with their pistols and shower DV and Cee Cee with bullets. With them dead, the boat should go back on the market, and Harry Dog could purchase it for Dudus. And best of all, revenge would not only be theirs, but they would be demonstrating their potential future value to the posse. They would be replacing their old shit jobs with prestigious jobs with the posse. It seemed a brainy, resplendent plan in his drug-addled mind. Moto Mouth agreed. Pacman was showing both imagination and leadership ability, and he felt privileged to be a part of it all.

Mi brilliant. Mi be making chicken salad out of chicken shit.

Pacman saw the raft approaching from his perch in the tree. He whistled to Moto Mouth and told him to be ready to swing out. When the raft seemed to be perfectly positioned, he signaled Moto Mouth to launch himself. Hitman was the first to notice them and saw they each had a pistol. When he saw both men converging, he dived in the water and began to swim out of the way. Then the limb that Moto Mouth had attached his rope to began to crack, and he began swinging out of control straight into the path of Pacman. They collided in midair over DV's raft.

"Ooooh, boxcova! Yu blood fyah **(blood fire)**!"

"Ooooh, shit! Who yu call blood fyah, raasclaat **(bum cloth)**! Kiss mi rass!"

"Rhatid! Damn, that hurt!"

"Yu bafan fool **(clumsy fool)**!"

"Kiss mi rass too, bat waste man dunce **(useless dummy)**!"

"Oh, suck yuh madda **(go suck your mother)**!"

The collision jarred the rope out of Pacman's hand and made him drop his gun. His foot got tangled in the loop. He suddenly found himself swinging upside down.

As he dropped the pistol, he accidentally pulled the trigger sending one errant shot into the trees where a flock of crested quail-doves were perched. Their wings began to flap up and down at a furious rate in a flurry of motion as they tried to escape, their fluttering wings creating a high-pitched whistle.

Moto Mouth hit butt first on the bow of the raft and ricocheted into the water. About this time Pacman disentangled his foot from the loop and came plunging down on top of him. The limb finally broke all the way and then it and the wad of rope tied to it came down on top of them both. Hitman stopped swimming long enough to swim back and untangle both men so they could all scramble for the shore. They all disappeared crawling on all fours into the undergrowth.

The force of Moto Mouth's landing jarred both DV and Cee Cee off the love seat and into the river where they hung onto the side of the raft. Both Henry and Rose's and Will and Betsy's rafts were not far behind and rounded the bend. When their captains heard the gunshot and saw the flutter of birds, they thought their guests were under a terrorist attack. They too dived into the river and vanished into the thick undergrowth. The now captain-less rafts collided with DV's raft, throwing all of them overboard as well. Will and Betsy began to swim their rafts to shallow water where they could stand. The other two couples followed their example and did the same. They helped each other pull up their rafts to keep them from drifting off and then sat down on the riverbank to regroup.

When they had caught their breaths, Cee Cee said, "Wasn't that our harbor master from Danny's Marina?"

"And also our ex-mechanic?" Betsy added. "

"I didn't tell you before," Henry said, "but Mikey Mo told me The Colonel made 'arrangements' for both of them have the opportunity to seek fresh opportunities with a new career."

"You mean he got them sacked," Will said. "No wonder they were rabidly P-Oed and wanted to try to even the score. Well, I'm glad their plan didn't work out. You know what they say about the best laid plans of mice and men — they usually go awry."

DV added, "The way I heard it is that they all get filed away somewhere."

"No, my friends, in this case we Jamaicans know how to best describe the scene we just witnessed. The higher the monkey climb the more he expose."

"I hate to disagree, darling," Rose said, "but I think the appropriate proverb is 'When crab walk too much, him lose 'im claw.'"

Will turned to his wife and said, "Well, darling, you're the only one who hasn't put her two cents in yet."

"I guess my only comment on plans are 'Not all foot in a boot a good foot.'"

"Hear, hear, my dear! Spoken like a true Jamaican, or should I say Jam-erican."

"There he goes again, my husband, the poet, who don't know it."

Will and Betsy then chimed in together, "Yes, indeed — a real Longfellow."

"Oh, please. Not again. Is that the only rhyme you know?"

"I know another one. Ready? Try this on for size. I eat my peas with honey. I've done it all my life. It makes my peas taste funny. But it keeps them on my knife."

"We may not have captains, but I guess at least we still have our sense of humor."

"And our lives."

MAKIN GROCERIES

Chapter 32

Pacman and Moto Mouth were not the only ones in Port Antonio plotting against the *Spirit of the Seas* group. Monkeyman, and Mighty Mouse had arrived with their own agenda and plans as well. They too initially went by the Errol Flynn Marina to verify that DV's boat had arrived.

"I see that my old friends who own the *Spirit of the Seas* are docked here," he told the harbor master. "Just thought I'd stop by and tell them hello. They're *really* super nice people. Are they staying on the boat?"

"No, mon. They're staying at Trident. They really must be good people. You're the second folks from out of town who have stopped by here asking about them to wish them well. And I also got a phone call about them."

Monkeyman briefly wondered who the other parties might be but quickly put it out of his mind. He had found out what he wanted to know. That the boat was unoccupied, and he now knew where the party was staying. He called Queisha Hamilton, introduced himself, and asked if he could visit with her. She told them when she'd be off. When he and Mighty Mouse arrived at her house, she offered them a Red Stripe.

"We're on a special mission for da President," Monkeyman explained. "The *Spirit of the Seas*, which is currently docked at the marina, is rightfully his, and he wants his property returned."

"So, what does that have to do with me?"

"He supported you in your time of need, and now it's time for you to repay the favor. Plus, some of the people who committed this injustice I'm told are people from your past."

"Who's that?"

"Colonel Winter, Mikey Mo Mullins, and Betsy Black."

Queisha's blood pressure began to rise as her mind began to flash back to a series of unpleasant events. A few years back, Queisha had gotten wanderlust and had moved to Lake Worth, Florida, where she became one of the hip-hop-rap group Top 6's resident bimbos and sex objects. By playing her cards smart and using her gangster Uncle Neville's influence, she had graduated from servicing the entire band to being their lead singer Dub Bootee's "personal assistant," making her his girl Friday and *very* personal hostess. Eventually, Dub affiliated himself with the Reverend LeRoy Cho-Arturo in Key West and became his second in command. Reverend LeRoy was not only a county commissioner but also the spiritual leader of the ashram, the United Spiritual Cathedral of the Redeeming Saints, and its offshoot, the Green Rainbow Ministries. They provided a very lucrative outlet for both marketing Shower Posse drugs and also laundering the posse's illegal profits.

Things had looked up for Queisha until Dub began to get bored with her and consider replacing her with a fresh assistant — that bitch, YoLanda Davis.

Her thoughts then reverted to Will and Betsy Black. Their meddling had eventually caused Reverend LeRoy to flee to avoid arrest and go into exile. Dub took over the ministry at that point, and with Uncle Neville's help, she became the organization's CFO and fund-raising chairman —until the Blacks once more intervened. When the end seemed inevitable, Queisha had escaped back to Jamaica and attempted the secure her future using a blackmailing scheme of her own design.

But that had not been the end of her involvement with the Blacks. They, with the help of Colonel Winter, had brought Dudus Coke's corruption scheme with the Highway 2000 building program down and helped jail many of his partners. The Teflon Don, Dudus, of course, avoided prosecution, but he was out millions of dollars and forced to rebuild his organization and operations.

The final act of this drama was when The Colonel and Mikey Mo had arranged for the murder of her uncle and her cousin, forcing Queisha with Dudus's assistance to move from her Browns Town hometown to Port Antonio and to have to take a conventional job at the Port Antonio Hospital.

Yes, I have an axe to grind. If these two only knew. Sure, it's important to repay Dudus what I owe him, but even more important for my self-respect, it gives me an opportunity to finally even the score.

"Why is this boat so important to the President? He can afford a fleet of boats if he wants them," Queisha asked when she finally got her mind back to the present. "Was he running drugs on it?"

"No. Keep in mind that we're only lowly posse soldiers, but I'll tell you what I've overheard if you give me your solemn word that this information will go no farther. If Harry Dog even suspects that we have loose lips, we'll all end up in a nameless cave in the Cockpit Country."

"You've got my word. But I'll tell you right now. I'm not getting involved in anything unless I know what I'm getting into."

"OK. Cash. Millions of dollars of posse unlaundered cash that The President's accountant, Weasley Lineitem, was supposed to invest and convert into untraceable gold bullion. It's all hidden somewhere on that boat. The pressure is on big-time. It was Harry Dog's fault that the boat and money were lost, and if he doesn't recover it, there's no telling what Dudus might do to him. That's why we've got to get our hands on that boat."

Larcenous thoughts began to enter Queisha's head. She was sick and tired of working at that damned hospital.

"Maybe if you steal it, we could just keep on going. We'd be set for life."

"Don't even think about it. Dudus would spare no expense to track us down. We'd be on the run for the rest of our lives — and that might not be long."

Monkeyman pulled the boat key out of his pocket, held it up, and dangled it in front of her.

"I've got the boat key. It's not occupied. The crew is staying at Trident. Harry Dog has arranged a place to hide the boat. What I need you to do is distract the harbormaster long enough for us to steal the damned thing. That's all you need to do. Your role should be simple. You've been enticing men for years. I'll make sure you get credit for your part of this operation, and I'll push Harry Dog to compensate you generously. After all, his ass *is* on the line."

"OK, let's do it. As my Uncle Neville used to say, 'No ketchie no habie' **(nothing ventured, nothing gained)**. Besides I need a little excitement and a chance to practice up on my man-power. Give me time to change. By the way, how am I supposed to get home again when this is over with?"

"No, problem, sexy mama. I'll give you the car keys when we get there. We can't just leave the car at the marina."

WE SPECIALIZE IN
BATHROOM   SPACE SAVER
HAMPERS   BIN
                    CUTTING
                    DRESSING

ALSO BUILDING OF HOUSEHOLD FURNITURE
UPHOLSTERING   CAR SEATS PLANE SEATS
FIX CAR LOCK WIND SCREEN RUBBER
    HAIR DRESSING DONE HERE

Chapter 33

When Queisha came out of the bedroom, she was dressed for the business at hand. She was wearing skintight, crotch-clinging, peg-leg, ankle-length mesh toreador style pants. They had alternating, see-through, black, yellow, green, and red stripes. Her top consisted of a bright yellow bikini bra that showed plenty of cleavage. The outfit left little to the imagination. Her purse had her usual ganja paraphernalia. She never went anywhere, even to work, without it. After all, you never knew when a girl was going to need a toke.

Monkeyman whistled.

"Mighty Mouse, give me your phone so I can call the cops. It's got to be illegal for this gal to look that good."

Queisha smiled. That was just the reaction she was hoping for.

They drove to the marina.

"You stay in the car," Queisha instructed them. "Give me a little time with the harbormaster alone. I'll signal you when I think it's safe for you head down to the boat."

She then did her sexiest strut down the pier and into the ship's store. Her attitude sent the message that she thought she was God's gift to men.

"Mi looking fo a handsome hunk a man to help me," she said as she leaned forward to give him a good peek down her cleavage. "Can yu take care of mi needs?"

"Empress, as gud as yu look good enuh, a mi only fe tek care a dah body deh enuh (**Empress, as good as you look, I'm the only one who should be taking care of your body.**). Ding Dong at yu service."

"Mehbe. Wi see. If yu da man yu look ta be, mehbe afta mi get to know yu, mehbe we play carpenter. Mehbe we'll get hammered, and mehbe mi let yu nail mi. Just call mi Clapper because mehbe, if yu lucky, mi gonna ding yu dong."

"Das a lotta mehbes. And mehbe mi wud climb a makka (**thorn**) tree naked fi yah (**to be with you**)."

"Or mehbe wi play UPS instead, and mehbe yu let mi handle yu package."

"And mehbe mi do a 68 which means mi go down on yu and den yu owe mi one."

"Yah! Rose are red. Violets are fine. Mi be yu six, and yu be my nine."

Queisha lit a reefer and offered him a puff. Soon the party was on.

When Queisha thought the time was right, she flipped her roach butt out of the open window and signaled her accomplices that it was time for them to make their move. They looked around, and when they saw no one milling about on the dock, they began to work their way down to the boat. When they got to the ship's store, they tried to crab-walk on all fours until they were past it. This worked great for the short Mighty Mouse but wasn't as easy for the taller Monkeyman. Just as they almost got by, Monkeyman caught his hand on a nail sticking up out of a warped board. He inadvertently uttered a cry of pain. Mighty Mouse clamped his hand over his partner's mouth, but their cover was blown.

Ding Dong tried to go to the window to find out the source of the noise, but Queisha tried to pull him back down. Instead, he staggered to the door just in time to see Monkeyman and Mighty Mouse right themselves. He grabbed his pistol out of his desk drawer, and yelled, "Hey, yu two. What yu doing here?"

He got off one shot, but it went into the air since Queisha was trying to wrestle the gun away from him. He pushed her away, ran back into the building, and called the police.

The two unlucky hoodlums righted themselves and began to run down the dock towards the boat. Monkeyman jumped on the boat and tried to get both the key and dead man's switch both into the ignition, all the while yelling for Mighty Mouse to untie the boat. The engine cranked. He yelled for Mighty Mouse to get on board.

In his fright and haste, Mighty Mouse forgot to untie the last stern line. Monkeyman jammed the gear lever into forward, but being a novice boatman who was panicking anyway, he shoved the lever too far into forward. The boat responded and leaped ahead before Mighty Mouse could get onboard. The powerful engine ripped the cleat and the old, weak boards around it out of the dock. Mighty Mouse leaped to get aboard, but being as short as he was, the jump was too far for him. In desperation, he grabbed the stern line, and the boat dragged him as well as the pieces of the dock behind it. He let out a gurgled scream as his mouth filled with water.

Monkeyman looked back at his struggling partner wondering what he should do, taking his eyes off of where he was going. When he looked forward again, he was headed straight for an incoming boat. Both boats veered to avoid collision, and the boatowner's wife and Labrador retriever were thrown overboard. The captain began to scream curse words at him.

About this time, Mighty Mouse lost his handhold on the rope. His momentum propelled him straight into the dog. He hung onto the dog for dear life. The drowning Lab began to snap, and he bit Mighty Mouse's arm and held on to it. He managed to shake the dog loose and then grabbed on the next closest thing, the dog's owner. The wild woman began to knee him and claw his face.

At this moment, Mighty Mouse saw something that terrified him more than the furious woman — a fin was swimming towards him in the water. He hyperventilated and yelled, "Shark!" in terror at the lazily approaching barracuda. When the barracuda saw the confusion, it turned and swam in the other direction. By this time, the boat owner had turned around and returned to rescue his dog and wife. He whacked Mighty Mouse over the head with his paddle before reaching out with it so his wife could grab hold to it.

While all this had been occurring, Monkeyman tried to guide the boat while he simultaneously tried to cut the rope dragging the debris with his pocketknife. It accelerated and veered off course. When he finally severed the line, the rope bounced back and gave his Adam's apple a painful blow before wrapping itself around his neck. As he staggered back towards the helm, the veering boat made him lose his balance. He grabbed for the steering wheel to right the boat but turned it in the wrong direction and whacked the windshield. As he staggered, he momentarily blacked out. When he regained his senses, he turned the boat towards the shore. When he got back into shallow water, he cut the engine, finally bringing the *Spirit of the Seas* to a halt. He half jumped and half staggered into the water somehow managing to get back on the bank. He felt for the the key and the dead man's switch, but it had been lost in the uproar. He disappeared into some nearby trees.

The police and an ambulance arrived at the marina about this time. Ding Dong drove them out into the harbor where they successfully rescued all the participants in the fiasco. Mighty Mouse was detained, loaded into the ambulance, and sent to the hospital first to have his injuries examined and if necessary treated.

By some miracle, the *Spirit of the Seas* was about the only thing uninjured.

In the confusion, Queisha disappeared, and since she had been using an alias, remained unidentified. Even if he had had her real name, Ding Dong would never have admitted that he and a girl named Clapper had been partying on company property on company time. When she got back to the car, she found Monkeyman hiding in the back seat.

When they got back to Queisha's house, Monkeyman insisted that she go to the hospital and assess how he might get his partner out of there. Queisha resisted at first, but Monkeyman convinced her that if she wanted to continue to maintain the Shower Posse's good will, it was necessary. She never knew when she might need their support in the future.

Plus, he added, she knew the hospital inside and out from working there. As he reminded her, "De new broom might sweep clean, but de ole broom know ebery corner."

D DOUGLAS

ELECTRICAL SERVICE DONE HERE
REPAIR AND DUCKTERING
REFRIDGERATOR
GASSTOVE POLISHER
ELECTRICAL IRON
WASHING MACHINE
STOVES ETC.

Chapter 34

The ambulance took Mighty Mouse to the Port Antonio Hospital. He was given a mild sedative along the way. Mighty Mouse played along, pretending to be in worse shape than he really was. He was checked into a room and given a hospital gown. He was also given another medication that made him feel somewhat drowsy, and he nodded off.

Queisha arrived for the beginning of her regular shift several hours later. She immediately checked and found out which room Mighty Mouse was in. When the coast was clear, she took a clipboard with an order for an MRI and a paper cup with a placebo of Tylenol and walked into his room. Mighty Mouse was napping, but she woke him enough to talk to him. She told him that Monkeyman had successfully escaped capture and was hiding at her house.

"Does Johnny Law know who he is?"

"I don't think so."

"Yu gotta get mi outta here so wi can get out of this parish. Dey will tek me ta jail from here, and mi'll really be screwed."

She held up the clipboard and said, "I know. Which could mean, honey bun, that I'm screwed as well if somehow you lead them back to me. I can't take that chance. So, here's my plan. I'm going to take you down to second floor for an MRI. I've got an order right here. You will have to figure a way to escape from there."

"How'd yu get da docta to gib yu da order?"

"Oh, he doesn't know he did. I made this order up myself. Now I'm going to wheel you in a wheelchair down to the lab. There shouldn't be anyone in there this time of day. After that, it's up to you. It's not a perfect plan, but it's the best I can do under the circumstances."

They rode the elevator down to second floor, and she left him there. He waited until he thought the coast was clear and sneaked down the hall. He heard someone coming from the other direction but was too far away from the lab by now to make it back. He ducked down another perpendicular hall. When he peeked around the corner, he saw that it was a security guard. A vacant hospital transport stretcher with a sheet on it had been left in the side hallway. He jumped on it and covered himself with the sheet.

As soon as he thought the coast was clear again, he tried to get back up with the sheet still on him, but both his equilibrium and his sense of direction were off. He shook his head to try to clear it and briefly wondered just what the medication was that they had given him back in his room. As he tried to get back off the transport stretcher on the wrong side with the sheet still covering him, he blindly kneed the wall.

"Damn that hurt like rhaatid (**hell**)!"

The pain caused him to reach for his throbbing knee and blindly bend forward. When he did, he headbutted the wall.

"Mighty Mouse, yu stakki mengkeh (**you lunatic idiot**)!"

The transporter rolled out from under him. He twisted around trying to catch it, but instead he hit the floor wrenching his back.

"Kiss mi rass, fassyhole!"

He kicked the transporter in retribution, stubbing his toe in the process. It bounced back and bounced off his tibia. Now his toe hurt, as well as his knee, his head, his ankle, and his lower back. And as if this wasn't bad enough, his nose was bleeding, and he had bit his tongue. Total frustration now took hold, and he let loose a garbled string of words containing almost every four-letter word in his vocabulary.

A male orderly heard all the racket and peeked around the corner to investigate. He saw a sheeted figure, cursing for everything he was worth. Mighty Mouse attempted to stand. As short as he was, the sheet continued to cover him completely and gave the illusion that it was magically floating up from the floor. Mighty Mouse's bloody nose and the blood from his bit tongue began to seep through the sheet, and he yelled "bloodclaat!" as he blindly limped towards the orderly.

The orderly screamed "DUPPY! DON'T GET ME!" and ran in the opposite direction down the hall. Mighty Mouse stumbled hard into the transporter and tried to use it to right himself.

It shot out from under him and began to roll after the desperately fleeing orderly.

"Baamborasspussyholeclaat!"

The rolling transporter convinced the orderly for sure that the duppy was chasing after him. It seemed to be following him.

"Bongopushdigrasskvaat!"

He stumbled into a mop bucket that had been left in the hall by a lazy janitor. He grabbed the mop and tried use it as a weapon to hold off the rabid, bleeding duppy that just kept on coming after him. Just as he got to the stairwell, he wildly swiped the mop back and forth, accidentally whacking the mop bucket sending soapy water everywhere. He fled again, jumping into a utility closet, and slamming the door on himself. The still blind Mighty Mouse hit the slippery, soapy water and slid into the stairwell door and jerked it open, banging his knee once again.

"Batty hole!"

More soapy water caused him to pitch forward.

"But a wah di rass (what the fuck)!

Before he could catch himself, he went careening down the stairs to first floor taking the mop bucket with him.

Mighty Mouse finally shook off the sheet and stumbled outside through the exterior fire door where he saw an unchained bicycle leaning against a tree. Despite everything on his body screaming pain, he managed to mount the bike and begin to wobble down the street on it. At that moment the bike's owner returned. He took up the chase.

Mighty Mouse's hospital gown was streaming and kept getting tangled in the bike's spokes. The hospital gown finally ripped, and Mighty Mouse found himself riding completely naked. With every bump, the bruised ankle and his testicles felt like they were being hit by a train, dragged down the track, and then thrown into an erupting volcano.

The rabid owner screamed, "Thief! Thief!" Mighty Mouse pedaled harder and rounded a corner. He looked back to see if the bike's owner was still chasing him. When he looked forward again, the dazed, naked, sawed-off, snake-bit degradant plowed into a fish monger selling his wares. He flattened both himself and the fish monger. Now he found himself covered with smelly fish and fish water. The furious fish monger jumped up and swiped at him with his fillet knife.

A street cop witnessed the incident. Despite all his years on the force, he had never seen a naked man riding a bike plow into a merchant before. He approached Mighty Mouse intending to make an arrest for something, debating with himself what the charge would be. His dilemma was simplified when Mighty Mouse abandoned the bike and picked up a slimy fish. He whacked the cop and took off running with both the fish monger and the cop chasing him.

As he cut through the straw market and zigzagged through the maze of stalls, he grabbed the first piece of clothing that he could reach. It turned out to be a sundress.

He then hid in a nearby alley. Once he was sure that he had lost his pursuers, wearing the stolen sundress, he approached a shocked ganja-dazed Rasta stranger and begged to borrow his cell phone to call Monkeyman to come pick him up.

On the surface Mighty Mouse's apparel didn't seem to immediately faze the stoned Rasta in the least. Only later, when he had reassembled the mental picture, did the scene's impact sink in. That was when the zonked-out Rasta finally commented to one of his friends, "Mon, earlier today mi met da ugliest, mowly (**smelliest**) batty gal (**dyke**) in da country or da most repulsive buggaman (**sissy**). Mi still not sure which."

As they rode over to Queisha's house, Monkeyman asked his partner, "Are you OK, my friend? Want a spliff?"

"No, mon. We need to talk about this with a clear head. I'm not OK, and admit it, neither are you. Recovering that boat's a losing proposition. It's haunted. I almost went to jail back there, or worse yet, I could've gotten killed. And admit it, mi brudda, you did too."

"You're just frustrated because we've just had a run of bad luck. Tired feet always say that the path is long. You'll feel better tomorrow."

"No, mon. You're wrong. This deck has been stacked against us at every move. And any element of surprise we once had is gone. Plantain ripe, can't green again."

"So, what are you suggesting?"

"That we cut our losses and disappear."

"You don't just run out on Dudus Coke and Harry Dog. You talk about dying? That's the best way I know to get killed."

"Is Dudus going to get us out of prison or even come to our funeral? It's time we took control. Time we run t'ings and t'ings no run we."

"But da posse all wi only family."

"Want all, lose all. So, we find new family. I know some people with the Spangler Posse."

"Let's give this more thought. After all, too much hurry and get there tomorrow. Tek time, get there today."

"Don't say anything around Queisha. She can't help us , only hurt us. She still has future debts to pay to square her account with Dudus. The hungry belly and the full belly do not walk the same road."

```
╔══════════════════════════════════════╗
║          XXX  NOTICE  XXX            ║
║      I.K. LEWIS, YOUR DENTIST       ║
║   WILL BE HERE FROM THURSDAY EVERY  ║
║     TWO WEEKS AT ALVIN BARNES       ║
║    HOUS IN SEVEN CORNERS, IS        ║
║   EXTRANT COOL OF ICE AND NICE      ║
╚══════════════════════════════════════╝
```

Chapter 35

By the time Monkeyman got Mighty Mouse to Queisha's house, he was totally exhausted from his ordeal. His head hurt. His knees hurt. His toe hurt. His ankle hurt. His tongue felt so swollen, he wondered if it would ever be normal again. He wondered if his nose was broken. And he was walking bowlegged since his bruised scrotum still hurt from bouncing naked on the hard bicycle seat. Overall, he felt like Lucifer had taken over his soul, cut it to pieces, burned it, and put it back in his body.

But miraculously I escaped from the rhatid hospital.

Queisha laughed when she saw Mighty Mouse's sundress.

"I told you that you had to devise your own plan, but I certainly didn't expect this. To disguise yourself as a clown's man (**loose woman**) or a sodomite (**transvestite**)? Instead, you look like a senseh fowl (**plucked chicken**)."

Mighty Mouse answered with his third finger.

'What's that? Your age, IQ, or your batting average? Cat got your tongue mighty midget?"

He tried to speak, but when it came out garbled, he just flashed his third finger again.

"And smell! Dead people smell betta than you do. What'd you do, swim outta the hospital through their gutter? Go take a bath, before I throw up. After that, mama's got a recipe that's guaranteed to make you feel better."

"I could use a pick-me-up too," Monkeyman said.

"I'll take care of you as well. Now, Mighty Mouse, go take that bath and get the stink off your body. And for God's sake, don't put that dress back on. It's not your color or your bra size. But if this is going to be your new look, at least shave your legs and underarms. If Dudus and your posse brothers could only see their brave soldier now! I laugh just thinking how they'd point and call out. I can hear it now. 'Yu fish dat' **(you're a gay boy)**."

All she got in return was another third finger salute.

Queisha got busy making their cocktails. She mixed bananas, citrus juice, pineapple juice, along with whatever other kinds of fruit she currently had in the kitchen in the blender with some 151 proof Wray & Nephew rum. Her secret ingredient that only she knew about was a healthy portion of LSD as well. She sampled a drink while she was waiting for him to clean up and nodded her approval.

Ambrosia! Nectar of the Gods! This'll get these boys right with the world again. Won't hurt me none neither.

Queisha's house was unairconditioned. After his shower, Mighty Mouse returned wearing only a pair of shorts and plopped down in front of a floor fan to stay cool. A pitcher full of Queisha's icy-cold concoction and some Tervis tumblers were already on the table waiting for their early happy hour.

"And now, have some of Queisha's sought-after recipe for fruit punch. Drink up, boys."

She poured a glassful for each of them.

"Biba **(Cheers)**."

"Anoder day, anoder bender. No retreat, no surrender."

"Down the hatch!"

"Oh, mama. Dis gooder dan good."

"Have as many as you want. And if we run out, mama'll fix another batch."

Within minutes, both thugs dozed off until Monkeyman was awakened by singing. Queisha was in the kitchen barefoot and topless, clad only in her panties, merrily drinking, chopping vegetables, and singing "I Can See Clearly Now" and "Wild World." But instead of singing one song and then the other, she was mixing the lyrics. A forgotten spliff was burning in an ashtray. She paused occasionally to drink more fruit punch.

I can see clearly now all obstacles in my way.
Since baby, baby it's a wild world. Gone are the clouds that had me blind.
Because it's breaking my heart that you're leaving because baby, I'm grieving.
But it's going to be a light bright sunshiny day.
Because I can make it now since the pain is gone
Since baby, oh, baby, it's a wild world and it's breaking my heart in two.

She was dancing in place as she chopped onions and peppers. She tapped rhythm with her butcher knife on two glass bowls she had set out on the counter. They were both overflowing with cut vegetables since she didn't seem to know when to quit since there were still a few of both remaining in their original mesh produce bags. Other peppers and onions littered the counter, and some had begun to fall on the floor. She trampled these, unaware that they were there. When she tried to play a drum solo on one bowl with the knife, it broke, sending glass and onions cascading to the floor. She didn't seem to notice until she stepped on a shard of glass and her foot began to bleed. She then stripped off her panties and used them to wrap her bleeding foot and began to rap to one of Dub Bootee's old numbers.

I really had to bleed so I shot my mother's dog.
Shot the bitch in the head, she bled like a hog.
And now there's blood in the subway, Blood in the underground.

The exhausted Mighty Mouse continued to sleep.

Suddenly Monkeyman's own LSD trip kicked into gear. The blood on Queisha's foot suddenly turned into cotton candy just as the sun came out from behind a cloud and sunlight streamed in through the open doorway. The *Spirit of the Seas* appeared, floating on the sea of cotton candy. A hazy woman's figure stood on the bow and beckoned to him. She began to sing.

227

Oh Cee Cee, Cee Cee rider. See what you have done.
I said Cee Cee rider. Oh, see what you have done.

The hazy figure became clearer. It seemed to be Cee Cee Craig.

"I dare you to come and try to get this boat," she taunted. "If you can, you have a future with the Shower Posse. If not — then I guess shit happens — you're just another shitty loser."

The room was suddenly flooded with a kaleidoscope of bright colors. Monkeyman rubbed his dilated eyes, took another big chugalug on his rum drink, emptied his glass, and then refilled it.

Jeezah! Kiss mi neck back! This is good, good shit!

He looked again for Cee Cee, but she had vanished in the light.

Queisha picked up a handful of onions and peppers and threw them into the air. They transformed themselves into a cascade of multicolored gems and began to float back down. They turned back into chocolate boats as they hit the floor. Queisha's dog, Rapper, leaped on them as they bounced thinking they were food for him, but their engines cranked, and they outran him. They ran head-on into each other and merged into a chocolate mound that began to take the shape of a beautiful nude Cee Cee with a gold-braided captain's hat that said *Spirit of the Seas.*

She beckoned to him and called out, "Take me if you dare. I'm yours for the taking."

A housefly flew in through the open doorway and buzzed around Queisha's head. She began to swing the butcher knife drunkenly at it. The peppers on the floor suddenly turned into more flies. These flies became three grasshoppers, each having a different human face, the faces of Dudus Coke, Harry Dog, and Hi-top. Antennae began to grow out of their heads, and their toothy mouths began masticating and dripping saliva as they attacked snakeheads that began writhing out of the almost empty onion and pepper bags.

"This will be your fate if you fail," they announced in unison.

Queisha stepped back and began to wave the butcher knife at them as if it were a musical baton and she was conducting an orchestra. Then she began to use the knife to play an air guitar.

A Nautical Conspiracy

The grasshoppers began to follow her lead and sing a Jerry Butler song in harmony.

Take it for what it's worth. You can't hide.
Go to the end of the earth. You can't hide.
You can run, run, run, but you can't hide from love.
Try to leave it behind. You can't hide.

Monkeyman's heart began to race as paranoia set in and took hold of him. The snakes now began to hiss and rap repeatedly.

"Sink the bakra's boat, Jack. Make sure it never comes back, Mac. If you fail, you go to jail. And I'll walk on your grave, slave. Cause you're my cow. I own you now."

Queisha's dog Rapper came over and began to lick him. But his tongue seemed to turn to sandpaper as his head grew and became a timber wolf before morphing once again into a scaly, fire breathing dragon. The dragon tried to jump up on him to play. Its licking tongue became a fiery one that seemed like it was trying to singe Monkeyman as the dragon sang an Arthur Brown song.

I am the god of hellfire and I bring you.
Fire. I'll take you to burn.
Fire. I'll take you to learn.
I'll see you burn.

The face on the dragon began to melt into the image of Cee Cee again. Her flaming lips began to sing a newly penned version of a Simon and Garfunkel tune.

I'm Cee Cee 'Celia, I'll break your ass.
Unless you get me, I'll shake your confidence daily.
I'm Cee Cee Cecilia. Come and get me please.
They'll beg for me to please come on home.
Hey, hey, hey, hey.

The dragon returned and began to sing again.

… unless you'd rather burn, burn, burn in the fire, fire, fire.

It let go with a blast of yellow and orange flame that smelled like burning, rotten eggs.

Monkeyman had had all he could stand. He picked up a kitchen chair, threw it through the kitchen window and dived out headfirst behind it. He grabbed Queisha's moped and drove it into her bougainvillea where he collapsed. A scratched Monkeyman woke five hours later still trembling from the experience but convinced that God had shown him the answer.

Through it all, Mighty Mouse continued to sleep.

When Mighty Mouse finally did wake up, Monkeyman told him that he had had a message from God with a mandate for the two of them. The spirits had ordained that they should see this job through. Anything less would be a blasphemy to all celestial beings and would draw their wrath. God had not only willed it to be so but had also told him how to accomplish it.

"We've been going about this all wrong. We shouldn't be trying to steal a four-ton boat. We've already seen that that plan hasn't worked. What we should do is steal a hundred-and twenty-five-pound woman. And then we can trade her for the boat. Dudus and Harry Dog will be happy because we recovered their boat, and then we can stay in the Shower Posse where we belong. Agreed?"

"OK? I guess. If you say so."

"And since God almighty has given us the answer, we had better not doubt his wisdom, or we're sure to get his lightning bolts in return. Right now, more than ever, we need God on our side. As mi granny used to say, "Nuh dash wey yuh tick before yuh dun crass riva (**Don't throw away your stick until you cross the river**)."

Mighty Mouse wasn't convinced, but he went along anyway.

He reminded his partner though, "Yu not the only one with a wise granny. Yu know what mi granny used to say? "Ef yuh get your han inna devil mout, tek eeh out (**If you put your hand in the devil's mouth, take it out**)."

Chapter 36

Port Antonio police detectives drove over to Trident and notified DV that someone had tried to steal his boat. They said that they needed to investigate the attempted burglary and to file some paperwork before the boat would be free to leave. Both events would not be completed until later that afternoon. By then DV reasoned that it would be too late for the *Spirit of the Seas* to depart, so he and his company would need to spend another night at Trident. DV called everyone together to give them this latest development.

"Well, guys and gals, I have some good news and some bad news. Bad news is someone tried to steal our boat. The good news is we'll be forced to spend another night in this posh, five-star resort while the police investigate the crime and get their paperwork in order."

"Someone tried to steal the boat?" Betsy said.

"Yep, while we were out on the Rio Grande. But their own ineptness foiled their plan."

DV gave them a brief description of what he understood the events to be concerning the attempted robbery. He concluded saying, "But continuing my good news bad news analogy, as I understand it, by some miracle, our boat was unharmed. But the bad news is that the culprits escaped, and since there were other damaged properties, not only is law enforcement involved but insurance adjusters as well."

"All this ineptness is reminding me of the story about a guy — we'll call him Clumsy Clem — who dropped his knife and cut off his toe," Will said. "A surgeon was engaged to surgically reattach it. After the operation, the doctor told him he had some good news as well as some bad news. He told Clem that the surgery was successful, but that the surgery team mistook his toe for a piece of candy and now he had a ... Tic-Tac toe."

"Oh, please, dear," Betsy said. "I think with Clem's toe woe, you've hit a new low."

"I thought that joke was a real toe-tapper, but since you didn't, I'll get back to the topic at hand, I thought we engaged *our* adversaries on the river."

"Apparently they weren't our only adversaries," Rose pointed out.

"Does everyone in Jamaica suddenly hate us?" Betsy asked.

"My dear, with our past with Colonel Winter in this country, I would have to say that it's not sudden. This boil has been festering for a while. And that boil is most likely Dudus Coke."

"Was one thief tall and one short?" Henry asked.

"Uh-huh."

"That's exactly who it is then," Henry said. "We're back on Dudus's, excuse me, ladies, dung docket. ...."

"Don't you mean excrement enumeration?"

"Just say it, shit list."

"Ahem! As I was trying to say, only time will provide the answer as to how long this poo purgatory with the police will last. ...."

He paused and waited for the next wisecrack. When it didn't come, he continued.

"My friends, as long as we're stuck here, may I suggest something that might be more fun than just hanging out at Trident today? Why don't we go to Boston Bay? It's only nine miles away."

"What's Boston Bay?' Cee Cee asked.

"Only the birthplace of jerk," Rose said. "Do you want me to tell you more?"

"I'm all ears," Cee Cee said.

"No comment," DV replied and nudged her in the ribs.

"Let's start this story at the beginning, and that beginning is 1655. That's when the British ran the Spanish out of Jamaica and over to Cuba. The Spanish were forced to leave their slaves behind. Some became freedmen; others became British slaves. The disorganized freedmen and the escaped slaves were all dirt poor. They began to live in small villages high in the Blue Mountains with what was little more than a subsistence farming existence. They became known as the Maroons. Their only way to get most of their much-needed supplies to raid British sugar plantations."

"That couldn't have made the British too happy," Cee Cee said.

"You're right. Especially since the slaves the British still owned helped them do it ..."

"And sometimes defected and joined them," Henry threw in.

"Not a good situation. It escalated into a guerilla war with the British fighting back. While the supplies the Maroons got from the raids helped keep them going, they still needed food. So, they began to hunt the wild hogs that were so abundant in the hills. But they needed to find a way to prepare the pork in such a way that their fires didn't lead the British to their encampments.

"The solution was to butcher and debone the hogs, score the meat, and then fill it with salt and sometimes wild bird peppers. Then usually they'd leave it in the sun to cure, but if they were feeling safe, they might use a low-smoke, covered fire to process it. Eventually Scotch bonnet peppers and allspice replaced bird peppers in their recipe. They called this 'jirking,' spelled with an 'i' instead of an 'e.' No one's quite sure how it evolved into being spelled with an 'e' instead."

"I guess it was kind of like Cayo Hueso evolved into being Key West. In Key West's case, they say it was because the Anglos couldn't pronounce Spanish and therefore bastardized the word," Will said.

"And like ragga became reggae," Betsy added.

"Good comparisons," Henry said. "But let me jerk this conversation back around to jerk pork ..."

Eyes rolled, and Rose said, "I think I'll lock you in a room with Will and see who sprouts into corn first."

"This process was not only simple, but it left nothing to waste, and it was discreet. It served its purpose well. The Maroons' finished product probably tasted sort of like what we now call jerky," Henry said. "They claim it was pretty tasty."

"I wonder if the word jerky is derived from jerk or vice versa."

"Don't know, but it's a thought. By the late seventeenth century, the British found themselves increasingly on their back foot. They needed more slaves to work on the ever-growing sugar plantations, so they imported more African slaves. A lot of these were from the highly warlike Ashanti tribes of Ghana. These were not subservient peoples and were soon in rebellion. They joined the Maroons and brought organization to their society. Before long, the only part of the country that the British were able to be in firm control of was a narrow strip along the coast. The interior belonged to the Maroons."

"This is getting good," DV commented. Cee Cee nodded.

"So, in 1728 the British brought in more troops and struck back. This is what we Jamaicans call the First Maroon War. They planned to separate the strongest Maroon faction, the Windward Maroons, from the weaker group, the Leeward Maroons, and then conquer the Windward faction."

"Divide and conquer. That strategy goes all the way back to Julius Caesar," Will said.

"But in this case, it didn't work. Because the Windwards were led by a remarkable Ashanti woman who called herself 'Nanny,' while the Leewards were led by her brother Cudjoe. By 1739 the British were exhausted, and Nanny and Cudjoe forced them to a stalemate, which we now call today the Kindah Treaty. The British were forced to recognize the Maroons as an autonomous nation. The Maroons agreed in return to fight for the British if ever called upon to do so and to return runaway slaves. The societal issues this led to eventually resulted in the second Maroon War, but I'll save that story for another day."

"Fascinating."

"But the point of my digression, is that after the Kindah Treaty, the Maroons were able to come out in the open, and selling jerk became one of their major sources of income. At first, they would cook the meat up in the hills and then take into the towns to sell it. But the demand for the meat by the mid-nineteenth century became so strong that they began to move to the coast to cook it and sell it there. One of the first places they moved was Boston Bay. The dish became less of a Maroon preserve and almost a national dish. Even the British army began cooking it. And of course, chefs began tinkering with the original recipe, now using ingredients like onion, scallion, ginger, wild cinnamon, nutmeg, and thyme."

"And so that's why we'll take you to Boston Bay today," Betsy said. "Change into our bathing suits before we leave since we'll be dining at Boston Bay Beach."

"Then, by golly," DV said. "Let's do it to it."

Since Henry was a commercial driver and member of JUTA, Mr. Levy let him drive one of the hotel vans in lieu of sending his driver to escort them. A half hour later they arrived at the Boston Jerk Centre. Mighty Mouse and Monkeyman, who were already high that morning from smoking ganja, followed them there.

The Jerk Centre was not what the Craigs expected it to be. It wasn't one building but a series of seven open air rustic stalls, each in a different building that flanked the unpaved road that ran through the middle of this "food court." The buildings were painted bright yellow with a royal blue trim. They were completely open from about the waist level up. The roofs were mostly well-seasoned galvanized tin, but some roofs were partially covered with rough logs or planks as well. As they drove up, they could hear canned dancehall reggae music being played on outdoor speakers by the resident DJ, D.J. Sheppy. Venders yelled, "Hot and ready, taste and buy."

Henry parked the car, and they got out.

"Here's the plan. As you can see, this is not one restaurant, but a series of independent vendors competing against each other. As you can imagine, some are better cooks than others. Two of them, Ivy's and Shaggy's, are among the oldest jerk shops in the entire world but don't feel obligated to buy from them. It is customary for prospective customers to ask the cook for a taste before they buy. The menus vary from one shop to another. I don't guess I have to tell you that lobster is the highest priced food on anyone's menu. The side dishes will vary from one shop to another. Peas and rice and festivals are probably the most popular, and pork is the biggest selling entrée."

"What's a festival?" Cee Cee asked.

"A deep-fried dough stick sort of like what we call bammy. You'd like them," Rose said. "The breadfruit … I'm not so sure if you're ready for that yet. … It's kind of a cultivated taste."

"The ambiance is not what this place is noted for. We'll get our food to go, and I'll drive you to the public beach near here to dine. Any questions? Don't think you have to stay with the group. Just wander on your own, explore, and enjoy. And don't think you have to buy from the first vendor you meet. Sample his wares. He expects you to do that. And feel free to drink a Red Stripe or two as you roam. The Gold Teeth Bar over there, should have some good cold brews. I'm going to buy us some rum punch to go with our meal. They make it fresh and then rebottle it by the handle in the used Wray and Nephew bottles."

"What's a handle?" Cee Cee asked.

"One and three quarters milliliters, the metric version of a fifth of booze."

They began to walk around. The food was being cooked over open fires and hot smoldering pimento coals. The cooking grill consisted of rough-cut, green, pimento limbs. The meat was sometimes covered with corrugated tin but more often was covered by rough-sawn planks that were black from long use. All the scents mingled with the smoke, making everyone's stomach rumble with expectation despite the not-so-appetite-inducing sights and smells of meats of varying types being openly butchered in one part of each stall. Flies swarmed in the butchering areas and around the fifty-five-gallon drums containing the resulting renderings.

Monkeyman and Mighty Mouse parked their car as close as possible and, when they felt safe, began to track the Craigs as DV and Cee Cee drank a cold beer and roamed aimlessly from one building to the next. The hapless thugs waited for an opportunity to strike. Their half-baked plan was to try to catch Cee Cee alone, chloroform or subdue her, and deposit her back in their car. Then they would either force her to sign a bill of sale or trade her for the *Spirit of the Seas*.

"Hi-top and Harry Dog are sure to applaud our ingenuity and resourcefulness and tell Dudus how lucky he is to have soldiers like us."

"Ya, mon. If you say so."

When DV spotted a restroom after a couple of beers and told his wife he needed to use it, they sensed that their opportunity was at hand.

Monkeyman tried to sneak up on Cee Cee from one direction as she waited. Mighty Mouse approached her from the other direction. As Monkeyman tried to douse his handkerchief with chloroform and stick it in her face, her skills as a self-defense instructor came alive. Her immediate thought was that he was a purse snatcher.

As he approached holding the rag in one hand and the bottle in the other, she caught him in the gut with a spinning back kick. He dropped the rag, and the bottle launched from his hand. Mighty Mouse charged low, head-down, only to be greeted with a knee to the head. The bottle splattered on his face. He began to wobble and see double. Cee Cee then caught him on his jaw with a sweeping roundhouse punch as he stumbled by, sending him careering into a drum of pork renderings. She grabbed Monkeyman by his dreads and slug him in the same direction.

The barrel overturned, and both thugs found themselves swimming in a sea of blood, pork and chicken fat, organs, fish carcasses, and bones. A profusion of bluebottle and fruit flies, roaches, biting midges, and ants immediately appeared and covered the two unfortunate miscreants. Both tried to rise while swatting the invasion of biting insects, only continue to slip back down again into the stinking mire. A rat ran up Monkeyman's pants leg. He began to flip and flop and beat on himself in the pool of renderings as he tried to shake it out of there. It finally surrendered and took refuge up Mighty Mouse's pants leg. He then began to flail and gouge like an out-of-control dancer. When the rat finally reappeared, he pulled his now slimy pistol out of his pants and tried to shoot it, barely missing his own leg.

An employee of a nearby stall heard the shot and came running out with a meat cleaver in his hand. Mighty Mouse and Monkeyman both attempted to rise but slid down several times before they could get their footing. Monkeyman pulled over a second barrel of offal in the process of trying right himself, and they found themselves swimming in a second pool of guts and intestines. They took off slipping and crawling on all fours until they hit solid ground again, at which time they finally were able to stand and sprint for their car trailing pork, chicken, and fish offal behind them. By the time they reached the car, the cleaver-carrying cook and a black cloud of biting flies were only steps behind. He heaved the cleaver. It whizzed by Mighty Mouse's head and embedded itself in the car door.

Monkeyman managed to open the driver's side door, offal dripping from his hair, and hit the ignition button to crank the car. Mighty Mouse dived in headfirst through the open passenger side window. Within seconds, they took off down the road with Mighty Mouse's flailing legs still sticking out of the window. Monkeyman grabbed his shirt and tried to drag him in the rest of the way with Mighty Mouse getting purchase on the deeply imbedded meat cleaver. One last push on the cleaver sent him careening headfirst into the driver almost making Monkeyman lose control of the car and run into a ditch before he could stabilize the weaving car.

"Nobody told mi that dis girl was Bruce Lee's white sister," Mighty Mouse gasped. "Bet she could whup Mohammed Ali and George Foremen bof togeder. Mi jaw feels like somebuddy took a sledgehammer to it. It feels worse than da time I pulled my own tooth."

"Ya, mon. She sho' rumbled in mi jungle too. I think wi need to think wi plan out again."

"Mi tink yu right. And wi betta not say anything about dis to Hi-top and Harry Dog. If we do, you gonna be down here same height as me 'cause they'se gonna cut you off at the knees. We den be twins — Mighty Mouse and Mighty Short."

"Ya, mon. Yu right. Speaking of short, leh wi tek a short stop by da Breathe Ezzi Rum Bar and Car Wash. It'll be coming up on da right. I need a short shot or two, and mehbe wi pay dey to wash da car."

"Dey won't let us in smelling like we do."

"Den wi just get a bokkle of Wray and Nephew to go."

"Mek it two bokkles. Mi need mi own. Den, how 'bout wi go ta Frenchman's Cove. Wi can wash up there."

Monkeyman parked outside of Breathe Ezzi, and they walked in. A plethora of flies followed them. Within seconds the crowded bar emptied out.

"Get yu stinking bodies out of my shop."

"Wi just need to bokkles of rum ta go."

Monkeyman pulled out some smelly fat and blood-soaked bills from his pocket.

"I don't want yu money stinking up my place. Here, tek two bottles and go. Pay me later."

"Mi don guess you'd hab someone who would wash our car."

"Not only no, but hell no. Take yu stinking bodies and bottles and just leave. And tek those flies with you."

When they arrived at Frenchman's Cove, they saw that they had the place to themselves except for some teenage surfers. They took their bottles of rum and waded into the water. Within moments, the water around them turned from gin clear to murky, and flies began to amass. Monkeyman ducked under the water to cleanse his dreads. When he resurfaced, some roaches emerged along with some bloody pork and chicken livers. Within minutes they had Frenchman's Cove totally to themselves. It was if the surfers had just vanished.

"Yu know, mon. I've had enough of das covert roundabout shit plans."

"Wha yu mean, mi friend?"

"I mean that we just need go back ta being direct. Remember the good old days. When we wanted something, we would just draw our pistols, and tek it. Das wah we need to with da damned boat. Tek out our pistols and just tek da bloodclaayt ting. And if someone tries to stop us, we just shoot them. Like da old days. It's that simple. Da's what I mean."

"Mehbe yu right. Sometimes da old ways, da best ways."

"It worked den, and I don see wah it wanna work now."

After the action was over, DV emerged from the restroom and saw the mess on the ground.

"What happened here? Did I miss something?"

"Oh, not much, dear. I just had an encounter with a different kind of jerk than what we came here to buy. Two guys tried to steal my purse, but we were able to come to an understanding that was acceptable to everyone involved. They're gone now. It got a little messy for them, and they were in too big a hurry to leave to clean up after themselves. But it's over now. Let's get our lunch and go to the beach."

"This mess may have taken my appetite away."

"I'm sure it'll return by the time we get to the beach."

About that time the Davises and the Blacks rushed over.

"I saw your scrap from way over there," Will said. "You're pretty good with your feet, girl. Remind me to stay on your good side. What happened?"

"They tried to take my purse, but I stopped them. That's the first time I've ever had to use my self-defense training in a real fight. I'm glad to find out that the classroom drills work well in a real street confrontation."

I'm not so sure purse stealing was their primary objective, Henry thought to himself.

I think they may have had another motive, but right now I'm not sure just what that motive might've been.

He briefly excused himself from the rest of the group and called Mikey Mo to inform him of this latest incident and to express his opinions.

"Chicken, I know that you and Ferrin were hoping to get to the bottom of just what makes this damned boat so important to the Shower Posse, but despite what The Colonel thinks about alarming the innocent Craigs, I think it's time that we let our friends in on at least some of what's been going on. This has gone beyond just the boat, and the attacks are coming with increasing frequency. I firmly believe that Cee Cee Craig was in real physical danger today. This affair is escalating rapidly. And I didn't protect her today; she subdued her attackers all by herself. Most women couldn't have done that. Hell, most men couldn't have done that. You're endangering these people unnecessarily by keeping them in the dark. We've been damned lucky up until now."

"You're right. Let me brief The Colonel today. I'll be there tomorrow morning and hold a meeting with the whole group. It's time we quit being defensive and went on the offensive. Let me put some thoughts together. Don't let them leave until I get there."

MISS STEWART,
MODERN DRESS MAKER
FANTASRTIC STILES
TO FIT EVERY ONE. SHIRTS,
PYJAMAS, CHILDREN SUITS, ETC.
YOU ARE WELCOME

Chapter 37

When Mikey Mo arrived the following morning, everyone gathered in the sitting room of the suite occupied by the Davises and the Blacks. Mikey Mo had requested that the confidential meeting be held in a nonpublic place in the hotel.

"There has been a lot of unintended fallout going on behind the scenes since DV and Cee Cee bought the *Spirit of the Seas* and since you, Will, gave The Colonel the initial heads-up on what seemed to then be a possible impending situation.

"Will, we're so thankful you recognized it and reported it when you did. Colonel Winter and I, along with some help from Henry, have tried to insolate the group from some of the goings-on while we tried to understand the scenario ourselves and decide how best to protect you from harm as we both resolved to put an end to the threat. I now apologize for our secrecy since the matter continues to become more convoluted in lieu of less so and is no clearer than when we made our original decision.

"After yesterday's incident at Boston Bay that didn't just endanger the boat but could very well have endangered Cee Cee, Henry feels that it is time that we be frank about it. The Colonel and I discussed it yesterday and have concluded that Henry's right.

"I don't have to tell Will and Betsy about Dudus Coke and the Shower Posse, and how dangerous they can be. The Blacks have foiled

242

Dudus' plans on more than one occasion, as have The Colonel, the Davises, and I. Acting as a team, we have cost Dudus literally millions of dollars on multiple occasions and forced him to reorganize his staff and restock his portfolio of dirty politicos in his sphere of influence."

"What Mikey Mo is saying is very true. To be blunt, all of us are permanently on Dudus' shit list," Betsy said as she looked at DV and Cee Cee. "And apparently by buying this boat, I'm sorry to say, you're now on it as well."

Mikey Mo nodded his agreement and continued.

"The Colonel and I have tried to get to the bottom of why this boat is such a sore issue, but as of yet, we haven't figured it out. But we have, with Henry's help, protected you on more occasions than you can probably imagine."

"Like?" DV asked.

Mikey Mo looked at Henry and asked, "Should I tell them? It'll just worry them."

"Go on. They're adults. The purpose of this meeting is to be frank and open. They need to have a full grasp of the gravity of what we've been dealing with."

"OK. To begin with, there were three initial attempts at stealing the boat, one at the impound yard and two on the highway by two separate hijackers, while the boat was being trailered to Sy Sleaze's to be detailed. Si, Sly, and I managed to head them off.

"Then there was an attempt by a fake blind man to attack Henry at the Jubilee Market in Kingston while you, DV, were playing with Sly and Robbie and Ray Munnings. Henry queered that plan himself.

"Then there was the attempted break in at Big Boy's villa. I'm still not clear on why they did so or what went wrong there.

"After that, Henry broke up another threat that you didn't know was happening when you were taking supplies to the boat at the Port of Kingston."

"All this was going on right under our noses?" Cee Cee gasped. "I had no idea."

"Oh, I'm just beginning. With a homeless woman's paid assistance, Henry broke up another plan to harm you at Gloria's as well as still another one when you visited Sam de Sham's container shopping complex in Morant Bay. And the reggae singers you met, Sizzla and Turbulence, — they were in Dudus' pocket.

"We suspect that another failed attempt to take the boat happened while you were on the way to Bull Bay. Only dumb luck and the miscreants' ineptitude kept that from being successful."

"Tsk, tsk! Dudus has been a busy little bad boy, even outdoing himself lately … And that's saying a lot, even for Dudus," Will commented.

"Apparently under the direction of Harry Dog," Mikey Mo said.

"Figures," Betsy commented. "Seen that before. Anything else we ought to know about?"

"Oh, I'm not done yet. DV, the reason your boat wouldn't run at Bull Bay was that some of Harry Dog's hirelings put water in your gas tank when you refueled with the idea of stealing it after their mechanic siphoned it back out."

"That did seem awfully strange that it broke down when it did," DV said.

"The men that I had stationed on your boat while you were at the Wickie Wackie kept that from happening. And that guy who tried to hitch-hike with you under the pretense of being a mechanic who wanted to go home and see his mama, he was hired by the Shower Posse to do you dirty. The Colonel unveiled that ruse, and then *my* men took care of it.

"Colonel Winter also used his influence to have both Pacman and Moto Mouth fired from their jobs, which is why they attacked you on the Rio Grande. The motive on that attack was nothing more than drug induced revenge. You can thank Henry for his part in heading that off. Which leads us up to the recent failed attempt to do you dirty here in Port Antonio, leading us lastly to the attempt to attack Cee Cee yesterday. I'm still not clear what it was supposed to accomplish. But it was the final straw that prompted the meeting we're now having."

"I can't believe …" Cee Cee gasped. "All this over a boat?"

Will and Betsy silently looked at each other. They knew too damned good and well the atrocities that Dudus and Harry Dog were capable of.

"So far, we've been on the defensive, hoping to discover Dudus' motive, but that remains a mystery since we have yet to actually nab the culprits. All we've done is chase them off. There's nothing to be gained by grilling people like Pacman and Moto Mouth. They don't know anything. They were just hired to do a job. Same thing with Harry Dog's soldiers. They're just following orders. Probably the only people who really know what's going on are Dudus and Harry Dog."

"You're right," Will agreed. "And good luck learning anything from them."

"Maybe not so. The Colonel and I have decided it's our turn to go on the offensive. Apparently Dudus will never give up trying to recover your boat, and you'll never be able to enjoy it unless we do something dramatic. I have a plan to corner Harry Dog so The Colonel can once again put the fear of God in him. If we all work together, we can pull it off.

"When Harry Dog was determined to try to steal the Genovesa treasure from us, we managed to apprehend him. After a heart-to-heart talk with Colonel Winter in which The Colonel explained to him the price of interfering in Maroon affairs, Harry Dog came up with a way to satisfy Dudus while not losing face and called off his men. He made a promise then that that he would not interfere with The Colonel going forward. It looks like it's time The Colonel reminded him of his pledge in person and on The Colonel's turf."

"What kind of consequences are you referring to?" DV asked.

"The consequence of ending up in an unmarked grave in a remote limestone cave in the Cockpit Country. The Colonel left Harry with no doubt that he could make that happen if he so chose."

"And he can do it too," Will added.

NOTICE
IT IS MY INTENSION
TO APPLY FOR
SPIRIT LICENCE
FOR THIS PREMISES
AT THE NEXT SES-
SION IN M/VILLE

Chapter 38

Mikey Mo wasn't the only man with a plan. Monkyman was monkeying with a still new scheme of his own as well. Whereas Mikey Mo's plan had been hatched in sobriety as he sipped a Red Stripe and watched fit young men and bikini clad girls at play at Boston Bay beach, Monkeyman's latest scheme had been first conceived in his usual ganja and rum haze of the Just 1 More Bar.

As Mikey Mo watched, some sun worshippers were cavorting playfully on jet skis. They darted in and out of each other wakes and before darting away again and laughingly dared their friends to try to catch and pass them. A powerboat zipped by dragging a parasailer behind it. Another pulled a skier in the opposite direction. He could see a MiniCat out on the horizon. Windsurfers zigged back and forth. Two surfers in tank tops and boardshorts tried to catch a wave.

This is a regular circus, he thought. *All they need is three rings and a ringmaster and it would be SHOWTIME IN PARADISE.*

And then the first nuggets of a jaw-dropping plan jolted him like a bomb blast. When Harry Dog had become a constant nuisance once before as they sought the Genovesa treasure, they smoked him out and forced him into a confrontation with Colonel Winter. Once The Colonel set him straight — problem solved.

But Harry Dog would never knowingly let me get that close to him again. And even if I did, it could easily turn into a bloody confrontation.

Lord, I wish I knew why this is so important to Dudus. I couldn't find anything hidden on that boat. Harry's only a soldier. It's gotta be as The Colonel says, 'The soldiers' blood, the general's reputation.' I can't imagine that it's merely a case of 'Want i'want i', cyaa get i' an' get i' get i', no wan i'.' **(You want what you can't get, but then when you get it, you don't want it.).**

I'm in showbusiness aren't I? Well, let's smoke Harry Dog out with a long con using what I know best — SHOWBUSINESS! I will create a fake show that Harry Dog cannot resist attending, and … BINGO! … We'll take him hostage. And then I'll let The Colonel do the rest of the convincing. He had Harry shaking in his boots at the last "come to Jesus" meeting they'd had.

Whereas Mikey Mo's bolt out of the blue had occurred with sober contemplation, thus was not the case with Monkeyman's latest plan. It was first induced in a rum haze as he and Mighty Mouse drank at the Just 1 More Bar and then perfected at the Easy Hideout Bar.

"Remember where that rhaatid boat was the first time we saw it?"

"Ya, mon. Da impound yard," Mighty Mouse slurred back. "So what?"

"Das our answer. We return da boat to *our* impound yard."

"Da rum has gone to your head."

"Dahs de reason I'm da boss of dis here operation is because I do use my head for something other than keeping my ears apart. Here's the plan. We disguise ourselves, pretend to be John Law, plant some coke on da boat, and use that as our excuse to impound it again."

"We don't have a impound yard."

"Ediat! Did yu mama drop yu on yu head, skunt **(cunt)** breath? We don need a real one. Hidey ho! We just take off wid it and never look back."

"I see. And how we supposed to look like Jamaica Defense agents?"

"Das the easy part. Remember a couple of years ago, they changed their uniforms? Every thrift shop in Jamaica has the old ones. Dah dumb American bakra won't know dah rhaatid difference. We just visit a few stores until we find two uniforms that fit."

As usual, Monkeyman was only partially right. After visiting four different thrift shops, they found a uniform that would fit him but were not able to find a satisfactory one for Mighty Mouse because of his height and build. As they stood in the Salvation Army Thrift Store on Orange Street in Kingston, Monkeyman had an epiphany.

"Go pick out a white shirt with pocket flaps and some blue pants that fit you. I'll cut the patches and epaulets and pants stripe off this uniform. Then all I have to do is glue and staple them to the clothing you buy. Just stay behind me until we get control of the situation and try not to attract attention to yuself. After that it won't matter. We're just dealing with a dumb American."

Mighty Mouse looked perplexed like he wasn't convinced that this would work, but just said, "Ya, mon. If yu say so."

DV was alone on the boat the following morning when the dumb duo arrived at the marina. He had planned to take it out for a quick spin around the harbor to make sure the engine was running smoothly. Monkeyman approached him and told him that he had been sent to give the boat a final inspection since it had been involved in a crime. This was standard procedure and would only take a few minutes. Then the boat would be allowed to legally depart. He asked DV to wait on the dock. When Monkeyman reemerged from the cabin, he was holding two bags.

"How do you explain these, sir?"

"I've never seen those before in my life."

"Looks like the makings of a speedball to me. This changes the picture. I'm afraid I'm going to have to place you under arrest and impound your boat."

Both Monkeyman and Mighty Mouse pulled their pistols to emphasize their point.

"Please stand there and don't interfere."

He ordered DV to stand on the dock while he continued his search. With no warning, he cranked the engine. Mighty Mouse held his pistol on DV as he untied the lines. When the boat was still a few feet away from the dock, Mighty Mouse tried to push DV into the water but only succeeded in pushing him down. Monkeyman opened the throttle and began to run the boat parallel to the dock. The boat leaped forward. When he looked back, he saw Mighty Mouse chasing after him, waving his arms wildly. He had not jumped in time. Monkeyman slowed to neutral so his partner could catch up and ran back to the stern to try to help him.

"Jump, mon. I'll catch you. No problem. I'll catch you. I got you."

By this time DV was able to stand back up and began pursuing Mighty Mouse down the dock, only steps behind him. Mighty Mouse stopped and turned. He tried to deck DV with a wild roundhouse punch that DV sidestepped, causing the midget to lose his balance and fall on his face. DV's forward momentum carried him past Mighty Mouse. He leaped onto an ajacent docked boat and immediately bounded off of it onto the Spirt of the Seas. Mighty Mouse sprang back up and jumped just as DV got to the helm and pushed the throttle control into forward. Monkeyman went airborne off the stern. Flailing and kicking, he collided face to face with Mighty Mouse in midair, driving them both back onto the dock. They landed in a heap with their arms entwined around each other like two lovers in an embrace. Both heard and felt their noses break. Comingling snot and blood ran freely. DV jammed the throttle lever into reverse, and the boat began to speed backwards back towards the two nose-bleeding thugs.

Monkeyman and Mighty Mouse fled down the dock for their car. Once there, Monkeyman hit a car behind them as well as one in front of them in his haste to drive away.

"I need to find a rum bar to settle my nerves."

"Club Concussion's not far from here. I'll have to hand it to you, boss mon. Yu're one helluva fine planner. Das last one was a plan for dah history books."

"Gunkona, sawed off pussywool (**Go fuck yourself, sawed off wimp**)! All you had to do was jump on the rhaatid boat. You couldn't even do that right."

As he careered out of the parking lot, Monkeyman narrowly missed Henry and Will, who were just arriving at the marina.

"Who the hell was that?" Will asked. "They must be chasing some bad guy. They both had uniforms on."

"But not current uniforms," Henry said. "The JDF went to camo uniforms a couple of years ago."

When they walked out onto the dock, DV briefed them on what had just occurred.

"Mikey Mo's right. We've got to put an end to this once and for all," Will said.

"I couldn't agree with you more," Henry replied. "It's time we run t'ings so t'ings no run wi (**It's time we take charge of things before things take charge of us.**)."

Jamaican Parking Only—
Violators Will Be Deported
Who Jah Bless Leh No Mon Curse

Chapter 39

"My friends, do you know what a long con is?" Mikey Mo asked his companions.

"Sure," DV replied. "It's a big payoff seemingly insane con job that takes some preparation and planning. Like Paul Newman and Robert Redford in "The Sting."

"Kind of like selling the Eiffel Tower or the Brooklyn Bridge," Betsy threw in.

"Exactly, and the insana da betta," Will added.

"Insana da betta," Betsy chimed in. "There's my husband trying to be a poet again, but he's still a short fellow trying to be a Longfellow."

"Now, Now, guys. Don't do the poet-but-don't-know-it schtick again. It's becoming your who's-on-second routine."

"No, who's on first. What's on second," Will responded.

"I don't know ...," Betsy said.

"I don't know's on third."

"That exchange certainly opened up some deep and worthwhile questions that we should revisit on a more appropriate occasion. So, what's the plan, man?" Cee Cee asked.

"Here's the schtick, chick. We are going to set up a fake showbusiness extravaganza that will make Harry Dog's mouth drool. And then we'll invite him to a behind the scenes VIP sneak preview outside the three-mile limit. When he can't resist attending, we'll nab him just like we did before, haul him to Accompong, and let The Colonel make a religious believer out of him again. It worked to get him off our backs when we were looking for the Genovesa treasure. We are going to sponsor the First Annual Sea Spectacular Rodeo."

"Huh! Wha ...? Did I hear you right?"

"Yep. You heard me right. We're going to convince him that we're going to do everything and more that cowboy's do at a land rodeo, but our sea-boys will do it all ... and more ... in the ocean."

"Why not?" Will said. "After all, the Keys really does have an underwater music festival. As nutty as it may sound, it's quite popular."

"Let's get to work and design a program," Mikey Mo said. "And let your imagination go. I've also got a special treat for Harry Dog planned, but I'll let you know more about that later."

Mikey Mo's group let their imagination run wild. Nothing was too outrageous. The sea rodeo was being produced by Popeye's Posse Productions with entertainment provided through Nauti by Nature. These names would mean nothing to Harry Dog, but the board of directors of both companies in the fine print on the back of the page alongside the list of disclaimers would. The *Spirit of the Seas* was prominently mentioned as the host boat that would check each arrival in. Mikey Mo wanted to make damned sure Harry knew who was involved so as to motivate him to want to attend or know more. The objective was to raise Harry Dog's blood pressure.

The finalized invitation was then sent to Harry Dog's office via Federal Express and marked private. It stated that the event would be strictly a VIP RSVP affair and that the time and place would follow but would only be sent only to those who indicated that they would attend the event.

YOU ARE CORDIALLY INVITED TO ATTEND

THE FIRST ANNUAL
SEA SPECTACULAR SEA RODEO VIP SNEAK PREVIIEW
AND DRESSED REHEARSAL

• A DECORATED BOAT PARADE – PRIZES FOR THE BEST DECORATIONS
• MANATEE RIDING
• BARRCUDA AND TUNA ROPING
• EEL DUELING
• BUCKING SHARK RIDING
•SEA COWBOYS HERDING FLYING FISH THROUOGH GIANT FIERY HOOPS
• DOLPHINS PULLING TOPLESS SLALOM SKIERS
• BIKINIED HOSTESSES SEVING UNLIMITED COMPLIMENARY FOOD

AND ADULT DRINKS AND SMOKES

EMCEEING THE EVENTS WILL BE THE LEGENDARY DJ YELLOW-
MAN AND LOCAL FAVORITES

COLONEL FERRON WINTER AND MIKEY MO MULLINS
(PHOTO OPS AVAILABLE)

RSVP VIA EMAIL TO PPPROD@YAHOO.COM

INVITATIONS LIMITED TO THE FIRST 200 RSVPS AND ARE SUBJECT
TO MANAGEMENT APPROVAL

THE TIME AND LOCATION OUSIDE THE THREE-MILE LIMIT WILL
ONLY BE DISCLOSED TO THOSE
GUESTS THAT MANAGEMENT ACCEPTS.

THIS SPECTACLAR IS BROUGHT TO YOU BY
POPEYE'S POSSE PRODUCTIONS AND NAUTI BY NATURE LLC
AND HOSTED BY THE SPIRIT OF THE SEAS

The day the invitation was delivered had not been a good one so far for Harry Dog. He had been informed of the to-do Hi-top's men had made at Boston Bay and was waiting to hear Hi-top's latest excuses. He ripped open the envelope when it arrived and read the contents. He fumed after he read it. This was not improving his day.

"The nerve of these batty creases **(assholes)** throwing that boat in my face," he screamed.

"The Maroons are mocking me again. They have no respect for me or the Shower Posse."

He slung it across the floor. It laid there until Hi-top arrived to offer his latest predictable excuses for his continuing failure to resolve the *Spirit of the Seas* affair.

"Look at that," Harry Dog yelled before Hi-top could say a word. "And it's all your fault. This is some more of Colonel Winter's doings. Now, he's rubbing YOUR failures in MY face by parading MY boat in front of the VIPs who count from all over this island. ... IN PUBLIC. ... EVERYONE KNOWS THAT BOAT IS RIGHTFULLY MINE."

Harry conveniently forgot to mention that if Oney, Which Flava, and Twinie, the crew that *he* had allowed Bigga to dispatch to bring the boat into Black River Marina, hadn't gotten stoned and attracted law enforcement, ... who then confiscated the boat, ... that the boat would still be his today. ... Oh, no! ... This whole disaster was Hi-top's fault because of the crew *he* had chosen to right Harry Dog's wrong.

Why! Because in Harry Dog's world, shit flows south, and Hi-top was further to the south on the organization chart than he was. Harry desperately needed to kick someone, and at this moment, Hi-top was the only person immediately available to kick.

Now Hi-top wished he too had someone to kick, but right now he just had to suck up Harry Dog's anger and take what he was dishing out. His turn would come later with Mighty Mouse and Monkeyman.

Harry made an executive decision.

I will refuse give Colonel Dirtbag the pleasure of attending any function that he has anything to do with.

"I wouldn't attend an orgy cosponsored by St. Peter himself where he contributed every virgin in the Caribbean if Colonel Winter was involved in it. And as much as I would like to meet the legendary Yellowman, if Mikey Mo Mullins is going to be sharing the microphone with him, count me out.

"For the last time, GO GET MY RAHTID BOAT BACK! DON'T MAKE ME SAY IT AGAIN."

Hi-top quietly picked up the invitation and retreated out of Harry Dog's office.

Maybe the Sea Rodeo could present another opportunity to end this ordeal.

After reading the invitation, Hi-top took an unaccustomed risk. He began to ruminate and use his own imagination in lieu of just taking or following orders.

Hmmm! I don't care what Harry Dog thinks. This sea rodeo sounds like it could be fun. I've never seen anything like this before. I think I'll RSVP in Harry's name but tell them to email the confirmation to me. I'll get my crew together, and we'll go. If an opportunity comes up regarding the boat, we'll take advantage of it. Otherwise, we'll just have a good time. Topless skiers and almost topless hostesses serving all the rum we can drink! It doesn't get any better than that.

Hi-top was so excited at the prospect of an exciting extravaganza that he forgot his intension to pass on the ass-kicking he had just gotten to his men. As he expected, Mighty Mouse and Monkeyman found the upcoming show to be even more exciting than Hi-top had.

"This is something I really want to see," Mighty Mouse said. "But where are we going to get a boat?"

"I know. Pacman and Moto Mouth. Between the two of them, they'll be able to get a boat. Shit, they're in the boat business. Let's go see them. Let me borrow this announcement."

When they got to Moto Mouth's garage, he was sitting in a lawn chair smoking a reefer. The rolldown door was shut.

"Ya, mon. Yu takin the day off, or is that business slow?"

"Not slow, dead. The law is closing me down. Pacman lost his job at the marina too. Dah rhatid Maroon bastard Winter. I'm told he de blame."

Monkeyman and Mighty Mouse were stunned. Until this moment they hadn't been aware that neither of their cohorts had the ready access they once did to anything since Colonel Winter had used his influence to put them both out of business. They felt obligated to join Moto Mouth in a sympathy reefer … or two. An hour later, all of them were feeling no pain.

"You know, mon, I'd really love to see someone ride a manatee," Mighty Mouse said.

"Or herd flying fish," Moto Mouth agreed. "I didn't know you could do that."

"Yah, man. Cool. … But we need a boat ta go."

"Dere's a pontoon boat on a trailer out back," Moto Mouth suggested. "It's not pretty, but it floats. And even though Pacman doesn't have his job at the marina anymore, I tink he still can get in dere storage room, and we could borrow a motor from dem."

"Who care if da boat ugly," said Monkeyman. "We gonna decorate it for da parade anyway. I wanna win da prize. I never won no prize afore."

"But da decorations got to be cheap and easy to assemble since wi no hab much money."

"I gotta idea. Leh we spray paint it red with white hearts and call it da Love Boat."

"Yu hab red paint?"

"No, mon, but I got white. And it's already kind of white anyway."

"Then I gotta anodder idea. Leh's mek it white like a bathtub and hang white and blue balloons from it … Balloons are cheap."

"Yu means balloons to mek it look like a bubble bath. I like that, and yu right. Balloons will be cheap and simple to blow up using my generator."

"And we'll call it da *Rub-A-Dub-Tub.*"

"Cool, mon. I like that. Leh me send da email back so we get us invited.

CENTRAL
CAR WASH
&
HARBERDASHERY
6 MANCHESTER AVE.

Chapter 40

"Looks like our show is on," Mikey Mo said. "I got an RSVP from Harry Dog."

"And a really big sheeew it is," said DV in his best Ed Sullivan voice.

"Yes, we do, but we're not going to let them get to the sheeew's so-called location. What I see us doing is waylaying Harry Dog before he gets there. And I'm going to ask you guys to remain on shore during the confrontation. I don't want to endanger you if I can help it. I'll take Tom John and Froggie with me to handle Harry Dog. They're trained for this sort of thing."

"At least let me go to pilot the boat," DV said. "I'm familiar with handling it. And besides, unless I'm there, the insurance company may refuse to cover the boat in the event of a disaster."

"Good point," Mikey Mo agreed. "But let my men handle things. OK?"

"Agreed."

The morning of the big show, DV stood in the enclosed, elevated helm of the *Spirit of the Seas* alone with a cup of coffee watching the new day arrive. A lone cock crowed in the distance.

Sometimes it's worth not pushing the snooze button, and this is one of those sometimes, he thought as he took a deep breath of the crisp morning air.

The first rays of the sun were cool and bracing to his eyes. The beauty was beyond description since everything around him seemed bathed in yellow light. From his elevated position, he could see beyond the marina to a small beach that abutted it. The shimmering beige sand looked so soft that it reminded him of a blanket of candy floss. The pocket beach was hemmed in by towering rocky cliffs. He looked in the other direction at the open sea and streams of pulsating light saturated the surface with a golden haze. The sky began to blend from pink to orange as the sun floated lazily over the horizon. The scene filled DV with hope and renewed confidence that Mikey Mo's aspirations for that day would be realized and that this would end his own involvement with the Shower Posse once and for all.

Mikey Mo's email communique had indicated to the "participants" that Colonel Winter would make his opening remarks and cut a ceremonial ribbon to begin the Sea Spectacular at ten thirty that morning. They would depart as soon as Mikey Mo, Tom John, and Froggie arrived and waylay the Shower Posse boat as it sought the show's location. They were armed for the confrontation. If they were successful, Harry Dog would never learn that the whole show was a nonexistent con.

Mikey Mo was no murderer. He didn't plan to simply set Harry Dog's boat adrift with his thugs aboard. They would zip-tie their opponents, anesthetize them, and tow their boat into a remote harbor where Mikey Mo had already left a spare car. Harry Dog would then be driven to Accompong, where Colonel Winter would reimpress him of the seriousness of his previous pledge to forever stay out of The Colonel's business and again reinforce the consequences of failing to do so. He also hoped to possibly learn why the *Spirit of the Seas* was such an issue with Dudus Coke.

Mikey Mo thought, *I've certainly been unable to find any contraband on the boat.*

Monkeyman, Mighty Mouse, Pacman, and Moto Mouth's thoughts were much more frivolous that morning. As far as they were concerned, they were going to what had to be the party of the year. Barnham and Bailey on the ocean.

Party! Party!

They had towed Moto Mouth's pontoon boat from the salvage yard and launched it the day before. They almost named it the "Ship-Faced Titanic II" but finally decided that the name was too wordy and christened it simply the "*Rub-A-Dub-Tub.*" They spent the remainder of the afternoon decorating it as they smoked and drank and made sure that the old outboard that Pacman had "borrowed" was in running order. Some time after dark, all four passed out and spent the night on the boat. Any thoughts about capturing the *Spirit of the Seas* as a primary objective had long passed through their minds. It would be a perfect day for a party.

Party! Party!

"Afta all," Monkeyman observed when Pacman briefly brought the topic up, "wi come here fi drink milk, wi no come here fi count cow. **(We came here to drink the milk, not count the cows.).**"

"Mek sense to mi."

They were positive that they would win "Best Boat" in the boat parade and get to meet Yellowman. After all, their creation was a magnificent sight to behold. The cistern liner had been spraypainted white and secured to the pontoon boat with ropes. "*Rub-A-Dub-Tub*" had been graffitied on its side in scrawly black spray paint.

RUB-A-DUB-TUB

"Fine! Mighty damned fine. Unless da judging rigged, gotta be a winner."

The liner had then been partially filled with water. They had drilled a hole in the aft portion of the cistern's rim and mounted the fishing rod with the pirate flag saying,

HAVE A IRIE DAY, MATEY

Sky blue and white balloons were attached to the cistern liner to simulate bath bubbles. Mighty Mouse had even bought some bubble bath. He dumped a generous amount into the cistern liner now and planned to dump the rest once they arrived at the show. Moto Mouth's "diving board" remained protruding from the bow like a phallic symbol. A fresh supply of Red Stripes had been iced down in the Igloo for the ride out to the show's location. And of course, the boom box had been brought along. After all, what's a party without music!

"Harry Dog dunna know what he's missing. But we'll drink a few in his honor. His loss is wi gain. And who knows. Wi might meet some ladies who want to go for a swim in our pool."

Mikey Mo and his men arrived, and the *Spirit of the Seas* departed from the marina. They tried to estimate where Harry Dog would probably be coming from and put some fishing rods out to pretend to troll as Mikey Mo scanned the horizon with DV's binoculars.

Suddenly the oddest craft he had ever seen came over the horizon. He looked, wiped the lens on his shirt, and looked again. He began to hear dancehall reggae music blaring in the distance.

Me seh Tarzan a da di king a da jungle,
Cuz me seh Tarzan da king a da jungle
Come mon him bad like a spider
Badda dan a tiger

He turned to DV and said, "Do I look drunk to you, or am I hallucinating? I hear Yellowman. Could he really be here?"

"Oh no, man. Can't be. Didn't we just make that shit up?"

"Then why am I seeing and hearing his voice?"

Mikey Mo handed DV the binoculars. DV looked and couldn't believe what he was seeing — a floating pile of junk with something mounted on it. … And it had a pirate flag flying above it. Balloons flapped in the wind and would occasionally become untethered. Each time the junkpile hit a wave, a bubble bath cloud would arise. Four drunken men gyrated to Yellowman's accompaniment.

Cuz me seh ether or either him bad like a tiger badda dan di elephant and di jaguar

Tom John looked through the binoculars, shook his head, and then handed them to Froggie.

"I think that's a liner to a cistern on top of that junkpile," Froggie said.

"No way, mon," Tom John said. "You gotta be wrong."

"Uh uh, … I think Froggie's right," Mikey Mo said, agreeing with Froggie.

Froggie grabbed the binoculars again.

"And I know two of those men," he said. "It's the same two low-lifes we chased off after they tried to steal this boat from the marina."

"Do you see Harry Dog aboard it?"

"No, mon. All I see is a bunch of drunks."

"OK. Let's go get our man. I'm sure he's on that boat somewhere. Get ready for battle."

"Shoot! I'm not sure it'll be much of a fight since they're all shit faced."

"That's even better."

The crew on the *Rub-A-Dub-Tub* saw the *Spirit of the Seas* for the first time as well but couldn't immediately identify it since they had no binoculars and since they were all three-sheets-to-the-wind, things looked blurry. No one could read the boat's name.

"Look. A fishing boat."

They waved with a beer in each hand, and DV waved back.

The music blared.

Tarzan a di king na di jungle cuz mi seh Tarzan a di king of di jungle

Suddenly reality dawned on Monkeyman.

"Dah no fishing boat. Dahs da President's boat!"

"Then leh wi tek it den in da name of da President! ... Long libe President Dudus!"

"Ya, mon. Leh wi do dat. Since dey dun know who wi are, wi got da element of surprise on wi side. Pull up on dey side, and wi board dem, like Errol Flynn did in 'Captain Blood'."

The *Rub-A-Dub-Tub* charged. Monkeyman and Mighty Mouse were prone on the bow so they could use the protruding plank to as a springboard to board DV's boat. Moto Mouth oversteered and instead of coming up on the *Spirit of the Seas'* side, headed straight at them. The gap between the two boats closed. When he saw he was about to accidentally ram them, Moto Mouth threw the engine in reverse to stop the Rub-A-Dub's forward momentum, but he choked the old motor, and it died. The boat continued forward unabated. Yellowman's "Rambo" now blared out of the boom box. Balloons flapped in the breeze, some breaking off and floating away.

Each time the boat pounded into a wave, Monkeyman and Mighty Mouse yelled out in pain.

SLAP!

"Oh, shit!"

SLAP!

"Yu trying to kill mi, mon? Slow Down!"

SLAP!

"A wah di bloodclaat dew yuh **(What the fuck's wrong with you)**? Dah's mi fingers yu just kneed, yu little tif tif boy **(fag)** runt!"

"Den move yu fingers outa mi way, Rent-a-dread caca fought face **(fart face)**!"

The music blared.

Blow 'em up like Rambo, He's a killing machine
He's the best combat yet that you've ever seen
And now he's all alone and what you call hell he calls home

Monkeyman and Mighty Mouse somehow remained on all fours barely clinging to the plank and increasingly questioning their assault plan.

CRUNCH!

"Oh, shit!"

The music blared.

Blow 'em up like Rambo

The *Rub-A-Dub-Tub* collided with the *Spirit of the Seas*. The end of the diving board speared the portside window of the *Spirit of the Seas* and didn't stop until it collided with the mast support, partially ripping it loose from its mountings. Monkeyman and Mighty Mouse skidded headfirst the length of the plank onto the roof of the *Spirit of the Seas'* cabin, grabbing onto a mast line as well as each other to keep from going overboard on the other side.

Another wave hit, rocking both boats down and then up, ripping the mast support looser each time. The force of this collision partially broke the cistern liner loose from the ropes securing it, and it swayed back and forth and partially tipped, dumping gallon after gallon of bubbly water plus the inner tubes onto Monkeyman and Mighty Mouse as it careened back and forth. A third wave hit, and the cistern liner broke loose completely, slamming with all its weight into the mast support. It barely missed Monkeyman and Mighty Mouse. The Igloo full of beer shot by only to become snagged on some rubble. The bolts holding the mast support broke completely free and suddenly the air and the ocean were full of a cloud of Dudus's hidden currency. When Moto Mouth and Pacman saw the cloud of cash, greed took hold. They forgot everything else and rushed to leap over the gunwale onto the *Spirit of the Seas* to try to see how much dough they could grab. This left the *Rub-A-Dub-Tub* unguided and unmanned.

Rambo continued to blare.

But when they fucked with Rambo, they fucked up. R.A.M.B.O
Blow 'em up like Rambo

With the seesawing wave action, the screws holding the plank to the Rub-A-Dub completely ripped loose, and when the two boats rolled downward again, it shot forward again, this time through the *Spirit of the Seas* starboard window, ripping out most of the cabin on that side and part of the roof as well. Another swirling mountain of cash appeared and spun in an upwards circle with each updraft. Each time the wind subsided, the cash cloud began to sink back towards the ocean, only to be swept up again with the next upward gust of wind. A crosswind began to break up the pattern and carry some in every direction. Some of the cash stuck to the *Spirit of the Seas'* wet sails, giving them an odd patchwork effect.

Above it all, was the sound of Monkeyman screaming, "Get off mi fingers, yu little sawed-off bastard."

Both Mighty Mouse and Monkeyman lost their remaining grip and the momentum washed them towards the ocean. Mighty Mouse's belt caught on a cleat, and he ended up hanging by it with his short arms and legs flailing like a turtle trying to right itself. Monkeyman tried to grab onto Mighty Mouse to save himself, but Mighty Mouse's flailing ripped his pants and sent both of them careening into the water. The belt and torn pants continued to flap in the breeze. The Igloo broke free and followed, barely missing them as it shot by. When it hit the water, they grabbed it by its handles and used it as support device.

Mikey Mo yelled to his crew, "Abandon ship!"

Tom John, and Froggie leaped onto the *Rub-A-Dub-Tub*. Mikey Mo grabbed DV and pushed him in that direction. When Moto Mouth tried to confront them and prevent them from joining Tom John and Froggie, Mikey Mo shoved him. As he stumbled, Mikey Mo and DV grabbed him by his arms and legs and heaved him overboard. He hit the water, spreadeagle, and face first. They turned towards Pacman. He ran in the other direction and leaped overboard to get out of their reach. Another wave hit and drove the two boats apart.

Above it all, Yellowman continued to blare, singing his song "Crying for Love."

A Nautical Conspiracy

Say some a them a all and some a bawl
And everybody bawling, bawling for love. Jah!
Ca' everybody asking, asking for love

"For God's sake, cut that rhatiid thing off," Mikey Mo yelled over the racket.

Froggie grabbed the boom box and hurled it as far as he could throw it. There was silence.

"Thank you."

When they looked back, they saw Pacman trying to pull his fellow conspirators out of the ocean and back onto the *Spirit of the Seas*. Everywhere they looked, both above and below, millions of dollars of unlaundered Shower Posse money floated. Each time the boat rocked, the mast support regurgitated more money. A pelican dived for a fish and came up with a thousand-dollar bill in its beak. Cash continued to swirl in the air. The cistern liner bobbed all alone out in the ocean with the pirate flag on the fishing rod waving back and forth. A few of the balloons remained attached.

HAVE A IRIE DAY, MATEY

Tom John tinkered with the Rub-A-Dub's outboard motor. It sputtered to life. Mikey Mo clenched his fists with his thumbs erect in approval.

"Think we should rescue them?' DV asked.

"Not only no, but hell no. They've finally got the boat they've been wanting for so long. I think they deserve to finally enjoy it."

He looked over and saw that Pacman had been able to retrieve the Igloo and everyone was drinking a Red Stripe.

"But they might get away," DV said.

"No, no, no. Ain't no way, Jose. I grabbed the key as we abandoned ship," Mikey Mo said as he wagged his index finger as he held it up for all to see.

"I sure wish we had a marine radio to call water patrol," DV said.

"I've still got my cell phone."

Mikey Moe grinned, wiggled his forehead, and held it up with his other hand.

"How do you think they'll explain all that cash to water patrol?"

"Not my problem."

"Well, we didn't get to abduct Harry Dog."

"But we got something better. We found out millions of reasons why Dudus Coke was so hellbent to get this boat back."

"And eliminated those reasons a thousand dollars at a time. — Gone with the wind."

"Quite frankly, my dear. I don't give a damn."

"I wonder how much of Dudus's money was on my boat?"

"Let me put it this way. All I've seen so far is thousand-dollar bills. A million dollars in thousand-dollar bills weighs less than three pounds.

"Holy shit! There must be fifty million dollars floating out there."

"That's right! Dudus is out a bunch of money."

"To him, that's a hunk, a hunk of burning love. Woo wee! If that's the case, by the time Dudus finishes with Harry Dog, he'll wish we had kidnapped him."

"I thought I searched that boat from stem to stern, but it never occurred to me that the prize was hidden in the hollow space inside the mast support. I really thought I was looking for illegal drugs. I had no idea the prize was illegal cash. No wonder, the authorities didn't find it. Cash doesn't smell. I'm sure that's what their dogs were looking for."

"Too bad it got wasted," DV said.

"Not from our perspective. With this much moola at stake, this was the only way Dudus would ever have given up. Otherwise, you would have been looking over your shoulder for as long as you owned that boat. And if he thought you had found his money, he'd be after you for the rest of your life. Would it be worth that?"

"You're right. No, it wouldn't."

"I can't wait to report the morning's events back to The Colonel. He doesn't know it yet, but he's won another round with Dudus."

"And this time he wasn't even trying to. Once again, lilly (little) axe cut down big tree," said Mikey Mo with a laugh.

"My gramma used to always put it another way. She said, 'puss and daag nuh ar de same luck **(cats and dogs don't have the same luck.)**,'" Tom John added. "Today, we da dog."

"Not just da dog. Yu mean wi now da top dog."

"Yah, mon."

EPILOGUE

"You just don't know how great it feels to be home at Sundance," Will said as he hugged Leva Carter, Sundance's cook and head of staff. "We've sure missed you two."

"Thank you, thank you very much," Elvis Jesse, aka E.J., added. E.J., Sundance's houseboy, was wearing his "Jailhouse Rock" t-shirt that day.

"And I can't wait to meet your new friends who bought Mount Corbett," Leva said.

"Oh, you will, and you'll like them," Betsy said.

"The boat journey wasn't an easy trip thanks to Harry Dog and his men."

"So, Mikey Mo told me," E.J said.

"Harry again?" Leva snorted. "I thought we were through with that dirty dog after I beaned him with my iron skillet."

"And then threatened his manhood with your lethal backhand spatula swats. ... So did we, but things changed when the Shower Posse wanted the Craig's boat and would stop at nothing to get it."

"You know what they say, 'You can stop a bird from flying over you, but you can't stop it building a nest.'"

"Well, you look gooder than good despite Harry Dog's most recent meddling. As Mr. Davis says, 'Weh no kill, fatten'.'"

"We wouldn't have made it this time without Mr. Davis and Mikey Mo," Betsy added. "Wait'll you hear the whole story. I'm going to hold it until everyone gets here later today so each of them can add their own two cents."

"I hope I'm not too busy getting today's feast ready to listen," Leva said.

"No worry. You won't be. Mikey Mo says he's taking care of the catering."

"Are you sure? He's no cook. When he gets through cooking, his results make the onions cry. The only way he knows breakfast from lunch or dinner is that it's the meal that doesn't have Red Stripes. And I hate to see the mess he'll leave in my kitchen."

"Trust me … or I should say, him."

"I'm going to wear my gold lamé Elvis suit for the occasion," E.J. said.

"And I'm sure you'll shine as usual."

"Once again. Thank you. Thank you very much."

After lunch, there was a honk at the gate.

"Go see who that is," Leva told E.J.

"Excuse me, folks. Elvis has been ordered to leave the building."

The horn tooted again.

"You better get on outta here, boy."

"Yessim, Mizz Leva. Don't hit me. I'ze a goin'."

When E.J. opened the gate, a shiny black Lexus with darkened windows rolled down the driveway, and a handsome, clean-cut man with a shaved head and a teenage girl emerged from the car. Leva stood on the front stoop wiping her hands with a dishtowel. The man's smile was instantly engaging as he walked confidently towards the house.

"May I help you?"

"I hope so, ma'am. I was told you needed a cook for a function here later today, and I was hoping you would consider me and my niece, Imani, to help you prepare for your guests."

"And your name sir?"

"Mr. Brown. And you are?"

"I'm Mrs. Carter. And you have experience?"

"Yes, ma'am. I have references from both Trelawny and St. Catherine who I'm sure will vouch for me. And we work for reasonable wages and never take the silverware."

"And who sent you, Mr. Brown?"

"Colonel Winter, ma'am. You can call me Collin."

"Collin Brown? Surely, you're not *THE* Collin Brown, the famous chef. … My God in heaven! … E.J.! … E.J. … This is *THE* Collin Brown. He's even cooked for the royal family.

"Plea … Please come in, sir. I've been a fan of yours for years. I have one of your cookbooks. This is an honor."

"I hope I'm not being presumptuous, but I took the liberty of doing some grocery shopping for tonight's meal. A box of groceries is in the back seat."

"E.J., … bring Mr. Brown's groceries in the house before this hot weather ruins them. Welcome to Sundance, sir. May I get you something to drink?"

Collin Brown and Imani walked in the house, and introductions were made all around.

"Didn't I tell you that Mikey Mo said he was making catering arrangements," Will laughed. "Didn't I tell you to trust him? And he said he had other surprises as well."

"How can Mikey Mo top this?"

A little later there was another horn at the front gate.

"E.J., go find out who that is," Leva said.

"Yes, ma'am."

Leva then informed everyone present, "It seems we've got more company."

E.J. opened the gate. A bright yellow Mercedes Metris Weekender van rolled into the driveway. E.J. waited for it to pass before latching the gate again and then followed it down the driveway. Mikey Mo sat next to the driver. When the van was parked, the driver got out and opened the side door. The man who emerged was almost a yellow as the Mercedes. He walked up to Leva.

"Madam, may I introduce myself? My name is Winston Foster. I was told that you need entertainment for an upcoming social event."

"King Yellowman!" E.J. blurted out as he rushed over to shake the new arrival's hand.

Two other men then emerged from the back of the van.

"May I introduce my associates, Mr. Dunbar and Mr. Shakespeare?" Yellowman said quietly.

"Sly and Robbie!" E.J. gasped. Leva just stared dumbfounded.

Betsy snapped Leva back into a semi reality when she hugged her and said playfully, "And who said that the day couldn't possibly get any better?"

Sly bussed Betsy on the cheek, "It's great to see you again, Mrs. Black. And you as well, Mr. Black. The last time we met you were with my old friend, DV Craig, I believe."

"He and his wife will be joining us shortly. They bought Mount Corbett up the hill."

"Be sure to tell him to remember to bring his guitar. As you know, our association with DV goes way back, but my friend, Yellowman, has never had the pleasure of sharing a stage with him."

Robbie walked over to Collin Brown and said, "Mr. Brown, it's great to see you again as well. Are you here in an official capacity?"

"Mrs. Carter has graciously agreed to let me share her kitchen with her. I'm hoping she will give me a tip or two about real Jamaican cooking since I'm still somewhat of a novice."

Leva just continued to stare as if she were in a trance. Collin Brown! ... And now, Yellowman ... and Sly and Robbie ... all on the same day ... all at Sundance! This is going to be the party of the century!

She literally danced up the steps to get back in the house.

Will hugged Betsy and whispered in her ear, "Another affair to remember. Have I told you lately that I love you?"

"Not today."

"Well, I do! I do! I do! I do! I do!" he sang.

"Maybe you should just let ABBA keep singing that song."

Sly looked at Robbie and said, "Maybe we'll give that one a try before the night is out."

"Swedish reggae. I gotta hear that."

"Welcome to Sundance," Leva said as they all entered the villa.

Will stopped at the bottom of the front steps and broke out spontaneously in one of the songs from "Sweet Charity."

David Beckwith

Look-a where I am
Today I landed POW in a pot of jam
What a set-up, holy cow,
They'd never believe it
If my friends could see me now.

Betsy closed the front door and said, "I swear don't know that man. He just followed me home."

Sneak Peek
Excerpt from "Conclusive All-Inclusive Confusion"
by David Beckwith

CHAPTER 1

Beauregard Montgomery "Monte" Connors would have been more excited if he hadn't been dragging. He had been up since three to catch the 7:36 flight from Detroit to Miami. He was nervous anyway since he was a neophyte traveler, and the events of the morning thus far had not been totally reassuring. He silently thanked the good Lord that he had his family with him and didn't have to face this unknown alone. After all, Detroit Metropolitan Airport was the busiest airport in Michigan with over 1,100 flights a day that went to four continents.

He had been gotten up at three to make sure he didn't oversleep and miss the airport shuttle bus. His daughter, Eve, had assured him that riding the shuttle would be no big deal, and normally it wouldn't have been. He had bundled up, and it had been a good thing that he had, since the bus's heater wasn't working properly. But now he somewhat regretted having that bulky jacket and wool fedora to haul around on the plane and keep up with in the Atlanta airport as they waited for their connecting flight to Miami. He had been glad they changed planes in Atlanta since a grandmother and her two disruptive grandchildren had sat behind him on the packed Boeing 787. The whole way, all he heard was her repeatedly telling them to stop this and to stop that as they bumped the back of his seat and did other irritating things. He was a naturally nonconfrontational person who didn't want to make a scene if it was at all possible. He just gritted his teeth and told himself that it was only for a couple of hours. He reminded himself that maybe irritations like this were the reason he had seldom travelled out of Highland Park, but he knew the real reason was that until now he couldn't afford to do so.

Monte would celebrate his fiftieth birthday on this trip. This milestone was one of the reasons he had decided to go. He had spent his entire life in Highland Park. He was not by nature an adventurous person. He was a confirmed bachelor and only child who had always lived at home taking care of his divorced mother, Nevaeh, until the Lord had taken her to heaven. He had never even had a girlfriend. After Nevaeh's death, he continued to live there in the house where he was born and raised despite the radically worsening neighborhood. After all, the house had been Monte's only asset and would bring very little if he sold it. It was probably not worth more than the five or ten thousand dollars other houses around him had sold for.

So, Monte continued to work for the Saint Benedict Catholic Church on Church Street, the church he was raised in, as their sometimes organist and piano player. He also helped in the church's food kitchen and thrift shop. It wasn't exciting, but it was a comfortable, familiar place.

Highland Park was once a vibrant community with a rich history. It is here that Henry Ford began the mass production of automobiles on a moving assembly line. Mass production expanded from here and soon affected all phases of American industry as it set the pattern for twentieth century living. This was no longer the case in the twenty-first century, however. This three-square-mile city nestled in the heart of Detroit had evolved into one of the most economically depressed places in the United States as it faced a list of long and dire difficulties. It had shrunk from a peak population of over fifty thousand residents to one of barely ten thousand. Ford departed as did Chrysler afterwards. Even Highland Park's high school shut down, and the city found itself having the distinction of being the municipality that had been placed under emergency financial management for longest period of time in Michigan history. Highland Park residents endured inconveniences like water shutoffs and even had 1,400 residential streetlights repossessed and ripped out of the ground because the city of Highland Park couldn't pay their electric bills.

Crime, blight, and poverty were all entangled in this mess, both cause and consequence of a gutted school system and failing tax base and infrastructure. With the absence of streetlights and Highland Park's inability to provide anything beyond the most basic services, crime and gangs flourished. Despite this, the solitary Monte lived a quiet, ordered life with his main priority being avoiding trouble.

But Monte had not been totally alone after Neveah's death. In a move that was daring for him, he convinced Saint Benedict's priest to persuade authorities to allow him to adopt three girls, whose Highland Park single, drug addicted, homeless mothers had died, in lieu of having the girls thrown into the overburdened state welfare system. They were various ages when he adopted them. He had then raised them and helped them overcome the scars resulting from their former lives. Viv was now a customer service agent at the Lake Trust Credit Union. Eve worked at Highland Park's Powerhouse Gym. Viv and Eve had recently married; Nan was a still-single librarian who lived with Monte at home.

Now the six of them were all on their way to Miami. The ripple effect of an act of kindness had led to Monte and his new family being on this trip. It began when Monte gave an overcoat that had been donated to the church thrift shop to a Highland Park wino amputee and Viet Nam veteran to keep him from freezing to death. A few weeks later, the wino showed back up at the soup kitchen with a lottery ticket in his hand. He gave it to Monte as a thank you. The lottery ticket turned out to be a winner, and Monte was suddenly worth a hundred million dollars. Half of the proceeds went for taxes, but he was still a very wealthy man when all was said and done. Monte just knew that this was Nevaeh's manna sent from heaven. After all, she had always looked out for him and told him that if he did good for others, it would come back to him in unexpected ways. Soon after, he visited the cemetery to thank her and took some flowers to honor her memory.

Monte was overwhelmed by his windfall and didn't know where to turn. Fortunately for him, one of the priests told him that he was a fortunate man. He had a financial planner available to him right there as part of Saint Benedict's congregation as well as a daughter who was in the financial services industry. He suggested to Monte that he bring these two resources together. This made sense to Monte.

Once again all mighty God has provided the resources that I need.

Banks Bridges operated a marginal one-man independent investment firm in Highland Park. Most of his business was selling low-minimum mutual fund periodic payment plans. The broker-dealer that he was affiliated with did have a cash management account called the Golden Rewards Cash Management Service that came with checks and a debit card, but Banks' clients rarely had enough money to meet its minimums.

At the priest's suggestion, Monte made an appointment for Viv to meet Banks. He didn't accompany her since he trusted her and thought he wouldn't understand what they were talking about anyway.

Banks salivated at the thought of meeting with Viv. Word had gotten out around the church about Monte's good fortune. Rumors ranged from a few million to many millions. Either way, this would be a windfall for him if he could land it. Even if it was only one million, it would become his largest account.

Banks and Viv met. Banks insisted that he take Viv to lunch, and when she confided in him the amount of money that her dad had won, he took her out to dinner as well. An intense courtship commenced, complete with candy and flowers. The wallflower Viv was thrilled that a handsome, virile young man was so taken with her. Banks became relentless in his pursuit of Viv and his effort to close the deal. After gaining Viv's trust, he worked on her to convince her that his firm offered customized services and personal attention superior to any conventional banking institution.

"My dear Viv, banking institutions are hard, cold entities. They are marketing organizations like any other business. You shop at Glory Supermarket, don't you? How many brands of bottled salad dressing do they carry?"

"I don't really know. Lots, I guess."

"That's right, lots. Does anyone in there advise you about which brand might be not only be superior but would be a bargain as well? Do they tell you which brands taste horrible and might ruin your salad?"

"Uh. … No."

"That's right. And if left on your own, you're likely to choose poorly. Why? Because you're not an expert on salad dressings. Do you know what that store really cares about? I'll tell you. All they care about is that you spend your money and leave the store with a bottle of salad dressing in your shopping cart … and that you don't sue them later because what they sold you was garbage."

"I guess maybe you're right."

"There's no maybe to it. You know I'm right. But what if while you were in that store, an expert on salad dressings chose the store's best product for you? You'd go home with the good stuff. Well, I'm that person. Financial institutions offer a wide array of products. Some are good; some are not. But do you know the difference? I do. I'm that guy who will stand in front of the shelf and choose the correct 'salad dressing' for you. Why? Because I'm a highly trained fiduciary who has your best interests at heart and who will cause your father to prosper rather than fail and be disappointed like too many other people. … Does this make sense to you. I'm the guy on your side, not the side of the big, cold corporation."

What Banks said made sense. Viv was sold. Not only had Banks sold his services, but he sold himself as well … and became Viv's husband.

My scraping by days are over. With a big fish like this, I don't need the rest of the minnows anymore.

Banks' actual birth name was Khoury Haddad, but he had changed it to Banks Nathanial Bridges. Banks N. Bridges had a much better ring to it, considering his profession and since he called himself a financial planner. After all, it sounded so American. He was careful not to include the word "certified" in his title since he had only taken one CFP exam. He had flunked it twice before dropping out of the program all together. With Viv's help, he easily convinced Monte to trust him with his windfall. After Banks and Viv were married, Banks suspended his mutual fund business and became Monte's excusive investment advisor.

Banks wasn't the only person who saw opportunity due to Monte. One of the few Golden Rewards Cash Management accounts he had on the books belonged to Jax Magnus, an insurance agent in the parish. Jax used it for his agency checking and premium escrow account.

Jax, an independent insurance agent, was also a member of the Saint Benedict parish. Jax was a marginal agent who was scraping by selling debit life insurance to the low income residents of Highland Park. He would collect the premiums on either a weekly, bi-weekly, or monthly basis depending on the frequency that coincided with when the policy holders had the money to pay. When Jax heard about Monte's good fortune, he hoped this might lead to an opportunity to make some real money for a change instead of just nickels and dimes. He wasn't used to elephant hunting but now went all out to land this one since maybe God had finally put a bonified elephant within his reach.

It all hinged on whether Jax could convince Monte that he had a future tax problem, and that Jax had the solution. Despite not knowing how much Monte had won or being a tax expert, Jax guesstimated Monte's estimated estate tax liability based on the rumored amount of Monte's winnings. Jax made sure he padded the number in his favor to maximize his commission.

I'll even tell him I assumed that the assets failed to grow just to show him how conservative I am.

Jax still beamed at the final number he was now looking at.

Yes! That looks salable — and profitable.

A fifteen million dollar paid up single premium life policy. That was the answer. A two million dollar investment would buy Monte a policy that would cover this estimated tax liability. And best of all, Jax would get paid fifty percent of Monte's expenditure as a commission.

Oh, how sweet it'd be.

But after thinking about it overnight, Jax got an even better idea. Why not quote Monte three million. Monte would still think he was getting a bargain. He'd be spending three million to get fifteen million. And Monte would never know he was being overcharged. He'd write the three million dollar check to Jax's agency, and Jax would send two million on to the insurance company and pocket the difference.

Yessiree Bob, together with the million dollar commission plus another million from the overcharge, I'll be on easy street.

Now, all Jax had to do was get to Monte before some other shark did.

Monte's daughter, Eve! She's my answer.

He had met Eve before at Saint Benedict's but hadn't paid her much mind. This needed to change. … And was about to. … He knew Eve worked for the Powerhouse Gym. He had seen her there when he went to collect premiums for some debit policies he had sold to some of its other personal trainers.

I'm overdue for some self-improvement. I think I'll join the Powerhouse Gym.

Jax hired Eve to set up a workout program for him. He invited her to lunch. He took her to mass at Saint Benedict's. This led to a dinner and a movie date. He began to pick her up at Monte's several times a week, making sure that he bonded with Monte as well as Eve.

Before long he proposed, and Eve became Mrs. Jax Magnus.

Once this happened, selling Monte on single premium life became a forgone conclusion, and Jax graduated from being debit policy peddler to being a real insurance professional with a substantial balance for a change is his Golden Rewards account. This sudden phenomenon did not go unnoticed by Banks.

The family convinced Monte that he deserved a vacation. He agreed to the trip since he had multiple reasons to celebrate since within six months of Monte receiving his windfall, both Viv and Eve had met nice young men.

Yes, once again, God had worked his magic in a mysterious but wondrous fashion since Banks and Jax, their suitors, had seemed to come out of nowhere to court and marry them.

Monte prayed for guidance.

The good Lord has smiled on my family once again. Thank you God and Jesus. I guess it's true. Sometimes the best things happen unexpectedly and come from the most unexpected places and begin with 'all of a sudden.' If it's your will for us to take a vacation together as well, I shouldn't question your divine judgement. You haven't steered us wrong yet.

After all, Monte rationalized that a trip would have a dual purpose. It would be a delayed honeymoon trip of sorts for both of them as well as a vacation for him. Like him, none of the girls had ever been out of the state of Michigan. Besides that, none of them had ever flown. What excitement! They voted unanimously on a trip to the tropics and after some research decided to visit the Seascape All Inclusive Resort in romantic Runaway Bay, Jamaica.

Now they were enroute for the adventure of a lifetime.

There had been a little excitement at the Detroit airport, but it had been overcome. Nan had worn a cute, blue-flowered pullover with sequins outlining the flowers. None of them knew that the sequins would trick the X-ray machine into thinking she was wearing a bomb. After going through the machine, several TSA agents had come running over and asked her for permission to pat down the area with the offending decoration. She had experienced pat-downs before from the Highland Park police, but never one this extensive. The woman grabbed the front of Nan's blouse and firmly felt it in and around her breasts. Nan stood there speechless. Then the woman let go without so much as howdy-do. Shaken, Nan retrieved her shoes and belongings from the conveyor belt and shakily made her way over to a bench to put her shoes back on.

They changed planes in Atlanta with no incidents. The plane they reboarded was thinner than most, with two seats, the aisle, and then two more seats. It seemed as long as their original plane, but it was long and skinny. Monte heard the flight attendant tell a man that it was originally designed to be a commuter plane.

When they arrived at Miami International, Monte felt culture shock. Miami seemed to be a mosaic of cultures and diversities. It was an unfamiliar climate, with people speaking unfamiliar languages, eating unfamiliar foods, and wearing tropical clothing and footwear. He felt even more out of place in his wool fedora, flannel shirt, dark long pants, and clunky black shoes, lugging a heavy jacket. He saw Hispanics, Jews, Haitians, and people from seemingly every island in the Caribbean. He wasn't prone to be prejudiced but he was a taken aback by the throng of people of all sorts. The airport seemed to be overflowing with them all, creating an almost smoggy atmosphere. He felt like he needed to find a COVD mask and put it on.

The long walk to their gate was an uncomfortable experience with people bumping and shoving them along the way. There were no seats available at the gate, so they resorted to plopping down on the floor like some other people to wait for their plane to Montego Bay to board and take off. The hour-long wait seemed interminable. Relief would wash over them when they finally boarded.

As they sat on the floor waiting for their plane to Montego Bay, Monte's two sons-in-law were comparing notes. Jax Magnus had married Eve, while Banks Bridges was Viv's recent spouse. When four seats were vacated, Monte and the girls quickly snapped them up, leaving only Jax and Banks on the floor.

"This damned floor is killing my back," Jax complained. "And who knows how many germs it has."

"Don't complain," Banks replied. "When we get to Seascape, we'll be living the life of Riley. You'll be able to get whatever you want on an unlimited basis whenever you want it."

"I can't believe we're going to be in a five-star resort in Jamaica,"

Jax said. "This will be the first time I've ever been outside the country. Have you ever been abroad?"

"Nope," replied Banks, "but this should be the first of a lot of trips to come now that Daddy-in-law Warbucks's motherlode has come in."

"Do you know how much he got?"

"Guess."

"I dunno. Five mill."

Banks smiled and turned his palms upward and wiggled his fingers at the ceiling. Then he motioned upwards with his thumbs."

"Ten?"

Banks smiled again.

"Twenty?"

"You're getting warmer."

"Surely not thirty."

"You still ain't close, but you're closer."

"You're shittin' me!"

"Since I'm his investment advisor and a fiduciary, I can't give you a number, but let me say this. If we play *our* cards right, none of us are gonna miss any meals … ever again."

Clayton "Potsy" Potter was sitting close enough to overhear Jax's and Bank's exchange. His ears perked up, and a grin spread across his face.

Hark! A mark! Do I hear a mark?

He began to hum to himself the chorus to a Steve Miller song he had always liked.

> *Go on, take the money and run.*
> *Go on, take the money and run.*
> *Go on, take the money and run.*

Potter was a career flimflam artist. … A first-class bunko man, heading to Jamaica for a little r-and-r and to get his head back on straight. His last scam had backfired on him and ended up costing him money, making him wonder if he was losing his touch. Now he knew where he was going to spend the week — Seascape Luxury Resort in Runaway Bay, Jamaica. The infinite hour-long wait suddenly seemed finite, and he couldn't wait to board the plane.

As if the airline had read his mind, the announcement came over to PA that boarding would begin. He heard Jax grumble, "About damned time, my back couldn't take much more of this floor."

After everyone boarded and got settled into their seats, the attractive head flight attendant gave her welcoming speech. She had a pleasant island lilt.

"Hello and welcome to American Airlines flight AA1502 to Sangster International Airport. For my fellow countrymen I say, 'Gud day. Wah gwaan? Mi, mi deh yah. (**Good morning. How are you all? Me, I'm going well.**)' If you're going to Montego Bay, you're in the right place. If you're not going to Montego Bay, you're about to have a really long day."

This brought a giggle from some of the passengers. Potsy thought to himself, *If the amount of that honeybun that I just heard about in the gate is even close to accurate, I'm definitely in the right place, and it's only going to get righter over the next few days. And if I'm right, this is a family tree with an enormous crop of nuts, and they're about to meet one squirrel who likes to get his share.*

The flight attendant continued.

"We'd like to now tell you about some important safety features of this aircraft. The most important safety feature we have aboard is …. The flight attendants. Please look at one now. May I say with all modesty that American Airlines has some of best flight attendants in the airline industry. Unfortunately, none of them are on this flight."

Some zoned out veteran travelers zoned back in. A few chuckled. Monte looked at Nan uncertainly. She just smiled.

"There may be fifty ways to leave your lover, but there are only four ways out of this plane."

The flight attendant went on to tell where all the exits were, told people to look around, identify the one closest to them, and count how many rows they were away from it in case the lights went out.

"If you are traveling with a small child and if we must use oxygen masks, … that's that margarine cup that'll descend from the ceiling … do us all a favor. Stop screaming and then put yours on first. After that you can decide which child is your favorite and help him or her mask-up next.

"Remember, your seat cushions are designed to be used for flotation. In the event of an emergency water landing, please paddle to shore and keep them with our compliments."

This brought on a few sniggers. The flight attendant continued her well-rehearsed speech.

"In the seat pocket in front of you is a safety feature pamphlet. It makes a very good fan and one I use when I am having my private summer. It also has pretty pictures. You have my permission to play with it now. One last thing. Your seat belt. It's a pulley thing, not a pushy thing like in your car because you are … on an airplane."

After takeoff, the flight attendant came back on.

"Just to remind you, this is a nonsmoking flight. … For both cigarettes or anything else that will take you higher than our planned cruising altitude … And that includes in the lavatory. If we see smoke coming from one of the lavatories, we will assume you are on fire and put you out. This is a free service we provide. We do have two smoking sections, one outside each wing exit. Oh, and I'm about to forget, we do have a movie. Let's see, … hold on, until I can check and see what it is. Here we go. … Today's move is 'Gone with the Wind.'

"Now, have an irie flight."

End Chapter 1 Excerpt

Thank you for reading.
Please review this book. Reviews
help others find Absolutely Amazing eBooks and
inspire us to keep providing these marvelous tales.
If you would like to be put on our email list
to receive updates on new releases,
contests, and promotions, please go to
AbsolutelyAmazingEbooks.com and sign up.

About the Author

David Beckwith is a three-generation native of Greenville, Mississippi, with a BBA and an MBA from Ole Miss. His parents owned an independent cash commodity trading firm which also cleared securities trades through Goodbody & Co. David spent 40 years in the securities business, the first half of his career with Bache & Co. and its successors, the second half with Morgan Stanley. He retired as a Senior Vice President with approximately $500 million in responsibilities. For 25 years he has served as an adjunct professor at five different universities.

His first book was a narrative nonfiction work published by the University of Alabama Press in 2009 entitled *A New Day In The Delta*. The Mississippi Institute of Arts and Letters chose it as the runner-up for nonfiction book of the year. The book is often compared to Pat Conroy's *The Water Is Wide*. David started writing the Will and Betsy Black Adventure Series in 2010.

Moving to Key West, David Beckwith was tapped to write a book review column for the Key West *Citizen*, which David continues to produce on a weekly basis.

For sales, editorial information, subsidiary rights information
or a catalog, please write or phone or e-mail
Absolutely Amazing eBooks
Manhanset House
Shelter Island Hts., New York 11965-0342, US
Tel: 212-427-7139
www.ibooksinc.com
bricktower@aol.com
www.IngramContent.com

For sales in the UK and Europe please contact our distributor,
Gazelle Book Services
White Cross Mills
Lancaster, LA1 4XS, UK
Tel: (01524) 68765 Fax: (01524) 63232
email: jacky@gazellebooks.co.uk

www.ingramcontent.com/pod-product-compliance
Lightning Source LLC
Chambersburg PA
CBHW070443030726
47503CB00004B/876